VIPERS OF ROME

Alistair Forrest

SAPERE
BOOKS

VIPERS OF ROME

Published by Sapere Books.

24 Trafalgar Road, Ilkley, LS29 8HH

saperebooks.com

ISBN: 978-0-85495-401-8

For Lord Cormack (1939-2024) who, long before he became Baron Cormack or even the esteemed historian, author and politician Sir Patrick Cormack, taught me how to accept criticism as my English Teacher at Wrekin College. I am grateful for the endorsement he found time to grant me during his illustrious career.

PART ONE: THE MISSION

CHAPTER ONE

Philippi, Macedonia 42BC

Dawn was grey and still. No birdsong, nor a mammal's death cry under the raptor's claws. No breeze to clear the air of the stench of thirty-six legions yawning their indifference to yet another standoff day.

Titus Villius Macer parted the tall marsh reeds and studied the fortifications before him. 'These are weak, thrown up in haste,' he whispered to his *optio*, Crispus, who lay alongside him on the damp ground. Crispus swatted a mosquito and grunted in agreement. The Fifth Alaudae Legion was not known for taking a step back — certainly not the First Cohort led by the indomitable Titus Villius — so the red-haired former gladiator knew what would happen next.

'Look there.' Titus pointed to the palisade before them, its earthworks a gentle incline. 'The posts are not even. What does that tell us?'

'That they are driven into rocky ground. Shoddy. One push from a team and they'll be over.'

Titus looked back to where his men waited. One century was waiting in the marshes, betrayed only by the occasional slap and muttered curse at biting insects, with the rest of the cohort ranged behind. How they had mustered so quickly and quietly was not a mystery — every soldier had been told to dress and arm in complete silence, and each knew the price of clumsily disturbing the cook's pots and pans. They had no horse and light shields only, or even none. And definitely no camp dogs. Stealth had been the command, surprise the watchword.

He could see no watchmen on the fortification. Cassius must have grown lazy or over-confident since his men had discovered the makeshift road of reeds and rubble through the marshes to his south, Marcus Antonius's attempt to circumnavigate Cassius's camp. He must think his brave palisade would deal with that threat. As if a blockade like this would stop the Fifth!

'Hand signals only, no trumpets or whistles,' Titus commanded. 'Send to the centurions that when they see me advance, they are to follow at a trot. Then use the catapult method to scale the ramparts — if they do not fall over at the first push.'

As Crispus crept back towards the First Cohort, Titus thought how he loved this method of attacking defences. Again and again tribes in the north had been surprised as hundreds of well-trained soldiers locked hands to launch comrades onto poor ramparts with blood-curdling war cries, and it would work again here. Cassius would barely have time to turf his woman from his bed before the Fifth's swords were at his throat. 'Find a way,' Antonius had said, and Titus had found it. His men would probe the defences and the general himself would decide whether to pull them back or send in his legions.

Crispus returned, grimly smiling confirmation of the *primus pilus*'s orders. 'On three,' Titus said quietly, slowly drawing his *gladius*. It was their ritual performed many times before, taking three deep breaths together. The third would ignite heart and muscle in an explosion of power and fury.

They ran from the cover of the reeds, legs pumping, swords seeking blood. They did not have to look back because they knew the First Cohort was at their backs, organised and determined. Titus was first to the palisades, his studded boots smashing into the posts, feeling them give slightly. Then Crispus was next to him.

There was no response from the other side.

Titus turned to his approaching century. With swift hand-signals he showed where he wanted the most muscular men to shoulder-charge the ramparts and where the catapult team should make their attack. They all knew the drill, and he was always the first to fly at the enemy.

The first two soldiers to arrive at his side dropped their weapons and locked hands. Two steps and Titus was over the ramparts, expecting to land on soft earth behind but finding himself falling into empty space. He landed on top of a sentry, driving the wind from him that moments before had been a gentle snore, with two others stirring nearby. All three died before they had properly woken. Next to him Crispus had landed, his sword unbloodied, looking menacingly around for a victim.

There were many, and they were waking.

Silently, more men from the century were dropping to the ground around them, and the wooden palisades nearby were beginning to collapse inward as the men shoulder-charged them.

'On me!' shouted Titus, silence now unnecessary. His men formed up at a trot either side of him as he moved forward, drawing his dagger with his left hand, *gladius* in his right. More of Cassius's guards died before they could grab weapons or shields, and at the same time the palisade collapsed inward with a groan. Eighty men armed for close combat poured through, another thousand to follow behind them.

Now the enemy had been rudely awakened to the threat and Titus, his sword arm already slippery with gore, weighed up the task that would have to be completed swiftly. Alarms were sounding and his opponents were forming up. They did not have time to don armour, but each wielded either a *gladius* or spear.

Titus wasted no time and ran at them, disappointed that he had not been as quick as Crispus, who was just ahead. He made for the biggest man, his beard betraying him as an auxiliary. With a sword and a *pilum* to use against Titus's smaller weapons, close combat was the priority. Titus swatted aside the spear with his short sword and sank the dagger into the man's neck. He didn't wait to see the shock in the man's eyes because he knew it was a killing blow, and the next man was on him with a wild slashing of his sword. Titus knew he would kill this soldier, but before delivering an upward stab to the gut he felt the sting of a blade on his upper arm. As always, he ignored the pain as his opponent died. More wounds to sew, more scars to mark his years of service to Rome.

Now he was ahead of Crispus at least, and the men of his century were heaving and hacking to his right. He felt more wounds as he forced his way through, slashing and stabbing. He looked around to see that this short battle was won, or soon would be. He then turned to his left, where Cassius had pitched his camp on a hill overlooking the plain outside Philippi.

And he caught his first sight of Gaius Cassius Longinus, senator of Rome and assassin of Julius Caesar, and brother-in-law to Marcus Junius Brutus who, little did Titus know, was at this very moment preparing to lead his legions in an attack on Octavian's camp on the far side of the plain. Cassius was standing outside his ornate tent, watching the battle unfold below while his generals and captains rushed around him to organise the defence of his camp. Titus knew that now was the moment to strike at the heart of the enemy. After all, these were Romans and they would soon form an impenetrable wall of iron. He reached for his whistle and blew hard.

'Form up on me!' he shouted.

Crispus, as ever, was first at his side. He, too, was blood-soaked but his eyes shone with the heady drug of killing. The century quickly formed two ranks behind him, and the rest of the cohort was running to form up behind.

Titus held his dripping *gladius* aloft, then in a slow arc pointed forward at the distant figure on the hill. No command was necessary.

Together, they ran at the hill and the camp of their general's enemy.

Even the well-trained men of the Fifth Alaudae's First Cohort were tiring, Titus sensed. The element of surprise had given him an inevitable advantage, but the enemy had quickly formed up and with their heavier shields were holding the line before Cassius's camp. Panting heavily, his sword arm weary and unresponsive, Titus pulled Crispus aside to allow the men behind to take their place. His throat was dry from the thick dust that enveloped the hill and he had lost his water leather in the attack. So had Crispus, with his entire body caked in dust and blood.

They looked back the way they had come to see that Marcus Antonius's legions had demolished virtually all of the defences and were advancing towards the hill where they stood. Against this force Cassius's Greek auxiliaries now surged forward from their vast camp. This was a fight Titus had begun but perhaps should not finish.

But that was not the way of his cohort.

He leaned close to Crispus to be heard above the din. 'Pull our century back so that the fresh legions can engage.'

'Pull back?' Crispus was incredulous. Not even in the face of Juba's elephants at Thapsus nor Hispanic warriors at Munda had Titus ever pulled back.

'Only very slowly,' said Titus. 'We are not retreating.' He motioned to his left where fewer men defended the camp. 'We'll break through there. Antonius can take over the main attack and deal with those Greeks. But I want it to be our men who reach Cassius.'

Even the crack century had lost too many men, but sixty were pulled and cajoled by Crispus away from the struggle. Disengaging did not come easily to them, but they were disciplined and did not question the tough *optio*. While the cohort's reserves took their place with fresh vigour, Titus and Crispus led them to the cover of a small copse away from the fighting.

'Take deep breaths,' he commanded them, 'and if you have water left, drink now. You are men of the Fifth's first cohort, men of my century, and over there —' he raised his sword to point at Cassius's camp — 'stands Caesar's assassin. We will bring judgement to him this day.'

As one, the sixty men pointed their weapons up the hill. Some shouted Caesar's name, while others yelled 'The Fifth' or 'Judgement'. Titus Villius Macer led what remained of his renowned century in an arrowhead formation towards where Cassius's guard was thinnest, his slaves and shield-bearers watching with alarm as the grim, bloodied sixty raced up the hill.

The fighting was brief and merciless. Felling the last of the makeshift defensive line, Titus walked into the camp of Gaius Cassius Longinus. Slaves cowered in the deepest recesses. An upturned table and several open chests, contents strewn across the reed floor, confirmed what Titus suspected: Cassius was now a fugitive from Antonius's wrath. He strode to the nearest slave, who collapsed before him, shaking with fear.

'Stand up, man,' he commanded. The slave did so, looking over Titus's shoulder at the fearsome men behind, his eyes darting, hands clasped in supplication. 'The only way you're going to live is by telling me where Cassius is.' He said this almost in a whisper, just loud enough to be heard over the clamour outside.

'Gone, sir,' the slave croaked.

'Gone where? And speak up, man.'

The slave merely shrugged, then as Titus's sword pricked his throat, he stepped back in alarm and tripped over a chest, sitting heavily. For a moment, Titus wondered whether the chest might be full of gold.

'Try again.'

The slave was snivelling now but managed to answer, 'Gone to the city.'

Titus realised the futility of questioning a slave and left the tent. He surveyed the battle below. It looked very much like a stalemate, but then his men had captured the enemy camp where there would be coin and provisions supplied by Ahenobarbus's fleet. The opposing legions would probably fight themselves to a standstill.

He looked across the plain to the north where he expected to see the legions of Brutus and Octavian engaging, but there was only a thick dust cloud. He hoped Brutus could be defeated too, then everyone could go home and live like human beings again. He would go home to Sicilia, marry his woman and teach his children how to build a barn and catch fish.

Crispus broke the spell. 'Sir, there's a rider approaching. Could be a messenger.'

The rider picked his way through the dead and wounded and came up to Titus and Crispus, whose rank could not be distinguished as they were covered in grime and blood.

'I seek General Antonius with a message from Marcus Vipsanius Agrippa,' he announced.

Titus waved to where the legions fought below. 'Over there somewhere,' he said wearily. 'I am Titus Villius Macer, *primus pilus* of the Fifth Alaudae, and I will convey your message.'

The messenger studied the two soldiers and saw from their bearing and what could be seen of their dress that this was indeed a senior officer and his *optio*.

'Sir, it is with regret that I report the camp of Octavianus Divi Filius has been overrun by the legions commanded by Marcus Junius Brutus.'

CHAPTER TWO

Titus resisted the urge to scratch at his wounds, still raw and inflamed where they had been roughly sewn by the cohort's surgeon. He waved away flies and poured two cups of watered wine, handing one to Crispus.

'Let's hope the general has something better to drink, eh?' he muttered, wondering why he had been ordered to attend Antonius in his command quarters. Twenty days had passed since the strange events of the first engagement. The legions of both sides were severely depleted, but still at a standoff. 'How do I look?'

'Dreadful,' Crispus smiled. He too bore the marks of a frontline soldier, including a broken nose and blackened eyes where a Greek had head-butted him. Not a new experience for the former gladiator, and not enough to prevent him from requisitioning clean tunics and the pick of provisions taken from Cassius's camp to be shared among what was left of Titus's century.

Titus wondered how the generals on both sides had fared. Rumours were rife among the Fifth that Cassius had taken his own life and Brutus had failed to push home his advantage, withdrawing to his original position. Nothing had been seen of the young Triumvir Octavian who had, so the rumours went, been recovering from sickness in a country retreat, miles from the battlefield and therefore not in his camp when Brutus's advance party had raided. The joke doing the rounds was that Brutus's men had murdered the fancy couch where the son of a god was not. Only Antonius had acquitted himself well, all passion and fire as he led his legions to rout Cassius's wing while on the other side of the plain, Octavian's legions had been embarrassed.

But the First Cohort had again proved its worth, and Titus thought back to the first time he and Crispus had fought together, at Thapsus in Caesar's campaign against Cato, Scipio and King Juba's Numidians. They had watched thirty elephants advancing in clouds of dust, brightly painted trunks raised to trumpet their fury, great tusks swinging to incite terror in their ranks. They had looked into each other's eyes, and Titus had known Crispus understood what to do. Their century had lost men beneath those stomping beasts, but their spears and arrows had turned them back upon their own men to wreak havoc, forcing the Numidian wing to retreat in chaos. War was in Titus's blood, but being summoned by his general was a different matter altogether, and he was glad that Crispus would be at his side.

'We'd better answer the summons, then,' said Titus. 'Time to find out what the plan is and finish this sorry war.'

'We?' Crispus shook his head slowly. 'The order was for you alone, Titus. No mention of your *optio* or any others of your brave century.'

'I decide who accompanies me,' Titus replied curtly. He looked suspiciously at Crispus as understanding dawned. 'Unless…?'

'If you are thinking that I have a prior engagement, you would be quite correct. We are honoured to be visited by a troupe of performers from the city, and I have arranged to discuss the works of Plato with the leading lady. Permission to attend, *sir*?'

Not a man normally given to outbursts of emotion, Titus couldn't contain himself and burst out laughing. 'So you're going to use that brain of yours at last? Of course, we both know where it truly lies, and it doesn't know anything about Plato! Permission granted.'

Crispus, unusually for him, blushed behind his bruises.

Marcus Antonius's command quarters were impressive if simple in design, a central hall built from rough-hewn local timber with ornate awnings that must have been carried from the general's campaigns in Cisalpine Gaul. The guards waved Titus through without hesitation — his heroics in attacking Cassius had given him a modicum of fame among the other legions, and he was clearly expected.

Antonius was hunched over a map table with several of his senior officers, none wearing armour as if accustomed to the long days of waiting. Titus breathed a sigh a relief that his simple tunic would be acceptable dress in this company and calmly stood to one side, unnoticed by the officers or Antonius. They seemed to be agitated by the lack of supplies reaching their legions, while Brutus's were abundantly supplied from the south where Ahenobarbus's fleet controlled the seas.

'We can't go on like this!' Antonius was shouting, jabbing at a worn map with his finger. 'We need to make something happen and crush Brutus before our men starve.' His officers were silent, none wanting to agitate their general further. Titus watched, intrigued. Antonius was the same age as him, about forty, powerfully built and well-groomed with fierce eyebrows above piercing blue-grey eyes. Not a man to be crossed, as Titus knew well after years of fighting under his command. He also knew better than to interrupt the general in full flow.

'There are three ways of doing this.' Antonius had calmed himself and was looking at each of his officers in turn, and as he did so he noticed Titus waiting patiently by the door. But he did not acknowledge him, continuing, 'One, we can continue to extend our right wing through the marshes to the Via Egnatia to cut off Brutus's supplies coming up from the south. This will take days to accomplish, and the men are hungry and weak. Two, we can unleash our Thracian cavalry to cut through behind him to attack his rear. Or three, we can have an old-fashioned battle, hand-to-hand. What do you suggest?'

The officers immediately began to debate among themselves, unable to agree on the right course of action. Antonius allowed the hubbub to continue for some time, taking the opportunity to give Titus a subtle wave, indicating that he should wait a moment longer.

'Enough, gentlemen.' He brought the debate to a close. 'Leave me now and come back at the third hour tomorrow with your answer, and I will tell you what we will do!' Each saluted and left, still muttering among themselves. None of them acknowledged Titus.

'Macer!' Antonius addressed him at last. 'Titus Villius Macer, hero of our time! Come, have some wine.' He clapped his hands to summon a servant. 'My officers don't get refreshment here, but heroes do.'

Antonius rested his hands on his guest's shoulders, causing Titus to wince where a cut was touched beneath the sleeves. 'How are you recovering? You were magnificent, I'm told, your century brave to a man.'

'It's no longer a full century, I'm afraid.'

'I will replace those you have lost. We're going to need you again soon, *primus pilus*.'

'At your service, sir.'

The servant brought wine and some sweetmeats. Titus noticed he was finely dressed and clearly understood what the general expected of him without being asked. Antonius led Titus to a corner table where the refreshments had been placed, two cups poured, and with the gusto for which he was well known invited Titus to drink with him, saluting several gods without reverence. The wine was smooth and mellow and immediately induced a conspiratorial mood.

'Now, before we get to a battle plan,' Antonius said, leaning towards Titus, 'you might be pleased to know that you have come to the attention of Octavian. Have you met him?'

'No, I've never even set eyes upon him. I heard he was sick.'

'Yes, unfortunately. Of course, he is young and inexperienced. Besides, this is my war and with men like you to the fore, who needs another general? But he does seem to be able to think ahead, and that's where you come in. You hail from Sicilia, I believe? You have family there? You're due to retire sometime soon, I suspect.'

His tongue loosened by the wine, Titus told him that he came from a small fishing village near Messana with its views across the strait to Rhegium, where merchant ships and war fleets funnelled in their voyages across the seas.

'It seems that you love the place,' Antonius observed. 'And you have a woman there?'

Titus nodded, forcing himself to be circumspect. He did not want to tell Antonius about his childhood sweetheart Zerenia and their young children, nor the vineyard he had bought on a soldier's pay. He especially did not want to mention the time he'd spent with the youngest son of Pompeius Magnus during his youth.

'Well?' Antonius pushed. 'Tell me about her, how beautiful she is and how you long to be with her. What's her name?'

'Zerenia.' Titus tried to tie his tongue and failed. 'We will marry when I am discharged and she will be a Roman citizen, as will our children.'

Antonius sensed Titus's reluctance to talk about his personal life. He gave him a playful punch on his shoulder, causing Titus to wince again. 'And in the meantime, there's many a fine young lady among the army's followers, eh?' Both knew this was not true: camp prostitutes were unfortunates, and Titus for one felt nothing but pity for them.

There was a moment's silence before the general's demeanour became more serious. 'You might be returning to Sicilia sooner than you think. I am going to recommend you to the *Divi Filius.*' Antonius scornfully emphasised Octavian's pretentious title. 'You see, we have a problem called Sextus Pompeius, who seems to be above his station. We gave him command of the seas around Italia, but instead of looking after Rome's interests he taxes the grain ships and robs the merchants. He's a pirate, and his base is Sicilia, your island, and he charges four or five times the accepted price for the local grain. While I will try to placate him, Octavian would rather destroy him, so either way we will need someone in Sicilia to keep an eye on him.'

'A spy, you mean?'

'Just a friendly soul with Rome's interests at heart. If you agree, and I know you will because it will be an order —' Antonius winked — 'you will be well rewarded, and you and your family will be living in peace on your island paradise.'

Titus's mind raced. He could be back home within weeks. His new assignment would mean an end to army life with its months of boredom interspersed with savage warfare.

'But first we have a war to win,' Antonius went on. 'Can you do it again? I'm relying on you.'

'Of course, sir.'

'Here's what we'll do. We'll continue to move men and defences to the south to make Brutus believe that we will soon cut off his supply lines. This will force him to attack us across the entire front in an attempt to bring a conclusive end to this folly. We will make him believe our efforts are concentrated on both wings, which will cause him to weaken his centre by moving men left and right. Of course, our centre will appear to be weak too, so he won't be concerned. But that's where you will be, Titus Villius Macer. Can you take his camp like you did Cassius's?'

Titus found himself wondering whether the plan could go wrong and Brutus would send in has cavalry through the centre. If Brutus won, he would have no hope of returning to Sicilia, and might even lose his life under the hoofs of enemy horse. *But Antonius is not a loser*, he thought, *and Brutus is a soft senator and his men largely mercenaries.* They were not Romans. Not like the Fifth.

'You have my sword, sir. Just tell me where to attack.'

CHAPTER THREE

Trumpets threw the First Cohort's camp into instant confusion. The call to arms always did, and Titus fought to control his own emotions as his men rushed to and fro, hurriedly strapping on armour and finding their muster points. Crispus, as ever, was at his side.

'As soon as their centuries are formed up, bring the five centurions to me at the agreed place,' he told his *optio*. 'But the men are to wait in the camp until told otherwise.'

Crispus thumped an oversized fist to his chest and obeyed while Titus ran to the edge of the camp and climbed the earthwork to get a clear view of the enemy's new fortifications some four hundred yards away, and the huge gates built into them. From its summit he surveyed the forces ranged opposite. From the gates, thousands of men spewed left and right to take up their positions in front of the defences. Exactly what Antonius had hoped for. A battlefront stretched across five miles before the city of Philippi.

He looked left and could make out Antonius's legions forming up and to the right, those of Octavian. Only the First Cohort of the Fifth Alaudae would be absent. The rest of the legion was not too distant to his left, within runner distance, under the command of the dependable Decimus Barba. *Make this plan work*, he pleaded with the gods, *so that we can all go home.*

He watched the enemy formations and thought how eager they, too, must be to enjoin at last. But he could see they were keeping to the higher ground, close to the defences, and if they were disciplined and held their position they would have an immediate advantage. He fixed his gaze on the great gates, certain they would remain open to allow retreat for those nearest should they be driven back. *Juno be with us, for we will enter those gates this day.* Once through them, the path to Brutus's camp would lie open.

Crispus brought the cohort's centurions, who crouched with Titus on the earthwork. These men had fought alongside him on many occasions and were now lauded for their success against Cassius three weeks earlier. Each held their helmets under an arm, hands on sword hilts, expectant and willing.

'Gentlemen, it appears we will fight this day.' The five said nothing; they knew that already from the way their blood coursed. 'But we will not be in the vanguard as we usually are.' Each looked disappointed, but they knew the sun would not go down before they had bloodied their swords.

Titus pointed to the gates. 'Our cohort has but one objective this day — to win those gates and hold them for Marcus Antonius and Octavianus Divi Filius. While we wait here and watch, the other legions will attack the wings of Brutus's positions, with the exception of the Fifth, who as you know are forming up closest to us and will follow us through the gates. Have your men move up behind the cover of this earthwork and play dice, tell stories or pray, but when I give the signal, we run together up that hill in an arrow formation and lead the Fifth to victory!'

The five centurions voiced their agreement, lost in the din of drums, trumpets and shouted orders. As they went to deliver his orders, Titus smiled to himself when he saw the Fifth had formed up not far to his left with minimal fuss and confusion, while the enemy dashed with some clamour to their positions. He could see dust clouds swirling where opposing cavalry moved to the wings and was pleased to note the centre opposite was clear of horses or artillery. Neither Antonius nor

Octavian seemed to be deploying heavy weapons. This would be a day for sword and spear. He checked his light shield's grip and tightened his cuirass after spotting archers on the defensive ramparts and some positioned in the enemy lines.

As the ninth hour approached, Crispus and Titus watched the drama of what they dubbed 'The Big Parade' as a colourful general — Brutus, they agreed — rode before his troops to exhort them to bravery and victory. Not long after, Antonius and Octavian did the same, but their words were lost in the lusty cheering of men suddenly freed from boredom. As Antonius passed before their position, he reined in and looked towards the enemy gates, then opposite to where the pair watched. No signal was given, as Antonius trusted Titus to deliver even if the odds were stacked against him.

One last time.

They knew the battle had begun when distant war cries and the beating of shields could be heard far to their right, followed by the incessant sound of battle as Octavian's legions engaged. Almost immediately, the closest legions either side of them began to move away from the centre. Titus hoped that the Fifth would not become caught up in the excitement and would stay where they were. Opposite, the enemy seemed confused with fewer opponents before them, but they had received no orders, so they simply waited.

'If they attack now, they could march straight into our camp,' said Crispus.

'The one weakness in the general's plan,' agreed Titus. 'Let's hope they take the bait soon, or it's you and me and five centuries against an entire legion, by the look of it.'

No sooner had he spoken than Antonius's Thracians came. Four thousand horsemen galloped right in front of the earthwork where Titus and Crispus watched, raising clouds of dust, lifting sword and spear high as they screamed a murderous announcement to the enemy that they would join the battle with Octavian's legions on the right. This seemed to anger the waiting legions opposite, whose soldiers shouted abuse back — to no avail, as the riders had disappeared in their own dust storm. The sounds of battle in that direction suddenly intensified.

'Move, you bastards,' muttered Titus, willing the enemy to lend support against this new threat.

A second wave of cavalry followed, and this was too much for Brutus's commanders near the gates. Several of his cohorts took the bait and moved off to the south, itching for a fight. At the same time, a rising clamour told him that Antonius had launched all of his legions against Brutus's right. That must draw more men away, thought Titus.

'Go now,' he ordered Crispus. 'This is our time. And send to the Fifth to hold their position until they see our cohort advance.'

'Don't go without me!' shouted Crispus above the noise as he ran to deliver the orders.

Minutes later he was back, throwing himself to the ground next to Titus. 'They're ready. Runner sent to the Fifth with orders to follow us to the gates.'

Titus didn't need to look behind him as he sensed the presence of his men, out of sight below the earthwork. 'On three.' Kneeling, they gripped light shields tightly, drew short swords and went through their breathing ritual, then they were up and running at the head of an arrow formation consisting of five hundred armed and dangerous men.

Too quickly, the enemy saw their approach, forming two ranks before the gates. The first arrows fell short, but then the archers on the rampart found their range. Titus felt the air part close to his neck, and Crispus took another arrow on his shield. A short scream behind told him he was a man down already, and not yet halfway to the enemy. He increased the pace. None of them wasted breath with war cries as they raced towards the enemy's throat.

Forty yards off, javelins rained from the sky, released from behind the ranks. Thirty yards, twenty. Titus knew he had lost more men to the *pila*. The cohort accelerated over the last ten, targeting a gap in the array of scutum shields before him. He stabbed down into the neck of the man to his right as Crispus took the man to his left, and they were through to the second rank. He knew his wedge of seasoned fighters would force the ranks apart as long as he and Crispus lost no momentum. His shield crunched into the face of the next man, the effort slowing him, but he redoubled and swung wildly at another with his *gladius*. He felt the familiar stickiness of blood on his arm and neck and knew that recent wounds had opened in the exertion, but he surged forward even when enemy reserves came through the gates.

Titus chanced a look behind and was gratified to see his men were tight-knit behind him, still in formation, stepping over bodies as they forced their way outwards to gain the bridgehead. Behind them the entire Fifth was surging up the incline, bristling with weaponry and embossed shields to push the enemy back.

But the look back was a mistake. Titus felt a blade cut deep into his thigh and with a grunt dispatched the man who had delivered it, unable to avoid another blow to his shoulder. The reserves they faced were no amateurs. He heard Crispus singing a gibberish song next to him as he hewed and hacked, his unusual method of maintaining momentum and rhythm.

But Titus's legs were leaden. The pain in his thigh was a raging furnace and his right arm would no longer do his bidding. He bit his lip in frustration and ordered his body to find renewed strength. He was about to stop when he felt the weight of the surging men behind him, pushing him forward. A voice close to his ear said, 'Sir, let me relieve you.' But he was *primus pilus* of the Fifth's First Cohort and would not take a step back.

'Just push, son!' he shouted back. He wanted to say more, but he didn't have the breath for it. He felt the weight of the soldier behind him and with an effort crashed his shield into the ribs of the man in front, sensing Crispus fighting with his customary fury next to him. Then he stumbled forward, almost falling to the ground as blood seeped into his boots, and they were through.

Crispus caught him, holding him upright as the First Cohort's centurions ordered their men to fan out in defensive lines inside the gates. Decimus Barba was dividing the legion's other cohorts: some would follow through the gates, others would continue to clear the enemy outside.

They had done it. *Surely this war is finished*, Titus thought as he passed out.

CHAPTER FOUR

The bruised face of Crispus came slowly into focus. Titus tried to work out where the pain came from, then he remembered the wounds he had taken as they stormed the enemy gates. He tried to speak, but his mouth was dry as an African desert.

'Welcome back,' Crispus smiled.

His took in his surroundings. There were the rich reds and purples of wall-hangings, several slaves and servants, and a bearded old man busying himself at a table laden with dressings, potions and surgical tools. And his bed was soft, luxurious, definitely not army issue. He couldn't speak, so instead he checked his torso for wounds. He looked at Crispus quizzically, his eyes demanding what his tongue couldn't deliver.

'You missed one hell of a party,' Crispus said and held a cup of water to Titus's parched, swollen lips. 'And no, there's no need to thank me for saving your life yet again.'

A wave of nausea made Titus fall back onto the bed. He tried again. 'The men...?'

'Mostly in good shape, all drunk as senators.'

'Where...?'

'First things first,' Crispus interrupted. 'Did we win and is the war over? I think so. Brutus is dead by his own hand, like Cassius before him, and the generals have you to thank for it. You are guest of honour in the quarters of Gaius Julius Caesar Octavianus. You may have a little difficulty saluting our victorious Triumvir, should he visit you, but I'm sure he will understand. Next question?'

Titus worked his jaw and croaked, 'How long...?'

'Oh, only a day, if you mean how long have you been lying here like a helpless old woman. You've been stitched more than a seamstress's curtains.' He indicated the old man at his apothecary table and added, 'You have the good doctor here to thank.'

The old man heard, shuffled over to the bed, lifted the linen cover and studied Titus's wounds with nothing more than a few satisfied grunts before returning to his work, nodding to himself.

'I think that means you will live,' said Crispus.

Titus's mind began to race, recalling what Antonius had said about him being posted to Sicilia — but how could he get there in his condition? Perhaps everything had changed. Maybe Octavian had different plans for him, or none at all. But why was he in this decadent room with servants and a doctor to care for him?

He dragged his focus back to what Crispus was saying. 'You are to be awarded *corona muralis*, but don't worry — they won't have any crowns to hand out in these parts. Even if they did, I can't see you wearing one...'

'Shut up and get me out here.' Titus had found his voice at last.

'Aha, the great warrior speaks!'

'I mean it, Crispus. This isn't right. I'd rather be among the Fifth, sleeping on hard ground and drinking their filthy brew. Like the old days when we first met on Africa's shores.'

'Pulling men from Caesar's leaky old tubs after that hellish crossing from Sicilia — yes, I remember it well,' said Crispus. 'Roughed it, we did — it made us into men. Lucky the enemy wasn't there to welcome us, or we wouldn't be here now.'

'So let's get back to our own tents. The men won't be happy if their *primus pilus* has special favours and a real bed.'

Crispus ran a hand through his wiry ginger hair. 'Unfortunately, I have orders from a higher authority. You are to stay here until told otherwise, and a slave has no doubt already rushed off to find General Agrippa to inform him that you will soon be ready to fight another war.'

'Agrippa?' Titus had only seen the young officer from a distance. 'I thought this was Octavian's lair?'

'They're thick as thieves,' said Crispus, pleased to show off his newly acquired knowledge of Rome's latest victors. 'Agrippa is now Octavian's man of the moment and from what I've heard, you're better off discussing politics with him rather than Julius Caesar's surly heir. Perhaps that's him now…?'

From the anteroom came sounds of barked orders and the hustle of servants attending someone important, before Marcus Vipsanius Agrippa entered. *So young,* thought Titus. *Rome is no longer ruled by old men.* Agrippa, wearing an embroidered off-duty tunic, had an air of authority about him, strong shoulders, a lean torso and an unreadable expression that bordered on grim until he set eyes on the reclining Titus.

'Don't get up, not that you can.' There was a hint of humour behind his no-nonsense visage.

'Sir,' said Titus and Crispus in unison. Crispus had snapped to attention as Agrippa entered.

'Relax, gentlemen. Mind if I sit on your bed? Looks comfier than camp chairs.' Agrippa didn't wait for permission and sat, hooking a sandalled foot behind his left knee. He turned to a servant. 'Bring wine, Octavian's best, not that he knows the difference.' At last the grim expression cracked and he winked at Titus. 'You're badly wounded so I won't stay long, but the Triumvirs want you to know that Rome is grateful to you — both of you, in fact.'

Crispus looked surprised and Titus shook his head. 'Only following orders, sir.'

'From what I've heard, you excelled, not once but twice — driving the enemy back with the strength of Hercules and the courage of Spartacus. I'm glad we're on the same side!'

For the first time since Titus had recovered his senses, the doctor chipped in. 'It's all senseless, this fighting and killing. All this bloodshed, and with it disease and rotting flesh. When are you soldiers going to stop? When you run out of people to maim and kill?'

Startled by the outburst, Agrippa shrugged. 'When will our patient here recover?' he asked the doctor affably.

'So you can send him back to war, I suppose? He mustn't be moved for a week.'

Titus shook his head, wincing at the pain behind his eyes. 'But I have duties to perform,' he protested.

'Not according to the great man in whose bed you lie,' said the doctor sternly. 'My orders are to get you well enough to travel, and that will take a whole week if not longer.'

Agrippa nodded his agreement, accepting the cup that was handed to him. 'Quite right, doctor. We have high hopes for this soldier and his *optio*, if they both agree.' They all drank, Crispus greedily, Titus cautiously. 'Now if you wouldn't mind, doctor, we have business to discuss, so with our gratitude, please leave us.' Standing, he addressed the servants. 'All of you, make yourselves busy elsewhere.'

When the last of them had backed out, bowing, closing the heavy curtains that served as a door, Agrippa turned to Crispus. 'The reports I have received refer to you as Crispus,' he said, sitting again on the bed. 'So that I am clear, what is your full name?'

'Just Crispus, sir. A freedman without fancy names.' Then, for fear of offending Agrippa, he blustered, 'I mean, sir, I've never seen the point...'

'I understand, soldier. I happen to know that you excelled in the arena as a *secutor*. That and your name and origin is by the by, although I suspect you are from a Gallic tribe?' Crispus affirmed with a puzzled look. 'But all I want to know about you is your loyalty.'

Crispus bridled. 'If anyone doubts...'

Agrippa held up a hand. 'Titus, do you have any doubts?'

'None, sir. Crispus was recruited to the Fifth by Marcus Antonius before Dyrrhachium, and we were teamed up four or five years ago in Africa. He is my right arm and my friend.'

'Good, then we can proceed,' said Agrippa. He reached into a pouch at his belt and took out a small scroll and a *fibula* brooch, handing them to Titus. 'Have you ever seen a *fibula* like this?'

Titus examined the brooch, a snake with two heads wrought in silver and bronze, its body a double S, the tail's end a clasp for the pin that was hinged where the heads joined. 'No, sir, not one with two heads.'

'That's because you've never met one of my *viperae*,' said Agrippa conspiratorially. 'It's yours; wear it to clasp your cloak or at your left shoulder. Where you're going, you will meet others with this symbol.'

'Antonius told me about Sicilia,' said Titus, mesmerised by the brooch's workmanship. 'Is this to be our assignment?'

'Yes,' said Agrippa solemnly. Pointing to the scroll, he added, 'There is a message written there, and if the good doctor is to be obeyed, you have a week to understand it and tell me what it says. I have business in Neapolis, which in case you didn't know is just ten miles south of here. I will be securing the port and persuading Brutus's legions to join our cause for the good of Rome.' He turned to Crispus. 'You will come with me.'

'But —'

Again, Agrippa interrupted the *optio*. 'You will be responsible for planning Titus's journey south and then across the sea to Sicilia.'

Titus was alarmed. 'But we heard the seas are controlled by Ahenobarbus. Are we to masquerade as the enemy, our enemies?'

'That won't be necessary,' Agrippa smiled. 'After what has happened here, Romans no longer want to fight with Romans. For our part, we will not waste Roman lives and Rome's wealth on further conflict. Most of our opponents accept this, or will come to accept it. Many will join us and all who do will be pardoned. If Sextus Pompey will come to his senses, all will be well and good, but if not…' He let the sentence hang, adding more weight to Titus's mission. 'Some will take ship with Ahenobarbus or Murcus. If they do, I pity them, as these are no longer admirals, just petty, aggrieved pirates. If any are sailing to Sicilia, you can go with them as long as you have coin — which, of course, you will.'

'Ahenobarbus I know,' said Titus, 'but who is Murcus?'

'Lucius Staius Murcus was Caesar's legate in Gaul and Africa but hitched his doubtful future to the assassin Cassius. He thinks he is Neptune's gift to Roman seamanship. He has a habit of choosing the wrong side, so he may well join with Sextus in Sicilia.'

Titus felt his wounds throb with the exertion of thinking about politics and impending travels. Agrippa noticed him wince at the pain.

'I have an important meeting to attend, so I will leave you now. Rest assured, in a week's time you will have a comfortable carriage to take you to even more comfortable lodgings in Neapolis port. You will have a traveller's trunk with the finest clothing and other requirements for the journey. This trunk will have a false compartment containing coin and gold, depending on what I can get my hands on, and instructions about who you will meet and how you will send messages to my secretary. All will be made clear. Crispus, you'll come with me. It's going to be a busy week.'

As soon as they had gone, Titus opened the scroll and read the contents. The message made no sense whatsoever.

CHAPTER FIVE

Titus leaned heavily on his walking stick as he breathed in the courtyard garden's herbal aromas. The *domus* newly acquired by Agrippa was conveniently positioned a short walk from the harbour at Neapolis, sufficient distance to escape the crowds of refugee soldiers and the overwhelming stench of rotting fish and human waste. The housekeeper, Philotas, had used some of the herbs to make mysterious poultices to bind his wounds, reducing the dull ache and freeing his stiff joints. Ten days had passed since the battle, and he was beginning to believe that he would soon be well enough to travel home.

Philotas interrupted his self-indulgence to announce that General Agrippa awaited his pleasure in the *vestibulum*, and for the first time Titus noticed he was wearing a viper brooch. He made a mental note to question the servant about his involvement in Agrippa's spy network, but for now there were more important matters to attend to.

Agrippa wore dress armour, a heroic bronze cuirass with patterned silver overlay, and he had a proudly plumed helmet clutched under his arm. But Titus noticed the sheathed *gladius* at his hip was not ornate, rather the functional weapon he was comfortable with in battle. The general obviously considered that defeated foes in Neapolis remained a threat.

'I see you are recovering well,' said Agrippa as Titus gestured him towards the *tablinum* where Philotas was laying refreshments on a low table between cushioned couches. They sat opposite each other.

'In mind and body,' Titus replied, laying his walking stick on the seat beside him. 'I have a message for you,' he added, handing a scroll across.

Agrippa untied it and read, a smile spreading across his face. 'This looks like perfect nonsense to me,' said the general. 'Please be patient while I puzzle its meaning.' On the table was a wax tablet and a stylus. Agrippa took it and swiftly penned the alphabet's twenty-three letters. Then, looking at the scroll's first word, he began placing a dot beneath each following letter, moved one place to the right, on the wax tablet. Frowning, he erased the dots with the flat end of the stylus and tried again. On his fourth attempt, his eyes lit up and he proceeded to the next word in the message, the stylus moving swiftly as he recorded the decoded message in the space below.

He chuckled and gave his pupil an admiring glance, handing him the tablet. Titus read aloud. 'Though confused at first, I have understood.' He looked up and added, 'I would have written more, sir, but this old soldier is not used to writing.'

'How long did it take you?'

'Not long, as you only moved one letter to the right each time. I assumed you intend the system to use more difficult substitution, as I have done?'

'Indeed,' agreed Agrippa. 'My message to you was based on Julius Caesar's method, shown to me by Octavian. As far as we know, it offers the secrecy we vipers need, but perhaps it should be made more complicated. A job for you in your autumn years…?'

'Oh, I don't know about that,' replied Titus, modestly.

'I happen to know that your Sicilian upbringing has made you proficient in both Greek and Latin — I have your legate to thank for that detail. Perhaps we can interchange languages too?'

'I also speak Sicilia's own dialect, but that would confuse both writer and reader.'

'This system will suffice for now,' said Agrippa. He called for Philotas. The servant entered immediately, proving that he had been listening at the doorway. 'Philotas has used the same system to keep the Triumvirate fully informed in recent months.' The servant bowed gratefully. 'In this way, we were aware of equipment and supplies reaching Brutus, and the unfortunate loss of our reinforcements at sea before the battle. Information can be as important as numbers of men, and you can help us in Sicilia as Philotas has helped us here.'

Agrippa invited Philotas to sit next to him. A servant seated with one of Rome's highest-ranking officers was just another strange turn of events that Titus no longer found confusing. 'I will now explain what we want, and together we will answer your questions.'

It soon became apparent that Agrippa's network extended to a Sicilian innkeeper at Messana, a harbour official at Panormus and a brothel overseer in Syracuse. 'You do not need to know how she was recruited,' said the general hastily. All wore viper brooches, but none had access to Sicilia's inner sanctum of officialdom, which was to be Titus's mission. Each of them could arrange for messages to be sent to Agrippa's secretary in Rome via friendly merchant captains and coastal traders.

'But how am I to seek passage to Sicilia when the seas are controlled by supporters of Brutus and Cassius?' asked Titus.

Philotas answered for Agrippa. 'No one at the port is asking. The captains, both merchantmen and militia, no longer care about factions. Only money.'

'The same applies to Sicilia,' said Agrippa. 'You are simply a wounded officer returning home. You have talents and knowledge that you can pass to Sextus to win his confidence, and I will even give you information that he will find useful. You will rank highly in his eyes.'

'Like a double agent, you mean?' Titus smiled.

For a moment Agrippa frowned thoughtfully, then shrugged. 'On double pay, if you play the game right,' he said. 'Now, where's your man, Crispus?'

The port was chaotic. Galleys and traders tugged at their moorings, fighting a brisk northerly. Soldiers and merchants argued on the dockside, flinging arms wide and cramming another twenty refugees onto their low-riding vessels. Sterns landward, ships jostled for position and access while their captains complained loudly about the damage being caused to bulwarks and steering gear as they lurched and swung together in the choppy harbour.

Crispus used his choicest language to find passage to Sicilia. He harangued and threatened until eventually a merchant captain pointed to a galley riding at anchor some two hundred yards offshore. 'That's Murcus over there,' said the hard-pressed captain. 'Try him.'

'What do you suggest? That I swim out there?' asked Crispus, exasperated. The man just shrugged and turned to yell at his crew to fend off the vessel alongside. Crispus grabbed him by the collar, pulling him close, a dagger pressed firmly at his throat.

'If you value your life, you'll talk to me in a calm, sensible way.'

The captain was clearly terrified. 'Spare me, sir,' he stammered. 'I am just a humble merchant's captain.'

'Then you will tell me how you know that ship out there is going to Sicilia.'

'The pennant, sir. It's blue. Blue for Sicilia.'

Crispus looked across and saw that a blue flag fluttered from the ship's mast, and noticed the crew were painting its archers' tower a similar colour.

'So how do I get to it?'

His victim found some courage. 'I'm just a poor sailor, sir. But I know that Murcus is not aboard that ship…'

'So you know where he is? How much?'

Greed shone in the captain's eyes. 'Ten.'

'Five, and you take me to him, or you die right here on the dockside.' Five denarii was nothing to Titus's swollen purse, and Crispus had fifty in his money-belt.

The captain nodded rapidly, pleased that he had secured a little extra cash for his pains, and he knew exactly where Murcus was — in a tavern just a short walk away.

The Sailor's Rest was no less busy than the port itself. Soldiers, seamen and civilians alike were crammed into its filthy rooms. The floor was sticky with spilled wine and the noise was overwhelming. Crispus, holding his terrified guide by the back of his neck, pushed him further inside, drawing curses from dubious customers. 'Show me.'

The captain looked around then craned his neck over the crowds. 'I see him.'

'Which one?'

'My money first, sir?'

Crispus paid him but did not let go of his neck. The captain pointed to a rotund, red-faced man who was laughing at someone's joke and in the process of throwing back whatever brew lurked in his cup. Without letting go, Crispus shouted, 'Murcus!'

The man immediately looked across the room, confirming his identity. Crispus let his guide go and elbowed his way through the foul-smelling throng. Murcus watched him come, hand on a dagger at his belt. *A man with enemies*, thought Crispus.

'You are Captain Murcus?'

'*Imperator* Murcus,' the surly captain replied. 'What of it?'

'You sail to Sicilia?'

'Who's asking?'

'Can we talk somewhere quieter?'

'These are my friends,' he snarled. 'No secrets here.'

'Very well, if I must shout. I act for my senior officer, who was wounded at Philippi. He seeks passage home.'

Murcus looked Crispus up and down, seeing before him a muscular warrior with a bulging money-belt and an oversized knife at his waist. What he saw dispelled any thoughts of a straightforward mugging. His friends had fallen silent, intrigued.

'Who is your client? From which side?'

Crispus smiled knowingly, his eyes remaining cold.

'It will cost you,' Murcus continued. 'One hundred.'

'Very well, but for that my master will have your cabin.'

Murcus burst out laughing, looking to his friends for encouragement. They all joined in the fake jollity, some shaking their heads. The captain put his hand on Crispus's arm to find it brushed angrily away.

'One hundred and fifty,' mouthed Crispus, his meaning clear despite the din.

'Must be a rich man, your master. Who is he again?'

'I didn't tell you his name, but you will not recognise him and neither will you repeat this to anyone.' Crispus knew this was unlikely, not least because those nearest had hung on every word. 'I will take you to him at the third hour tomorrow. Meet me here unarmed and with your senior officer.' He turned to leave, but hesitated. 'On second thoughts, you can bring your sword if you wish, along with your hangover. Won't do you any good, though.'

CHAPTER SIX

The Sicilian fleet did not take kindly to the approaching quinquereme and its three escorts, even though they showed the island's colours. Five fast *liburnians* cut through confused waters to intercept, sea wolves with teeth bared. Behind them Messana's imposing pharos lighthouse marked the island as a naval power in its own right. A fist shaken in the face of Rome.

Titus felt a surge of pride that his homeland's navy had come so far in the five years he'd been away, first with Caesar in Africa and Spain, and thence to the struggle against the Dictator's assassins and Philippi's bloody climax. Legs braced against the swell, the breeze roughing his untamed hair, he wondered whether Zerenia and his children were watching — the twins would be six now, grown fat on Sicilia's abundance — but then why would they care about a newcomer when the approach to the Messana straits never ceased to teem with shipping?

Murcus stood next to him on the quinquereme's command platform, grudgingly respectful after hearing how the battle-hardened veteran had earned his forthcoming retirement in so many decisive battles. The naval commander seemed not to consider Titus as a foe, just another returning soldier, crisscrossed with livid scars. His companion, Crispus, was another matter altogether. Murcus would happily have seen the giant murdered in his sleep and tossed overboard if he hadn't been the source of an unexpected supply of coin. He would have to make do with the satisfaction of seeing Crispus retch violently over his ship's bulwarks for virtually the whole voyage.

They watched the *liburnians* approach. 'Good seamanship,' observed Murcus. 'See how they use the strait's currents to aid passage.'

'A rich piratical history,' mused Titus, 'but these ships are much more impressive than the clumsy vessels I remember from my youth.'

Murcus smiled. 'That's why I'm here. A fleet to control Rome by squeezing her grain supplies. The starving hordes will soon bring down these pretentious triumvirs.' Whenever he had Titus's ear, he had enthused about Sicilia's organised piracy and seemed determined to continue the struggle despite the disappointment of Philippi.

As the Sicilians approached, white water creaming at their bows, Murcus's command to down oars was conveyed to the three banks of rowers, and the quinquereme began to slow, the helmsmen heaving on their steering beams to hold the ship's course. With perfectly timed strokes, two of the Sicilian *liburnians* surged either side of the larger visitor, the other three ranged between them and the port with its shingle breakwater guarded by the pharos. On the decks of both, grim archers held bows with arrows nocked. Murcus just laughed and called across to the nearest captain.

'Come any closer and you will be welcomed into Neptune's scaly arms!'

A response, shouted in Greek, floated across thirty yards of churning waters. 'Who comes hither?'

Murcus clearly didn't speak the language, so on seeing his puzzled look, Titus told him, 'They want to know who you are.'

'You tell them,' Murcus scowled, 'before they pass too far.'

Titus took a deep breath. 'We are from Neapolis in Macedonia, bringing reserves from the legions of great Cassius and noble Brutus.' He hoped Sextus would welcome such, given the man's stand against Caesar, who had vanquished his father Pompey Magnus.

'Enter under half-oars and report to the...' The rest was lost on the breeze.

'Better do as he says,' said Titus after translating the message. In a skilful display of seamanship, the *liburnians* took up position around the quinquereme, giving no room for sudden manoeuvre. Fifteen days out of Neapolis and foul autumn winds had put the crew in no mood for anything more than making port, partaking of local food and ale, then falling into a woman's embrace. The soldiers on board had been grumbling for most of the journey. While Crispus had suffered, especially where powerful currents collide south of Achaea, Titus had revelled in it. Now he sniffed the saltiness of the straits and turned his gaze to the very spot where his small parcel of land no doubt dripped with fruit and olives and his woman baked oatcakes and flatbreads at the kitchen fire.

Murcus pointed to an appropriate mooring as the *liburnians* lost interest and went elsewhere to police their waters. Meanwhile, Titus surveyed the vast natural harbour, making a mental note of the size of the Sicilian fleet for his first report as Rome's eyes and ears. It was plain to him that Sextus had spared no effort in transforming Messana into a naval base to threaten Rome — most of the ships riding at anchor or moored at quaysides were smaller triremes and *liburnians*, while several larger troop transporters dominated the deeper waters. Rows of newly built ship-sheds were a hive of activity both for construction and repair, while half-a-dozen galleys were beached nearby, propped with timbers to replace planking infested with shipworm.

As ropes were cast to swarthy dockers, an officious-looking Sicilian and a handful of nervous yet well-equipped guardsmen waited on the quayside. Their leader was a balding old man clasping a wax tablet, who waved his arms frantically as the gangway was being extended.

'Wait, wait,' he pleaded as Murcus stood at the rails, summoning men and crew to disembark.

'What do you want?' Murcus shouted scornfully. 'I have four hundred heroes of the Republic itching to lend their swords to Sextus Pompeius, and if you're going to stand in our way you will soon find yourself as fish food in this stinking place you call a port.'

But Titus was first to the top of the gangway, Crispus beside him. 'The first thing off this vessel will be my trunk, then the others can disembark,' he called to Murcus. He turned to address the port official. 'And you, send word to Sextus Pompeius that Titus Villius Macer has returned to Sicilia.' As the clerk looked at him aghast, he added, 'Now!'

Murcus roared with laughter. The official looked around, bewildered, then spoke to one of his assembled guards and the man ran off. Titus stepped onto the gangplank but hesitated at the rasp of swords being drawn and looked down at the half-dozen men blocking his way. Behind him, Crispus muttered, 'Looks like we're going to have to fight our way into this primitive land. This lot will soon be scurrying home to their mothers.'

Titus just smiled and advanced towards the guard, the clerk cowering behind his men. As one they melted back, because Titus and his *optio* didn't break stride. Murcus continued to indulge his amusement and ordered two men to carry Titus's trunk to the quayside.

The sound of an approaching squad distracted them. All turned to see a magnificently robed warrior astride a white stallion, at his back at least thirty foot soldiers armed with shield, sword and spear. The clerk hurried his guard away, allowing the newcomer to lead his men closer to the moored quinquereme. Titus and Crispus turned to face them while Murcus ordered his archers to assemble on the ship's deck.

'State your purpose,' demanded the mounted officer, his features concealed under a blue-plumed helmet. His silver cuirass glinted in the afternoon sunshine, and at his hip was the distinctive curve of a falcata blade, a weapon favoured by Mare Nostrum's pirates.

'Who wants to know?' Titus was beginning to lose patience.

Scowling, the officer dismounted and removed his helmet to reveal a shock of blond hair. The first thing that struck Titus was not the colour of his hair, so unusual in these parts, but his flawless, chiselled features and piercing blue eyes. *That is the face of a cruel man*, thought Titus. He sensed Crispus fingering his *gladius* next to him and put a hand on his shoulder. 'Be calm,' he whispered. 'Let me handle this.' The two men faced each other like bristling dogs.

'Before I tell you who I am,' said Titus quietly, 'you can tell me who you are.'

The officer spat at Titus's feet and smiled, cocking his head to one side in a display of arrogance. Then, with forefingers tensed, he pushed Titus's chest, forcing him to take a step back. Titus silently ordered himself not to reach for his sword, instead smiling back. On the ship, Murcus whistled to his archers to ready their weapons. The officer ignored them.

'A bully, then,' said Titus, still smiling. 'And a foolish bully at that, or are those not fifty very sharp arrows pointing right at you?'

'Perhaps you are the foolish one here, if you want to pick a fight with Azhar, commander of the armies of Sicilia.' His voice was silky and refined, yet his whole demeanour dripped with venom. 'Now that you know how perilous your position is, on *my* island —' here he raised his voice menacingly — 'you *will* state your purpose!'

Titus forced himself to stay calm, but he sensed Crispus might take a different approach, so he said firmly, 'If you must know, I am Titus Villius Macer, returning to my home after many years of campaigning in foreign lands.' He decided on the spur of the moment not to mention that he was a Roman citizen, but his name probably gave that away. 'Now, if you and your men would be so good as to clear the way, I am hungry, tired and not in good humour, and I wish to see my woman and my children, who await me not two miles behind you. Now *you* tell *me* —' he too raised his voice and pointed a finger at the officer — 'just how long we have to stand around like women gossiping in the market!'

Azhar's arrogant smile appeared again. This time, his eyes focused on the viper brooch that clasped Titus's cloak at his chest. He reached out to touch it, but Titus slapped his hand away. 'A pretty piece,' said Azhar. 'As pretty as your woman? And your pretty children? Do I know them?'

Crispus lost patience. He pushed past Titus, sweeping aside his cloak. His dagger was at the officer's throat before he could move. 'Now you back off, Sicilian, or your blood will stain this foul island before you can blink.'

The men behind drew their swords, all wielding menacing falcatas and drawing leather-clad shields to eye level.

'Wait!' cried Titus, pulling Crispus back. Titus knew a dockside fight was pointless and would defeat his objective before he had even begun. Turning to the officer, he said, as calmly as he could, 'In whose name do you challenge us?'

'My own,' came the reply. Azhar seemed unruffled by Crispus's outburst.

'Are you Imperator here? Or king? What of Sextus Pompeius? Is he not lord in Sicilia?'

'What of it? I am invested of all authority here.' But Titus saw doubt in his eyes, just a flicker, that betrayed his true position.

Murcus interrupted the exchange. 'Enough of this!' he shouted and strode down the gangplank, impatiently waving his archers to stand down. The crew cheered their captain as he pushed between Titus and Crispus and faced the regal officer. Shorter than all three by a head, Murcus puffed out his chest. His face was reddened by sea storms, and his riotous hair and beard were in need of a Messana barber. 'Get your ruffians out of our way unless you can immediately escort us to Sextus Pompeius himself, so that he can apologise in person for this unacceptable delay.'

Azhar smiled again, and Titus thought how sweet it would be to break his nose if Crispus or Murcus didn't do it first.

'I should arrest you for insolence,' Azhar snarled, 'all three of you.'

'You can try,' said Murcus, 'but somehow I don't think Sextus Pompeius would take kindly to that.'

'Indeed he wouldn't.' A new voice in the argument. Almost soft, yet with just enough authority to silence the dispute. All four turned to see who had spoken.

The man was dressed in a hooded peasant's robe, his eyes in shadow, yet beneath the folds was the hint of a lithe frame. He pulled back the hood to reveal the clean-shaven face of an amused young man in his mid-twenties, with dark, well-groomed hair and a crooked smile.

Sextus Pompeius Magnus Pius, son of Pompey the Great and scourge of Roman supply shipping, had come to greet — or arrest — the newcomers in person.

CHAPTER SEVEN

'I don't care one jot who you fought for,' said Sextus. 'You are a Sicilian before you are a Roman, and you saved my life, what is it, ten years ago?'

After ordering Azhar to accommodate Murcus and his men in the port's barracks, Sextus had retained his anonymity while leading Titus and Crispus to The Blue Flag, an inn favoured by visiting officials and merchants. Two slaves had carried the trunk to a first-floor room, while the three men procured a jug of Sicilia's finest wine and a large plate of delicacies to banish the memory of meagre rations, lurching decks and cramped quarters.

Titus recalled the days when he had taught the teenage sons of Rome's greatest general to fish among the tuna shoals off Syracuse. 'You broke all the rules by going out alone in that leaky tub of yours,' he said, 'and ignoring all the signs that Tempestas was in a foul mood that day!'

Sextus produced his habitual look of mild amusement, bringing back a memory for Titus of a youth who embraced danger and never doubted his unsinkable ability as a sailor. He had a sense of adventure that refused to abate, even when his father had suffered an ignominious death in Egypt and his friends and allies were defeated in Spain. 'Good thing you were making for port nearby when I lost the mast and went over. I was beginning to get slightly worried. And I was very wet.'

Crispus interrupted their reminiscences. 'Don't expect me to join your seafaring madness. Getting here was bad enough. Solid ground beneath my boots is all I ask.'

Laughing, Titus held up his cup to Crispus. 'Here's to solid ground, then, and a life of plenty provided by Sicilia's rich earth.' Turning to Sextus, he added, 'And to the sea, which if I'm not mistaken you rule from here to Greece. Quite the pirate and a thorn in Rome's side.'

'Perhaps. Perhaps not.' Sextus paused to drink. 'The senate gave me command of the seas, but it seems these overblown triumvirs hold all the power now. But I have a hundred ships and more join us every day, including Murcus and before long Ahenobarbus. And now I have a letter from Marcus Antonius seeking an alliance.'

Titus raised an eyebrow. Perhaps there was hope for peace at last, but did Octavian know? Crispus looked bored and instead turned his attention to a buxom serving girl who had been admiring the muscular soldier from across the room.

Sextus changed the subject. 'You'll want to rest, then go home to that beautiful woman of yours.'

Another shock for Titus. 'You know Zerenia? How? And the children?'

'Of course I know Zerenia — through her father. He came to me for protection.'

'Protection from what? Or who? Are they safe?'

Sextus threw up his hands to slow the interrogation. 'Rogues, that's all. It seems someone had designs on your land — I don't think it was any more than that. Besides, your slaves proved more than capable and had everything under control.'

'Not slaves,' protested Titus. 'They are paid servants. What of my family?'

'All safe. Azhar has posted men to keep a watchful eye on them.'

This worried Titus, who had already witnessed Azhar's questionable character, but he let it go. 'Thank you, Sextus. It seems it is now me who owes you.'

'I'll hear none of that,' said Sextus, calling for more wine. 'Zerenia and the children are safe. I will send a messenger today to announce your return and have a fine wagon outside in the morning to take you to them. And then, when you have done those things expected of a returning lover, we can discuss your forthcoming role in Sicilia's navy.'

Titus was about to protest when the innkeeper brought another jug of wine. Sextus introduced him. 'Ah, Niko, meet Titus Villius Macer, a hero returned from Philippi, and his man Crispus. Look after them well and always serve them your finest wine.'

Niko smiled, placing the jug on the table. He was stocky bordering on fat, with a jovial face and a shiny bald head. 'Pleased to meet you,' he said. His eyes took in Titus's viper brooch as Sextus poured.

And Titus found himself looking at a *fibula* exactly the same as his own, pinned to hold the shoulder ties of Niko's apron.

Niko maintained his cover well, busying himself in the kitchens while the three men concluded their business, Sextus eventually staggering towards the port to find Murcus to discuss the deployment of his ships and men. 'I don't trust Murcus,' Sextus had slurred, 'but his reputation precedes him.' He had revealed how Sicilia had seen an influx of slaves and freedmen escaping unrest on mainland Italia, many of them proving their worth as sailors and marines, including two capable officers, now his chief admirals, Menodorus and Menecrates. These did not even try to pretend they were not pirates, and with Azhar formed a trio of warlike officers under the command of Sextus.

They had talked at length as Niko's wine took its effect, trading tales of the sea and the fish they had caught, the tunny becoming steadily larger with each recollection. But Titus had touched a raw nerve when he mentioned Sextus's father, the great general who had once been Caesar's friend but who had fled east after defeat at Pharsalus, forgetting that Sextus had probably witnessed his father's murder on Egypt's shore. At this, Sextus had displayed a rare moment of grief but then, fuelled by wine, had become angry at Caesar's incessant pursuit of all Republicans and the subsequent deaths of all of their leaders. 'Except me,' he had slurred, 'and now since *Uncle Bloody Julius* got what he deserved, we have these upstart fools taking up his mantle. While I've got breath in my body, I'll give them hell. They'll get no mercy from me.'

Titus had tried to placate him, first by suggesting that he might treat for peace, and then by hinting that Antonius had money to burn and Sextus should relieve him of lots of it. 'I always respected you, Titus, but why, old friend, did you end up fighting on the wrong side?'

It was a question Titus had hoped to avoid, but he put a paternal arm around the young Pompey's shoulders and told him, 'I had no choice. I was in a Sicilian legion that owed allegiance to Rome, and I was enlisted in the Fifth Alaudae. I had no idea the war would continue in Africa and then in Spain. Believe me, if I had known I was taking up arms against you and your Republicans, I would have remained here and tended my vines — and caught bigger fish than you ever managed.'

'I know, I know,' a smiling and very drunk Sextus had replied, 'and I want you to know you're forgiven. You're here now, and when you've settled in with your lovely wife once more, we'll go fishing and forget that Julius Bloody Caesar ever set foot on this island.'

After Sextus left, Titus shrugged off the effects of the wine and found the landlord Niko in the inn's garden picking a basket of figs, and fished for clues as to whether he was Agrippa's man. It became apparent that messages could be sent with ease through Niko's network of well-paid trading captains, no questions asked and money passed secretly in order not to arouse suspicion. The next opportunity would be the following day, so Titus hurried to his room and unlocked the concealed compartment in the base of his trunk. Using a wax tablet for his notes and coding, he then transferred a message to vellum.

VIPERA was the agreed first word for every message. This would give Agrippa the key to the code used for that message. He wrote ZMSHVD thus showing that the code was three letters removed using the alphabet's twenty-three letters. Then he coded his message:

Hundred ships, sixty at Messana with more under construction. Murcus has brought four ships with many men. More follow. Antonius seeks alliance with S.P.

Not bad after just one day, thought Titus. Crispus, who had kept himself busy by paring his nails, peered over Titus's shoulder.

'But you can't read,' Titus said.

'So this makes even less sense,' laughed Crispus. 'What would Sextus think if he knew?'

'I don't think I've said anything that Agrippa doesn't already know. And if Sextus asks about the triumvirs, I'll tell him what I know. But I don't think Sextus really cares who knows what he's doing, as it's pretty obvious to everyone concerned, so

we'll just take the money and enjoy a quiet life. But Azhar …
now he's a different proposition altogether.'

'Any trouble from him and he'll feel how sharp my sword is.'

Titus snorted. 'You and whose army?'

The wagon, pulled by two well-fed mules coaxed by an elderly
veteran with little to say, was comfortable enough. Titus
directed him south, along rutted lanes, past ramshackle slums,
the stench of excrement mingling with rotting fish, past
mutilated beggars pleading for coin and gangs of grubby
children challenging the passengers with wooden swords. All
were ignored as Titus gave Crispus a running commentary
about the land of his birth.

Recent rain had made the going slow for all travellers, and
twice the pair had to put their shoulders to the wagon as the
driver cursed the mules forward. Eventually they approached
their destination, which Titus had described as an idyllic
farmstead with orchards and vineyards leading down to a
sheltered cove where his much-loved fishing smack would be
beached, longing for him to take her to sea once again.

But it was not as Titus had left it five years earlier.

Obeying his soldier's instinct to survey the territory, Titus
ordered the driver to halt while he and Crispus took in the
scene before them. A small military encampment guarded the
approach, and Titus could see two unusual galleys on the bay's
shingle, high-sided and shorter than traditional Roman fighting
ships, their crews cleaning the hulls and making repairs to
rigging and equipment. Smoke curled from several cooking
fires where makeshift kitchens had been set up, and the
murmur of coarse language disturbed the once-peaceful haven.

'This isn't right,' said Titus after a long silence.

'Not what I expected either,' muttered Crispus.

'Never seen ships like those before. Foreigners, maybe? And that camp looks too well organised to be anything other than military. Something to do with that nasty Azhar fellow?'

Crispus grunted, as he always did when he had nothing to add to the conversation.

'Better find out then,' said Titus.

The wagon turned into the smallholding that had once boasted sturdy wooden gates and a large sign reading PAX VILLIUS but was now marked only by the crumbling remains of a stone wall. Beside the track leading to the farmhouse was a regimented square of eight tents positioned around a firepit, over which a blackened pot hung from a tripod of spears. A dozen soldiers lazed nearby, one of them heaving his stocky frame to his feet as the wagon approached. He stood in the track and held up a hand to halt their approach, then sauntered casually around the mules and the wagon as if inspecting them for any slight fault. He looked at each of the three men in turn before undoing his trousers to piss on the wheel.

'You lost?' he asked, shaking the last drops and retying his waistband. Although young and clearly in need of a wash, he bore himself with a degree of arrogance that told Titus he might be able to hold his own in a fight.

'No,' replied Titus, 'are you?'

'Don't get smart with me, old man. Now state your business.'

'My business is nothing to do with you. Stand aside.'

The soldier instinctively reached for his sword but did not draw it. He narrowed his eyes, glanced over his shoulder to see if his colleagues would support him, then returned his attention to Titus. 'So that's how it's going to be, is it? You sure you're tough enough?'

In one swift, easy movement, Titus leapt down and was instantly close enough to the youth to prevent him from drawing his falcata. He placed his hand on the soldier's where it gripped his sword hilt, and with his other delivered a playful pat on the cheek. This startled the youth, who took a step back. He tugged at his sword, but Titus held his hand firmly. Crispus laughed.

Seeing the commotion, several of the other soldiers rushed to their colleague's aid, but by the time they had arrived, Crispus was at Titus's side, *gladius* in one hand and dagger in the other. 'Ready when you are,' snarled the former gladiator.

'Wait!' shouted Titus. 'I for one would like to know what these fine gentlemen are doing on my land before we kill them, don't you agree, *optio*?' He deliberately referred to Crispus's rank so that his opponents would realise that they were dealing with a senior Roman centurion. To a man, the ruffian soldiers hesitated.

Their leader regained his confidence. 'What do you mean, your land? This belongs to the People of Sicilia and is under my protection.'

'Well, thank you for looking after it for me,' said Titus. 'Now pack your bags and off you go.'

'Eh?'

'And when you report to your superior, tell him that Titus Villius Macer has returned. If he wants to come and enjoy my Pax Villius vintage, he is most welcome, but he will leave his sword at home.'

Though they were seasoned veterans, Titus and Crispus were outnumbered fourfold by these callow youths of Sicilia's army, and there was no doubt who would come off best in an encounter. But it did not come to that as a motley group made their way from the farmstead and the surrounding groves to see what was taxing the minds of their guardians.

Leading them was a tall woman in a full-length black robe belted at the waist, her dark hair held firm by a headscarf tasselled with silver bells. Beside and slightly behind her, cautiously peering at the newcomers, were two children, twin girls, fear etched on their young faces. On her hip was a child, who buried its face in her shoulder.

Zerenia strode to where the two veterans stood with the estate's self-appointed guardians. She did not smile as she passed the youngest child to an old yet sprightly man whom Titus instantly recognised.

Then she punched Titus, her fist finding his jaw with such force that the former *primus pilus* of the Fifth Alaudae, who had never retreated in his entire career, staggered backwards with a flashing behind his eyes.

CHAPTER EIGHT

When Titus recovered his senses, he found himself face to face with Eshmun, who held in his arms a child, barely two years of age.

'Hello, Great Father,' he said, rubbing his jaw.

'She is not pleased with you,' said Eshmun, the father of his betrothed.

'Bet that hurt,' said Crispus. 'I never thought I would see Titus Villius Macer bested in battle, and by a woman at that.' Gazing after her, he added, 'I like this woman!'

Titus was still rubbing his jaw and watching Zerenia and those who had come with her as they returned to the farmstead. 'And who is this?' He pointed to the child.

'That is your third child,' said Eshmun.

'But she is barely two. What are you saying?'

'Listen to me, son. You will accept this child as your own. I do not know who her father is. Neither will you know who her father is unless my daughter tells you. All I can tell you is that she has died a little and she has never betrayed you. She needs you now more than ever.'

'But she has birthed a child with another man. The law says—'

'Do not even think that. She was raped, you ignorant Roman bastard! Does that make her the one at fault?'

Titus fell to his knees as the enormity of what had happened dawned on him. Then he looked up at Eshmun. 'I will not fail her. I have always loved her. And now I will kill the man who did this to her.'

'Are you going to kill every man within a half day's walk of here?' Eshmun knelt beside Titus. 'I would already have done that, if I thought it would help. But it doesn't, you see? She will not tell me, and she will not tell you. But I think she blames you for not being here when she needed your protection.'

Titus cursed his weakness as tears welled. Crispus looked away. The ruffians who had challenged Titus scuffed their boots in the dirt. The driver of the wagon said, 'Am I finished here, sir?'

Crispus answered him. 'No, you are not. Deliver the centurion's trunk to the farmhouse over there, and then you can return to Messana. You will not speak of this to anyone, ever. Am I clear?'

The driver nodded solemnly and flicked the mules forward towards Pax Villius, leaving the group of hardened men to their misery.

Titus sat forlornly on the trunk near the farmhouse door, the child on his knee busying itself with the viper *fibula* on his jerkin, while Crispus wandered into the vineyard to talk to the men who worked there. Eshmun rapped on the door that had been barred on the inside, calling his daughter, pleading with her to open it. There was no response.

'There is another way in, but I think it best that we wait for Zerenia to allow us entry herself,' said Eshmun. 'She's not one to be crossed when she's in a bad mood.'

'I understand why she doesn't want to see me,' Titus mumbled, 'but what have you done to offend her?'

'Be born a man, probably,' Eshmun replied. The child, clearly a boy, had begun to wriggle.

'What's this little fellow's name?' asked Titus.

'We call him Smudge. He hasn't got a proper name yet.'

Titus managed a smile as a thought struck him. 'Smudge Villius has a ring to it, don't you think?' Awkwardly, he nudged the child's chin. 'Hello, Smudge. It seems I'm your new father.'

'A brother to Gaia and Marcia. They do not know you, but Zerenia has faithfully told them how you sailed away to Africa with Julius Caesar, and for many days they prayed together for your safe return. Eventually you became a distant memory, probably dead in a ditch many miles from home.'

'And here I am, returned from the dead and locked out of my own home.'

Both men turned at the sound of the locking beam being removed. The door opened just enough for a child to peer outside, her untidy dark hair covering much of her face. Eshmun crouched, his eyes level with the girl's. 'Come, Gaia, this is your father returned from the war. Where's your sister?'

Gaia looked suspiciously at Titus. The door was yielded further and another face appeared, almost identical. Titus watched them, hesitant but hopeful.

'This is the part where you sweep them up in a crushing embrace,' said Eshmun, and Titus reached out an arm to them, the other clinging to Smudge. Zerenia appeared behind her daughters, jaw set firm, but Titus thought he sensed a hint of softness in her dark eyes. He held her gaze, silently pleading with the woman he had deserted to fight wars in far-off lands she neither knew nor cared about, leaving her with two babies to fend for. He could now feel the pain and hurt he had caused, at long last understanding the cost of his stubbornness. He had been so enraptured with Caesar's zeal that he hadn't even said goodbye, nor kissed his daughters farewell. He had just obeyed the great man's command and herded his Sicilian auxiliaries onto the appointed galley and sailed south to fight the legions of Scipio and Cato at Thapsus. He'd even followed

Caesar beyond his death, to serve under Marcus Antonius and now Agrippa. For five years, he had deserted all that he had once held dear — a betrayal that Agrippa's gold and promises of land could never atone for.

He watched as Gaia and Marcia clung to their mother, hiding fearful faces from the stranger who had abandoned them, and slowly let his arm drop.

'Did you expect them to run to you and embrace you after all these years?' said Zerenia. Her voice was brittle, not the summer sea breeze he had carried in his memory.

'I... You look... I've missed you,' he stammered, and it sounded feeble. He tried again. 'Can you ever forgive me?' He handed Smudge to Eshmun and went to her. The twins cowered but Zerenia faced him, raising her fist to strike him again. She managed only a glancing blow on his jerkin, before falling into his arms.

'No,' she said, forcing back tears, wanting to strike him again and again, to hold him close, to forbid him from leaving her side. 'No ... maybe in time.'

Titus felt as though anything he might say now would spoil his slight chance of redemption, so he held her tight. She was mumbling incoherently into his shoulder. He wept, glad that Crispus was not near to see it. Eshmun shepherded the twins to their parents and was satisfied to see their grubby faces look up to their father as he held their mother, though they clung timorously to her rather than this strange man who might, one day, earn their respect.

'There,' said Eshmun. 'That's a start, at least.'

Three hours later, as the sun dipped behind Etna and the dish of goat, almonds and figs was wiped clean with flatbreads prepared by a jovial team of house servants, Eshmun whispered to Titus, 'Leave the children to their rest and come with me. I have something to show you. Bring Crispus.'

Dragging Crispus away from Zerenia was not easy, as he clearly worshipped her beauty and fiery character, but the three men soon made their way down a goat track that zigzagged to the bay below, where the two strange ships were beached. Crews and shipmasters were settling around beach fires for the evening's camaraderie, the sea's peaceful calm reflecting red and gold, bewitching even gulls and waders as dusk approached.

'I'll wager you haven't seen vessels like these before,' said Eshmun. He had a boyish enthusiasm for boat building; his craggy features were brought to life just by being close to the sea.

'Never seen anything like them,' replied Titus, 'although some fishing boats I saw in Utica had similar lines, though not so high-sided.'

They reached the first of the beached vessels, Eshmun waving to colleagues at the fires and resisting calls to drink with them. He ran an appreciative hand over the planking, and Titus noted that the gunwales were far higher than those of a traditional Roman galley. Eshmun sensed his unspoken question.

'Come alongside a galley and your archers are that much higher and shoot down,' he said with a distinct note of pride. 'And if the enemy tries to board, it's that much harder to climb up than leap across.'

Titus smiled, appreciating the point. 'Did you build these?'

'Not exactly. They came from the north, sailed past the Pillars of Hercules by adventurous Gauls. Veneti vessels originally, I think. Ships like these gave Caesar's fleet the runaround way back when he was eyeing up Britannia for invasion, and Sextus used these to escape after Caesar's triumph at Munda. But I have made some improvements. Apart from their height above the water, the big difference with these galleys is their dependence on wind. Look here.' Eshmun was in his element, animated as he pointed to the oar ports. There were few openings, positioned below deck, allowing nothing like the massed banks of oars that made Roman ships look like giant waterborne centipedes. 'These can outrun even a *liburnian* in a stiff breeze, but they're not much good in a flat calm, which is why Sextus isn't interested. The other problem is that they are flat-bottomed and tend to drift sideways if there isn't a following wind.'

Titus scratched his head. 'Not a lot going for them, then?'

'Not until I made some modifications. Come.'

Eshmun was first up a ladder at the bow, followed by Titus and Crispus. They looked across an upper deck that was wider and less cluttered than Murcus's quinquereme, with a central mast and a large sail furled around an unusual boom attached to an iron ring-pivot, hoisted vertically when not in use. Built into the high stern was a cabin and above it a lofty deck. Positioned on each side of the deck were four wooden contraptions that Titus instantly recognised as scorpios, the mobile catapults that Julius Caesar had used to fire iron bolts into his enemies' massed ranks to devastating effect. Titus ran his hand over the nearest, admiring the torsion ropes and the strength of the wooden frame. 'Different,' he said. 'I didn't realise these could be used on a ship.'

'Never mind those — we're making sprung iron cross parts for more power, but I've got something better to show you.' He pointed to a pulley contraption mounted just forward of the mast. 'Here is my invention,' he beamed. The three men peered into a narrow compartment into which two ropes descended from a two-man winch and appeared to suspend a large wooden blade with metal edging. Looking down into the enclosed opening, they could make out the beach's shingle below.

'There's a great big hole in the bottom of your boat!' said Crispus.

Eshmun feigned alarm. 'So there is.'

'I think I can see what you've done here,' said Titus, 'and it's very clever. As long as that opening is waterproofed, the sea can't rise above water level inside it, but your blade can be lowered beneath the boat where the water is deep enough. So you can lift it in shallow water or beaching.'

'Correct,' said Eshmun. 'But what's it for?'

'No idea,' said Crispus, betraying his seafaring ignorance.

Titus, who had spent much of his youth at sea in Sicilia's coastal waters, knew differently. 'This prevents the drag,' he said slowly. 'And it enables you to go in any direction except directly into the wind by adjusting the angle of the sail. Clever.'

'Precisely,' said Eshmun. 'Manoeuvrability.'

'But what do you do when there's no wind?'

'Ah,' Eshmun frowned. 'I'm working on that.'

CHAPTER NINE

Titus wanted nothing to do with Agrippa, Rome or even Sextus while he got his affairs in order, starting with his expanding family. He found it challenging to reinvent himself as a lover and father, and decided to bring Zerenia and the children small gifts every day until they welcomed him back. It seemed to be working, the bunches of wildflowers and brightly painted pebbles proving to be the best currency, as well as the model boats he made from offcuts cast aside by the ships' carpenters.

Crispus, immediately bored with family matters, had packed his sword and some coin and announced he was off to Messana in search of adventure.

'Come back soon and don't bother telling me about anything political, not Sextus's piracy nor impending invasion by Octavian's legions,' Titus told him as he left.

'You know I will,' Crispus replied, 'and I know that deep down that's what you expect.'

'Go, and don't catch anything unwholesome.'

He was gone for days, and Titus soon realised he missed the burly soldier's gruff ways and blunt opinions. He also missed his devotion to Zerenia and the children, and the way the household servants and field labourers looked up to the battle-scarred warrior.

But there was an advantage in not having Crispus nearby as a reminder of his lost years. Titus clumsily attempted to rediscover the freshness of young love, which Zerenia came to appreciate in a faintly amused way, but even when their lips brushed for the first time in five years, he knew he was not entirely forgiven, not least because the weight of her ordeal hung over him like a gathering storm. It was all he could do not to bring up the subject, and he groaned under the burden from which there was no relief, often waking in the darkest hour to curse the gods for their merciless torture.

He knew that none of the men who worked in the vineyards was responsible, yet he watched them all with suspicion. Every visitor was a suspect — the merchants seeking wine for Sicilia's nobility, suppliers bringing amphorae to be filled and stamped with the Pax Villius seal, seamen and captains seeking Eshmun's talents in ship design and repair. He scowled at every man and youth who visited and carefully watched Zerenia's mood on each occasion, looking for clues as to which man to kill — slowly and very painfully.

That urge was strongest the day Azhar and a small detachment of cavalry wheeled into the Pax Villius entrance, ostensibly to inspect the guard stationed there but in reality to make life uncomfortable for Titus and his household. They turned their horses free to graze in the vineyards and olive groves, Azhar slapping dust from his leathers while looking around for someone to bully. Titus watched him from a distance, hating the man's arrogance and longing to slide his sword between his ribs the moment he had proof that this was the degenerate who had raped his woman.

Zerenia had been in the fields with the children but when he looked for her, she was nowhere to be seen. Was this his proof? He chided himself for not keeping a cool head and went to meet the commander of Sicilia's land forces.

Azhar saw him coming and folded his arms, watching disdainfully. 'Ah, the hero of Rome has returned to his country hovel.'

Titus didn't break stride and moved close to him, eyes cold and unwelcoming. 'State your business and make it quick, then take your men and your horses somewhere they may be of more use than on my land.'

The response was not what Titus had been expecting. Azhar merely laughed and shook his head in mock disbelief.

'I have no intention of staying longer than it takes me to give my greetings to the Lady Zerenia —' at the mention of her name, Titus curled his fists and got ready to strike, but what came next was intended to wound more deeply — 'and to inform you that your man languishes in my dungeon, awaiting execution.'

'What? You lie! On what charge?'

'Oh, causing a disturbance, being drunk and reckless, stealing someone's wife, murdering innocents — you name it. He's guilty as Tartarus, and that's where he's going.'

'Now I know you are lying.' Titus locked his eyes on Azhar's and moved a step closer. 'So what is the real meaning of this?'

'Oh, none really. I just thought you should know. So you can bury him when I've removed his head.'

'You feel slighted that Crispus challenged you on the dock these weeks past. You didn't like him then and you don't like me. So this is your revenge? Does Sextus know you have arrested a Roman citizen and accused him wrongly?'

Titus watched for telltale signs that Azhar feared Sextus, or disliked him, and was satisfied to see that same flicker of doubt he had seen on Messana's dock. He was also interested to see if Azhar dared to deny that he had arrested an innocent man, and was not disappointed.

'In Sicilia, we do not care if a man is a Roman citizen,' said Azhar.

Titus sighed. 'So what will it take to free him?'

'You couldn't afford the price.'

'Try me.'

'You can start by telling me who you are working for.'

Titus was wrong-footed by that. His mind raced. What did Azhar know? How could he know anything about his mission for Agrippa? He ordered himself to stay calm and give nothing away.

'I work for no one other than myself. Explain what you mean.'

'Come, now. Your man has been heard singing the praises of Rome's armies at Philippi and your great generals, and these are Sicilia's enemies. Then you arrive arm-in-arm with Murcus, who may pretend that he is a friend of Sicilia, but we all know he loves nobody better than himself. So here is my price — which of these jumped-up despots are you working for? Tell me, and your man goes free. Remain silent, and he will beg for death long before I allow it.'

Titus played for time with a long, hard stare into the commander's eyes. He now knew that Azhar was clutching at straws. But why? Was he attempting to destroy both Crispus and himself so that he could gain free access to Pax Villius and Zerenia? He dismissed that thought instantly — it felt like jealousy, an emotion that was of no use to him. Was it pure hatred? Azhar's own jealousy of a man who had returned after battle feats that he could only dream of? That must be it.

'Your demands are just, Commander.' Titus kept his voice even, almost compliant. 'I will accompany you to Messana. When I have seen Crispus with my own eyes and have taken him to the baths to wash away the stink of your base hospitality, then and only then will I tell you all I know.'

Azhar was uncertain whether this was a triumph or a trick. His face betrayed him, so without hesitation Titus took and held the upper ground.

'As it happens, I will say this now to give you some assurance. I have spent time in the battle quarters of both Marcus Antonius and Gaius Julius Caesar Octavianus and have heard them discuss their hopes for Sicilia. And as Sextus Pompey is an old friend of mine — what, you did not know this? — nothing would give me greater pleasure than to tell you all that I know.'

Azhar almost visibly reeled.

'So now gather your men,' Titus continued, 'and form them up outside my land. Wait for me, and I will accompany you to Messana. Send a rider ahead to the Blue Flag to have Niko prepare rooms for me, and we'll have all of this nonsense cleared up in no time.'

'Here you go again,' said Zerenia as Titus fastened his sword-belt and packed a few necessities into a saddlebag. 'Do you really have to take a weapon?'

'That depends,' said Titus, watching her. 'What do you know of Azhar?'

She blanched. 'I know he was here; the men spoke of it. What's going on?'

'So you know him? In which case, you'll know that he is a complete goat's turd.'

'Yes, he is,' she replied. 'So whatever it is he expects of you, be careful.'

'He has locked up Crispus and is threatening to murder him. He's got a shock coming.'

'That's precisely the problem with you, Titus Villius. You think violence is the answer to everything.'

'It seems to work.'

'Only for soldiers. Try using your brain once in a while.'

Titus smiled at her. 'You know, I now realise that I should never have left Sicilia. You have a way about you, and yes, talking is sometimes good. It would have helped enormously before Philippi, but those Roman generals would rather shed blood than talk and I followed them to Tartarus and back. But somehow I don't think Azhar is very good with gentlemanly conversations, so I will have my sword at the ready.'

'Can't you take someone with you? Someone to watch your back?'

'I'm beginning to think you care,' he said, and risked taking her in a loving embrace. She melted and let him kiss her. 'I'll be back before you can say "Gaia, Marcia and Smudge"!'

'Don't come back in a box.'

Azhar was in no hurry to take Titus to his prisoner. The moment the detachment entered the fortified barracks that housed Messana's marines, the peacock commander ordered the baths to be prepared and food laid out in his quarters. As the horses were led to the stables and Azhar strode away, the dismounted marines shuffled towards Titus. His hand closed around the sword at his hip, and he studied each of the half-dozen seasoned men in turn, cursing his folly in entering Azhar's private realm alone. Did they mean him harm? Was he to be imprisoned too? He would fight to his last breath, despite the hopeless odds.

'Sir, we have some bread and cured meat, if you would care to join us?'

Titus breathed a sigh of relief and smiled. The man who had spoken was clearly a veteran, creased around the eyes, with a crooked nose, close-cropped grey hair and a beard.

'Is this a trick?' asked Titus.

'No, sir, no trick. You see, some of us remember you from the old days, when you served in our army before Caesar's war. Great days, them. Keeping the peace and not bothering with those fools in Rome.'

'I remember it well,' said Titus. 'Such a shame it couldn't stay like that. How is it you're not enjoying a quiet retirement, like me?'

'Not allowed to, sir. The commander says he needs every man in case those bastards come over with ideas above their station. Says the top men in Rome aren't very happy with us.'

'That may be true. I think your commander wants to discuss these matters with me when I've been to see Crispus. Do you know where he is held?'

'Certainly do, sir.' The soldier's face cracked into a smile. 'Probably waiting for us. Expecting his luck at dice to change.'

'He's not been beaten, then? Tortured?'

'We smothered him in pig's blood and told him to look all forlorn whenever the commander was around. He's a good actor — he moans like an old woman and walks with a limp. He stinks too — needs a bath.'

Titus chuckled. 'Can you take me to him?'

'Step this way, sir.'

They heard Crispus before they entered the barracks room where he squatted with several soldiers, cursing his luck at dice. He must have made use of a bucket of water to clean himself up because he appeared to Titus as he always did, strong and bronzed, although the tunic and trousers had seen better days. He looked up and exclaimed when he saw Titus.

'Come to rescue me, Chief?'

'Doesn't look like you need rescuing,' said Titus. 'I take it these men have branded you with hot irons and squeezed your balls to extract secret information?'

One of the soldiers slapped Crispus on the shoulder. 'We threatened to brand him if he didn't stop talking. He reckons the women in Italia are ten times more beautiful than our Sicilian women.' The men all laughed.

'Oh, he's one for the ladies all right,' said Titus. While the men continued their game, he wondered how he might extricate himself and his *optio* without further confrontation with Azhar. Could they simply walk out of the compound? Could these soldiers be persuaded to turn a blind eye while they made good their escape? Or perhaps he should defer to Azhar and make up some story to offer as currency in return for Crispus's release.

A commotion in the drill square outside snatched everyone's attention. A rider had arrived and, leaping from a sweating horse, was demanding to see the commander. One of Azhar's guards was blocking his way, while others sensed that something urgent was afoot and dashed to different parts of the barracks to search out senior officers. Titus stepped outside with the old soldier who had welcomed him, just in time to overhear the messenger shouting at the obstructing guard that he had a message from Sextus Pompey Magnus himself. At that, the guard let him pass.

'What happens next may interrupt our lunch,' the soldier muttered.

Whatever the message from Sextus, it caused a flurry of activity. Before long, trumpets were sounding and men arrived at the double to form up. Grooms brought the officers' horses from the stables. Soldiers arrived from all directions, most hurriedly strapping on armour as they ran. The dice-players disappeared to grab equipment and join the ranks, leaving Titus and Crispus alone, unguarded and extremely puzzled.

They sat together on the barrack hut's portico, sharing a cup of the barrack's wine ration, and watched Azhar's army march out.

'Looks like they're off to war,' mused Crispus. 'Wonder who they're fighting today?'

'Probably nothing more than a fishermen's revolt,' said Titus. 'They'll be throwing wet fish at each other down at the docks.'

'Element of surprise. We should have tried that at Philippi!' Crispus laughed. As the ranks marched out, the pair watched them until no one was left in sight. The sounds of shouted orders and the rhythmic crunch of two thousand boots slowly receded.

'Right then,' announced Titus, pushing himself to his feet. 'Nothing to stop us walking out. Better go see what's going on in Messana.'

Zerenia would be proud, he thought. *Mission accomplished without even drawing my sword.*

CHAPTER TEN

Why had the gods presented them with an easy freedom? Titus sniffed the salty air and looked south towards his homestead and his family, then back towards the bustling port where raised voices could be heard, mingling with the tumult raised by thousands of citizens and indignant seabirds. The choice was simple, but he chose wrong.

He should have hastened home and lived in peace and obscurity with vines to tend and fishing boats to maintain, a long-neglected family warming at last to his brusque yet gentle ways. He should have left Rome to fight its own wars and fashion its complicated intrigues and become an old soldier quietly fading away in the warm Sicilian sun. Instead he searched out his old mare, which by some miracle had not been taken by Azhar's cavalry, and led her towards The Blue Flag, Crispus grinning at his side. The pull was irresistible: one more flirtation with Rome's politics, then he'd take the money and hide.

The inn was virtually empty. The city's attention was on the interception of two Roman war galleys by Sicilia's fleet in the Messana Straits, and the arrayed ranks of Azhar's men at the port. Excited chatter in the streets was all about war, and whispered gossip insisted that the new Caesar himself had come to quell Sicilia's rebellion. That he would do it by sailing into the midst of the world's greatest naval power with just two warships was not considered — the people had something to talk about as they yelled insults at the visitors and cheered their loyal troops.

'Overkill, as usual,' commented Niko as he welcomed Titus and Crispus to his inn. 'All this fuss just because two ships arrive, and old ones at that.'

'So what do they want?' asked Titus. 'Sounds to me like an attempt at talks, which, let's face it, is better than all-out war.'

'You'd be right there,' said Niko, fingering his viper brooch. 'Let's get you settled in and then I'll tell you what I know.'

By the time Titus had stabled his horse and the pair had washed away the road's dust and grime, the city had become bored with the invaders' inactivity, disappointed that the Roman crews weren't slaughtered on the spot. The Blue Flag was gradually filling with people intent on discussing the day's events, and when two blue-cloaked officers arrived to quench their thirst, they were cheered ironically as if they had defeated a mighty foe against the odds. 'Show us your battle scars,' one old man slurred, and another shouted, 'What no prisoners?'

'Slaughtered them all,' one of the officers quipped. 'Now, who's going to buy two heroes a drink?'

Crispus was first to offer, seeing an opportunity to resume his engagement with Sicilia's militia and perhaps relieve them of some coin at dice. Meanwhile, Titus sought Niko, who was serving the house brew to two shady characters in the corner of the main hall. Titus caught his eye and fingered his brooch as a signal that he wanted to talk. Niko nodded and indicated the courtyard gardens.

'How much do you want to know?' Niko asked when they had found a quiet spot beneath a mulberry's canopy. 'And if you've anything to report to our masters, I can get a message to one of the Roman vessels before they return.'

'Hmm. That depends.' Titus was thoughtful. He had already decided he liked Niko, not least for his hospitality. 'I've nothing much to report, but part of me wants to know what's going on, if only to protect my family.'

'Of course. But this is an important time, because what happens next will decide whether we have peace and prosperity, or war between Rome and Sicilia. We — you and I — have only a small part to play in that story and sometimes, you know, a small piece of information can make all the difference.'

'So let's compare notes,' said Titus, 'and see where all this is leading.'

The inn had become uncomfortably busy as officers and civilians milled in the fragrant courtyard, so Niko drew close to tell Titus that while Sicilia's position was quite simple, Rome's was not. The triumvirs did not trust each other, a triple-headed monster that could barely rule together, but with Italia in upheaval and suffering famine, something had to be done. Their first instinct was for war, but Rome's legions were weary of fighting each other and because Sicilia was an island, and guarded by a far superior fleet, perhaps talks and compromise would bring a better resolution. So Rome had sent a delegation to explore the possibility.

'They didn't come here with weapons ready to fight, but you can be sure they came armed with lies,' whispered Niko. He fell silent as a customer passed, looking for somewhere to relieve himself. Niko continued, 'Sextus is naïve, but he can tell lies as well as the next man. You know, he actually believes that he is to be the new Lepidus. It's well known that Octavian and Antonius would like to be rid of Lepidus and rule the world between the two of them, although one of these would then fight the other until just one ruler emerged. But Sextus is eyeing the African territories that Lepidus holds, and all the islands from Peloponnesus to Melita and Sardinia. Pirate havens all.'

'Ambitious,' said Titus.

'Indeed. You know, it wouldn't surprise me if Sextus agreed to negotiate. He wants to rule the seas, tax the grain ships and charge a fortune for Sicilian grain, but he's not so hot when it comes to shipping large numbers of men to raid the mainland. That isn't his thing at all, not since he and his brother were trounced by Julius Caesar at Munda.'

'I sense there's a "but" coming…'

'There is. I think Marcus Antonius is playing a crafty game. I'm certain he has his own spies here and wants to befriend Sextus while he is of use to him.'

Titus looked puzzled. 'But it was Antonius who recruited me to Octavian's cause.'

'That doesn't mean he doesn't have others you don't know about,' said Niko. 'Or he probably thought you were too straight and honourable to fit in with his shifty methods.'

The feeling that Titus should wash his hands of this intrigue grew stronger. *I'm a soldier, not a spy. This will be my undoing.* But he found himself saying, 'So why does Antonius need spies in Sicilia when he has the wealth and the resources to buy Sextus's loyalty?'

'Keeping anyone loyal these days is like walking on shifting sand,' said Niko. 'And Sextus himself can't be certain of the loyalty of his own commanders. His right-hand men, his captains and generals, are either tearaway madmen like Menodorus or totally untrustworthy animals like Murcus. There are others who would gladly stab their grandmothers for a pocketful of gold. That sort of information might be useful to Antonius, not to mention all three triumvirs.'

Titus scratched his chin. 'You know, I feel for Sextus. When I knew him as a youth, he seemed to believe he was destined for greatness, yet with every move he makes he is dealt another unkind blow. And now he rules Sicilia with the same self-belief, but if he sails away to talk politics with Octavian and Antony, what's to stop these greedy men left behind helping themselves to Sicilia's riches? Or, for that matter, going with him and assassinating Rome's leaders, maybe even Sextus too?'

'Perish the thought,' laughed Niko.

The passing customer, duly relieved, was weaving his way back towards the now-crowded main hall. He brushed past Niko and lurched heavily into Titus, who pushed him away.

'Right now, we've got nothing to report,' said Titus, watching the stranger stagger back to his friends. 'The outcome of any talks with these Roman visitors will be interesting. Perhaps then we can see what Sextus and his admirals plan to do. Not that I care, as long as I can get a good harvest and pay no taxes!'

'Come, dear Titus, that's no way to talk when the future of the world hangs in the balance.' Niko was only half joking, but swiftly added, 'Your cup is empty. We shall drink to happier times.'

They found Crispus teaching his new friends a marching song, sufficiently crude to convince Niko to seek solace in the kitchens while Titus, who had declined another drink, decided he would take the air and see for himself the Roman ships in the harbour. Perhaps he would even discover more about the purpose of their visit. He went to the stables, where he had left his cloak on a nail close to the hay pile that fed his mare. He pulled it around his shoulders and reached for the brooch at his chest to pin it.

It wasn't there.

He knew he had been wearing it when he arrived at The Blue Flag. Did he leave it in his quarters, or lose it in the swell of carousing customers? No, he was wearing it when he contacted Niko earlier. He was wondering if Niko might have a spare when he heard movement behind him. He turned just in time to see the man who had pushed into him bring down a heavy cosh, catching him on the temple. He thought he heard an agonising groan as he passed out.

CHAPTER ELEVEN

The cell was cold and damp. Titus shivered as he tried to make out the shapes and shadows and determine whether he was blind or there was simply no light. A thick fog inside his head made his eyes throb with each heartbeat. His limbs were unresponsive, and his stomach was racked with searing cramps. He tried to move his hands from behind his back but found he couldn't. He felt cold iron clasping his wrists.

But he sensed there was light somewhere. He squeezed his eyes shut then opened them again. Yes, light from somewhere made smoky shapes on the cold floor. A steady drip told him he was probably below ground level. He groaned, willing oblivion to return. When it didn't, he forced his stiff neck muscles to turn his head to seek the vague source of light. There. A frame flickered, weak and yellow — in the door? Yes, there was a simple wooden hatch in the door, badly made so that it did not shut out the lamplight beyond.

He tried calling out. 'Hello?' He had nothing to lose — he had already lost so much through his folly and poor choices. 'Hello?' The only reply was the steady drip.

He pushed his weight forward, wincing as his crusted knees grated on stone, and tried to stand. He couldn't. He slumped sideways, his shoulders wrenching as his clamped wrists pulled on the chain that held him to an embedded iron ring.

He found the strength to pledge vengeance on whomever had done this, recalling the crooked smile of the man who had coshed him and promising that this was a face that would one day cry for mercy.

'Hello?' he tried again.

He noticed a subtle change in the light at the door hatch, telling him of movement outside his cell.

'I know you are there!' Titus called. 'Tell me what you want.'

Nothing happened for ten heartbeats, then the hatch slid aside, the light enough to make Titus turn his head at the brightness. He looked back and could make out the orange reflection in a man's eyes, promising more pain and sorrow to come.

The man said nothing, his eyes dancing in the light, silently mocking Titus's predicament.

The hatch slid back, and darkness ruled again.

There was no way of telling how long Titus lay crumpled on a wet, cold floor. Waking moments were painful, and he could only quench his raging thirst by licking drips from the rough wall.

The hatch slid back, forcing him to recoil from the light.

'Still alive,' a harsh voice said.

'Bring him,' came a muffled reply.

The door groaned open. An iron hammer smashed the chain from the cell wall, the savage blows bruising Titus's wrists. He was dragged from the cell, the stone floor tearing scabs from his knees.

Pushed into a bare room with a crude table, he was left standing as the questions began.

'What is your name?'

'Titus Villius Macer.'

'Sicilian or Roman?'

'Both.'

The slap was sharp. 'You cannot be both.'

'Well, I am.' This time a punch broke his nose, not for the first time in his violent career, though this instance was probably the most painful.

'You will be respectful. Why do you say you are both?'

'Because I was born here, if indeed I am still in Sicilia, and I served here for many years before Gaius Julius Caesar recruited me for the Fifth Alaudae to fight in Africa.'

There was a long silence. His inquisitors, whom he could barely see as they were in shadow, probably didn't know their history. One up to him, even though it had cost him severe pain and his good looks.

Eventually, one asked, 'Who commanded the Fifth?'

'A tribune, and a general. Marcus Antonius.'

Further silence, then: 'Did you fight at Philippi?'

'Yes.'

'What was your rank?'

'*Primus Pilus.*'

'Why are you here?'

'I was wounded. I am retired. I am no longer in the Fifth.'

'Where is your allegiance? Rome or Sicilia?'

'Neither. I am a farmer. I have land near here. I don't care about your pathetic little wars, so let me go home.'

A face came close to Titus's. After talking to shadows, he could now see that his inquisitor was a fat, red-faced man with bad teeth and foul-smelling breath.

'I'm going to hurt you,' the fat man said, 'and then you are going to tell me the real reason you are here.'

'Everything you do to me will be returned to you ten-fold.'

The blow brought sharper pain than the last because the inquisitor was holding sharp corals in his hand. Titus felt blood trickling to the corner of his mouth.

Another voice, one he vaguely recognised, said, 'Stand back.' The dispassionate face of Azhar came close. 'What is this?' He held Titus's viper brooch close.

'Looks like a *fibula* to me.' Titus swallowed blood and felt droplets running down to his filthy tunic.

'Where did you get it?'

'My wife bought it for me.' Titus realised his mistake and instantly regretted it.

'The lovely Zerenia?' Azhar drew out the syllables of her name as his eyes reflected lust and desire. 'That little fact can be checked. Want to change your mind?'

'No. But tell me this. Why are you so interested in a little trinket that may or may not be mine, and how such a meaningless possession came to me?'

'Because I have seen such items before, worn by your accomplices. You are a spy for Rome, and these are the emblems by which you can identify one another. You can confess now.'

'You are talking through your anus, Azhar. Go and pick on someone who actually cares about your pathetic little games.'

Momentarily, Azhar was taken aback. Titus saw the surprise his defiance brought to the commander's face. Azhar stepped back and turned to the fat man.

'Take a finger and give him time to reconsider.'

Titus's head swam. He had been manhandled back to the cell, which seemed more enclosed and damper than before. His whole right arm throbbed with pain, and he was glad there was not enough light to see the wound where his hand had been mutilated. He knew it was unbandaged and would likely fester in this rat-filled dungeon. He spent the hours that passed imagining the revenge he would inflict on Azhar the Cruel.

When he was led into the bright light of a ground-level refectory and food and wine was placed before him, Titus was struggling to maintain his sanity. The sounds around him were exaggerated; the scrape of a knife on a plate was like screeching vultures, the murmur of a dozen voices was like distant thunder, and the floor seemed to move beneath his feet.

Bile rose in his throat when he saw the food laid before him: roasted fowl, mountains of cracked wheat, garlic and onions, fruit piled high — and all out of reach, but he didn't care. He would rather die than surrender to these animals.

Beyond the table stood Azhar and the fat man. The pain in Titus's arm intensified, and the room fell silent.

'Eat,' said Azhar. 'You will need your strength for your confession.'

'You will get nothing from me,' hissed Titus.

'Come now. You and I should be friends. There is so much we can enjoy together as Sicilia takes her rightful place as ruler of Mare Nostrum.'

'Our sea?' Titus was incredulous. 'Is that how you see it? Who rules the seas rules the world?'

'Indeed. You know it to be true. And I am here to welcome you into a new world order. All you have to do is confess to your underhand dealings, then everything will be out in the open and you and I can work together to put everything to rights.'

Titus struggled to control his astonishment at Azhar's outrageous expectations. But he saw his chance and assumed a sympathetic tone. 'If that is for the good of Sicilia, then I am all ears.'

'Then listen. If, when I have spoken, you do not confess your allegiance thus far to Rome and your willingness to join with me, I will remove your hand. Not the one that has only four fingers, the other one. And then, if you do not conform—'

Titus interrupted. 'Get on with it, man. Your threats bore me.'

'Very well. I think you know that the new Caesar and his underling Antonius will likely entreat with Sextus Pompey Magnus Pius —' he snorted at the over-inflated titles Sextus had given himself — 'to divide power between themselves. But there are some who have a different opinion.'

There was a moment of silence, and Titus suddenly became aware that it was Azhar the Cruel who was about to confess, not he, the inopportune spy for Agrippa and Octavian. He willed Azhar to continue, but there was a commotion and raised voices, then Sextus himself appeared in the room, accompanied by a guard of well-drilled soldiers.

'Gentlemen,' he said. 'I see you have a feast prepared. How kind. Let's eat.'

CHAPTER TWELVE

'Now then,' said Sextus, crunching a stuffed sparrow. 'What's all this about? My dear Titus, you look pale and bruised. What ails you?'

Titus looked down at his mutilated hand and said nothing.

It was Azhar who spoke. 'This man is a spy for Rome.'

Sextus continued chewing, extracting a tiny bone from between his teeth, then scooped spiced barley with a piece of flatbread. He watched Azhar icily as he ate.

'He was an officer in the Fifth Alaudae and was sent here by Octavian to spy on us,' said Azhar, looking down as he spoke.

Sextus waved a piece of bread. 'Well then, show me your evidence. And remember, this is Titus Villius you accuse, who saved my life many years ago.'

Azhar produced the viper brooch. 'They wear this, to identify their circle of spies.'

Sextus turned to Titus, who shrugged.

'That's it?' asked Sextus.

'Two of these spies were seen plotting against you two days ago,' said Azhar, blinking rapidly. 'They wore identical *fibulas*.'

'Where is the other spy?'

'We are watching him, expecting other spies to meet with him so we can expose more of this treachery.'

Sextus looked at Titus and saw his wounded hand. 'Have that wound bound — now!' he ordered.

Azhar nodded to one of his officers, who rushed to find vinegar and bandages. Sextus shook his head sadly as he took in Titus's pitiful appearance, making the soldier straighten his back.

'Are you a spy, Titus?'

'Do you believe this of me?'

'Even if you were such, I wouldn't care. Perhaps there is truth in this childish game of vipers, who knows? I might have cared more before the Roman ships came, but in truth what could you have told them that they didn't already know?'

Titus saw his opportunity to change the subject. 'What did the Romans want?'

'That you don't know pleases me. They want to meet me. The new Caesar and Marcus Antonius want to acknowledge the son of Pompey the Great and clasp hands together for the good of Rome.'

At this, Azhar stirred. *He didn't know either*, thought Titus.

'Spy or not, you are important to me, and it would help if you could tell me what kind of men these are,' Sextus went on. 'You have fought with them and seen their ambition. Are they honourable?'

Despite the pain, Titus laughed. As an officer came to pour vinegar and bind his wounded hand, he explained that he and his men had always obeyed their commanders and believed their cause to be honourable. But now, away from the heat of battle and with news of a growing rift between the triumvirs, perhaps power and wealth came before honour. 'Be careful, Sextus. These are men in the image of Gaius Julius Caesar, and look what happened to your father.'

Sextus closed his eyes, no doubt recalling the murder of Pompey the Great on Egypt's distant shore, a savage end for Rome's greatest ever general. He sighed. 'Can it be mended?' he asked, almost in a whisper, forgetting that he was surrounded by his own officers who followed only the stout-hearted. He looked around the room, then back to Titus. 'I don't believe you are a spy, but if you are, tell them that Sextus

Pompey Magnus Pius looks forward to meeting them on the seas that divide the lands we rule, and that together we will forge a treaty to relieve the suffering of Italia and make our enemies quake with fear.'

There was a stunned silence.

Sextus wasn't finished. 'Here is my ruling. Titus Villius Macer is to be taken to my villa, where he will be cared for and questioned further.' Turning to Azhar, he added, 'You tell me there are spies operating within Sicilia on behalf of the triumvirs, but I'm telling you that if there is a nest of vipers, Titus is not one of them. Far more likely the greatest threat comes from those who profess to be enemies of Rome and seek power among us, and I'm ordering you to seek them out. Start with that shark Lucius Staius Murcus.'

Accompanied by two solemn guards, Sextus helped Titus out of the austere building where he had been held. There to greet them beside a garish, four-wheeled *carpentum* were Crispus and Eshmun. Two harnessed mules ignored the attention of a hundred flies.

Seeing the state of his senior officer, Crispus immediately drew his *gladius* and demanded to know who to kill first, while Eshmun and Sextus helped Titus into the carriage. Crispus, still brandishing his sword, and the two guards followed on foot.

Titus refused food and wine until he had washed in the sea that lapped close to the villa, then accepted his host's invitation to join him and Eshmun in his hot baths. The steam smelled of wealth, and the water was a healing balm. Women waited at the massage benches with skills that Titus had not thought would ever be offered to a mere soldier. He was relieved that Crispus had not been invited — he would not know how to behave.

He let his body relax beneath the warm caress and closed his eyes. He became so drowsy that he hardly realised Sextus was speaking.

'…all of the world's leaders in one place, so I think that achieving something without cutting each other's throats could be challenging…'

Eshmun interrupted him. 'Why not meet on board a ship? That way, you keep away from Octavian's legions.'

'But then he will be at my mercy, on my ship.'

'I see your point. But you cannot set foot on Italia's shores or there will be a swift end to you and your ambitions.'

'We'll work it out,' said Sextus. 'Speaking of ships, how are you getting on with those strange Veneti vessels? Why aren't you building new quinqueremes for my fleet?'

Eshmun laughed. 'Oh, those. Just a hobby. They're of no use to you as they depend on wind, and we don't always have that. Not like the north where they come from. But give me a brisk breeze and they'll outstrip anything under oars, so they may be useful as traders.'

'Speaking of oars, I have a new flagship. I shall call her *Andromeda*, because she's better than any sea-monster Octavian can come up with. She has more oars than any ship sailing the ocean, and she's unsinkable. Maybe I should sail her to meet the triumvirs.'

Titus let his mind surface. 'Surely your advantage is speed, not size?'

'Ah, the Roman spy awakens,' laughed Sextus. 'But you are right: in sea warfare my smaller ships will conquer any and all. But for a show of strength, ruling the waves, my *Andromeda* will have the new Caesar gasping in astonishment.'

'All beyond me. I'm just a soldier.'

'Come with me. You know these waters as well as I.'

'Absolutely not,' said Titus firmly. 'I am retired, remember? And I don't care about Rome.'

'Very well. Eshmun?'

'Nor me,' said Eshmun. 'I have a daughter and grandchildren to care for, given that this errant father here insists on aggravating everyone he meets.'

'It's the way of the soldier,' said Titus, feeling slightly more himself in the baths. 'Although I'd rather be a simple farmer.'

'I can manage without simple farmers and very ancient boat-builders,' said Sextus. 'But I have one more favour to ask.'

'You have favoured us greatly today,' said Titus. 'Ask anything and it's yours.'

Sextus massaged his chin for a moment. 'Your man Crispus. He seems like an honest fellow, and one not to be bested by any of my marines. Would he be up for a bit of spying himself?'

'Go on,' said Titus, intrigued.

'I am not convinced about my own commanders, least of all Azhar. Could Crispus track him? Watch what he does and report back?'

'You mean spy on the commander of your land forces? That would mean I am spying on you and my man is spying *for* you!'

'Correct. Shall I have you executed now for spying on me?' Pointing to the massage benches where several women waited, Sextus added, 'Or shall I condemn you to the ministrations of those angels over there?'

Oils infused with thyme, worked by skilled fingers, eased Titus's aching body still more and made it difficult to concentrate on talk of the new ship *Andromeda* and the best locations for a conference of world leaders. But he was vaguely aware that Sextus wanted to trust Octavian and Antonius, although he was scornful of Lepidus and clearly saw himself as the more obvious choice as the third triumvir. Eshmun was grunting approval whenever Sextus paused.

Titus slid into blissful slumber.

He awoke to find himself alone, his body tingling with healing and renewed vigour. He was very hungry. Dressing quickly, he went in search of his host but found only servants about their daily tasks. He wandered into the gardens, following the sound of a child's laughter. Pushing aside foliage, he saw Crispus on his hands and knees playing the part of a pony for a small girl. She clung to his tunic, giggling with delight, while her mother steadied her. Titus coughed to get their attention. The woman — well-rounded with aristocratic hair and a colourful, floaty dress — turned to smile at him while her daughter tumbled from her mount's back and burst into tears.

'You must be Titus Villius,' she said, leaving Crispus to comfort the child.

Titus bowed. 'And you must be Scribonia, lady of this house. I hope your daughter is uninjured?'

'Pompeia? Nothing wrong with her. She would scream properly if she was hurt.'

Sextus came running but relaxed when he realised that his daughter was already demanding to be remounted. Eshmun followed at a more sedate pace.

'Ah, Titus, back with us I see,' said Sextus. 'We've left some food for you. We thought it unkind to wake you.'

He put an arm around Titus and led him to an atrium table, where sufficient food had been left to restore him. While he ate, Sextus took advantage of being alone with him. 'I've decided you are no spy, but just in case you feel the urge to betray me to anyone, the location for my talks with Rome will be one of the smaller Lipara islands.' He winked as he said it.

Titus nodded his approval; he knew the Lipara archipelago well, not least for its fishing grounds. 'Makes sense. Not too far to the north, yet impossible to accommodate more than a few soldiers, let alone a legion.'

'Of course, Octavian and Antonius have other ideas and wouldn't go anywhere near the Lipara islands, because they would be at the mercy of my fleet. Try this, it's delicious.' He offered a sweet pastry. 'And I'm telling nobody except the captain of *Andromeda* and a few trusted friends where the true location is.'

'So you don't mind me mentioning Lipara to Crispus and anyone else I meet?'

'Exactly. You catch on fast, Titus. You would make a fine spy.'

'I'd better brief Crispus about his new adventure. I know he's bored and will probably relish crawling to Azhar to beg forgiveness for escaping and join his army. Can you give him a recommendation?'

'Couldn't think of a finer addition to Sicilia's legions,' smiled Sextus. 'I'll have my secretary draw up papers immediately.'

CHAPTER THIRTEEN

The Veneti ships were trialled when autumn breezes deposed summer's heat. Crispus had been gone for a month, all had returned to normal at Pax Villius, and Titus had busied himself working with the carpenters and foundry men, readying the vessels for trials. By common agreement among the crews, *Boreas* and *Eurus* had been named after two of the four winds and celebrated with much wine and feasting, with Zerenia and the children joining the gaiety. The vessels were then launched with a traditional song.

Titus gripped the rail, white-knuckled with unfamiliar fear as *Boreas* heeled for the first time, the main lateen sail and a smaller foresail straining before the brisk easterly. He fought nausea as creaming seas surged towards him and wondered how Eshmun and his crew could keep their feet. Some of them were whooping at the sheer joy of their new discovery; others braced at the unexpected strain of the ropes hitched around coiling posts. Eshmun ordered the ship about to test the crew's discipline in the chaos of the tack, and Titus gasped when he saw the nearest of two steering paddles lift clear of the broiling wake as *Boreas* picked up speed again, *Eurus* following.

That evening, as the wind dropped, the crews practised with the scorpios, an old fishing boat anchored in the bay disintegrating under a barrage of iron bolts the length of an arm. 'Quite enough to see off a pirate,' said Eshmun as the splintered target wallowed in the shallows.

'You surprise me,' laughed Titus, 'a man of your age seeking adventure on the seas and taking delight in such lethal weaponry.'

Eshmun reminded him that these were uncertain days when every man should be ready for the unexpected. But Titus wasn't listening; his gaze was fixed on the figure making his way down the track to the bay.

Crispus had returned.

'I am now a deserter.' These were Crispus's first words as he sat with his back to a beached *Boreas* and accepted a skin of wine handed to him by Barek, a carpenter whose stature and demeanour afforded him equal respect in the eyes of his colleagues to that shown to Titus's *optio*.

'Start from the beginning,' said Titus, 'and don't leave anything out.'

'I think you need to hear the end of my story first,' Crispus said with a wry smile. 'Sextus has set sail in that big fancy ship of his to meet with our former commanders.'

'How can you know this, when as I understand it you were in Syracuse with Azhar, not Messana where Sextus has his main fleet?'

'Because I have met the lovely Saverina. She wears the viper *fibula*.' Crispus revealed that he had been a customer in the best brothel in Syracuse. Eventually, after several visits, he had noticed the brooch worn by the keeper of the house and had discovered that Agrippa's network reached further than either he or Titus had realised. Winning her confidence in him had cost much coin but he had convinced her with small pieces of information, in return for a gradual understanding of her sources. It was his reference to Azhar's treatment of Titus that had opened a greater flow of information before a mysterious visitor had brought news that Sextus and a full crew of five hundred men had sailed north at dawn six days ago. 'It cost more than you can imagine,' said Crispus with a wink, 'but now we know where that conference is to take place, and it's not an island called Lipara.'

'So where is it?'

'My knowledge of Italia's coast is not good,' said Crispus, 'but talk is that it is in a bay called Puteoli — a place called Misenum. Don't ask me to draw a map.'

'Does Azhar know this? And Murcus?'

'Those two are thick as thieves. Azhar's legion moved out at the same time as Saverina had heard about Sextus leaving Messana. I stayed with them until I was certain of their destination — Panormus, on the north coast. What's more, Murcus sailed out of Syracuse with four ships on the same day as Azhar marched. Something has stirred the hornet nest, and we both know what it is. But are they supporting Sextus, or causing trouble?'

Titus knew instinctively that it was the latter. Murcus and Azhar were in league together, but what were they planning to do? With no time to send a coded message to Agrippa's secretary, he had to take matters into his own hands. He whistled to Eshmun, who was chatting to some of his crew.

'Eshmun, do you think *Boreas* and *Eurus* are ready for some proper action?'

'No. Why?'

'Because something's going on.' Titus was grimly conspiratorial. 'Sextus has sailed to meet Octavian and Antonius, and suddenly Murcus and Azhar are rushing to Panormus. Why is that? It may be nothing, but I think there's a plot afoot that has the stench of betrayal. And no one is in a position to do anything about it — except someone who has a fast ship. Two, in fact.'

Eshmun stared at Titus for a moment. 'I have no idea what you are talking about,' he said. 'But if you need to get somewhere fast, then let's put our ships into action.'

'How long to sail to Panormus?'

'With fair winds and an early start, a day. But what do you want to do when you get there?'

Titus shrugged. 'Maybe fight? There's always someone who needs defeating.'

'Then we call at Messana first. There's someone there you should meet.'

The two ships were provisioned overnight, scorpio bolts gathered from the shallows around the wrecked fishing boat. Bundles of bolts, bows, arrows, swords and spears, together with several chests of leather armour and shields, were carried from the foundry to both vessels. Titus ran to the farmstead to give swift explanation to Zerenia.

'Who do you want to save this time?' she asked, but Titus was relieved to sense a note of resignation in her voice and merely smiled.

'If I knew, I would tell you. But perhaps it is myself who needs saving,' he said.

She laughed. 'I wish you would let me do that, for once.' He kissed her and the children, then went to assist the crews, grabbing a sack of loaves as he left.

Boreas and *Eurus* were launched before dawn. There was no wind, just a glittering moon's sheen on calm waters. With just ten oars on each vessel, progress out of the bay was slow, sails hoisted but hanging limp. Past the headland between Pax Villius and Messana, a slight rippling of the waters gave the crews hope, then a barely perceptible protest in the sails. 'Here it comes,' said Eshmun. 'Ship oars and lower keels.' The ships' namesake winds awoke.

The sun had barely climbed over Italia's mainland as they tacked into Messana's harbour. 'The man we will meet here is not a nice person,' Eshmun told Titus as they approached the dock where a ramshackle trireme was moored. 'But he is a man you will always want on your side when it comes to a sea battle. His name is Menecrates, ugly as sin, but his falcata is as sharp as his knowledge of these seas. He's a Sicilian to the core — he hates all Romans unless they are friends of his friends. So be cordial.'

Crispus, standing beside them, said, 'My kind of man.'

'Then you talk to him,' Titus told him. 'Show him all that charm you are famous for.'

Boreas nudged close to the trireme and moored, *Eurus* following alongside.

Looking down on an untidy deck, where dozens of crewmen slept amid ropes and filthy sails, Titus wondered how this trireme could possibly be part of Sicilia's slick and powerful fleet. A few of the sailors awoke and stared with puzzled expressions at the high-sided ship that had moored to theirs. Seeing no threat, they returned to their slumber. Crispus threw an onion at one of them and a rotund bearded face glared up at him, then lay back down again.

Crispus threw another onion. 'Get your captain. I'm coming aboard.'

The bearded man, at least the size of Crispus, gave a lazy wave in the direction of a framed leather shelter at the stern. Crispus vaulted down onto the trireme deck, landing surprisingly lightly for a big man, and picked his way between prone bodies to the captain's quarters, pulling aside a salt-encrusted flap to peer inside. He wasn't surprised when a woman peered at him, a slight smile forming at the corners of her mouth. 'Come to join us?' She patted a mountain of blankets, which stirred and farted. 'You have a visitor,' she said, looking Crispus up and down and admiring his muscular frame.

'I'm looking for the famed seaman Menecrates. Would that be him under that untidy pile?' asked Crispus.

A face appeared, several days' stubble giving it a grubby appearance. 'Who wants to know?' The words were rough, accompanied by a waft of stale wine and garlic.

'I am Crispus, *optio* to *primus pilus* Titus Villius Macer who has sent me to inform you that his friend Sextus Pompeius may be in danger.'

Menecrates gestured to the woman to leave. She pulled a grubby dress over her her naked body as he said, dismissively, 'That man's always in danger and me with him, so what's new?'

'You know he has sailed to meet two of the triumvirs, Octavian and Antonius?'

'Of course. Nothing gets past Menecrates. Now, why is young Sextus in danger?' he asked, reaching for a leather flask, swallowing a draught then handing it Crispus, who squatted beside him.

'We think Murcus is up to no good. He set sail with four ships at the same time as Sextus left from here. Of course, he may be going to support the Sicilian cause…'

Menecrates laughed. 'The only person Murcus ever supported is Murcus.' He stood, unembarrassed at his nakedness, running his hands through his dark, lank hair.

'There's more,' said Crispus. 'Azhar is marching his legions north, towards Panormus.'

'Hmm. Now that is intriguing. He may be the biggest turd in Sicilia, but Sextus seems to have faith in him. Never trusted the man myself.' Menecrates studied his visitor. 'I am going to wash and then we will eat together, at which point I want you to explain why you have come to me and how you know all this.'

With that he brushed past Crispus, still naked, and dived over the stern of his ship.

CHAPTER FOURTEEN

Menecrates's trireme led the two Venetis north around the Messana headland then steered west on what they hoped would be an interception course. The sweeps of the traditional galley, rhythmic and powerful, belied the state of her crew, who had all appeared hungover and lethargic not two hours previously. Their rowing song and the shrill of the pipers drifted over the calm seas as *Boreas* and *Eurus* dropped ever further behind.

Eshmun called across from a wallowing *Eurus*, 'If that wind doesn't come soon, I'll rename this ship hippopotamus.'

'We should let Menecrates run ahead while he can!' yelled Titus. 'Catch up with the next blow.'

But the wind had gone elsewhere, and eventually the despairing crews on *Boreas* and *Eurus* lost sight of the trireme as it skirted the shimmering shadows of the Lipara islands to the north. The sun was high before a warm and gentle breeze picked up from the south and the ships were making way once more. 'Stay together,' was Eshmun's call. 'Make for Panormus in case Murcus is still there.'

They came up to Panormus harbour at dusk, running at a brisk pace before lowering sails in a perfectly judged manoeuvre that brought them, keels raised, almost to the dockside with just simple poling, using the oars to leave them nestled side-by-side before a gathering crowd intrigued by the strange vessels. There were few boats in the harbour, none of them Murcus's galleys. It wasn't long before stalls selling hot bread and sweetmeats had been set up, and officials arrived wanting to know who they were and why they were here.

Eshmun, Titus and Crispus conferred before disembarking. 'There's no point in returning to sea tonight,' said Titus. 'We should go ashore to find out what we can, but the crews should stay on board and be ready to depart as soon as we know what's going on.'

Crispus nudged Titus and pointed to a number of blue-cloaked soldiers milling near the water's edge. 'Those are Azhar's men. I recognise those ugly bastards.'

'We'll go ashore,' Titus replied. 'Eshmun, you stay here to keep an eye on things, but be ready to leave at any moment. Have your meanest men landward; allow no visitors.'

Without waiting to be told, Crispus donned his cuirass and strapped his *gladius* and knife to his waist. Titus did the same and nodded at his *optio*. They dropped to the dockside and strode into the busy streets of Panormus, where yelling vendors and the aromas of local street food enticed.

The legless beggar reclined against a stone wall, a worn legionary helmet upturned beside him as yet bereft of coin. Titus turned to Crispus and shrugged, reluctant to leave an old soldier without a donation. Crispus fished in his purse for a coin and tossed it into the helmet. As he did so, Titus's eye fixed on the viper brooch pinned to the beggar's soiled coat. Seeing the bearing of his benefactors, the beleaguered soldier seemed to be attempting to stand. Remembering he couldn't, he thumped a fist to his chest and saluted with a breathless, '*Salve!*'

'Where did you get your *fibula*?' asked Titus. 'Nice workmanship, that.'

The beggar's hand instinctively covered the brooch. 'Young officer at Munda gave it to me,' he said, looking around for enemies as an old soldier might.

'You fought at Munda? Which legion, soldier?'

'Seventh Claudia. At Pharsalus, too.'

Titus squatted so they were eye to eye. 'I was at both.'

'Great victories. Those elephants were scary, though.'

'Indeed.' Titus reached out and touched the brooch. 'So where did you get this?'

'From a fellow by the name of Marcus Vipsanius Agrippa,' the soldier announced proudly. 'I watched his back when the battle got messy.'

Titus looked around, seeing several militiamen nearby who were likely with Azhar's forces, and kept his voice low as he touched his own brooch. 'We, too, are with Agrippa. What do you know, soldier?'

'Old Manius doesn't miss a thing,' he growled. 'They're up to no good, that lot in their fancy armour, stood right next to me with their plotting and planning. Just because I haven't got legs, it doesn't mean I'm deaf too.'

Titus sent Crispus to buy food for the old soldier and sat next to him. 'Tell me everything.'

Only too happy to be of use, Manius told them how he had listened to three officers — 'dressed like peacocks they were, fancied themselves rotten' — discuss their objectives while the four ships were provisioned and armed for action. Titus gently fished for details about the officers, what kind of ships they boarded, and clues as to where they were heading. While they shared a large bowl of fried fish, a picture emerged. Both Murcus and Azhar were distinctive characters, Murcus short, rotund and furious-faced, Azhar the opposite, so Titus was convinced Manius had been listening to the two main suspects in a conspiracy, if indeed there was one. He let Manius ramble, encouraging him with grunts of approval and friendly touches to the shoulder, nodding sagely even when the story became as much a reminiscence of old times as an imparting of intelligence.

Manius clearly knew nothing of the talks taking place between Rome and Sicilia, so Titus patiently picked helpful details from the meandering discourse. Eventually, he asked, 'Did they say where they were going?'

Manius waved a hand vaguely to the northwest, adding, 'I heard them mention "the islands".'

'Lipara? They were going to these islands?'

'Oh no, they said they would go north of the islands.'

'To Italia, then? Did they mention a place in Italia?'

Manius had the look of an old man who struggled to make his memory work. 'Began with an M, I think.'

'Misenum?'

'Could be. No idea where that is but yes, could be. Over by Puteoli, they said. That's where they would do it.'

'Do what?'

'Kill them all, of course.' Manius looked into Titus's eyes. 'All three of them.'

The rest was easy. Dozens of fully armed men had boarded, and the four ships had sailed late morning, giving them time to approach Misenum in two days' time if they sailed by the stars. Sextus and the triumvirs would not suspect them to be anything more than part of the Sicilian naval guard, giving Murcus time to pick his moment to attack and change the world, no doubt setting himself on Rome's throne with Azhar as his greedy accomplice. Or the other way around.

'Not one of them gave so much as a half-copper,' said Manius.

'Pay this man well and find him a blanket,' Titus told Crispus. 'He's a hero of Rome.'

'Bring everyone on deck, both crews,' called Titus as he climbed the ladder to board *Eurus*, closest of the two vessels. Crispus followed him to join Eshmun on the stern platform as the two crews came alert, those from *Boreas* leaping across to her twin. A hundred men eager to hear about their mission gathered in the light of a full moon and the port's torches.

'First, the bad news,' Titus announced. 'We are hopelessly outnumbered.'

All were silent save one man, the broad-shouldered carpenter named Barek who stood, stout legs placed firmly apart, clutching his favoured mallet. 'Outnumbered by who? If it's those ladies in blue, they'll be no match for real men.'

All laughed, including Titus. 'Four ships are heading for the coast of Italia. Each will no doubt be crewed by around two hundred men with a further fifty marines on each. That's a thousand men to our hundred.'

'What about the other ship? The one we picked up at Messana?' This was a fidgety youth, his first beard barely formed. Eshmun whispered 'Felix' in Titus's ear.

'Well, Felix,' Titus smiled, 'if we can find Menecrates, he has two hundred or more, all bloodthirsty types and each man worth double any of those we chase. But we're still outnumbered.' He paused before pointing to the scorpios that lined the sides of both ships. 'But the enemy doesn't have anything like those! And fifty men on one of our ships can hold off boarders because we'll shoot arrows down on them.'

Felix, bold beyond his years, said, 'I'm not afraid of a fight, sir, but we're two ships going after four Sicilian navy ships. Why?'

For several heartbeats, Titus wondered why it was so important to stop the conspiracy. Who was he to decide who should live or die? 'Because…' he began hesitantly, 'since the death of Julius Caesar and the evils that followed, we have had enough of all this killing. However, the new Caesar and Marcus Antonius rule by divine appointment, and Sextus has gone to them looking for peace. You may not know the men who would murder all three, but I have met them, and they are mere opportunists hungry for power they don't deserve. If they succeed, we will have yet more war. And I tell you now, Felix, there will be no end to it.'

There was a murmur while the men looked to one another. They were uncertain of Titus and Crispus, who they barely knew, but when Barek called to Eshmun for his opinion as a man they respected, they fell silent.

'I am certain of one thing,' said the old man, 'and that is we have had enough of war.' Another murmur of approval. 'And if that means we fight once to save Sicilia, then that's what we should do. And who knows, we might save Rome at the same time. Mark my words, men, this is a cause worth fighting for, whatever the odds against us. The gods are with us.'

These were simple folk who saw things in black and white, just like the three leaders who stood on the platform before them, and this time the murmurs became cheers. But Eshmun had one more thing to say. 'I know how to build ships,' he said after calling for quiet, 'but does anyone here know how to steer by the stars?'

'I do,' said a small voice that came from the dockside. 'I do!'

Eurus lurched as a hundred men crowded to the side to see who spoke.

'Well, are you going to let me aboard or leave me standing here when Neptune himself has commanded me to help you poor ignorant souls?'

A woman's voice, thought Titus, *and a young woman at that. What foolishness it this?* The men had formed the same opinion despite the speaker being shrouded in a hooded cloak, her face darkened by shadows. Hands reached down to help her aboard.

'Bring her to me,' Titus commanded.

'What madness is this?' exclaimed Crispus but then, as she pulled the hood away to let loose a cascade of dark hair, he added, 'Welcome aboard, lady!' Titus and Eshmun were stunned into silence.

'Where do you want to go?' she asked.

'A strix? Or a seer?' Titus asked. The young woman was attractive and had an authority about her.

'Just a navigator,' she said. 'Name of Marina. Now, where do you want to go? North-east from what I've been hearing while you discussed politics among yourselves.'

'Yes, north-east,' agreed Eshmun. 'We have a crude map.'

'That will help. Get it for me and cast off.'

'But…'

'I thought you were in a hurry. Let's see what these strange ships can do. And wrap you cloaks tight — there's a chill wind and it's choppy out there.'

CHAPTER FIFTEEN

Eurus led, catching the wind immediately on leaving harbour and lowering her keel on the command of Eshmun. Meanwhile, Marina positioned her map on the deck and, kneeling, gazed to a part of the clear night-sky where she traced a line of stars with her hand, then moved it right, past the seven stars of *Septentrio*. She held her hand steady. 'There, that way.' Eshmun peered over her shoulder, struggling to see the map's outline in the moonlight as her finger traced a straight line to a large bay that could only be the mainland's Puteoli.

Boreas fell into line astern, heeling in the night wind. On the platform, Crispus struggled with nausea but found his voice. 'So we're trusting a woman to guide us?'

Titus laughed nervously. 'It seems so. I'm going to check the scorpios are ready. They're our best chance.' He went down to the main deck and moved unsteadily among the men, chatting to Felix whom he had already identified as someone to trust in a crisis, however young. He checked the winding mechanisms for elevation and ensured that each weapon had a stockpile of bolts beside it. They would not be needed for some hours, but it was best to be prepared. The men were in good mood, though nervous, sensing their lives were on the line but trusting in the confidence of their commanders. *Carpenters, ironworkers and farmers*, thought Titus, *salt of the earth*.

On *Eurus*'s platform, Eshmun stood with Marina, the two steersmen behind them holding course. 'I can hold this course if you need to sleep,' he said.

She snorted. 'Sleep below with these men? Give me a ship like this and the stars to steer by. Better than the attentions of any man I know.'

'Who are you, Marina?'

'I am a child of the sea,' she said wistfully, 'and you are lucky to have me on your ship.'

'What of your parents? Do they know you are sailing into the jaws of death?'

Marina laughed. 'My father is Neptune. I have never seen his face, but I hear his voice every time I go to sea. My mother is every woman in Panormus who shows me kindness and knows better than to tell me what to do.'

'And where is your boat? Who do you go with when you traverse the seas?'

'Fishermen, mostly. I even show them where the best fish lie. I can show you if you wish, though I sense you have other reasons to be out here.'

Eshmun looked back at the sparkling wake. 'Come daylight, we will probably be entertained by dolphins, but the last thing on my mind is fishing,' he said. 'Something tells me we are coming to the day of the gods and we are their playthings, put here on the great ocean to see what transpires between mere mortals.'

Marina looked up at him. 'Perhaps it is already written. I, too, sense divine forces at work. But what do you think will happen?'

Eshmun explained that the three leaders would meet offshore, probably on ships moored together or even on Sextus's *Andromeda* with soldiers and crew disembarked apart from a few servants. A swift attack by Murcus's fast ships could leave Octavian and Antonius cut off from their legions and Sextus caught by the element of surprise.

'We have to catch them before they attack,' he said. 'But whatever comes, I'm ready.' As if confirming momentous events to come, the heavens gave a brilliant display of stars falling to earth, the gods at play.

On *Boreas*, Titus kept watch as Crispus slept.

The horizon before them was filled with the haze of Italia's mainland backlit by the rising sun. To the south were the islands where perhaps Menecrates searched for Murcus; beyond these, Vulcan's breath crowned Sicilia's mountain.

Titus had slept fitfully and now he searched for ships but saw only murky emptiness. A mouthful of water and fruit from the ship's basket restored his spirits. Crewmen adjusted the mainsail as the wind shifted, still strong but now following so that *Boreas* slowed and wallowed in the swell. Crispus heaved over the side. *Eurus* lay astern, passed in the night but now closing again, so Titus ordered slack sails to allow her to reach them, then called to Eshmun, 'We can tack to use the wind, north to a count of a hundred, then south-east.' Eshmun signalled his agreement and the ships turned together in harmony, a pod of dolphins soon frolicking in the creaming bow-waves.

The wind was their ally for most of the day, dying as the sun dropped astern. It was only then that Crispus, recovered at last, called Titus and pointed to distant movement reflected by the dying sun — two ships, maybe more, dwarfed by Italia's shadowy mass. Titus alerted Eshmun and signalled that they should turn north, as these were probably Murcus's fleet. 'We should not appear to be chasing them,' he called across. 'They will not attack in darkness, so if we turn away now we will not alarm them. But we must stay close.'

On *Eurus*, Marina marked on her map where she thought the enemy ships lay and plotted a course to intercept them at dawn. 'It's guesswork, and we have to count out each beat so we turn together and stay close, but if the gods are truly with us we'll find them tomorrow.'

Eshmun looked closely at the map and put his finger on the northern end of the great bay of Puteoli. 'What's the chance of us getting there first?'

Marina smiled. 'There's a challenge,' she said, and Eshmun went to call across the new plan to Titus and Crispus.

Both ships went about together, two innocent traders perhaps bound for Rome, yet all aboard them readied for what they knew lay ahead.

They crossed paths with Murcus's four ships a few miles off the rocky cape that guided ships to Misenum. The quinqueremes were making for the channel between the island of Aenaria and its smaller neighbour, out of sight of the port itself. The wind had dropped, and a morning mist shrouded the galleys so that they heard the rush of the sweeps before they saw the sleek vessels emerge; the two Veneti ships were becalmed, and Titus cursed their lack of manoeuvrability. He sent word to try to appear foreign and harmless, and to show no weapons. He hoped Eshmun would do the same on *Eurus*. They waved to the Sicilians as their wash gently rocked the Venetis, grateful not to be challenged.

But Murcus, grim-faced, standing on his aft platform just fifty paces from *Boreas*, was not interested in two traders and did not even turn to acknowledge them. He was straining to see where *Andromeda* was moored, no doubt planning his attack as his ships moved towards the bay.

The mist cleared swiftly and as a small tide tugged them towards the coastline, *Boreas* and *Eurus* moved close and moored to each other within view of Murcus's ships and the giant *Andromeda* where the world's leaders would be meeting. The suspect vessels took up position behind the smaller island, the perfect place to watch without being seen. A tender was lowered, and Titus watched as someone stepped onto the island, presumably to observe and report back to Murcus and Azhar.

'Check all the scorpios,' Titus commanded, pleased to feel pulse-quickening anticipation once again, 'and everyone get yourselves armed.'

'Forgive me if I'm missing something,' said Crispus, 'but don't we need a strong wind for these tubs to be any use in a sea-battle?' Even as he spoke, the gods granted his wish and a light breeze snatched at his hair.

Titus looked toward Vesuvius and the mountains beyond, where thick cloud promised stronger winds. 'We'll need far more than this if we are to be any more than onlookers.'

Marina called across, 'The gods have heard you. Look there.' She pointed towards distant *Andromeda*, where a single blue pennant atop her mast's rigging flapped with new vigour. She was moored to what appeared to be a wide platform on which were awnings and more flags, beyond this a narrow mole leading to an encampment which must be the home of Octavian and Antonius for the duration. The set-up puzzled Titus — how could Murcus spring a surprise attack with perhaps several legions watching over the deliberations? Unless... The mole was narrow and could be defended if Murcus landed a handful of men to control it. It would be even easier if the leaders they targeted were on the flagship and the attacking marines boarded swiftly to cut her adrift.

We have to stop Murcus reaching them, he thought.

The distant sound of horns, wavering in the now strong gusts, broke the boredom of both crews. Two figures wearing distinctive togas strolled along the mole, cheered by the soldiers massed behind them. Stepping across from *Andromeda* a solitary man, similarly dressed, set foot on the palatial landing stage, arms outstretched in welcome. They met beneath the biggest canopy, while secretaries and scribes stood back and the servants on board Sextus's ship lined an outrigger deck.

'Can't see any soldiers on the ship,' muttered Crispus, whose eyesight was sharper than Titus's.

'They must be ashore, or possibly below decks,' said Titus. 'This has the look of a friendly agreement, don't you think? The way they are dressed, showing affection, and so few guards. Even the support ships are standing off.'

The figure that must have been Sextus turned towards *Andromeda* and appeared to shout an order. Almost immediately two more pennants, one red the other yellow, were hoisted to fly next to Sextus's own flag. All three flew proudly in the stiff breeze. On the ship's stern, hidden from view by the outriggers, another figure waved a makeshift flag in the direction of the island that hid the Sicilians. Titus studied the crest of the island where another flag was waved, apparently in response. He called across to Eshmun, 'Look there. A signal from Sextus's ship to Murcus.' Turning to Crispus, he went on, 'So they have a spy among Sextus's people! No wonder they knew where the conference was to be — not Lipara, as put about by Sextus himself.'

'Looks like it's time for action,' said Crispus.

'Wait … yes, see there, all three are boarding *Andromeda*. Do they not realise how vulnerable they are? Have the men cast off.'

As the moorings between *Boreas* and *Eurus* were loosed and the men raised sails, Titus addressed both crews. 'The odds are against us,' he called, 'but we know the gods are with us. Our first objective is to prevent Murcus from reaching Sextus. Use the scorpios to destroy them and when they are done, we shoot as many of the enemy as we can with arrows. But do not grapple them; they are too many. Better to ram them, as our ships are made of sturdy oak, theirs of flimsier stuff. Light the braziers should we need fire. If they attempt to board us, fight like demons. I promise you all, we will be well rewarded for what we do today.'

Both ships caught the offshore wind simultaneously and came about. Side by side they nosed towards the island where Murcus no longer hid as his four ships emerged, sweeps rising and dipping, white water spraying at their bows.

CHAPTER SIXTEEN

Boreas and *Eurus* sailed so close to the wind that Titus thought their masts would surely snap as they heeled bravely, but both held their course. Smoke trailed from their braziers, dissipating as it drifted seaward. He looked across to Eshmun on *Eurus*, whose jaw was set firm, feet braced as his oaken vessel proved her resilience with every surge and crash through foaming seas. Beside him stood Marina, who had donned armour and was leaning on a short spear for support, and Barek, muscular arms bared and glistening with sea-spray, clutching his mallet. On *Boreas*, Titus stood with Crispus and young Felix, who whooped with delight at the prospect of his first battle.

The four galleys they opposed were rounding the island to come into full view of any who watched from *Andromeda*, but there were none and no alarm was raised. Which one was Murcus? Titus cursed himself for not taking note of his vessel as it had slid past at dawn, for surely to destroy the leader was the first rule of warfare. And on which was Azhar? *We will have to stop all four*, he thought grimly and singled out the lead ship to target.

'We pass to the left of that ship,' he called over the wind singing in *Boreas*'s rigging. She was heeling at a considerable degree and moving faster than at any time over the past two days. 'Ready scorpios, maximum decline.' The scorpio crews were well drilled; the four catapults were winched to point downwards, bolts loaded. 'On my command, one to four, aiming for their helmsmen and their steerage.'

As they closed, Titus looked across to see that Eshmun had singled out a second ship and was adjusting his course to pass close, perhaps even take out rows of oars as well as fire a broadside. Then he focused on the oncoming enemy ship, giving hand-signals to the steersmen beside him for slight adjustments to their course. Such was their closing speed, they were almost upon it before he saw any reaction from their target, but it was too late.

'One, loose.' There was a loud snap as the sprung iron drove its bolt outwards, then three more on Titus's commands. He barely had time to see the havoc they had caused before seeking his next target, ordering a change of course to bring the scorpios on the opposite side to bear on the next ship in line. He risked a glance over to *Eurus* to see that Eshmun's target had slowed with its oars in disarray, then to the ship he had fired upon — but it held its course. Surely they hadn't missed? Perhaps targeting the oars and their rowers was more effective. Titus hoped the scorpio crews on the other side had adjusted their trajectories — it was far easier when not having to shoot downwards.

He made his decision. He waited for the right moment as *Boreas* smashed into the target's oars. He imagined the devastating scenes on the rowing benches as rowers were being crushed and maimed, hearing their screams. 'Loose all together.' Four bolts added to the chaos and the enemy ship began to turn, one bank of rowers obliterated as the opposite side continued on.

Then *Boreas* was through. 'Come about,' commanded Titus, stabbing his hand landward, but the vessel struggled coming into the wind. He tried again, seeing that Eshmun had made his turn successfully and was chasing their quarry, two ships clearly ruined, the others turning towards *Andromeda*. He ordered his four lee oarsmen to assist, and she slowly came about, but now he was far behind. Felix leapt from the platform to help tighten sail and slowly *Boreas* began to pick up speed.

But the enemy was fighting back. From one of them a hail of arrows and spears rained on *Eurus,* and she momentarily lost way as her crew reached for shields, reeling from the onslaught. He saw several men tumble, screaming, into her wake. Grappling irons were slung by the enemy, dozens of them, probably intended for *Andromeda* but now used on this strange vessel that dared to assault them. But their action slowed their progress.

'Reload scorpios,' Titus yelled. Looking at the steersmen, he pointed to the enemy's opposite flank. As they came up to them, he saw that *Eurus* would soon be boarded as the enemy heaved themselves upwards, too many, while Barek cracked skulls with his mallet and the crew fired volley after volley on their attackers. *Boreas* came alongside, almost unnoticed. The enemy vessel visibly shuddered as four bolts splintered her below the waterline. Titus ordered slack sails and demanded the scorpio crews reload — they needed no call to urgency as they wound their weapons taut and fired another volley, this time raking the rowing decks where screams and curses told him they had caused bloody devastation.

But all three ships were now stationary, tangled together in confusion, and Titus knew that hand-to-hand combat would surely follow. He risked a moment to see where the other ships were and was horrified to see that although two floundered, one of them was unharmed and making for *Andromeda* — could this be Murcus with his murderous intent? Yet there was another vessel, too. And it was on a clear ramming course for that one remaining enemy ship.

An arrow thudded into the transom beside him. He took in the scene. Crispus had not waited for his 'on three' command

and was stabbing downwards at the marines who were attempting to board. Felix was at his side, thrashing with a rusting falcata. The crew was outnumbered but had the advantage of height.

Titus knew what he had to do.

The brazier glowed in the freshening wind, its ironwork blistering his hands as he lifted it. He ran across the deck and launched it, an explosion of sparks distracting their attackers as small flames caught ropes and sails. Some broke off their attack to attempt to douse flames, but soon the enemy's deck was ablaze, fanned by the wind, and the assault slackened.

'Are you thinking what I'm thinking?' It was Crispus, standing beside him, *gladius* and dagger in his hands, eager for bloody work. Beside him, Felix clutched his falcata blade.

'I am indeed. We must draw them away from Eshmun's ship.' Titus saw that the enemy marines on the deck below them were in chaos, some trying to douse the fire while others continued to scramble up the side of *Eurus* to board her. He searched among them for Azhar and Murcus, but the soldiers were all helmeted and none bore the familiar Sicilian cloak, an unsuitable garment at sea. He called to the crew to hold *Boreas* steady and remain on board to provide covering fire and be ready to throw ropes for their return. He turned back to Crispus.

'On three.'

They leapt down to the burning deck, two seasoned soldiers and a callow youth outnumbered by an enemy crew yet with the advantage of confusion and fear. All around them, men screamed as the crews from both *Boreas* and *Eurus* loosed arrows and spears, and for a moment the enemy hesitated. Then there was the familiar fury of hand-to-hand combat, a knot of marines rushing at them with falcatas raised. Crispus was at Titus's side, already singing his tuneless battle song, and Felix was showing courage beyond his years.

Crispus stepped forward to take the full force of the collision, scattering the enemy left and right with his size and strength, allowing Titus and Felix to dispatch off-balance soldiers with ease. But now the enemy came in greater numbers, and still too many were trying to board *Eurus*. 'Arrow wedge!' Titus yelled to Crispus and the burly *optio* immediately advanced, Titus and Felix his flanks. Shieldless, all three took wounds, but the enemy took more.

A plumed helmet caught Titus's attention. Most of the enemy helmets were unsophisticated and functional, but a marine with elaborate headgear? Azhar, surely. Titus found the breath to draw Crispus's attention, but they could not afford to break rank. Yet Crispus hated Azhar as much as Titus did, and with renewed vigour the three cut their way towards their archenemy.

The fire took hold all around them, the wind sending bright sparks back towards *Boreas*. Titus strained to reach Azhar. The commander was close enough for Titus to look into that cruel face; their eyes met across the confusion, and now Azhar knew the architect of his doom. Titus pointed his *gladius* at Azhar's eyes, but he was not close enough to wound.

And he knew they had to retreat before both Veneti ships caught fire too.

He saw that their diversion had worked, and the enemy was no longer attempting to board *Eurus*. He tugged at Crispus as the big man dispatched another marine and pulled Felix back from his frenzied stabbing and slashing, noticing that both were dripping blood from multiple wounds. They understood when they saw the strength of the fires around them. They backed away as *Boreas*'s crewmen threw ropes, Crispus as ever the last to board, scowling and cursing the enemy to the last.

'Tell me we didn't retreat,' he said to Titus as he clambered aboard.

'We've got a worse enemy to escape from.' The fire was so hot that many of the enemy soldiers were leaping over their galley's stern and bow. He called four of the oarsmen to him. 'Grab your oars and push us away. Get us clear of that ship before the fire catches us too.' He looked over to *Eurus* to see she, too, was edging away from danger. He looked more closely through the smoke and flames and saw Marina stooped over a prone figure on *Eurus*'s command deck, an arrow protruding from his chest.

It was Eshmun.

They left the burning quinquereme to its fate, *Boreas* and *Eurus* bound in sisterhood as they limped away under half sail. They saw two more enemy ships floundering on the rocks beneath the cape, then the fourth, broken and wallowing with the seas lapping across its deck. Nearby, an untidy trireme stood off.

'Hail Titus,' came a booming voice.

'Menecrates?'

'The same. Seems I arrived in the nick of time. Want to join my pirate fleet?'

'What kept you? We were just coming after this fourth ship, but I see you had the easy pickings.'

'Ha! If not for me, Sextus and these two jumped-up Romans would all be dead by now. But you have done well, defeating three ships with those two ancient tubs of yours.'

'And what of Sextus?' Titus looked over to *Andromeda* and saw no sign of concern.

'Two of his *liburnians* came sniffing to see what was going on, but when they saw it was a minor skirmish and that I am Sextus's friend, they went back to their lazy duties and excess wine rations. And what of you? How have you fared?'

'Eshmun took an arrow. I think he may die.' Titus paused, thinking. Part of him wanted to report to Octavian, Antonius and Sextus, but he knew Zerenia would never forgive him if her father died while he delayed. 'Will you escort us back to Messana?'

'Of course. But first come alongside; I have some medicine that will help the old man.'

The three ships, two heroic Venetis and a pirate's trireme, set a course south to Messana, the sun setting crimson on the shimmering ocean. Titus, Crispus and Felix doused themselves with buckets of seawater to wash away blood, clean wounds and cool burns. Marina broke the shaft in Eshmun's chest, leaving a hand's breadth protruding, then poured Menecrates' strong spirit into the wound. Each of the men looked on solemnly, willing the old man to live, speechless as they shared the bottle to relieve their own aches and bruises.

Behind them, Octavian, Antonius and Sextus celebrated their agreements, congratulating themselves on the riches to be reaped from their allocated lands, their new trade deals for grain and goods, and new betrothals to seal their promises to one another.

PART TWO: BETRAYAL

CHAPTER SEVENTEEN

Rome, early 38BC

The three men reclined at a working lunch, nothing elaborate in deference to Octavian's delicate constitution. It was, after all, in his house where they met. Just bread, cheese and fruit. Agrippa thought nothing of that, being used to the frugal fare of Gaul where he had been assigned to free the region from the last vestiges of Antonius's influence. The third man was Gaius Cilnius Maecenas, patron to Rome's struggling poets, broker of well-connected marriages and repairer of broken diplomatic relationships.

'That's settled, then,' said Maecenas in a smooth, hypnotic tone, looking into Octavian's expressionless face, 'a new marriage and a firm grip on our western territories while Antonius busies himself in the East with Cleopatra.'

Octavian frowned. He knew of his fellow triumvir's flirtation with the Egyptian queen, playing Dionysus to her Aphrodite and demeaning the name of his sister, Octavia, barely a year married to Antonius. 'We must keep him close while we have such unrest at home,' he said. 'We may need his ships.'

'To deal with our friend Sextus?' asked Agrippa, flicking the edge of a scroll. 'I hear he's still not happy and his piracy has resumed. That will mean more riots among the starving masses.'

Octavian managed a cold smile for his two confidants. 'Then we do what we should have done in the first place, instead of listening to his ridiculous demands.'

'But to do that we need more ships,' said Agrippa, 'not to mention fully trained crews and better weapons.' He picked up the scroll and smiled, inviting his co-conspirators to lean across to inspect it.

'Something from your man in Sicilia?' asked Octavian.

'Ah, your trusty spy network, eh?' Maecenas murmured.

'Indeed. I have reports from my vipers that say Sicilia is in turmoil and Sextus is consumed with rooting out the traitors that dared to attempt to assassinate him along with Octavian and Antonius at Misenum. But he still has a much bigger fleet, and his ships are faster than ours. Now he also has new weapons which were used to great effect to foil Murcus's attempt to take control.'

This time, Octavian's smile was warmer. 'I hope the heroes who did this have been well rewarded. A sea battle raging while we were on board Sextus's flagship, and we knew nothing about it!'

'My man will be well paid,' said Agrippa, 'but it's best if we keep quiet about the episode — not just for the embarrassment that you were so exposed, but because we must protect my viper's identity.'

'Of course. What else do you have?'

'Well,' said Agrippa, 'we've heard from our man in Sardinia. You've met Menodorus, of course?'

Octavian nodded. 'Yes, unsavoury fellow as I recall, a bit of a tub-thumper at Misenum — typical pirate.'

'The same. Sometimes goes by the name of Menas. Now he's Sextus's governor for Sardinia and Corsica. From what my spies tell me, you might want to wave some medals and a bright new uniform at him.'

Maecenas interjected. 'Sounds to me like we could have a renegade double-crosser on our hands. What can he bring to the cause?'

Agrippa referred to the scroll. 'Looks like three legions and sixty ships.'

'Get on to it, Marcus,' said Octavian, 'but be careful; these pirates are all the same. But he does have ships and soldiers...'

'Poor old Sextus,' mumbled Maecenas. 'Not long for this world, then.'

'One more thing,' said Agrippa. 'The last message from our man in Messana said that he had fulfilled his mission, thank you very much, and he was going to retire to tend his garden. I will tell him otherwise, of course, but you might want to make it worth his while?'

Octavian thought for a moment. 'Aren't there some rather nice estates in Bruttium that richly deserve a new, *loyal*, owner? Right next door to Sicilia?'

'Perfect,' said Agrippa, his hand reaching instinctively for his own viper brooch. He rubbed it with his thumb, for luck.

CHAPTER EIGHTEEN

Messana, Sicilia, 38BC

Titus read the first line of the message he had decoded: *You have our gratitude, but your mission has barely begun.*

He sighed.

Crispus held a sharpening stone still on his sword blade. 'What now?'

'Seems we are still employed by Agrippa.'

'Good.' He resumed his task.

There was silence while Titus read on and Crispus sharpened. Outside their small armoury, wind and rain lashed at Pax Villius. They could hear Zerenia and Marina laughing with the children in the kitchen as they prepared a feast for Sicilia's version of Agonalia.

Three slow and deliberate strokes of the stone later, Crispus eyed Titus with a quizzical look. 'What does he want this time?' By 'he', Crispus meant Agrippa, whom he admired for his no-nonsense approach and military bearing.

'He says there will be war.'

'Good,' Crispus repeated, then paused. 'Will we be involved?'

'Looks like it. Agrippa has heard of the scorpios we used to destroy Murcus's ships. He wants to know more. And he wants us to sign up to sail with Sextus when Octavian's legions come knocking.'

'Good. You go to sea, and I'll stay on dry land.'

'He says he will make it worth our while.'

'What does that mean? More coin? Gold? We're running a bit low.'

'That's because you spend too much on the ladies. Maybe Marina will rein you in a bit.' Titus had noticed how much time his *optio* had been spending with the young navigator lately. 'Actually, it says here that Octavian wants to give us an estate in Bruttium, just across the strait, along with all of its slaves and servants.'

'Then what are we waiting for? You can oversee the plantations and I will run the gymnasium. I might even start a gladiator school.'

'And a brothel, no doubt.'

'Not me. I'm a reformed man,' said Crispus with a wry smile. He sheathed the sharpened sword, pulled a leather cuirass from the pile of armour, unstopped a bottle and began to work sweet-smelling oil into the cracked surface.

Laughter in the kitchens rose to a crescendo and Zerenia called, 'Titus! Crispus! Food's ready.'

The former *primus pilus* and his *optio* put down the tools of their trade and obeyed the summons. In the kitchen, the children were laying dishes of vegetables around a huge platter of roasted goat.

To the side, reclining in a comfortable chair, Eshmun managed a smile that added only a little colour to his dulled visage. One arm hung limp by his side and his breath rattled. He raised a hand feebly to acknowledge the two men.

'Hail Eshmun,' said Titus reverently. 'I see you have instructed my family well in the skills of preparing a feast.'

'You haven't tasted it yet,' laughed Zerenia. And Titus thought, just for a shortest of moments, that perhaps he had found true happiness at last with his woman and his family.

His happiness dissipated as soon as he thought of Agrippa's latest expectations. Zerenia would not take kindly to his adventures, even if it did offer him a fine estate on mainland Italia.

But he had a far more important mission to fulfil. He knew from the pain in his heart that he must find the man who had defiled Zerenia while he was away with the Fifth Alaudae. He smiled at his betrothed and promised himself he would find his quarry.

But first he would marry her. And he knew what she would say: 'What took you so long?'

CHAPTER NINETEEN

The *liburnian* tracking north out of Syracuse rode a slight swell, a hundred rowers at half speed to conserve energy for the fight ahead. Despite his portly frame, Lucius Staius Murcus stood steady on the command platform, a veteran of numerous voyages and many a naval encounter. They were mostly successful, apart from the last one when his attempted coup at Misenum had ended in disaster, an event that he could only wipe from his memory if he could find revenge against the lowlifes that had intervened.

Standing next to him was a tall figure in full armour, helmetless, his face bearing the livid scars of that same intervention when his galley had burned. Azhar, once the shining prince in command of Sicilia's forces, had lost his good looks, his dignity and his military career in that momentous sea-battle when a flaming brazier had been lobbed into his ship. He had been lucky to escape with his life when searing pain and burning hair had given him no option but to leap overboard. It had been a slow and agonising swim, but time enough to swear to himself that one day he would catch up with the bastard that had thrown that brazier.

He muttered a curse as the image of Titus Villius Macer floated into his mind. His pulse quickened as he recalled the two strange vessels coming out of nowhere as he and Murcus were about to raid the huge ship where Rome's new leaders were meeting with Sextus. It had been right at the climax of Murcus's plan to kill them all and rule both Sicilia and Rome for himself. The scorpio broadsides from the fast Veneti ships under full sail had destroyed two of his small fleet, the third immobilised soon after, and the daring plan had come to nothing. Azhar's disfigured face twitched at the memory of the final insult, the burning brazier, his ship ablaze, and a desperate plunge to escape the conflagration.

Azhar narrowed his eyes and pointed to a promontory that shielded from view the port of Messana some miles beyond. 'There. The bastard's lair is just around that point.'

Murcus grunted and gave a hand signal to the steersman to adjust the ship's course. He looked at Azhar's ruined face and wondered if his co-conspirator was grinning or grimacing. 'Have the crew and our marines ready to land. We'll beach and sweep this pest into the next world. Kill them all.'

Sensing that action was near, the rowers renewed their efforts and white water surged at the *liburnian*'s bow.

'You are Gaius to me, and I am Gaia to you.'

Zerenia smiled through her veil as she spoke the traditional marital pledge, and Titus felt his legs go weak. He had never experienced this except in the heat of battle after hours of shoving and stabbing, his ever-reliable century with him as his enemies gave way.

And now he welcomed the weakness. Zerenia, his betrothed, was agreeing to be his wife right there on the beach beside his homestead, their three children gazing up at them in awe, the priestess lifting her staff aloft, all of his freedmen and ships' crews holding their breath for his reply. The harpist's hand had frozen on the strings. Even a pair of oystercatchers hesitated in their hunt on the rocks nearby.

Titus had longed for the moment when he could make the formal response, when he could finally call Zerenia his wife and make her a Roman citizen, to share in the rights bestowed after so long with the Fifth.

No longer. It was time for marital bliss and harvesting oil and wine.

Nervously, he began his formal response. 'You are Gaia to me...'

From the corner of his eye he saw movement at the southern point, just visible beyond their two beached ships, and tried to ignore it.

'...And I am Gaius to you.'

The priestess shook her staff, its silver cymbals announcing the gods' blessing on the marriage, and the gathered audience cheered as one. All except Crispus, ever the guardian warrior, who had followed Titus's momentary distraction and was watching the war galley, its oars dipping and rising with familiar urgency.

Zerenia sensed their alarm and frowned. It was she who had insisted there would be no weapons at the wedding feast. It was to be a celebration of peace and laughter among friends. Behind, her father Eshmun tensed, knuckles white where he gripped his crutches, the dull ache of old wounds reminding him of the recent time his people had faced ships like this one. Was it merely crossing the bay, heading for Messana's bustling port, perhaps on some mission out of Syracuse on Sicilia's southern coast?

The ship cleared the point, sea frothing at her bow, and turned in the unmistakable manner of a vessel readied for action.

Crispus, always the suspicious warrior whose talent had been honed in Rome's arenas where gladiators never assumed honour in an opponent, looked to Titus. His friend was troubled. Beside him, his woman Zerenia and their children were lost in the joy of the moment.

'Could it be Sextus?' he mouthed.

Titus shrugged. 'Best to assume the worst,' he said. 'None of Sextus's ships have that device on their bow.' At this, Crispus looked again and saw the large black eye dripping red blood painted on the bow of the approaching ship. It looked like a demon from Tartarus. And the warship showed no familiar colours, not Sicilia's blue pennant nor Rome's red. War shields lining her flanks indicated that the rowers were also marines, armed and ready to fight.

The wedding party, fifty men with their women and children, bore no weapons.

'Damn you and your wars,' said Zerenia. Her voice was steady, but her dark eyes flashed with anger.

'Take the children and run to the house,' Titus ordered, then turned back to Crispus. 'Send men to the ship shed to gather swords and spears, as many as they can carry, but you stay here in case they are upon us before we are armed.'

Marina, Neptune's daughter who had found a home at last with these simple folk, stepped forward. 'I will lead your women to bring arms.'

Titus nodded and Marina ran to gather the women. Crispus was already breaking down the wedding bower, splintering its struts across a muscular thigh to use as weapons. The men gathered for orders, most of them fearful but some eager for the fight, not least the broad-chested carpenter Barek and the youth Felix, who had both excelled in the fight at Misenum.

The approaching warship was close enough now for Titus to see the familiar figure of Murcus on the command deck. *So you survived, you wily old fool*, he thought to himself, *and now you seek revenge.* But who was the tall, disfigured man standing next to him? *Surely not? Azhar?* Azhar the Cruel, Titus's torturer and surely the man who had raped Zerenia. *This time I will have your life, but not before you have begged for mercy*, thought Titus. His right hand throbbed as he made this vow, the one from which Azhar's gaoler had removed a finger.

Eshmun tugged at his sleeve and Titus forced his anger to subside, turning to look into the craggy features of his father-in-law.

'We can use the scorpios.'

Of course. The *ballista* crossbow weapons that had proved so successful at Misenum, firing broadside after broadside of heavy iron bolts into the enemy ships. But these were mounted on the two ancient Veneti ships that were beached nearby and could not easily be manoeuvred into position.

'How?' asked Titus.

Lungs ruined by the arrow he had taken, Eshmun could only speak in a whisper. Titus strained to hear him. 'They can train left to right and up and down,' he croaked. 'Look, do you see? We have four on the nearest vessel, *Boreas*, pointing in the right direction, and if the enemy lands anywhere within their range, we can fire them. Even at the ship before it beaches.'

Titus grasped Eshmun by the shoulders. 'Old father, you are right. How many men do you need?'

'There are bolts stored on *Boreas*. I only need four to operate the scorpios, and two to supply them with bolts.'

Titus called four of his crewmen and two of the younger servants. He saw the fear in their eyes.

'You will not have to fight on this beach today,' he told them. 'But you can win this fight for us. Go now with Eshmun and do exactly as he tells you. And when we come to our wedding feast tonight, you will have the choicest cuts.'

CHAPTER TWENTY

The approaching *liburnian* did not slow and was now heading for the shallows, where gentle waves lapped at the shingle on which fifty unarmed wedding guests stood together at the shore of Pax Villius. It was so named for 'peace', but here was an aggressor who did not understand the word. Most of those on the beach feared for their lives; a few didn't care because they had faced death many times. It was their land and their livelihood under threat.

Titus looked back to see the women straining to carry weapons from the ship shed and knew they might have to take the first attack unarmed. He ripped his cloak free from its clasp, the precious viper brooch, and turned to his men.

'Do this,' he called, wrapping the cloak around his left forearm. 'Use any cloth you can find, then pick up driftwood and stones — anything you can use as a weapon.'

Crispus, who had dismantled the wedding bower, was passing out pitifully few lengths of wood.

'You have no shields on which to beat. You have no swords or spears,' Titus called to the men. 'But you have your strength, the spirit with which we defeated Murcus and Azhar at Misenum. You have your lives and your families; you have your very being with which to fight and destroy this enemy that bears down upon us in cowardice and disgrace on this day of joy. What will you do to them?'

There was a moment's hesitation, then a solitary voice called out. It was the carpenter, Barek. 'We will fight them!' This was echoed to a man.

'What will you do to them?' Titus repeated. He did not need to turn seaward to know that Murcus approached, as he could hear the grunts and chants of the enemy as they rowed.

'We will destroy them!'

Titus looked beyond them to his beloved homestead, where his wife and children waited in fear. 'Hail Pax Villius!' he yelled.

They responded together: 'Hail Titus!'

There was a loud crack, then three more, from the direction of the beached ship, *Boreas*. Titus turned to see the devastation that scorpios could wreak on a vessel, splintering the enemy's superstructure and ripping into the rowers behind. The oars on one side immediately tangled in confusion and the approaching ship slewed as it came to the shingle, its draft of half the height of a man finding the seabed without the thrust to take it onto the beach. Murcus stumbled on the command deck as his ship lurched and Azhar grasped a rail to steady himself. There were shouts of confusion and pain from the rowing decks, then immediately another volley of the deadly bolts.

Titus hoped the numbers had been made more even by the scorpio volleys. He was counting the heads he could see gathering weapons before their advance through the shallows, when he felt a tug on his tunic and a sword was handed to him. He saw that others around him were being armed with spears and short swords, some with grappling hooks and pitchforks, but at least they now had weapons. In his mind, he blessed the womenfolk for their speed in responding to the threat.

Crispus advanced past him — ever the fearless hero, ever the fool, but a lucky fool who this day would take more wounds and no doubt live to tell his tale in Sicilia's inns and whorehouses. He carried a long-bladed *spatha*, the best weapon to wield when shieldless, and immediately scythed it expertly above his head as a dire warning to the enemy who were now leaping from the bows of the ship.

Another volley from the scorpios took out more of the enemy as they advanced through the shallows, but the surprise weapon would be useless once both sides had engaged, for fear of harming the Pax Villius defenders.

The Syracusians came on, wading against the shore's undertow. Titus rushed past Crispus to thrust a killing stab at the neck of the first marine, then took a heavy blow on his padded left arm. The cloth blunted the cutting edge and for a moment he felt the arm go weak. Then Crispus was at his side, swinging his *spatha* like a reaper's scythe, the enemy unsteady and uncertain. But the gruesome figure of Azhar was now at the ship's prow urging his men on, Murcus behind him looking uneasily in the direction of the beached ship from where the stinging volleys had come.

But these were seasoned warriors that came leaping over the bulwarks, wading ashore with shield, spear and *gladius*, and Titus knew it would take courage and luck to hold them. From the corner of his eye, he thought he saw the lithe lad Felix kill a soldier twice his size and the brute Barek wielding a hefty piece of driftwood to reduce the odds, but still they were driven back, now on dry shingle. As he took further blows on his padded arm to allow him more killing thrusts to groin and neck, aware that Crispus with roaring courage was holding the advance as best he could, Titus sensed rather than saw the moment his wife was orphaned.

Eshmun had limped to the battlefront. The old man, Zerenia's ingenious father, was no warrior, his contributions to sea warfare always limited to ship design, like the two leaky Gallic ships he had adapted for speed and surprise. His was the mind of a peacemaker and a sensible father and grandfather, but now he was enraged at the sight of armed men threatening his family. As frail legs propelled him towards the battle, he swung a gnarled crutch at the invaders with strength not befitting one so old and infirm. He died with a blade in the sternum, three of the enemy face down on the shingle around him where his life force bled out.

The men of Pax Villius would have been beaten back into the wilds of Sicilia and massacred if they had not been saved by the sound of trumpets blaring across the bay. The sound halted the cut and thrust and the shouts of Murcus and Azhar from the safety of their ship. Every man stopped where they stood and looked to see where the sound came from.

Two triremes sailed serenely into the bay of Pax Villius, both flying the blue pennants of Sicilia's fleet. The larger vessels boasted more power and three times the number of men who fought on the shore, and their presence was not lost on Murcus and Azhar. They called their men to retreat, pushing the unwelcome *liburnian* back from the shingle and clambered aboard. They knew their chance for revenge had passed, and while the bloodied men of Pax Villius stood agape on the beach, the enemy fled.

Sextus Pompeius Magnus Pius, self-styled governor of the islands of Sicilia and Sardinia and piratical thorn in the flesh of Octavian and Antonius, had come to join the wedding.

CHAPTER TWENTY-ONE

Marcus Vipsanius Agrippa was tired. He had barely slept since receiving the summons at his headquarters in Gallia Narbonensis, from where he had put down the Aquitani rebellion. Despite a long journey leaving him in need of the baths and a massage, he thrust the thought aside and went straight to the home of the new Caesar, Octavian, who had written 'come immediately' and probably meant it.

Ordering his escort to wait with Octavian's guards, he approached the house, thinking how inadequate it was for the man who was calling himself 'son of a god'. The entrance was modest, twin columns in need of repair and a heavy door faded by the sun. Wiping a finger of dust from a carving of what might have passed for Jupiter, Agrippa rapped with his fist and was about to use his sword hilt when the door opened to reveal the inquisitive face of an immaculately dressed slave. He announced himself and was waved inside, the door shutting on the noise and smells of the Forum.

It was refreshingly cool inside, with very little natural light. The slave beckoned but Agrippa held up a hand. 'Are you not forgetting something?' The slave shrugged as Agrippa removed his *gladius*, saying, 'Suppose I am an assassin? It has happened before to a Caesar.'

'My master has told me you are as a brother to him, but if you insist…' The slave took the sword and laid it on a table. 'If you would follow me, sir?'

Agrippa looked around as he followed the slave and wondered why Octavian had not made more of the riches now at his disposal. Perhaps the money had all been spent on putting down Italia's own civil unrest. He was shown to a large room at the back of the house, lit by a little sunshine from a rare window, supplemented by lamps which gave the gaunt figure of Octavian a yellowish hue. The triumvir looked up from his desk.

'Ah, Marcus. Welcome.' He rose from his chair and began to remove tablets from a couch.

Octavian did not look like the son of a god, unless the gold and purple braid on the fringes of his simple knee-length tunic indicated divinity. He had often been ill when on campaign, more than once delegating authority to Agrippa, whose inner strength and boundless energy always enthused the men, but now he looked worse than ever. Perhaps it was just the poor light. Whatever ailed him, Agrippa thought, he had not lost his devotion to matters of state: he was surrounded by scrolls and tablets with accompanying writing implements. It was a disorderly mayhem that only a divine mind could unravel to make sense of where Rome was heading.

'Greetings…' Agrippa was uncertain how to address Rome's ruler.

Octavian ignored the hesitation. 'We have much to discuss. Come, sit.'

'I hear you have married again,' said Agrippa. 'Is Livia here, and her child?'

'She is in the country with *both* her children.'

Agrippa gaped in confusion.

'My dear Agrippa, you've been away too long,' laughed Octavian as if his marital incongruity was of no consequence. 'Not only did I take on Livia and young Tiberius, but she was with child when we married, plain for all of Rome to see.'

'Such haste. You must be in love.'

'Ah, love…' Octavian was wistful. 'It gives us such bliss and it causes such strife. Even wars. But Livia is no Helen, and I am no Paris.'

'Except —'

'Except what? Her husband Claudius gave his blessing. He was gracious enough to attend the wedding and even gave me the hand of Livia.'

Sensible man, thought Agrippa. 'But what of Libo's sister?' he asked, wondering what had become of Octavian's second wife, who was aunt to the wife of the Sicilian pirate, Sextus Pompey.

Octavian narrowed his eyes, and for a moment Agrippa wondered if he had gone too far, but that marriage had been an important part of making a pact with Sextus to allow the grain ships safe passage and end the famine that had ravaged Italia. And now Octavian had put her aside with indecent haste, even divorcing her on the very day that she gave birth to his daughter.

'That rat Sextus was never going to keep his word,' said Octavian. 'Which is why I have summoned you.'

'Pleased to be of service. How can I help?'

'Have you heard from your man in Sicilia of late? His name escapes me — the centurion who fought so well at Philippi and foiled an attempt on my life at Misenum…'

'Titus Villius. Brave man. I have yet to catch up with my secretary here in Rome and no message reached me in Narbo. But as I recall, he was reluctant to continue, so we tempted him with an estate in Bruttium.' As he spoke, Agrippa fingered the viper brooch at his chest.

'Are you telling me we gave this Titus a valuable estate what, four months ago, and he has done nothing for us in return?'

Agrippa stiffened. 'I have no doubt that Titus remains in our service. He has simple values in life; he obeys orders and remains loyal to the hand that feeds him.'

'But what if Sextus offers him more? What's to stop him betraying us to that pirate scoundrel?'

Agrippa raised an eyebrow. 'He is clever enough to take Sextus's silver and feed him a handful of useless morsels. But even if he is a double agent, he is too far removed from Rome to know anything of our plans.' He fidgeted again with the brooch. 'Of course, we could summon him…'

Octavian interrupted. 'And feed him some false information?'

'If we want to feed information to Sextus, false or true, we can ask him to do that for us. Titus is definitely our man, but if it makes you feel better about him, you can look him in the eye and ask him yourself. But I have another reason for wanting to see him.'

'Oh? And what might that be?' asked Octavian.

Agrippa knew how to manage Rome's new master. 'My dear Caesar,' he said with his warmest smile, 'I have come such a long way. I'm hungry and I probably smell like an old goat. Can we not discuss this in more leisurely surroundings?'

For a moment, Octavian was aghast and for a second time Agrippa feared he might have offended his friend. Then his features softened. 'Please accept my apologies. An army marches on its stomach, even if it rarely washes.' He clapped his hands and the slave appeared at the door. 'What delights do the cooks have for us?' demanded Octavian.

'Very little, sir. Since the lady departed, you have barely required anything of substance. Might I suggest the poet?'

'Maecenas? A grand idea. When his kitchens have satisfied us we can attend the baths, or the other way around. Go and inform him of our imminent arrival.'

The three most powerful men in Rome relaxed at the nearby Forum baths and dined at the home of Maecenas. They discussed global politics, from the Parthian threat to the pacification of Gaul, what Marcus Antonius might do next, and how to deal with the Sicilian problem and Sextus Pompey.

This brought up the subject of sea warfare and Rome's dearth of fighting ships and crews, which Octavian thought might be resolved by an arrangement with Antonius. 'He needs men, so we can give him legions; we need ships, so he can provide us with a fleet in return.'

'We can't defeat Sextus without a fleet,' Agrippa agreed. 'But we need more than some worm-eaten Egyptian monstrosities crewed by starving slaves. We should build our own ships, equip them with new weapons and train our own crews.'

'But that will take years,' sighed Maecenas, and Octavian concurred.

'Then the sooner we get started, the sooner we can take Sicilia back for Rome,' said Agrippa, 'and if we are going to do that, we need to know our enemy better.'

Octavian looked at him. 'Better send for your man Titus, then. He can tell us what we're up against and while he's at it, he can show us the plans for those ship-mounted scorpio weapons that our engineers are talking about.'

'Ah,' smiled Agrippa, 'I've been working on that myself.'

CHAPTER TWENTY-TWO

Pax Villius, Sicilia

Sextus Pompey was a changed man. Sicilia's de facto ruler shouted orders to the second trireme to pursue Murcus's retreating galley and waded ashore, leaving his crew aboard.

Titus waited for him, expressionless. Around him lay the dead and the dying, equal numbers of invaders and men of his homestead; the latter were simple folk who tended olive, almond and grapevine, or who repaired ships, or who cooked and cared for the extended family that lived at Pax Villius.

And at his feet was Eshmun, master shipbuilder in his youth and father of his woman. The old man's blood seeped into the sand where he lay. 'Mercurius speed you to Elysium, Great Father,' Titus had said as he closed Eshmun's unseeing eyes. The women had keened their sorrow as Zerenia ran to them, her wedding skirts hitched, her dark hair streaming behind her, an anguished cry escaping as she knelt over her lifeless father.

Now she stood with Titus as Sextus waded ashore, his arms outstretched in supplication. 'Do not let him set foot on our land,' she hissed as the son of Pompey the Great came towards them.

'Why not? He is my friend.' Even as he said this, Titus thought how easy it had been to betray Sextus by sending reports to Agrippa, yet he had not expected it would ever lead to war. But now? The bloodshed on his own beach told him differently.

'You can trust no one, especially not him,' said Zerenia. With that, she turned away to help the other women tend to the wounded.

As he approached, Sextus seemed to Titus to have aged. The smiling, careless attitude was no more. Instead, there was anger etched on a face lined by the tensions of Rome's politics and Sicilia's own internal wrangling. Gone was the golden warrior who once sought to bring down the architects of his father's demise. Sextus had become yet another ambitious local dictator who saw fame and fortune whenever Rome was not looking.

'Titus! What has happened here?' he asked.

'Murcus. And Azhar. That's what's happened.'

'I thought I was coming to my friend's wedding, and instead I find destruction. Murcus will pay for this.'

'And Azhar? He was here.'

'I still have faith in him,' replied Sextus, surprising Titus. 'He was always an efficient general, and there must be a reason why such a man should find himself under the control of Murcus. We shall see.'

Titus spat. 'He deserves to die, and I will be the one to relieve you of your precious general.'

Sextus put an arm around Titus. 'Well, it seems I will not be feasting with you today, although if there is food and drink we should not let it go to waste. But perhaps you can help me destroy Murcus?'

'Not me. I have to send the dead to their ancestors. You can fight your own battles. I want nothing to do with Sicilia's petty wars anymore.'

Sextus adopted an air of conciliation. 'Come,' he said, tightening his grip on Titus's shoulder, 'I will help you, my

145

crew too. Let us put this day's evil behind us and look to a better future. For all of us.'

The pyres burned brightly as the sun dipped behind Etna. The families of Pax Villius sang an ancient Greek song that they had brought with them after escaping from slavery in Italia, and long after they had gone to their beds, Titus and Zerenia stood as the embers glowed and the souls of Eshmun and their departed friends were ferried by Charon across the Styx. The enemy dead went with them, forgiven for their sins, though not for their masters'.

Zerenia buried her face in Titus's shoulder. 'Is there no end to this? War follows you as flies descend on rotting meat.'

Titus said nothing. He looked across to Sextus's night camp where the pirate's men caroused, gathering close to warm themselves at the fires on the beach. They had helped themselves to bread and sides of mutton that were to have fed the wedding party and drunk from skins of Pax Villius wine. The second trireme had returned empty-handed; Murcus and Azhar had somehow managed to lose their pursuers in a fortunate sea mist, despite their damaged ship and reduced numbers. And now Murcus was back in his Syracuse stronghold, where no doubt he would continue to plot and scheme. Sextus had no choice but to confront him, but should he, Titus, be drawn into the conflict?

Yes.

Zerenia would not understand, but here was his opportunity to avenge the wrongs committed against her by Azhar the Cruel, rapist and torturer, and now co-architect of the devastation that had blighted his wedding day. Murcus he would leave to Sextus — Titus cared nothing for the would-be imperator's designs on power.

He stroked his wife's hair. 'One more time,' he whispered, knowing it would hurt her. 'One more time, and then I will be free to be a husband and father.'

Pale moonlight lit the path back to their home.

Crispus always knew when battle was at hand. With dawn's brittle light, Titus found him in the armoury, sharpening weapons for both of them. Without looking up, Crispus asked, 'When do we march?'

'Better to ask *why* we march,' snorted Titus, picking up a brightly polished sword. 'Sextus wants us to help him flush out the traitor Murcus, and I want to stick one of these swords in Azhar's heart. You don't have to do this, old friend. It's not your fight.'

Crispus put down a gleaming *gladius* and looked his commanding officer in the eye. 'Oh, but I do have to do this. When have we not faced the enemy together? Or are you forgetting Philippi, when we twice stormed the battlements against the odds? Do not your old wounds twitch at the expectation? Mine do.'

Titus pulled up a stool and picked a cuirass from the war chest, running his fingers over its oiled leather. 'You're right. You'll need me to watch your back when you charge like a Gallic bull.' Crispus laughed, and Titus continued, 'But it will be some days yet, because Sextus will want to rally a cohort and decide whether to attack Murcus from the sea or by land. I suspect the latter, because Murcus is an old sea dog and will have too many tricks up his sleeve, but he might not be so eager for a land battle. And that would be why Sextus wants us, because we have done this so many times before.'

'Just you and me, then?' asked Crispus.

'Felix and Barek too. They have twice proved their fighting strengths, first when we burned Azhar's ship at Misenum and then yesterday on the beach. I want them with us, and a few of the strongest among our people. But that begs the question, who will guard Pax Villius while we are away?'

Crispus smiled as he put down his sword and sharpening stone. 'Come with me, and I will show you who is already doing this.'

They heard the bright ring of sword upon sword and the clash of shields turning away spears even before they had entered the olive grove. A guttural female voice demanded thrust and parry as they made out around forty of the house servants and grove tenders practising their tight-knit drill.

'Marina?' asked Titus as they ducked the low branches of an ancient olive tree.

'Yes, Marina.' Crispus winked at Titus. 'Did you expect me to choose a woman merely to darn socks?'

The men were wielding sword, spear and shield while Marina countered the attack of one of the vintners, finding breath to shout encouragement to the others. She was slight but well balanced, her auburn ponytail dancing with every step and parry, her slender arms and legs glistening with sweat even in dawn's chill. She was a true warrior and leader, and none questioned her authority.

Titus slapped his *optio* on the back. 'You have chosen well. Pax Villius will be in good hands with your Marina, my Zerenia and all of these good people.'

Crispus grinned. 'I'm glad they are not my enemy. The legions of Cassius and Brutus weren't this good!'

'Let's not get ahead of ourselves,' said Titus. 'This little war over Sicilia may have to play out over many days, even years, but at the end of it our Pax Villius family will not only have survived, but will prosper.'

'And by Neptune's fishy beard, so will we all,' said Crispus.

Titus took a skin from the war chest, dipped a stylus in cuttlefish ink, and wrote the letters ANTIXE. Decoded, it would spell VIPERA as the agreed first word in every message, enabling Agrippa to decipher the rest of the message. Then, using the code as indicated by his first word, he wrote: *We fight Murcus with S. Pompeius. Sicilia riven with dispute and unrest. Take this advantage if you can land your legions but beware fast Sicilian ships.*

He placed the message in a leather cylinder to pass to Niko in Messana for despatch, then sought Zerenia in the kitchens. 'Come,' he said softly. 'It may not be the ultimate luxury, but we are going to Messana for a few days of relaxation.'

She looked at him doubtfully. 'But who will look after the children?'

'Crispus of course,' he replied, 'and Marina. They need the practice for becoming parents, which will surely happen one day soon.'

Zerenia found that amusing: she had watched love blossom between the tough soldier and the lovely navigator.

'As long as they don't teach them to fight,' she said.

CHAPTER TWENTY-THREE

Titus and Zerenia took a lateen-rigged skiff, just the two of them, sailing away from the setting sun. Titus relived his childhood by catching lively fish using a trace made from chicken feathers, and they beached just past the headland that partitioned Pax Villius from the bustling port of Messana. There he built a small fire and grilled the blue-backed fish while Zerenia prepared a dish of wild berries and herbs. Gulls, warblers and rock sparrows provided background music while they watched an eagle hunt for lizards and snakes on their deserted promontory.

They made love beneath the stars, and afterwards Zerenia laid her head on Titus's chest. She smoothed the tight curls of dark hair, a sign that she was about to give voice to her thoughts.

'Are you delivering that message you've brought, or are you taking me shopping?'

Titus fell into the trap by assuring her that this trip was all about her and she would have a new dress and shoes on the morrow.

She slapped him playfully. 'Liar.'

They pushed off from their wild paradise at dawn and when a warm southerly picked up, they made for Messana's port. Titus worked sail and tiller to manoeuvre between several war galleys and captured grain ships to nudge against the shallow end of a pier, where dockhands were loading amphorae of wine and oil onto carts. He tied up with the skiff's bow resting on shingle, leapt into the shallows and, before she could protest, lifted Zerenia onto his shoulder to carry her to dry land. Several workers stopped to applaud, one of them shouting, 'Next time, bring her sister!'

They made for the port's market, but it was not lost on Zerenia that to get there they had to pass The Blue Flag. She clutched Titus's arm and smiled at him. 'Isn't that the place where you trade your secrets?'

'How did you know that?' asked Titus, eyes narrowed. 'Have I been talking in my sleep?'

'Crispus, of course,' she laughed. 'He told me you might have business there. Come on, introduce me to your fellow spy and make sure he crosses your palm with silver — enough to buy a necklace to go with a fashionable silk gown.'

The inn was buzzing with customers; they spilled across the forecourt and onto the rutted track that led to the market. A lad aged no more than about twelve, wearing a scarlet bandana around spiky blond hair, was carrying jugs of ale to those outside, placing proffered coins in a bag belted to his waist.

Titus, arm-in-arm with Zerenia, hailed him. The boy's wink acknowledged them and with the last coin pouched he was at their side, ushering them to join the crowd. 'We have Niko's finest brew and a new shipment of wine just in from Rhegium, perfect for the lady.' His sharp eyes looked around as he spoke, as if protective of the new customers.

'Lead us inside and bring us two cups of the Pax Villius wine that I know you have,' said Titus.

'A good choice, sir,' said the boy. He paused as he made the connection. 'Are you...?'

'Titus Villius Macer? Yes, and this is the Lady Zerenia.'

'Sir, I regret we have no room inside. You see, their lordships are all inside.'

'Which lords?' asked Titus.

'Army types, sir. Generals and such.' Then, leaning closer to Titus, he went on, 'The lord Sextus Pompeius is planning something.'

Zerenia bridled, pulling at Titus's arm, but he held his ground. 'And Niko?' he asked the boy. 'Where is he?'

'He is inside, sir. Looking after the generals. I think he is expecting you, because he told me to look out for a tall soldier with lots of fighting scars who makes wine and goes by the name of Titus Villius Macer. Now that I know that's you, sir, I think you should know that you are being followed.'

Titus raised an eyebrow and held the boy's gaze, but Zerenia was alarmed and nervously looked around. 'Go on,' said Titus, realising that this was a bright young man and probably an ally.

'There's a fat man looking at pots and things.' A swift movement of his eyes indicated the edge of the market, then he glanced to Titus's right. 'And there's a thin man with a big nose sweeping the flagstones in front of the house next door. Both suspicious, and both looking at you, sir.'

'Smart lad.' Titus reached into his purse and extracted a coin. 'What's your name?'

'Leo, sir.'

'Pleased to meet you, Leo.' Titus rubbed the coin between forefinger and thumb. 'Now, tell me why I should trust you.'

Leo looked at the viper brooch that clasped a neck scarf at Titus's chest. 'One day, I will have a *fibula* like that,' he said, 'like yours and Niko's.'

Titus gave him the coin. 'Good enough for me. Now, bring us that wine and tell Niko that we will want the best room in the inn for tonight and the finest cuts from his kitchens.' Leo nodded eagerly and turned to go. 'One more thing,' said Titus, 'when we dine tonight, we'll have a jug of Pax Villius vintage. None of that Rhegium muck.'

Leo disappeared on his errand.

'You've made a friend there,' said Zerenia. 'What are we going to do about these men who are following us?'

Titus turned to look at the fat man on the edge of the market. His hand suddenly throbbed with the memory of torture. 'That one's dead,' he said coldly, 'but not before I have removed more than a finger.'

Zerenia shuddered. 'I want all this to be over. If you must be involved, please end it quickly so we can all live in peace.'

'My thoughts exactly,' muttered Titus.

He left Zerenia in the capable hands of an African woman who had bolts of cloth and racks of colourful dresses, promising to return as soon as he had found some new toys for the children. He meandered among stalls selling weapons, hats, rare birds in gilded cages, more clothes and sparkling jewellery, then followed the aroma of roasted nuts and flatbreads.

He knew the fat man was following.

He bought some nuts, tossing them into his mouth as he sauntered towards a stall with a fine array of swords and daggers. He picked up a *gladius*, its wide blade polished and glinting in the midday sun.

'A fine blade, that one. It suits someone of your bearing.' The trader was squat and bearded with small, close-together eyes and wore an oversized robe. 'Seen some action, has that blade — used to belong to Caesar.'

'Which one?' Titus asked with a smile. 'The dead one or the new one?'

'Why, Julius Caesar, of course. Dealer out of Rome brought it here a week ago. Look here —' he pointed to the pommel — 'you can see his initials.'

Titus ignored the scratches on the pommel and instead held the blade close to his face. A reflection of a fat red face watching him confirmed his quarry was close. Casually he fingered the sword's point. Suitably sharp. In one swift movement he turned, strode towards the fat man, noting the surprised look on his face, and thrust the *gladius* point down into the man's sandalled foot. The shock and pain must have paralysed his vocal cords because he made no sound, just stared vacantly at his ruined foot. No one nearby seemed to have noticed the assault.

'Remember me with every limping step you take,' Titus whispered in his ear. 'You took my finger, and you are only alive because I don't have time to visit your magistrate on a murder charge.'

With that, he melted into the market crowds, where he bought three carved monkeys for his children.

Niko, landlord of The Blue Flag and viper courier for Agrippa, had prepared a private room for the couple's feast, away from prying eyes. Zerenia wore a shimmering, close-fitting Egyptian dress set off by a simple silver necklace set with three sapphires, her dark hair coiled and held in place with a jewelled comb. Even phlegmatic Titus had gasped at her beauty. Niko, too, was besotted as they reclined on couches to feast on dishes of fish, venison and suckling pig brought to the low table by Leo. They sipped rose-gold Pax Villius wine.

'There was something of a commotion in the market today,' remarked Niko as he washed his fingers in a bowl of scented water, a smirk on his face as he watched Titus raise an eyebrow. 'Apparently, some hapless fellow dropped a sword point-down on his foot by accident. Poor chap left puddles of blood everywhere.'

Zerenia looked suspiciously at Titus, who shrugged.

'Poor fellow,' said Titus, crunching a honeyed almond. 'Anyone we know?'

Niko couldn't resist looking at the stump that used to be a finger on Titus's hand. 'Once was a gaoler, apparently, probably working for that cruel bastard Azhar back in the day. A sharp sword through the foot is the least he deserves.'

'Sounds like justice, then,' smiled Titus.

They fell silent as Leo and another servant brought trays of aromatic delicacies, pushing through the heavy curtain that separated their private room. When they had left, Niko was ready to change the subject. 'We have a trader leaving for Ostia tomorrow —' He trailed off, looking from Titus to Zerenia.

Titus read the unspoken question. 'Zerenia and I have no secrets,' he said. 'She knows why we are here…'

'You don't think we came to Messana just for the shopping, do you?' Zerenia interrupted.

Niko laughed. 'So you have a message?'

'Indeed, neatly trussed up in a leather case ready for Rome. Is anything coming in the other direction? I expect your couriers pass messages to you. For that matter, what have you heard of what transpires here in Sicilia?'

'How long have you got?' asked Niko. 'The answer is yes and yes, we have heard from our master in Rome, that rising star Agrippa, and I have listened carefully to the plans of Sextus Pompey in this very inn today. You'll be pleased to know that Sextus mentioned you in his plans to strike at Murcus.'

'That's no surprise,' said Titus. 'He asked for our help when he came uninvited to our wedding. But come, viper to viper, tell me what news from Rome?'

Niko dropped another surprise into the conversation. 'You've been ordered to the mainland to meet them, so you can take your message and report in person.'

There was a moment's silence. Titus closed his eyes and took a deep breath. Zerenia sighed. 'First Sextus, now Agrippa,' she said quietly. 'Where does it all end?'

Niko answered for Titus. 'If you ask me, there's going to be war, no question, a war that will probably destroy Sicilia. And we are caught up right in the middle with no way to escape.'

They ate in silence, pondering the implications of an invasion by Octavian's forces. Titus was about to speak when Niko suddenly held a finger to his lips and looked towards the curtained partition. Silently, he crept towards the curtain. Thrusting it aside, he reached out to grab a startled Leo by the ear and pulled him into the room as the child yelped. 'So my young helper turns out to be a sewer rat, listening at the door to matters that are not his concern!' Niko boomed.

Titus laughed, Zerenia had the look of a concerned mother and Niko, who knew the value of this industrious and crafty youth, withheld the blow that he had been about to deliver to the back of Leo's head.

'Explain yourself!' Niko demanded.

Leo gathered himself with an admirable expression of defiance combined with guilt. 'I … well… I heard…' he began. Then, looking straight at Titus, he went on, 'I know I'm too young to be a soldier, but if there's going to be a war I want to be a spy like you.'

Both men were shocked into silence, but Zerenia found her motherly instinct. 'What would your parents think about that?' she enquired gently.

'I don't have parents,' said Leo. 'I don't even know where I was born. I think I was meant to be a slave in Rome, but I've been running for as long as I can remember — until Niko took me in.'

Niko was flustered and didn't know where to look, but Zerenia held her arms wide, offering motherly concern. Leo held his ground with a look that said real men don't need that sort of love. But when she said gently, 'Come,' Leo softened and fell into her embrace.

'Looks like I've just lost my best waiter,' said Niko.

'And I've got another mouth to feed,' added Titus.

It soon became apparent that Leo would have his uses. They allowed him to stay while they discussed the quandary of Titus being expected in two places at once, especially given that Agrippa's orders insisted that Titus attend a meeting at Puteoli on the Ides — just three days hence — while Sextus was planning to march on Syracuse the next day.

Leo proved resourceful and enthusiastic, offering to escort Zerenia home to Pax Villius while delivering a message to Crispus. Reluctantly, Titus could see the advantage in that he could either take the ferry to Rhegium and travel along the coast to Puteoli, or better still sail with the merchant who was already expecting to deliver messages for the vipers. He could deliver his message and more to Agrippa in person.

'That's settled then,' said Niko as Leo hungrily finished the remnants of a honey-cake. 'I will arrange passage for one former centurion to be dropped off at Puteoli. You, Leo, will escort the lady Zerenia to Pax Villius. For extra protection, I will find someone who looks mean enough to keep any nasty robbers away. And Titus, don't worry about your little boat; I will have someone look after it until you next have need of it.'

'I'll look after you, lady,' said Leo, putting on what he thought was a manly expression.

Zerenia smiled. 'I feel safer already,' she said.

Titus failed to conceal his unease, then thought better of expressing concern. 'Pull this off, young Leo, and you will have a viper badge like mine when I return. But there's one more thing you can do for us.'

'Sir.' Leo stood to attention, happy with his assignment as a protector and spy.

'I have fresh orders for my *optio*, Crispus. I will write them down and explain them to you. Remember that you are on a vital mission, so pay attention.'

Wide-eyed and concentrating hard, Leo received his first briefing as a member of Agrippa's vipers.

CHAPTER TWENTY-FOUR

Outside the gates of Pax Villius, a scowling Sextus Pompey grudgingly accepted Crispus's word that Titus had been unavoidably detained on business somewhere on the island of Sicilia and he would have to make do with the small band of warriors that stood before him, each armed and looking dangerous. After all, Crispus explained, he was a seasoned *optio* who had time and again been in the van as the Fifth Alaudae had swatted Rome's enemies aside. And now he had used all his experience as a former gladiator to turn this handful of farmers and sailors into a lethal fighting machine.

What's more, he told Sextus, he had a plan.

Sextus, astride his white charger at the head of a cohort of blue-cloaked Sicilian foot soldiers, archers and slingers, looked over the ten men under the command of Crispus. 'You'll have to do,' he barked. 'Have your men fall in with mine and you will ride beside me to explain this plan of yours.' Then he pointed to Leo, who was lurking behind Felix and Barek, clutching a dagger. 'And send that boy home. This is no place for children.'

Felix put an arm around Leo and whispered in his ear. The boy turned and in an evident sulk, traipsed back towards Pax Villius. When Crispus raised an eyebrow, Felix said, 'I told him he was to protect Zerenia and the children. I think he got the message.'

Crispus was quietly surprised at the discipline in the ranks of the Sicilians, given that most of them were former slaves, retainers and household servants who had fled the triumvirate's proscriptions following the assassination of Julius

Caesar. The cohort, some eight hundred men in all, was not organised by century so much as by the weapons they bore — spearmen carrying large *scutum* shields, swordsmen with lighter shields and leather cuirasses, and slingers and archers wearing only padded tunics over knee-length leggings. Not all wore helmets, but the heavy blue cloaks were clearly standard issue and would double as sleeping blankets. All carried a travel sack with basic provisions. Several large carts drawn by oxen brought up the rear, presumably carrying more provisions, tents and other equipment. Three shifty-looking scouts were sent ahead and were soon out of sight.

'Is Murcus expecting us?' Crispus asked when Sextus had satisfied himself that the column was in order and had motioned them southwards, towards Syracuse. He felt awkward in full, polished armour while Sextus was lightly dressed — perhaps his armour was being carried in one of the carts — making him an obvious target in an ambush.

'He is most likely expecting us,' Sextus replied. 'He has his spies, but then, so do I.'

'So what can we expect? And what of Azhar?'

Sextus smiled knowingly. 'We won't have to fight Azhar, only Murcus, but he commands a small army of his own.'

'Why not Azhar? I saw with my own eyes his attempt to destroy you at Misenum, and he was with Murcus when they attacked us at Pax Villius.'

Sextus shrugged. 'Not everything is as it seems. Now, tell me about this plan of yours.'

Crispus reminded Sextus of the mission on which he had been sent to find out what Murcus was up to in the days before the Misenum pact between Sextus and Rome, although he didn't mention the time he had spent at the finest brothel in Syracuse with Saverina, the she-wolf who wore the same viper brooch as Titus and Niko. But what he did say was that he had scouted the countryside around the city and had explored the huge limestone quarry carved out by Greek slaves in a bygone era, including its network of caves and tunnels — the perfect place to trap Murcus. The difficulty was how to lure him there.

'Leave that with me,' Sextus said. 'I like a plan with an element of surprise, and we have three days' marching to think on it.'

At the second night's camp a few miles north of Syracuse, Crispus took the men of Pax Villius aside to their own campfire. He sacrificed two lambs he had bought from a shepherd on the road south, then Felix skinned and cleaned them ready for the spit constructed by Barek. The other men busied themselves gathering wood and making crude shelters from acacia and olive branches. None noticed the tall warrior brought to Sextus by the three scouts; if Crispus had seen this man, with his face ruined by fire, he would doubtless have challenged him to a fight to the death.

Dawn brought a cold mist rolling in from calm seas, cooling the blood as the men of Pax Villius went through their sword drill. 'Today we fight,' said Crispus, 'and when we return to our home, I want every one of you marching with me unaided, so stay close and remember everything you have learned.'

'Don't worry, Crispus. We'll look after you,' said Felix with a wink, bringing nervous laughter from their small squad.

For a moment, a scowl crossed the rugged features of their leader as he wondered if his men doubted his ability to lead without Titus. Then he too saw the funny side. 'Carry on with your practice while I go to teach these good-for-nothing Sicilians how to win a battle, and be ready to march within the hour,' he said. He went to find Sextus to plan the last day of Murcus's insurrection.

The ancient quarry, hewn into a hillside, formed a hollowed crescent shape with sheer cliffs four times the height of a man around most of its circumference. It faced the untidy city of Syracuse, its rock-strewn floor providing sufficient space for a well-concealed camp for the cohort while yielding enough brush and dead wood to supply that night's cooking fires.

Sextus ordered his men to make camp in the quarry while Crispus, Felix and Barek explored the caves and tunnels at the back. These must have taken Greek slaves years to hew out of the limestone. While most ended abruptly in harder rock and many showed signs of earlier collapse, they found a larger cave with a fissure that widened into a tunnel, offering a route out of the quarry, if only in single file and in some places on hands and knees. It was damp and dark, lit only by Barek's flickering lamp, a crushing space shared with hundreds of bats.

Felix toed a pile of bones. 'I hope many slaves found their escape here, but at what cost?'

'Before nightfall, a hundred men will owe those slaves a debt,' said Crispus, eyeing the bones in the dancing glow, 'and it will be Murcus, not us who shares the fate of this poor soul.'

Later, Sextus took Crispus aside. 'You will be in command at the mouth of this quarry when Murcus comes,' he said.

'And how do you know he will come to us? Have your spies told you?'

'Better than that.' Sextus stooped to pick up a stone, which he tossed absently from hand to hand. He was in full armour now, as if ready for a planned encounter. 'Your plan is a good one, Crispus, but it depends on us being able to lure Murcus here. Azhar is seeing to that.'

Crispus spat. 'But he is an enemy and not to be trusted. How can you know he will not betray you again?'

Sextus laughed and looked across to the city just as several ravens took flight towards them, settling in the tangled woodland overlooking the quarry. 'There is risk in everything I do, but I think today the auspices are clear. Now, let's put our plans together. You know what to do.'

Sextus looked back into the quarry where tents were being erected and cooking fires lit, and the first raucous songs of soldiers rose in anticipation of the coming night's supply of wine. Putting his fingers to his mouth, he whistled to summon his cohort. The ravens continued to argue in the trees above the quarry's edge.

Ordered by company, the Sicilian slingers, archers and spearmen were swiftly marched out of the quarry, leaving Crispus with just a hundred men and a camp to command.

CHAPTER TWENTY-FIVE

Puteoli, Western coast of Italia

Titus regretted not bringing with him a trunk with weapons, spare footwear and a change of clothing. He had stepped ashore at Puteoli dressed in a salt-encrusted tunic, sandals that chose this very day to begin to fall apart, and an old cloak clasped at the shoulder by his viper brooch. His only weapon was a dagger, no better than a thief would carry, thrust through his belt next to his purse. He felt naked.

But he was carrying enough coin to resolve the unfortunate circumstances in which he found himself. He took a spacious room at a dockside inn, washed away the sea's residue and spent an afternoon shopping for respectable attire. He then enjoyed a spicy fish stew chased down with a delightful local wine. Feeling better about his lot, he enquired politely of the host about who else might be in town to explain the unusual presence of what appeared to be a legion of well-turned-out soldiers on just about every street, and the many Roman war galleys anchored in the bay or moored in the harbour.

The host, a wiry man with innkeeper's eyes that flitted and scanned his busy tavern throughout the conversation, was astonished. 'You haven't heard? The new Caesar is going to teach that Sicilian pirate a lesson in manners and he's here, in Puteoli. What would that do for business if he came in here for his supper!'

'He could do worse,' said Titus, wiping his bowl clean with a crust.

'No, their lordships have villas everywhere for their scheming, and besides, I don't have any of that fancy food they would insist upon, let alone a decent vintage.'

'Nothing wrong with your wine, and I should know.'

The host stopped scanning the crowded room long enough to look Titus up and down, taking in his forearm scars and wondering if there were more concealed by the crisp, new tunic. 'You're in the wine trade?' he asked suspiciously.

'Yes, but that's not why I'm here.' Titus slid a coin across the table. 'I might stay for a few days. So tell me, where might I find their lordships?'

The innkeeper looked at him with renewed interest and leaned closer. 'That depends whose side you're on. I mean, we don't want trouble here, so if you mean to do the new Caesar harm…?'

Titus smiled. 'No, I just want to wish him well. We fought together at Philippi.'

The innkeeper studied him with respect. 'I knew it the moment you walked in. "That's a real live war hero," I said to the missus, "the sort that made Rome great".' He nodded towards a swarthy man sitting alone across the room. 'See that gentleman there? He's been here a few times with official types — very secretive they are, but I happened to overhear —'

Titus laughed, interrupting. 'An eavesdropping innkeeper — now there's a surprise. Go on, what did you overhear?'

The host fingered the coin on the table before him, subtly sending a signal to his richly attired guest. Titus slid another coin towards him but sent his own signal by keeping his forefinger firmly on it and arching an eyebrow.

'They came in from Sardinia. Seemed to be very important seafaring types.'

'How do you know that?'

'Sailors are usually rowdy, especially when they drink my ale. These were whisperers. And they had money. Lots of it.'

Titus kept his finger on the coin. 'So? Pirates, maybe? Spending their ill-gotten gains?'

'Not these. Pirates don't have scrolls with lots of writing on them.'

'Merchants, then?'

The innkeeper shook his head. 'Look, I know a pirate when I see one and I know all the merchants and traders in these parts. Besides, I'm sure they were talking about a meeting with the new Caesar. They called him Octavian.'

Slowly, Titus turned to look at the man the innkeeper was talking about. He took in the cut of his clothes and noted the quality of the *gladius* at his left hip and the Arabian dagger, things that would set him apart as a military official of some sort. But the thing that caught his eye beyond clothing and weaponry was the *fibula* brooch on his chest.

Titus took his finger off the coin.

His name was Miclio and he didn't seem surprised to be approached, warmth crossing his bronzed, bearded face as he fixed his gaze on Titus's viper brooch. He gestured to an empty chair. 'Vipers drink together, then talk,' he said, snapping his fingers to summon a serving girl. Then he introduced himself and as Titus was about to return the courtesy, he held up a hand. 'I know who you are.'

'Then you have me at a disadvantage, because I've never heard of Miclio.'

'I came in from Sardinia yesterday with, shall we say, an interesting cargo.' Miclio looked around to ensure nobody was listening, especially an eavesdropping innkeeper. 'Agrippa told me to look out for a fellow viper coming in from Sicilia, and I picked you out as soon as you set foot on the dockside. Good shopping here, don't you think, Titus Villius Macer?'

'You followed me?'

'Wasn't hard. Besides, you weren't expecting to be watched, so I thought I'd let you settle in before getting down to business.'

'Ah, business,' sighed Titus as Miclio poured two cups. 'I sense you know more about that than I do?'

'Not sure I do,' replied Miclio, another conspiratorial smile flashing behind his beard. 'Let's find out together. But first we drink and get to know each other. I hear you fought at Philippi?'

They discussed campaigns and the generals they had served under, Miclio reserving the highest praise for Agrippa, who had recruited him in much the same way as he had picked out Titus four years ago. Miclio had been sent to Sardinia, a large island far to the west that was also controlled by Sextus, with orders to sew discord and if possible recruit its rulers to Rome's cause.

Titus suspected this charismatic man, flamboyant in both dress and gesture, had succeeded in his mission.

Miclio and Titus strolled in the shady gardens of a large villa, waiting for an audience with Agrippa. Heady floral scents disguised the region's tendency to a sulphurous atmosphere. There was no breeze and high clouds — the sort of day that would have made wearing armour distinctly unpleasant.

'We're both here to betray Sextus Pompey,' Miclio was saying, swatting an insect aside.

Titus glanced at his new friend. 'Maybe. But I'm here to destroy his general, Azhar the Cruel.' His mutilated hand throbbed at the thought.

'Seems we're trumpeting the same notes. But it's all going to be orchestrated by Octavian and Agrippa.' He put a hand on Titus's arm and indicated a group of men wearing togas, deep in conversation in a cypress glade. 'And there they are, with my secret weapon.'

There were two men with Octavian and Agrippa, both powerfully built, older than the triumvir and his spymaster. Titus was certain he had seen one of them before and knew it was in Sicilia, but he couldn't put a name to the face. Weatherworn and bearded with wild dark hair, he did not carry the same upright bearing of the other, who was clearly a high-ranking and trusted officer. Titus had the immediate impression they were both navy types — the obvious clue was in the array of vessels in Puteoli's waters that must have been summoned by Rome's leaders.

'Which is your secret weapon?' Titus asked.

'You're about to find out.' Agrippa had spotted the new arrivals and was walking towards them, arms wide in greeting.

'Greetings, friends,' he said. 'Welcome to Puteoli.'

After greeting Agrippa wrist to wrist, Miclio turned to the scruffier of the two strangers.

'Menas,' he beamed. 'Are you content with our arrangement?' Then, turning to Titus, he introduced the governor of Sextus Pompey's territory of Sardinia. Titus was shocked. He realised that he was looking at one of Sextus's right-hand men, Menas, an admiral who had led many a pirate raid on Italia's coastal communities and had subsequently been rewarded with his own island to rule. And now he was a traitor. What would this do for Sextus's chances? Titus racked his brains in an effort to determine the size of the Sardinian fleet, at the same time pondering how Sicilia's defences had been compromised at a stroke.

Pulling himself together, Titus greeted Menas and Agrippa, nodded curtly to Octavian who, he thought, looked healthier than the last time they had met, and turned to the other man for an introduction.

'Gaius Calvisius Sabinus,' said the stranger, offering his hand, and Titus recalled that this was last year's consul and Rome's foremost naval admiral, a man who fought against the odds as traitorous knives were thrust into the body of a dying Julius Caesar some six years earlier.

'At your service,' said Titus, and immediately wondered if he meant it.

Agrippa interrupted the formalities. 'Gentlemen, we have some serious discussions ahead of us. May I suggest we retire to the villa, there to plot Sicilia's liberation?'

'About time too,' said Octavian. 'All this backslapping is making me hungry.'

Titus was impressed by the speed with which Rome's war machine had been mobilised, and surprised at how much detail the commanders were imparting given that he would soon be returning to Sicilia. Of course they could trust him — he was convinced that Sextus should be ousted and Azhar destroyed — but what if he was suspected, captured and tortured? Although he knew he would never betray Agrippa's network, the thought did not appear to have crossed the Roman leaders' minds. Or perhaps they knew that a tough centurion with his reputation, and a well-paid one at that, would never talk.

Reclining around a lavish feast served by a small army of slaves, the commanders of Rome's land and sea forces questioned him about the Sicilian fleet and its tactics and weaponry, perhaps to confirm what they already knew from Menas, who remained silent as Titus answered. The only time the defector became agitated was when Titus spoke about another Sicilian admiral, Menecrates, now the commander of Sextus's fleet at Messana; all sensed there was no love lost between the two admirals. Octavian interrupted with a question about Murcus and became animated when Titus reported that several days ago his *optio* Crispus had marched with Sextus to put an end to that admiral's rogue intentions.

'I can assure you he is either dead or captured,' said Titus, solemnly. 'Crispus will make sure of that, and at the same time destroy Sextus's general, Azhar.'

Agrippa asked about the ship-mounted scorpios and whether Sextus had adapted these on his own ships. 'I suspect he's working on it,' Titus replied.

Agrippa nodded sagely. 'We are mounting something similar on Menas's ships, much the same as the field scorpios that you used at Misenum but mounted with barbed spears to pull in enemy ships for boarding,' he said. 'But the credit will always be yours — an ingenious weapon!'

He explained that a crucial part of the invasion plan was to divide the Sicilian fleet and asked Titus to help spread the word about the gathering of legions and ships around Puteoli. 'You are here as a producer of fine Sicilian wines, looking for a market in Italia,' he said with a wink. 'If anyone needs proof, you will have full order documentation to supply our garrison here and quite a few senators who have villas in the area.' He explained that this information — or disinformation — might divide Sextus's fleet and open the way to land Rome's forces on Sicilian shores.

'With the greatest respect,' Titus said slowly, 'this may provide sufficient cover for me as one of your vipers, but I of all people know what a victorious Roman legion can do to the innocents who get in their way. When your legions land on

Sicilia, how will my family and my people be protected from the very invaders we have sought to help?'

Agrippa reached for a delicacy then reclined thoughtfully. 'We always look after our own,' he said. 'Since Philippi, we have found it necessary to take precautions on several occasions to protect our most valued spies. All of our commanders from centurion up to legate know the rules and will spare any property marked with our symbol.'

'And that symbol is…?'

'I'll give you one guess. But your viper sign must always be red and daubed onto every gate, door and tree. Some of our soldiers are none too subtle and get carried away. If they don't heed the signs, you might try yelling my name in their faces!'

'Let's hope it doesn't come to that,' said Titus. 'You know what happens to anyone who enters my land with sword drawn.'

'I don't doubt it for a heartbeat,' replied Agrippa. 'That's why we're on the same side.'

Octavian leaned back with a smile. 'Take your time returning to Sicilia,' he said. 'And while you're here, cast an eye over the legion that Menas has brought with him from Sardinia. See if you can't knock them into shape in time for their march south with my army.'

Menas scowled but thought better of arguing with Rome's new Caesar.

The next morning, Titus went down to Puteoli's docks to seek out the merchant who had brought him to the mainland, only to discover he had sailed north at dawn. He returned to the inn, where a few more coins brought him face to face with the jovial captain of a shabby-looking merchantman that was taking skins, timber and statues to Messana to exchange for a cargo of lava jewellery, pottery and art for Rome's genteel society.

'If we can dodge the pirates,' he laughed, 'but they usually ignore my old tub.'

'Will you take a letter, and deliver it in person?'

'It'll cost you,' smiled the captain, 'and it depends where you want it delivered.'

'You'll be familiar with The Blue Flag at Messana?' said Titus, dipping his fingers into his purse and stirring coins.

'Who isn't? I always look forward to a night in Niko's company.'

Titus counted four coins into the captain's palm. 'That's for your trouble,' he said. 'And when you see Niko, ask for a drop of his Pax Villius wine and he'll know who sent you.'

'So, this letter. Important, is it? Message for a lover, or some secret plot to murder a senator?'

Titus opened an unsealed leather pouch. 'Look,' he said, 'I know you will no doubt open this and read it the moment you set sail, so I have saved you the bother of having to break the seal.' He handed the parchment to the captain. 'Go ahead, read it. Let's get this part out of the way so we have no secrets. Because we trust each other, don't we?'

The captain laughed and couldn't resist the temptation. He ran a finger under each line and mouthed the words as he read:

My dear friend Niko, greetings.

With this letter you will find an order for the finest Pax Villius vintage to be delivered to the prefect at Puteoli. There are many ships and legions here, so demand has never been higher. Have Zerenia prepare and seal the amphorae for the first shipment and arrange passage. Also send word to Crispus to meet me at The Blue Flag on Aprilis Nones. Tell Crispus to bring young Leo, who may be useful to run errands and by now may want his former job back.

Give the bearer of this letter a fine dinner and a cup of our now famous vintage, and I will recompense you on the Nones. Also plead with Sextus and Menecrates on his behalf for safe passage in perpetuity.

Your friend, Titus Villius Macer.

The captain smiled his appreciation for Titus's generosity. 'You can be sure I will deliver this to Niko. Is there anything else?'

'Indeed there is. Here is the merchandise order, sealed only to protect my business, from which I hope you will profit many times over if this goes well.'

Titus took the second parchment from the pouch. Its wax seal bore the imprint of his viper brooch. What the captain didn't know was that inside it was a second message that opened with the mysterious word YLRGTC, spelling VIPERA in their code. The message, deciphered by Niko, would read:

Rome's ships gather at Puteoli under Calvisius. Octavian marches south with his legions where there will be more ships. You may allow this rumour to reach Menecrates and Sextus. Until Aprilis Nones.

The captain was delighted to accept his mission and as he disappeared into the dockside crowds, Miclio was at Titus's shoulder.

'That went well, no?'

'Are you still following me?' Titus asked him without taking his eyes off the departing seaman.

'Only because we are going to get very drunk together. You can tell me all about Sextus Pompey, and I will tell you all about my perfidious friend Menas.'

CHAPTER TWENTY-SIX

Syracuse, Sicilia

If the approaching scouts were meant to be concealed, they failed miserably. Crispus saw the three men attempting to blend into scrubland and ruins that could easily have masked a skilled legionary scout from his old century. He looked across the rolling hills to the distant city and knew for certain that the enemy was positioned within easy striking distance of the quarry, and whatever arrangement had been agreed in secret between Sextus and Azhar had worked: Murcus was here. They had probably two or three hours of daylight remaining. Now all he had to do was summon his few men and make Murcus believe that the whole cohort was camped within the quarry, just waiting to be trapped and slaughtered. Sextus's archers and slingers would do the rest — if they got their timing right and their aim was true.

Smoke rose from campfires within the quarry, and the hundred soldiers within enthused in their ribald singing and laughter. The quarry echoed and amplified the sounds that could easily be mistaken for a larger force.

Still watching the enemy scouts, Crispus put his fingers to his mouth and gave a shrill whistle, the signal to Felix and Barek to join him at the mouth of the quarry. He smiled as the scouts froze, then sought better cover. His lieutenants were at his side within a few heartbeats, fully armed and ready, the other seven Pax Villius recruits following behind.

'They're here, as expected,' said Crispus. 'Is everyone ready?'

'Yes, sir,' said Felix. 'The men in the quarry know to keep the fires burning, but as the enemy advances they will fall back as if in disarray.'

'Good. Look casual, like unsuspecting guards.' He pointed to the hill that would most likely conceal a small force. 'They will come from there, so don't stare at it. We ten will face the enemy here, but of course we won't notice them until its almost too late. Remember to look terrified as you fall back.'

Felix was about to extend an arm in salute, then a grin crossed his fox-like face as he motioned the others to sit on the ground for a game of dice. They leaned shields and spears together in pyramids. Barek made a great show of being dice-master. Crispus stood aside and watched them, weighing each up as their first encounter with an enemy approached. Some were genuinely happy to be playing dice, others nervously pretending. Somehow he must keep them alive. He could trust Felix and Barek to do right when faced with death, but these others? They were young men with so much ahead to savour and enjoy; he did not want to see them throw themselves onto cruel steel and bleed away a lifetime of opportunity.

He tapped the nearest on the shoulder, the lad Marco who had fumbled the dice at his turn to throw.

'Nervous, Marco?'

'We all are, I think, except Felix and Barek.'

'Stay close to me and you'll be all right. Remember, if your opponent's arm is high, you strike low. Not so very complicated.'

A shout went up as one of the lads won the whole pile of pebbles and the others moaned their disappointment. Crispus felt the skin between his shoulder-blades prickle and knew that he was being watched. He hoped no arrow would fly before Murcus attacked.

But Murcus didn't attack with war cries and savage intent. The wily old seadog calmly led his small troop of less than a thousand men at a cautious walk from exactly the spot Crispus had expected. His men were not uniformly dressed for war, but they were well armed and to a man looked mean and powerful.

Crispus and the men of Pax Villius turned to face them as they approached, hoisting shield and spear, forming a line that was ready to defend.

The enemy calmly marched before the quarry entrance and formed up in four ranks, facing the ten of Pax Villius. Behind, inside the quarry, the remaining hundred maintained their raucous pretence as if nothing untoward was happening. The enemy's front rank parted to allow their leader to advance two paces before them, then closed again. They were disciplined, thought Crispus, and perhaps not as stupid as they had been led to believe.

Murcus was the only one that Crispus could see who wore a bronze cuirass, inlaid with silver, over a mail shirt. His helmet boasted a fine plume of blue and yellow feathers, and he bore no shield or weapon other than the *gladius* sheathed at his side. For a long moment he stared at the few men who formed a line before him.

'I am wasting my time,' he said, loudly enough for the men of Pax Villius to hear, a mere six spear lengths between them. 'I come here because I am told that Sextus Pompeius wants revenge, yet I see before me just ten peasants!'

'So you can count,' said Crispus. 'Bet you don't know what comes after ten.'

Murcus refused to take the bait. Instead he looked around, his gaze drifting to the heights above the quarry, then back to Crispus. 'I know you, soldier,' he spat. 'If I am not mistaken, you're that soldier who was puking up on the deck of my ship when I brought you here out of the kindness of my heart. You were with that other enemy of the true Rome, Titus Villius Macer. Where is he, soldier? Up there with Sextus, waiting to cut us all down with arrows and spears?'

Just loud enough for his men to hear, Crispus said, 'One step back.' As one, they retreated a pace.

'That's right, lead me into your trap. Do you think I am stupid?' Again, Murcus looked to the cliffs above the quarry, then back to Crispus. 'Send your man Sextus to parley, if he is not up there waiting to ambush us when we walk into his trap. If he does not appear, then I know where to find him.'

Crispus did not reply, except to order another step back. In his heart, he knew the plan had failed. Perhaps Murcus was brighter than Sextus had thought.

'Thought so,' said Murcus, and with a series of sudden hand signals, he sent the rear two ranks moving off to their right. He, too, went with them at a trot, belying his age and weighty figure.

And Azhar the Cruel stepped forward.

Crispus could see even behind Azhar's cheek flaps the scars of fire on his face and the fury in his eyes. But he also knew this man was a coward, and his impression was confirmed when Azhar signalled the remaining ranks to attack, standing his ground while the two ranks streamed past him and charged at the Pax Villius ten.

'Shields tight, back two.' Crispus's command was immediately obeyed. But he knew how strong the temptation would be to run in the face of such overwhelming odds. Shoulder to shoulder, his men barely filled the quarry entrance, about three cart lengths, and although they should fall back to lead the enemy into the trap, running would expose their backs and they would die.

But their shields blunted the first blows, and Crispus sent a silent prayer of thanks for the hours of training. None of his men responded to the war cries of the Syracusians, but just watched with cold intent. Spears and swords protruded beyond shields, porcupine quills hampering each wave of attack.

'Back two and hold,' he called left and right, and the line retreated. He heard Marco scream as his shield gave enough for a spear to be thrust through the gap, but he couldn't spare a moment to see if the lad was injured as a heavy axe crashed onto the rim of his own shield. He locked eyes with the burly, sweating soldier whose axe was now trapped just long enough for a seasoned warrior's *gladius* to find the attacker's groin. The man's eyes showed fear then shock before he let out his death scream.

Men from within the quarry came up behind them, giving the appearance of hurriedly donning helms and armour, but Crispus knew Murcus had seen through it all and now they would be lucky to escape with their lives. But he had to try. The new arrivals added noise and swirling dust to the tumult, swelling the ranks just enough to cause the enemy to hesitate and allow Crispus the chance to look to the men of Pax Villius. All were covered in dust and grime, rivulets of sweat and blood streaking their faces, necks and arms.

'Fall back!' He hoped that Sextus would be able to deliver his attack from above, but they needed to make space between themselves and the attackers if they were not to fall to the missiles that would surely begin their death-rain soon. Backward steps became more frequent now and some turned to run, but the men of Pax Villius held their line, facing the enemy as they withdrew.

Now, thought Crispus. *Shoot now, Sextus.*

But the arrows, spears and slingshots did not fall from above.

Crispus risked a glance upwards, to the place where Sextus should have his men arrayed. He thought he could see confusion there: Murcus had found him and foiled the attack. Now they had no choice but to fight to the death against the odds. Their heels were edging closer to the tents and campfires, dangerous hazards for his men, so he had no choice.

'To the back of the quarry — run, now!'

A hundred pairs of running feet now caused dust to rise like a sandstorm. Bloodthirsty, the enemy followed blindly, many of them tripping over guy ropes and cooking gear as they gave chase in the choking dust-clouds. Some threw spears randomly, and Crispus hoped that the retreating men would remember where to rally. They had to buy more time and hope that Sextus could keep to his part of the plan. As he thought this, Barek was at his side and he saw Felix encouraging the others to keep running and not let go of their heavy shields. 'Have we lost any?' he managed. Although Barek shook his head, Crispus could tell from his expression that there would be wounds to bind.

They reached the back of the quarry. 'Form up here!' yelled Crispus, then turned to Barek, making himself heard above the din. 'We can buy time if we make them gloat. Send word to begin the escape.'

'They are already doing that,' spat Barek. There was confusion at the cave mouth, where men pushed and shoved to be first to crawl through the tunnel. 'Looks like it's down to us, then?'

'Not all of us are cowards,' said a blue-cloaked soldier that Crispus recognised as one of Sicilia's more reliable officers. A dozen men stood with him, eyes on the advancing enemy that had recovered their composure and were now reorganising, ready to slaughter the trapped men.

'Good,' said Crispus. 'We are outnumbered, but if we form our shield wall on that ledge —' he pointed to the wide platform of rock smoothed by the feet of hundreds of slaves, in front of the cave entrance — 'then we can hold long enough for your men to escape.' As the men began to climb onto the ledge, he turned to face the enemy. He looked for Azhar and would have challenged him to single combat to settle the matter, but he could not see him, neither could he establish which of the men he faced in the heat and dust was the senior officer. He risked a glance at the cliff-top and could see no sign of fighting there; perhaps Sextus had recovered his position, and though the tactic had failed thus far it was not too late. *Mars be with us* was his silent prayer.

'Who commands?' he called to ranks opposite, and when the Syracusians shuffled and looked at each other, he thought: *A leaderless rabble! The odds are even now.* 'Where is Azhar? I would speak with him.'

Silence. Then more unease.

'I see you have no leader, so who will step forth to fight me man to man?'

One man in the enemy ranks found his tongue. 'We will all fight you,' he said, and encouraged by murmurs of agreement, he went on, 'because we are many and you are pitifully few.'

'And what do you hope to achieve by that? We few may die, but so will most of you.' To emphasise the point, Crispus cast aside his shield and drew a hefty serrated knife to pair with the bloodied *gladius* he bore. His stance was gladiatorial and his eyes flashed death. Several of the Syracusians took an involuntary step back.

From the corner of his eye, he saw movement on the cliff-top and knew this was the stealth of bowmen and slingers getting into position. He must keep doubt in the enemy's mind, keep them talking, waiting for leadership, and hope they would delay long enough to be caught in the open away from his own men.

'Why do we fight?' he called again in the general direction of the voice that had spoken in their ranks. 'Who tells you that you must kill us? Is it Murcus, who sought to kill Sextus Pompey and the new Caesar at Misenum? Is it Azhar, who even while you slept in your beds last night was entreating with Sextus?' This brought fresh murmurs among the Syracusians. Doubt spread through the ranks like a breeze disturbing a calm sea.

'So tell me,' Crispus went on, 'where is Azhar now, and more to the point, where is the pretender Murcus?'

'Here he is.'

This new voice came from the cliff-top and every eye turned to see a line of archers, bowstrings stretched to chins, shafts pointed at the Syracusians. At the highest point, where the drop was steepest, stood Sextus. He wore no helmet and his cuirass was bloodied. In one hand he held his *gladius*, and in the other he held a rope that was tied around the neck of a bound and wild-eyed Murcus.

'Will you fight for him now?' Sextus called. 'Or will you throw down your arms and return in peace to your women and children?'

Again, the Syracusians looked at one another in dismay, but another voice joined the discussion.

'I command you to fight!' screamed Murcus. 'Avenge my death!'

The next move seemed obvious to everyone. No one could tear their eyes from the imminent death of the once-famous Roman, victor of many sea-battles and now self-imposed ruler of Syracuse.

Sextus turned to his line of archers and held up a hand. 'Aim.'

Swords and spears clattered to the ground in surrender. Sextus whispered something to Murcus, whose eyes widened in horror.

'Loose!'

CHAPTER TWENTY-SEVEN

Messana, Sicilia, Nones of Aprilis

Titus Villius Macer stepped ashore at Messana, summoned a cart-porter and ordered him to take his brand-new trunk to The Blue Flag.

Inside the trunk were gifts for his wife and children and a new *gladius* for Crispus, the blade engraved with the words 'For the enemies of Pax Villius'. There was also a copy of several diagrams on navigation by Eudoxus of Cnidus, which he thought would appeal to Marina, some woodworking tools for Barek, a fine ring clasping a blood-red gemstone for Felix and a bronze *fibula* brooch, bearing what might be construed as a viper, for Leo. There was a small *lar familiaris* cast in bronze to stand by the hearth at Pax Villius, in honour of Zerenia's father, Eshmun. He also carried clear instructions on the symbols that were to be painted on every tree, wall and fence post to protect the homestead from any Roman invader.

But Messana was not in the mood for jubilant homecomings. Warships were being fitted with new weapons and squads of soldiers drilled on the open spaces near the docks. The marketplace was bereft of merchants and sellers, and citizens walked the streets with heads held low and a worried look in their eyes. Whether via rumour emanating from Titus's message to Niko or word from visiting merchants, Sicilia knew she faced the wrath of Rome.

Crispus was waiting at The Blue Flag.

'What kept you?' the ex-gladiator said before embracing Titus.

'Negotiating with our paymasters,' he replied. 'Delighted to see you survived your trip to Syracuse. What about the others?'

'Some scratches and bruises, but all alive, which is more than I can say for Murcus and his band of ruffians.' Crispus did not impart this with any sense of triumph. His face darkened as he studied his boots.

Titus put an arm around his shoulder. 'Then we'll find somewhere quiet where we can break bread, and you can give me your report. Where is Niko? And did you bring Leo?'

'I did — also Felix, Barek and Marina. They are with Niko in the port, finding out what's going on. And while we wait for them, I have a pitcher of wine that requires a vintner's opinion.'

The wine was good, but the news from Syracuse and the story of the battle in the quarry was not. Titus listened intently as Crispus explained the plan to trap Murcus inside the quarry, but even for a hardened warrior like Crispus, the treatment of the enemy was painful. Murcus had been forced to watch as most of his small force was slaughtered by a hailstorm of arrows and spears, then by the swords of the Sicilian cohort, although the men of Pax Villius had refused to take part. Crispus had pleaded with Sextus to stop, but he had revelled in the slaughter, laughing evilly throughout. Just a few of the Syracusians survived to face a life of slavery. *Not a good way to keep an island united when Rome threatens*, thought Titus as he listened.

But that was not all. The next day, Murcus was crucified naked at the entrance to the quarry while Sextus's cohort stripped the victims of weapons and valuables and roped the survivors for the return march. It was a hot day, and it was many hours before Murcus's screams became a whimper.

'Sextus just laughed,' said Crispus, 'even though it was plain his men were disgusted.'

'And Azhar?' asked Titus. 'I hope you spared him for me to deal with?'

'Now, that is interesting. It seems that all along Azhar has remained Sextus's man. He helped to lure Murcus into the trap, but the last I saw of him was outside the quarry when his men advanced, but he did not. You can be sure you will meet him again.'

Titus was aghast. 'But he plotted against Sextus, as well as Rome!'

'That's how it appeared to us. Guilty as sin. But either he was at Misenum to somehow prevent Murcus from murdering Sextus, or Sextus is completely mad and Azhar's smooth words have seduced him. Either way, Azhar is still our enemy and always will be. And what's more, after what I have seen, I doubt you can continue to count Sextus as a friend. All honour has deserted him.'

Shaking his head sadly, Titus contemplated these events. 'The truth is, when everything is laid bare, we opposed Sextus from the moment I struck a deal with Agrippa. I did not expect it to come to this, but Sicilia is going to experience Rome's wrath. And the way Sextus has behaved makes it easier for me, and for you, Crispus. He has changed from the carefree youth that I knew into a bitter despot. And we have seen what Zerenia thinks of him, and I trust her judgement. This makes it easier to do what we have been ordered to do.'

'It was never in doubt,' said Crispus. 'Not for me, at least. How many times have we gone into battle together after counting to three and doing what must be done?'

'We have the wounds to show for it,' smiled Titus.

'But this wound,' said Crispus solemnly, 'might be the hardest to bear.'

'Crispus! Where are you?'

It was a juvenile shout with a distinct note of panic.

Crispus and Titus looked at each other in alarm. 'Leo,' they said in unison and rushed from the back room, overturning stools and shoving past the few customers who preferred midday ale to the confusion in Messana's streets. They found Leo and Marina at The Blue Flag's wide street entrance, both dishevelled and flushed with exertion.

Leo ran to them, stammering incomprehensibly, but when calmed by Crispus, Marina said, 'They've taken them.'

Titus felt a stab of alarm. 'Who has been taken?'

'Barek and Felix, with Niko,' said Marina, recovering her composure.

Leo twitched with anxiety. 'We were watching the ships being readied, and there were soldiers and shouting and —'

Crispus squatted before the boy, a hand on his shoulder, then looked to the young navigator. 'Marina?'

'They needed rowers,' she said. 'We were in the wrong place at the wrong time. We were in a crowd watching the ships being loaded with provisions and arms when a whole squad of soldiers started pulling men aside. I think it was for Menecrates' ship.'

'They can't do that,' said Titus.

'But they did,' Marina went on. 'Barek tried to reason with them, and so did Niko. They tried to stop them taking ordinary citizens and the soldier in charge turned on them, and Felix too, but we were unarmed. Barek hit one of them and threw another to the ground, but there were too many and they were taken, all three. Niko called to us to find you. That's why we're here.'

'We have to stop them,' cried Leo.

Titus turned to Crispus. 'Weapons? Mine are in my trunk.'

'I'll bring three swords,' said Crispus. He ran to his quarters, swiftly returning with the swords and a dagger for Leo.

They ran to the dockside, pushing through crowds, their progress frustratingly slow. Several war galleys were making their way out of the harbour into the straits, oars rising and falling rhythmically, the sound of shrill flutes and monotonous singing marking the time, sails flapping as they were hoisted to catch a rising southerly. More ships were casting off to form a steady procession, the leaders now turning north to meet the threat of the naval force that had gathered off Puteoli.

'Which one?' asked Titus.

Marina pointed seaward to the lead trireme, now heeling to port as its two sails filled.

'That one.'

Titus and Crispus studied her lines and markings, Neptune's trident in sky blue on her bow, her archer's tower boasting the same symbol, and an extra-long blue and gold pennant flying from the main mast that set her apart as the flagship.

'Menecrates,' mumbled Titus. 'If he leads, Sextus is still here.'

'And we don't want to treat with him,' said Crispus. 'Besides, he would hardly recall his admiral, even though he owes us. There's no catching Menecrates now.'

'If only we had our ships here, or at least one of them, we could overhaul them in that breeze.'

Leo tugged on Titus's tunic. 'We could steal one.'

'And what would we do for a crew?' Crispus scoffed.

Titus was deep in thought. He would not let this go; these were his people on board that ship, and Niko was a fellow viper. 'We *do* have a crew,' he said, 'only not here.'

Marina was first to understand. 'But if we return home, launch one of our own ships and then follow the fleet, we will be a day behind at least. They will have engaged by the time we catch up — then what will we do?'

'I don't know,' said Titus, 'but I would rather be there in case we can do something. I for one do not want to wait around here in Messana, hoping that nothing happens to harm my friends.'

'Nor do I,' said Crispus.

Marina and Leo sprinted back to The Blue Flag stables to find, or steal, four horses or mules.

By nightfall, *Boreas* was provisioned and armed and the chosen crew ordered to rest for departure at first light. And that crew did not include Crispus who, if he was anything but a reliable soldier who always followed orders, would by now be sulking or breaking furniture at the homestead he had been asked to protect in the absence of Titus, Felix and Barek.

'Sicilia is at war,' Titus had told him, 'and that means soldiers from either side could come rampaging across our land. You know what soldiers do when their bloodlust is up.'

'But you are sailing directly into that war, and you will need me to win any fight you throw yourself into,' Crispus had replied. 'Marina is more than capable of defending Pax Villius.'

'Marina is a much better navigator than you are, my friend, and as it happens she is a natural at sea, whereas you will just throw up everywhere in the slightest swell. I need you here to protect Zerenia and the children.'

Having won the argument, Titus had thrown himself into preparing *Boreas* for departure the next day, casting worried looks at Marina as they loaded water casks, food, armour and weapons, and giving helpful words of advice to young Leo, who took great pride in his promotion to 'officer of the watch'.

At the darkest hour, robbed of sleep, Titus and Zerenia watched the night breeze play with the driftwood fire, shawls pulled tight around their shoulders. The two Veneti ships were dark shadows, *Boreas* moored in the shallows, *Eurus* high and dry on shingle, braced with staves for hull repairs.

Titus recounted his experiences in Puteoli, how the fate of their island was now in the lap of the gods and there was nothing more to do except rescue their friends who had so wrongfully been pressed into service on Menecrates' ship.

'But how will you do this?' Zerenia asked softly. 'Even if you catch them, how can you stop a war long enough for you to politely remove Barek, Felix and Niko from a fighting ship?'

Titus shook his head.

'But you will try,' she said, laying her head on his shoulder, 'and that makes me proud.'

They sat in silence as dawn fanned delicate light behind the dark mass of Italia's mainland. Marina led the men of Pax Villius to the shore, twenty grim seamen and the lad Leo, all willing to follow Titus into storm and danger, women and children following to see them off, wrapped in blankets against the chill.

The crew splashed through shallows, tossing their weapons onto *Boreas*'s deck. Some shinned up rope ladders while others put their shoulders to her stern to bounce her afloat with each incoming wave. Titus embraced Zerenia, whispering, 'We will all return.' He was last aboard, wet to the waist.

Four oarsmen pulled *Boreas* to deeper water, where the iron-rimmed keel was lowered through Eshmun's ingenious central casing and the huge lateen sail was hoisted. Titus himself manned the tiller and nursed the bows seaward, feeling a surge of power as the sail filled and his men fastened sheets. The wind was fresher now and the direction ideal for their course north; the old Veneti vessel belied her age and nosed impatiently into the strait that separated rebellious Sicilia from her would-be masters of Rome.

CHAPTER TWENTY-EIGHT

'You need to get some sleep,' Marina told Titus as darkness fell after a full day at sea. 'Trust me, I know we're on the right course. We've been here before, if you remember.'

It was rare to sail at night, scudding clouds intermittently obscuring Marina's night sky and her guiding stars, but Titus had learned to trust the navigator, who had an uncanny ability to plot a course in her mind and even predict the weather. And he liked the bond she had formed with Leo, who brought her cups of spiced *posca* from the galley below and helped the steersman whenever Marina ordered a change in course. Now she had sent the boy to the bows to use his cat-like vision to watch for any looming obstacles — more likely to be traders or warships than unexpected landmasses now that they had passed ash-flanked Strongyle at dusk.

Titus reluctantly went below, doubting he would sleep as the swell and gusting wind made *Boreas* heave and tremble. He wondered how Felix, Barek and Niko fared, no doubt confined to a rowing deck on Menecrates' ship, with only hard biscuit and putrid water for sustenance. Felix and Barek could survive harsh conditions, but he was not sure Niko would cope away from the comforts of The Blue Flag.

Menecrates, with the best part of Sicilia's fleet, was so far ahead they would not be able to catch them until well into a second day's sailing, and perhaps the Sicilians would already have engaged with Calvisius and Menas by the time *Boreas* arrived at the bay of Puteoli. This was where they had hoped to draw the Sicilian ships while Octavian gathered his legions and a second fleet at Rhegium far to the south, close to the rebellious island and perfect for invasion. Titus had spotted only a few of Sextus's ships patrolling the strait as they left Pax Villius, which indicated that Octavian and Agrippa had succeeded in dividing their enemy.

But he did sleep, if fitfully, and with dawn's first light he was on deck to smile a greeting to a windswept Marina before finding Leo asleep in the bows, curled in a tight ball against the chill. Only a grey, confused sea lay before them, the shadow of Italia on the horizon. He went below again to help the crew ration a simple breakfast, taking bread and cheese and a cup of *posca* to Marina.

'Hardly a drink I'd expect from you,' she winked, 'but it'll do.'

'Find Menecrates today and we'll drink our fill of Pax Villius finest when we get back home. Your turn for rest. I'll take over here.'

'We'll find them,' replied Marina, steadying herself against the cross swell. 'But the seas and the wind are no longer our friends, so it may be tomorrow. If you sight any ships, wake me.'

She went below. Titus watched her depart, thinking how fortunate he was to have such an assured navigator. He gazed at the grey coastline to starboard then ahead, straining to see through the haze, willing *Boreas* to hasten and find the Sicilian fleet. Hours passed, the empty sea ahead hypnotic.

They sailed into Puteoli late in the afternoon and there were no Roman warships to be seen, just a handful of deserted traders moored together as if seeking mutual protection. Titus ordered the four scorpios to be covered with spare sails as he nudged *Boreas* to the quayside, the crew ignoring the crowd that gathered, mostly children wielding wooden swords and getting in the way of dockers as they secured the new arrival.

Titus summoned Leo and gave him a handful of copper coins. 'We're going ashore, and you're going to help us get through this crowd of children,' he said with a wink. 'You know what to do.' Leaving Marina in charge, the pair went in search of supplies and information. The children mobbed them as soon as they leaped down to the dockside, outstretched hands pleading for a coin or tugging at Titus's tunic. Leo smiled at them and opened his palm, instantly getting their attention. He lobbed the virtually worthless coins into the street, where they made music that no child-beggar could resist, and suddenly they were alone.

Titus made for the inn where he had stayed only a few days before, on the way paying for the entire contents of a fruit stall to be delivered to *Boreas*, fresh bread at another. As expected, he found the innkeeper regaling a small group of despondent merchants. He performed a classic double-take as Titus and Leo walked in.

'Back so soon?'

'The lad is hungry, and I am thirsty,' said Titus. 'We have come a long way to sample your excellent fare but make it quick as we're in a hurry. More importantly, we have some questions.'

The innkeeper's eyes lit up, as he knew Titus was wealthy enough to pay for information. He called to the kitchens for food and wine and indicated a table where they could talk, the merchants looking relieved to be left to their own devices.

'Where are all the ships?' Titus got straight to the point, but the innkeeper merely shrugged, knowing that money would soon slide across the table. He was met with a steely stare from the former *primus pilus*, but it was Leo who broke the spell.

'I kept some of those coins back,' he said, slapping down two half-moon shaped pieces.

'Well,' said the innkeeper, laughing, 'in that case, I can tell you they're not here, and you can keep your money.'

Titus showed him a fistful of denarii. 'Look,' he said, 'I have returned here because three of my friends have been kidnapped by one of Sextus's captains, so I'm not just looking for Roman ships. Tell me what you know and while you're at it, whether you have seen Sicilians in these waters in the last few hours.'

He didn't wait for an answer but poured the coins onto the table in front of the innkeeper, who had to swiftly sweep them up as a large bowl of steaming stew was placed before them, with bread, a pitcher of wine and a jug of water. Leo was first to ladle the aromatic meat and vegetables into his bowl and ate hungrily, oblivious to the ensuing conversation.

'The Sicilians were here this morning, a hundred of them, I'd say,' the innkeeper began. 'They swept into the bay then went towards Misenum and Aenaria without stopping when they saw none of Octavian's ships here. Shame. Bet they were hungry and thirsty too…'

'Get to the point,' said Titus. 'Where are Octavian's ships?'

'Not Octavian's — he marched south days ago. Calvisius and Menas, now there's an unlikely pair.'

'Well?'

'North. I've heard they're at Cumae, the next port up from the Misenum promontory.'

'I know where that is,' snapped Titus. 'How many ships?'

'Doesn't matter how many ships they have — they are no match for Sicilian seafaring. Don't think much of their ships either — all new, not seasoned and tested, and crews who don't know an oar from their elbow.' Titus took some of the stew and drank some wine while Leo consumed a third helping. 'Your boy?' asked the innkeeper.

'Favourite son,' said Titus, 'but don't change the subject. So Calvisius is at Cumae with an untried fleet. It's getting dark now, so where would you go if you were the Sicilians?'

'That's easy. They'll be hiding behind Aenaria island. When Calvisius comes out at first light, all Tartarus will break loose. My money's on those pirates.'

Back on board *Boreas*, Titus called the ship's crew together. The light of a dozen oil lamps shone on grim but determined faces, many of the men still sharing melon, figs and pears and passing a jug of *posca* around.

'As far as we know,' began Titus, 'Calvisius and Menas are at Cumae.' He pointed towards the distant Misenum promontory which, with two islands beyond, was now in total darkness, then rolled his hand limply. 'A few hours' sailing around the Misenum headland. Menecrates lurks there too. So we sail before dawn, and when the sun is up we will look for his ship and our people.'

A lone voice said forlornly, 'What can we do when we find them? Do we engage Menecrates?'

'The truth is,' replied Titus slowly, 'I honestly don't know. But if we do our part, the gods will do theirs. Our mission is noble and just. It's not about Rome or Sicilia for we few, it's about the Pax Villius family. And we will do what it takes to rescue them. So take your cloak, wrap it close around you, and sleep. You will need your strength for tomorrow, come what may.' He put a fist into the centre of the huddle. 'Pax Villius.'

'Pax Villius!' responded twenty men, one woman and one boy.

CHAPTER TWENTY-NINE

'I see them!' Leo shrieked.

Titus narrowed his eyes and could just make out the bare masts of three ships under oars. They were shrouded by the dark cliffs of the innermost island, moving east towards the mainland and what he knew to be the mouth of a channel that provided a shortcut to Misenum. Dawn's silver light flashed confirmation as it caught polished shield bosses.

He turned to Marina beside him. 'Only three? Where are the rest of them?'

'Looks to me like Menecrates is springing a trap for Calvisius. If the Roman fleet is using that channel, it will take only a few ships to trap them. My bet is the main force is behind that island waiting to attack Calvisius's rear.'

Titus tried to imagine the lay of the two islands and calculate the distance they might have to sail. The morning breeze was freshening and promised more speed through the water than a trireme's banks of rowers could achieve.

'Make for those three ships,' he ordered. 'If none of them are Menecrates, then we will sail around the island until we find them.'

They knew they hadn't found Menecrates or their captive friends as they approached an hour later. Heaving to within hailing distance of the lead ship, rolling in the swell beneath the cliffs as their sails flapped loosely, *Boreas* was challenged first.

'Name yourself and your purpose,' a strong voice called.

'Titus Villius Macer out of Messana, seeking Menecrates with a message from Sextus Pompeius.' The lie came easily. 'Whom do I address?'

A pause indicated that the Sicilian captain was deciding whether this could be a genuine mission. 'I have heard of you, Titus Villius,' he said eventually. 'I am Demochares, second in command, and you can give me your message.'

'I am tasked with delivering this message in person, but as you are an officer of the Sicilian fleet, I can tell you it involves news of Octavian's advance into Bruttium with several legions. Sextus urges your hasty return as soon as you have finished here.'

Another pause. Then Marina's theory was confirmed.

'You will find Menecrates on the other side of this island, but you will not catch him before he engages the enemy. Good luck, Titus Villius, and to those in your strange vessel!'

Boreas's lateen sail was already catching the stiffening breeze as Titus replied. 'May Neptune protect you, Demochares.'

At first they made painfully slow progress as Marina was forced to tack against a strong southwesterly wind, but the unique keel proved its worth as they rounded the island's point. *Boreas* heeled under tightened sail and leapt eagerly in pursuit of the main Sicilian fleet.

Leo saw them first and Titus joined him in the bows. The scene was confusing, a forest of masts close to the mainland shore at the northern mouth of the narrow channel that separated the inner island. But a smaller second fleet in the distant north was approaching the mêlée.

Titus re-joined Marina on the stern platform. 'It appears Menecrates has driven the Roman ships against the shore, but who commands those other ships that approach from the north?'

'Menas?'

Titus agreed with his trustworthy navigator. 'If that is so, we must make for the heat of the battle, because that is where we will find Menecrates.'

'He is there,' she said, pointing. 'Look.'

They could now see that the blue-flagged Sicilian triremes were more organised than their opponents, sailing in a line to pass close to the Roman ships that were being pressed against the rocky shore, firing missile after missile into the hapless and confused enemy, some of them ramming with a glancing blow to damage steering gear before moving off to repeat each attack. And in the van was Menecrates' distinctly marked flagship.

'How long until we close with them?' asked Titus.

Marina looked up at the mainsail, taut with the wind's power. 'Another hour?'

Titus felt helpless despite a renewed surge beneath a heeling *Boreas* as Marina risked tightening sail against the beam reach. But as they watched the Sicilians crushing the Roman fleet, both noticed the flagship appeared to be breaking away from the fight.

'If that is Menas approaching out of Cumae, and Menecrates has seen him, there's going to be a bloodbath,' said Titus. 'They hated each other even before Menas betrayed Sextus. And our people will be right in the thick of the fighting.'

Marina took a moment to gauge Menecrates' new course and estimate an interception point, then ordered the steersman to turn slightly to port. 'It's going to be tight,' she said. 'I fear there will be three ships in this encounter.'

'And I still don't have a plan. Do you?'

Marina managed a taut smile and didn't answer.

No time was wasted as scorpio bolts were stockpiled next to each of the catapults so that on either beam they would be primed and ready. The men were already in light armour and were placing bows, quivers of arrows, and the long spears used to repel boarders beneath the gunwales.

But Menecrates was closing in fast and the lead ship of the approaching flotilla, which must be Menas, was increasing speed and a head-on clash now seemed inevitable. Driven by his hatred, Menecrates must be exacting superhuman effort from his rowers — presumably including Barek, Felix and Niko. Unless Barek with his bulky carpenter's frame was being readied with the other marines to board the enemy ship, if they could? The oncoming speed brought white water spraying over the bows as the Sicilian came on, bent on vengeance, and Menas too seemed intent on total destruction. Were they whipping their rowers? That was unheard of in Rome's navies, but the intent was such that Titus could only stare and gasp at the fury both ships displayed. He knew he could do nothing to intervene and sent a silent prayer to Neptune that his friends would survive.

The ships closed, three of them — Menecrates and Menas set for head-on collision, *Boreas* heeling under full sail, closing from the south but still too far off to attract attention. At the last minute, Menecrates veered, possibly an ill-judged manoeuvre as he exposed the oars on one flank to the onrushing ship's bow and risked the lives of every rower on his port side. Titus cursed as the oars splintered, and although he could not hear them, he felt the agonies of thick oars sent thrusting into the chests of every man that held them, not knowing what was coming, and now the stricken ship was out of control.

But somehow, whether it be weakened by the glancing blow or shoddy fitting, the metal-encased ram on Menas's prow fell off, causing the traitor's ship to buck and plunge at the moment of apparent success, both ships disabled and floundering alongside each other. The men on Menecrates' ship recovered first and flung grappling hooks across with the intention of boarding, and as *Boreas* closed, the arrows, spears and slingshots began to fly.

'This side,' commanded Titus, pointing to the starboard side. 'Arm scorpios.' The men frantically wound the two catapults to full tension, then placed bolts in both.

Marina ordered the helmsman to pull *Boreas* to port and was gratified to see young Leo lend a shoulder to the tiller as it resisted their efforts. The old Veneti came about and now Menas's ship would be presented as the perfect target while her crew was focused on Menecrates. As he watched, Titus saw Agrippa's new weapons unleash their fury, a broadside by Menas of the fearsome spears, barbed iron missiles flying from tensioned catapults that scythed through the men on Menecrates' vessel.

Now you get the same, thought Titus. 'Fire both!'

The scorpio bolts ripped through superstructure and tore through marines and rowers alike. He saw Menas turn as the devastation struck, and at that moment an arrow burst through his shoulder. With a stunned look on his face, he crumpled face down on the deck.

'Go about, arm scorpios!' yelled Titus as *Boreas* cleared the awful scene.

It took an age to come about, the sail flapping impotently as the helm was worked to bring *Boreas* first into the wind, then to catch it and begin to reluctantly turn back to the fray. She heeled and surged again, the men hauling on sheets as they sought to close once more. But the crew on Menas's ship had had enough, perhaps because their commander had fallen or because they feared attack from both sides. Cutting free from the boarding grapples, the turncoat vessel was moving away from Menecrates towards the continuing naval battle beyond.

'Heave to,' commanded Titus, but there was no need, as Marina knew exactly what to do. They came up to Menecrates' stricken ship, observing the bloody mayhem on her decks. They threw ropes to surviving crewmen to bring the two ships waist to waist.

Titus surveyed the scene. Blood ran through the gunwales to drip into the ocean. Men wept and groaned. And there, in the centre of the flagship's decks, lay Menecrates, a barbed spear protruding through his hip, his lifeblood draining onto the deck.

Beside him knelt Barek and Niko. Felix was at the gunwale, waving to *Boreas*, ready to receive more welcome ropes of rescue. Titus and Marina stood side by side, knuckles white where they grasped the railings.

Despite the weight of the spear and the agony he must be experiencing, Menecrates heaved himself up to rest on an elbow and surveyed the higher vessel now alongside.

'Where were you when I needed you, Titus Villius?'

CHAPTER THIRTY

Titus knew that Menecrates would soon die. He knelt beside the stricken pirate and forced himself to look at the wound. The heavy, barbed spear had pierced his hip and must have shattered bone before bursting through his lower back. He was passing in and out of consciousness and gasping for breath, his hair lank with sweat and his face drained of colour. No longer did he resemble the bronzed, carefree pirate who had helped Titus end Murcus's attempted coup in these very waters just a few months ago. He would be a great loss to Sicilia, compounding the damage done by the defection of his rival admiral, Menas.

'If it takes us until Saturnalia, we will get you home.'

Menecrates attempted a smile. 'Where is that bastard Menas? I haven't finished with him yet.'

Titus gazed at the scene beyond, where battle still raged between the Sicilian and Roman ships, and took in the sight of Menas's galley moving slowly away from them. He had seen an arrow take the Sicilian traitor but doubted the wound was fatal. However, he said, 'You killed him.'

Barek, Niko and Felix, who had been helping the sailors and fellow rowers tend to the wounded and move the dead ready for burial at sea, squatted with Titus. Eyes closed, Menecrates' breathing was shallow.

'He treated us well,' said Niko. 'He did not know who his gang leaders had pressed into service until we were at sea, and by then it was too late. He promised us wealth in return for our work.'

Titus studied the men standing nearby. 'Who is second in command here?' he asked them. A thickset older man with a grizzled countenance, still in armour but helmetless, stepped forward. 'I am, sir. Name of Draco.'

'Well, Draco, have your men make a hammock for your captain and find somewhere to suspend it so that he is more comfortable when your ship rolls. And ask my navigator if she thinks there is a way to remove that ugly spear from his side.'

A sour look crossed Draco's face. 'I'm not taking orders from a woman,' he grumbled.

'Oh yes you are,' Titus said firmly, 'and one day you'll thank the gods that you crossed paths with Marina.'

Draco shrugged and turned to go about the task he had been set, but Titus called him back. 'One more thing, Draco. Was it you who stole my people to crew your ship?'

'Yes,' he replied, 'them and many more. Just obeying orders because we were short of rowers.'

'And how did they do?'

Draco scowled. 'As good as any.' Then he looked thoughtful, as if realising the men he had stolen had been instrumental in saving his life, if not that of his commander. 'I suppose they brought you and your strange ship here in the nick of time. I reckon they were worth it,' he growled.

'You're in charge now, Draco, but me and Marina are going to help you and your chief get back home. When you're done looking after him, come across to *Boreas* and we'll work out how we're going to do it.'

He beckoned to Marina as he strode to the ship's stern, the highest part of Menecrates' ship, where he took in the distant battle scene. Most of the Roman fleet was floundering on the rocky shore and the Sicilians were withdrawing.

'Looks like Rome is defeated here, but it's not over yet,' he said.

Marina sniffed the air and looked towards the hazy horizon. 'We could be home in two or three days, unless…'

'Unless we bring Menecrates with us, and his ship. So, how long with this added burden?'

'How many men for rowing?'

'My guess is around two hundred fit, but probably tired. Many of the oars were shattered in the attack, and I think she's breached close to the waterline, which will slow her. When the wind is right, they can use their sails and we can tow, or we can lash both ships together and go the whole way under sail. What do you think?'

'Or both, depending on the conditions?'

Titus looked at his navigator. 'You seem to me to be a far better captain than power-crazed Romans or Sicilians.'

It took seven days. Menecrates died on the second and only then was the barbed spear removed from his side, releasing a stench of rotting flesh. They sewed him into a spare foresail and left his body in the bows to commune with Salacia and Neptune to guide them home. They found provisions at a small settlement on the larger island, out of sight of Roman ships retreating to Puteoli to lick their wounds, and more lavish supplies on the island of Lipara, which lay close to Sicilia. They paid local farmers from Menecrates' treasure chest, which had been opened by Titus and Draco. The pirate had done very well for himself in his years of service as Sextus's chief admiral.

The keel beneath *Boreas* proved its worth when both ships were lashed tightly together, and they made reasonable progress using four sails sheeted close to the wind. When there was none, progress was slow under oars, all crew now weary beyond anything they had known in local Sicilian waters. They saw no reason to put into Messana on the seventh morning, happy to allow Titus and Marina to guide them through busy shipping and beyond towards Pax Villius's remote bay, observing the build-up of warships near the Bruttium coast opposite.

It was evident that the war had only just begun.

The men, women and children of Pax Villius streamed down to their beach as *Boreas* glided into the bay, sailors hauling on pulleys to lift her keel as the old Veneti approached the shallows and crunched onto shingle. The broken Sicilian trireme followed under oars to nudge the shore beside her rescuer.

Titus and Marina were first to leap down to a raucous reception. Titus took Zerenia in his arms, kissed her, then knelt to embrace his three children, whose enthusiastic greeting pushed him onto his back. Crispus seemed unsure whether to bark orders or join the celebrations, until Marina threw her arms around his neck and kissed him.

Others helped the weary crews to secure both ships while Draco and three of his men carried the body of Menecrates ashore. Barek led a detachment to gather wood and olive branches stockpiled from the winter pruning to build a funeral pyre while Felix organised a nearby campsite for the crew of Menecrates' ship. Zerenia took charge of feeding the Sicilian crew by organising the slaughter and cleaning of several goats, which would be roasted over fire pits while large cauldrons were rolled to the beach to stew vegetables seasoned with seaweed.

The Sicilian crew and the people of Pax Villius gathered at dusk around the funeral pyre and sent Menecrates to the underworld, their silent reverence broken at last when Draco began to sing. Titus recognised few of the words, a mixture of Greek and the local dialect.

There would be many sore heads in the morning and Pax Villius would be relieved of several vats of good wine, but as the homestead's people mingled with the visiting crew, a warm sense of camaraderie pervaded. The songs became increasingly incoherent and the women quickly retired. The wine warmed the blood so that none seemed to care as the wind picked up, and the first spots of rain went unnoticed.

A wet, blustery dawn found Titus and Crispus at the shore, cloaks pulled tightly around their shoulders, gazing across the storm-lashed strait to Bruttium. The ashes of Menecrates' pyre still glowed red despite the slanting drizzle; his surviving crew was mostly sleeping off the night's excesses in various untidy clusters across the beach and its grassy borders. Ships swarmed like bees against the hazy mainland opposite.

'Looks like the fight resumes,' said Crispus dourly.

'Hard to tell who's who in this weather, but this storm will favour Sextus,' said Titus.

'As long as they remain over there and don't land on our shores. I for one don't feel like fighting today.'

'When has too much wine ever stopped you before?' Titus would have laughed, but he didn't feel up to it either.

They watched what appeared to be a repeat of the sea battle of a week earlier, when the Romans had hugged the coast, allowing the Sicilians to hound them at will and keep them penned in. Once again, Octavian's fleet seemed to close in on the distant shore, with Sextus's triremes pushing at them in a line, not using ramming tactics but sailing close enough to unleash a hail of spears and arrows and the occasional fireball.

If Octavian wished to bring his more experienced troops to Sicilia's shores, he would have to break through, yet his naval commanders seemed incapable of penetrating the Sicilian line.

'We should have a leisurely breakfast,' said Crispus. 'Not much happening here to alarm Sextus.'

Draco dragged himself wearily across sand and shingle to join them, a threadbare blanket pulled tight against the chill. 'What passes yonder?' he asked in his gravelly piratical tone.

'Nothing to concern us,' replied Crispus. 'Your ships have Rome at their mercy, by the look of it.'

'Doesn't surprise me,' said Draco. 'Those Romans know nothing about the sea. Storm suits us.'

They watched in silence until a loud rumble from Crispus's stomach indicated it was time for food. They dragged themselves away from the distant spectacle to find the campfires stoked despite the driving drizzle, and groups of men hovering around pans of lentils and fritters formed from the previous night's leftovers. Zerenia and the women had brought jugs of spiced *posca*, brewed with local herbs, all combining to offer a tempting aroma to many a sore head.

'Better than fighting in a storm, this,' mumbled Draco, to the approval of those seated on the ground nearby.

'Stay as long as you like, boys,' smiled Zerenia. 'We've got plenty of fences to fix and vines to tend.'

The visitors laughed appreciatively. Her jest might be taken seriously.

But Draco was distracted. Chewing on a mouthful, he touched Crispus on the shoulder and strode away towards the shore, where the wind was driving angry breakers to claw at shingle. He pointed at Italia's far coast, where battle raged.

'No mistaking, that's an enemy ship that's broken through.'

'How do you know?' asked Crispus.

'I know. Sextus hasn't got any ships like that.'

They watched the scene. A large ship, far bigger than the Sicilian triremes and *liburnians*, was plunging through the angry swell, a following wind filling its red and white sail. It was alone, and it was heading towards the Pax Villius shore.

'*Merda!*' exclaimed Crispus, reaching for the sword that wasn't at his belt. Turning to Draco, he asked, 'How many men on a ship of that size?'

'Four hundred, maybe more.'

Crispus watched the ship lift her bows and crash down into a trough, spray flying high.

'We have to stop them landing here,' said Crispus, 'or we'll be overrun.'

CHAPTER THIRTY-ONE

Titus was decisive.

'Felix, have *Boreas* and *Eurus* armed with scorpio bolts and muster men to launch them both. I will command on *Boreas* and Marina will command on *Eurus*. Crispus, form up all of the men on the shore in case they land.'

Wearily, the men of Pax Villius and all of their guests readied themselves for war. Titus knew it was too soon after the exertions of recent days, but this was his land, his family and his people, and he knew the approaching vessel was unlikely to be convinced that he was a friend of Agrippa. Worse, Draco and his Sicilian crew did not know of his mission for Rome and would look upon him as a traitor, just like Menas. He knew the onrushing Romans would be frustrated by their reversals of fortune and would be eager to demonstrate their fighting prowess at last.

If that ship landed with its superior force, Pax Villius would be captured and would no doubt be used as a beachhead for Octavian's invaders.

While the men detailed by Felix used logs to roll *Eurus* to the sea and relaunched *Boreas* into the breakers, Crispus led the remaining men to the ship shed to arm themselves. They emerged bearing shields, swords and spears, Crispus himself wearing a light leather cuirass and a Greek-style helmet with white plumage. He ordered the men of Pax Villius and those from the Sicilian vessel's crew to form up on the shore, then handed something small to Titus, no words passing between them. Titus pinned the viper badge to his chest, saluting his friend before running to the floundering ships, each now manned by a dozen crewmen.

Felix gave Titus a leg up to board *Boreas*, then sought to use a knotted rope to clamber up behind. But Titus, looking down from the deck, held up a hand. 'Stay with Crispus!' he shouted. 'He'll need every man to repel the invader.' Felix obeyed, turning to see Crispus barking orders and attempting to bring order to the ranks of the few.

Too few, thought Titus, *but the gods have brought us this far and will not desert us now*. He touched the viper brooch for luck, then looked across to *Eurus* where Marina was already ordering the keel to be lowered and giving hand-signals to the steersman to come almost directly into the wind. Titus did the same, feeling the grind of iron on seabed with each wave trough, but then *Boreas* was free of encumbrance and leapt to follow her sister ship into the freedom of deeper water. Both ships tacked at the same moment and heeled in unison as they found the easterly's power, lateen sails dangerously taut. The white-crested swell proved incapable of slowing them as they cut a course towards the approaching warship at twice the speed any ship could manage under oars.

But the Roman vessel was already close to Sicilia's shore and their Pax Villius haven. Knowing that only their vessels between the quinquereme and the shore would halt their progress, Titus gave a frantic hand signal to Marina to heave to before the approaching warship, calling out against the wind and spray, 'Block their path!'

Again, both Venetis moved as one and came about, sails flapping impotently as they lost way, forming a barrier. The oncoming vessel could only ram them or change course.

And they saw how well armed and determined was this great ship, filled with armed marines in her bows and grim commanders on her stern platform. Her red and white mainsail was filled with the following wind, her bronze bow-beak in the shape of a sea-serpent plunging and heaving with menace.

Now we'll know, thought Titus, realising that if the Roman did not change course, one of his faithful ships would be lost. He ordered the deckhands to man and load the two scorpios on the starboard side and hoped Marina would do the same. But the swell, now side-on, would make accuracy almost impossible as both ships wallowed and rocked alarmingly.

But the great ship did not ram either *Boreas* or *Eurus*. Shouted orders lost on the wind brought her slewing to port just a javelin's throw apart from the Veneti pair. Three hundred oars dropped to slow her motion. On the poop deck was a resplendent admiral, his Rome-red cloak flying in the wind, his attendants grim-faced as they peered at the impudent challengers. A hundred archers rushed to her starboard bulwarks, bows armed and ready to let fly their deadly hail.

'Name yourself!' came the shouted command.

'Titus Villius Macer of the Fifth Alaudae, friend of Marcus Vipsanius Agrippa, seeking only peace and protection for my people.'

There was no reply, but the commanders had heard and were discussing something. One man pointed to the shore where Menecrates' ship was beached.

'We see a Sicilian ship yonder,' one of the commanders replied. 'Tell us why we should not destroy you.'

Titus signalled to the two scorpio crews who had been looking at him throughout the exchange, as if hoping for the signal to unleash their bolts. His signal was *hold, ready*.

'Now you name yourself!' he shouted across the small stretch of choppy sea. 'Before I destroy you.'

He knew he heard laughter, but held up a hand for the scorpio crew to wait.

'Marcus Valerius Mesalla Corvinus.' The name was all but lost on the howling wind, but Titus heard the name "Mesalla". He filled his lungs, hoping his memory served him well.

'You lost at Philippi. Why do you now fight for my friends?'

Again there was laughter, as if Titus was unfamiliar with developments since that great battle that had decided the future of Rome. Eventually, the admiral called, 'Stand aside!'

'Loose!' yelled Titus and two bolts flew harmlessly above the Roman. Seeing this, he didn't hesitate. 'Reload!'

The peacock admiral on the invading ship rushed to the railing, steadying himself with one hand, the other held up towards Titus. 'Do you mean to fight?' His words floated uneasily through the howling wind.

'Try me!' shouted Titus, but it was Marina's scorpios on *Eurus* that responded, and this time the bolts found their target, ripping through superstructure and sending splinters flying through the air. Some of the Roman commanders managed to duck, while others screamed in pain as their flesh was ripped by debris. One of the bolts drove through a steersman's chest, killing him instantly.

Arrows flew thickly, mostly aimed at *Eurus*. Titus feared for them, but he saw many shields raised and hoped none had suffered.

'Loose!' he ordered again, and this time his bolts struck home, smashing through the Roman's flanks where oarsmen must have died or been maimed.

The great Roman ship immediately came about and began to pick up speed, heading towards the Pax Villius shore. Thinking to track her and fire more broadsides, Titus ordered his steersman to run parallel and find wind in *Boreas*'s sails, but the shore was too close. He ordered another salvo, which flew harmlessly above the invader and was about to turn away when he heard a great crash from beyond the attacking vessel.

Marina had rammed *Eurus* into the side of the galley, near its stern and steering gear. Mesalla's huge vessel began to slew out of control. With just enough clearance for the keel, *Boreas* again edged between the attacker and the shore. More arrows flew, this time in desperation, and now Titus felt that he had control thanks to Marina's courageous endeavour.

'Yield!' cried Titus. 'And return whence you came. None of your allies follow you. Landing here is pointless.'

'Never!' came the reply. 'We are here to bring Rome's justice.'

'And so am I,' replied Titus, 'but not with more bloodshed.'

By now, everyone on the shore could hear the exchange, and a great roar went up. They were all weary of warfare and wanted no more killing. But a lone voice took up the challenge.

'I will fight. Name your champion and we will resolve this man to man, right here on the shore of Pax Villius.'

Titus knew who had spoken before turning to look.

Crispus stood on the shore, ankle-deep in frothy breakers, his helmet proud. He held his *gladius* in one hand and his serrated knife in the other. Above, the gods growled their expectation and Hermes' wind snatched at the hem of his tunic.

Again, there was no immediate response from the command platform of the other ship. Eventually, Mesalla spoke, his voice ringing across the decks and the narrow strip of sea between his vessel and the Sicilian shore.

'Flaccus!'

The man who emerged was fully armed. He moved deliberately, powerful limbs holding him steady on the swaying deck. He was helmetless, his bald head glistening with sweat, and he carried a light shield and a *spatha* sword. He moved to the ship's bulwark and surveyed the scene, his gaze fixing on Crispus where he stood in the shallows.

'When I defeat this little flea,' he said in a strong voice that carried to all, 'am I right that everything that he holds dear becomes ours?'

'Yes,' said Mesalla.

Titus struck the deal. 'And when your man Flaccus is cut down by my man Crispus, everything you have, including your men and your ship, is mine to do with as I please?'

'Yes,' said Mesalla, and Flaccus leapt down into the surf.

CHAPTER THIRTY-TWO

For a moment, Crispus found himself back in the arena in Rome. His scalp prickled with expectation, and he involuntarily swept his *gladius* from side to side, advancing a few steps as if to mark his territory in the foaming shallows.

He noted his opponent was left-handed, his *spatha* held limply but his shield firm in his right hand. There would be an opportunity there, if he could negate the shield by getting close to Flaccus and stabbing low and upwards. But he would have to get inside the arc of the long sword. If he could do that, the advantage was his.

But Flaccus did not look like an inexperienced swordsman. He advanced deliberately, not showing any dexterity yet, just expecting his quarry to back away in fear.

Crispus stood his ground. 'You are as flabby as your name,' he said, hoping for an angry response.

Flaccus advanced, saying nothing. He may have carried excess weight, but this didn't hinder his muscular strides through the shallows. He moved straight towards Crispus, and his first sword-swing was powerful, slashing through air as Crispus swayed aside, keeping his balance, *gladius* and dagger held low.

He took a step back — against the rules of the Fifth Alaudae, but not in single combat.

Flaccus smiled confidently. Crispus watched his eyes, looking for any sign of his intent. Every shout of encouragement was shut out by the menacing Greek helmet that only allowed him to focus on his quarry.

The *spatha* swept in an angry arc towards his neck, and the first bright ringing of the blade-clash rang out across the bay as Crispus parried the blow. The shield followed quickly in an attempt to connect iron boss with Crispus's chin, but it swept past harmlessly. Crispus noted how the onshore wind caught the inside of the shield and held it for the briefest of moments before Flaccus brought it back. He would not miss his chance a second time.

He thrust low with his *gladius*, but Flaccus was nimble enough to leap backwards, and then, with astonishing speed that belied his size, he seemed to surge forward again with another sweep of his sword. Crispus took a glancing blow on his helmet and bright lights flashed behind his eyes, momentarily blinding him. He swayed with the blow, stumbling to his left, almost losing his footing in the shifting sand and shingle. But instead of trying to halt the movement, he followed through and pushed off his right foot to leap into the air and swivel almost entirely around to catch Flaccus unawares with a downward slash of his *gladius*. It opened a bright cut on his opponent's forearm, but the look in Flaccus's eyes told Crispus that it would not hinder him. Yet the cheer all around was for first blood.

'We can stop now, if you want to be sensible about this.'

Flaccus spat and the wind carried away a muttered insult as he lifted his shield to cover his face.

He seemed to be waiting for Crispus to make another move. But Crispus had always fought best when his opponent was advancing, so he dropped his hands to his sides, dagger unbloodied but *gladius* dripping red from the flesh wound it had inflicted.

Flaccus was strong. His next blow, aimed in white-hot anger, rang sharp against Crispus's parry and slid ferociously onto his shoulder, scraping on bone. But before Crispus registered the wound, his dagger slid into his opponent's undefended belly.

Both men looked each other in the eye, Flaccus's wide in shock and pain. They clasped each other for several heartbeats.

It shouldn't have been possible, but Flaccus thrust Crispus backwards and again held his *spatha* high. Crispus wanted to look at the wound he had inflicted, but his training and experience told him to watch his opponent's eyes. Flaccus swept his *spatha* downwards with a grunt that betrayed, for the first time, a hint of fear. It must have brought pain surging through his body. Crispus barely parried the blow and took another wound, this time on his left shoulder, and his opponent's shield came round with a crushing blow to his chest. Suddenly he was down, seated on damp sand, foaming waters dragging away his blood and Flaccus's.

For the first time in his life he expected the killing blow: he was unaccustomed to being at the mercy of an opponent.

But it never came.

Flaccus dropped his sword, his shield at his side held only by a leather thong, and with his left hand clutched his wounded midriff. Intestines peeped out. His eyes glazed, and he collapsed to his knees.

The men of Pax Villius and on the ships offshore held their breath.

Crispus struggled to his feet and came towards Flaccus, holding him beneath his arms as if to keep him upright.

'Brother?'

'I am done,' gasped Flaccus.

Crispus held him close, his blood mingling with the sweat that seeped from his opponent. 'Stay with me. You are a warrior, and you will not die.'

Flaccus looked into the eyes of his vanquisher. 'You are worthy —'

The light went from his eyes.

Crispus held him in that embrace until Zerenia came forward and knelt beside them.

'He is gone,' she said gently, 'and you are our champion.'

There was no euphoria, not on the shore as the people of Pax Villius watched aghast, nor on the Roman warship where the spirits of crewmen and marines sank under the expectation of defeat.

Titus was first to break the silence. He turned to address Mesalla on the larger ship. '*Domine*, how do you wish to proceed?'

Mesalla paused. 'We will beach in peace, Titus Villius, but do we have your word that you will not assault us?'

Titus wondered if he would be stupid to allow this, given the greater numbers of the invader, but he still believed in Roman honour. 'You may land,' he called, 'and we will break bread as friends.'

'Agreed,' came the reply. The commands were shouted to bring the giant quinquereme to the shore, but her greater draught made it impossible to come up to land. She leaned in submission, with choppy water between ship and shore.

Four men, clearly the friends of Flaccus, were first to leap into the surf and rush to their colleague. Taking him gently in their arms, helped by Crispus, they laid him face up on the beach. One of them pressed an ear to his mouth to confirm that he was dead. Silence and respect pervaded as Pax Villius watched on and the Roman crew waded ashore. Marina ran to Crispus, tearing her headband away to dab at the blood on his arms as he waved away her concern.

Several of the younger men on the beach advanced, swords and spears in hand, but Titus called out in a strong, clear voice, 'Stand back! Give these visitors to our shore your respect.' The aggressors edged away, and the Romans held up empty hands to show they had no malicious intent.

Ashore now, Titus approached Mesalla, hands spread wide in peace. The Roman general affirmed, pulling off his helmet and casting it aside, and the two clasped each other's wrists.

'You may beach your ship for repairs and my men will assist,' said Titus, 'though we are short on supplies for victuals, as you are not the first to seek our aid.'

Mesalla looked seaward, where no Roman ships followed. In the distance, a great sea battle seethed where the storm raged foulest. 'I fear we are alone here,' he said, 'and we are at your mercy.'

'We see no enemy here,' replied Titus. 'We will do our best for you and provide aid where we can for the stricken and the hungry, but we cannot assure your safety if Sextus follows. He is bound to have seen your ship break his lines and he is intent on holding this island.'

'We gladly accept.' The Roman was dignified, upright and square-shouldered, but had warmth in his eyes as he looked Titus up and down. 'Your man fought well. Flaccus has put many in the ground before this day. Can we send him to the gods where he belongs?'

'A great man, the Sicilian admiral Menecrates, goes before from this very shore. Flaccus will be in famous company and will be well received across the Styx.' Titus half expected

Mesalla to spit and curse the name of Menecrates, but he didn't. It was clear there would be no more bloodshed this day.

The people of Pax Villius and the crews of Menecrates' and Mesalla's ships gave Flaccus a noble send-off to the underworld, but they knew the camaraderie they all found that night on the beach opposite Rhegium would be short-lived if Sextus came to seek the one vessel that had broken his line. The wine and ale put this thought to the back of every mind.

CHAPTER THIRTY-THREE

Leo was wishing something would happen. These were the best days of his young life; he'd experienced excitement and adventure at sea and the thrill of becoming an apprentice spy, and now he was on scouting duty to forewarn Pax Villius of any approaching soldiers. But he had become bored, grubbing around for hours in the bushes beside the road that led south from Messana. His favourite diversion was capturing a scorpion, holding it by the tail so its legs and claws became frantic, then placing it near an asp viper to see if they would fight. His second-best pastime was trapping a lizard by its tail so that it could only escape by shedding the appendage, then seeing how long the detached tail would thrash around on its own. The record for that day was a count of twenty; as it happened, this record could not be broken because Leo didn't know what number came next.

He heard the steady tramp of soldiers long before they came into sight. His first instinct was to immediately begin the long jog back to Pax Villius to warn Titus, but Leo knew he would be asked for numbers, even though this was not his strongest talent. He climbed to the top of the knoll from where he would have been watching if not for his preoccupation with snakes and scorpions, lay down and began to count.

He knew they were Sicilians for two reasons. Firstly, he was pretty sure no invading Romans had landed on the island, apart from the huge warship now being repaired at Pax Villius, and secondly he knew the blue cloaks worn by the soldiers and the pennants of the same colour set them apart as the local militia. Two mounted officers, resplendent in shining armour and blue-crested helmets led a large column of foot soldiers. He counted twenty of the men, then estimated a further twenty blocks of a similar number and knew that from this information that Titus and Crispus would be able to work out the number of soldiers that would soon arrive at their homestead.

He edged away from the knoll and ran home as fast as could. It was more than a mile, probably two, and he was so out of breath when he arrived at the gates that he could barely speak to the small group of men guarding the entrance to Pax Villius. But they knew from his wild gestures that men were coming and hurried him on his way to find Titus. The veteran soldier wasn't there, nor Crispus. Zerenia was, and she brought her calming influence to bear, eventually establishing that around four hundred soldiers, probably led by the unwelcome figures of Sextus Pompey and his commander Azhar, were approaching. She hoped they would pass Pax Villius by, but in her heart she knew that that these men would cause trouble.

She gave Leo water; he gulped half of a jugful and poured the rest over his head. 'We must warn them,' he said.

'They are on the beach,' said Zerenia. 'You run ahead, and I will follow.'

When he heard the news, Titus looked north, and a dust-cloud confirmed the approaching threat. He hailed Mesalla who was on his ship overseeing repairs, the huge vessel anchored in the shallows, stern moored to the shore. Crispus, Felix and Barek, who had been assisting, came ashore with the Roman captain. Menecrates' Sicilian vessel lay beached further away, where her crew continued to work on damaged planking.

Zerenia joined the five men and noticed with a smile that Leo had a look of importance about him as he tried to explain who was approaching. 'About four hundred men,' she said, knowing that Leo had some difficulty with numbers, 'probably Sextus and Azhar too.'

At the mention of his nemesis Azhar, Titus spat on the sand. 'They are looking for you, Mesalla, and much as I would like to fight beside you I cannot risk my people again.'

Mesalla smiled. 'A tactical withdrawal, then. We would not wish to offend your land and your home by spilling Sicilian blood here.' He whistled to his crew and signalled immediate departure, then turned to Titus and Zerenia. 'I wish we could have met in better circumstances. I am grateful to you, although I sorrow over the loss of one of my men —' at this, Crispus involuntarily touched a bandaged shoulder — 'and I will convey your kindness to Octavian when I see him. I wish you well.'

'Go quickly, and may Neptune and Mercury protect you,' said Titus as they clasped hands.

There was no time to give the Roman quinquereme a send-off as her crew busied themselves about departure, the great ship soon serenely heading to open sea.

'We must arm ourselves,' said Titus.

'Why?' asked Zerenia. 'We should not provoke so many men.'

Titus thought about their predicament and pointed to the departing quinquereme. 'That is a Roman ship over there, and Sextus knows it landed here. He may accuse us of colluding with Rome.'

'Let him,' said Zerenia. 'He will also see that one of his vessels, which you helped, is beached over there. Why not just tell him the truth of it, how Crispus fought the Roman champion? Surely that is enough?'

Titus reluctantly concurred. 'I will feel naked without my sword, but you are right. We should meet him up at Pax

Villius, and perhaps he will not notice that a Roman ship has been here.'

'Too late,' Crispus interrupted, pointing to the clifftop above their bay, lined with soldiers bearing shields and spears. On the pathway leading down to the beach, a smaller group approached.

'Sextus,' muttered Crispus.

'And Azhar,' said Titus. 'I would know that peacock bastard's walk anywhere.'

The approaching group halted where grassy scrub became shingle and pebbles. For a few moments, they stood and stared, taking in the scene on the beach, looking towards the retreating Roman ship and back to where the damaged Sicilian ship was being repaired. They seemed to know who stood in the closer small group on the shore.

They debated, pointing. Then the two leaders separated from their colleagues and walked towards the small knot of people where Titus stood, unarmed and watching suspiciously.

'What do they want?' asked Zerenia, nervously. 'I don't like these people.'

'If Azhar comes any closer, I'll kill him with my bare hands,' whispered Titus and Crispus grunted approval.

But they didn't come closer. They stopped halfway to wait and watch, the invitation clear.

'Come on,' said Titus, glancing sideways at Crispus. 'You and me, like old times, only this time words are our only weapon, so be careful what you say.' They advanced purposefully until they were no more than five paces apart from the Sicilian leaders.

'Sextus!' Titus called.

'Old friend,' replied Sextus. 'What happens here?'

'All will be explained as soon as you send that weasel standing next to you back whence he came.'

Azhar snarled. 'If you want to fight me,' he said, fingering the pommel of a falcata sword at his hip, 'I am ready, and I see you are not.'

'Whenever you like, Azhar. You have a big sword and I have my fists.'

'Calm yourselves, gentlemen,' said Sextus, motioning downwards with his hands. 'There are bigger matters to discuss.'

'Ready when you are, old friend. But keep that animal beside you away from me.'

Azhar did not seem ready to take a backward step. 'You are a traitor to Sicilia, and I know that you would see Rome rule here.'

'Prove it, snake,' replied Titus, taking a step forward, but Sextus interrupted before they could come to blows.

'First, we must establish what has happened here,' he said. 'Is that Octavian's vessel we see retreating?'

'Yes,' said Titus. 'We gave battle on this shore.'

'Liar!' shouted Azhar. 'Where are the bodies? Where is the bloodshed?'

It was Crispus who answered for his *primus pilus*. 'That you will never know, and why would you? Where were you when our people fought for Sextus at Syracuse, sneaking away when swords were drawn and good men would die? And were you not at Misenum when our people prevented your scurrilous plans with Murcus? You should bow your head and allow me to lop it off, if Sextus will lend me his sword. You do not deserve to live.'

Like Titus, Crispus had reason to want this end for Azhar, but he had said his piece and hoped it would end the charade. It did not.

Sextus, not wanting personal battles to interfere with his mission, changed the subject. 'I also see one of our ships on this beach,' he said. 'I require an explanation for this also.'

'Before we explain these things,' said Titus, 'tell us how you have fared in the war with Octavian.' He pointed across the strait towards Rhegium. 'We saw the battle yonder but do not know the outcome.'

Sextus smiled. 'This so-called Caesar has been driven away and his ships ruined, as much by the storm as by us, and now we seek answers about the one ship that was able to break through our lines. Who commanded?'

'Mesalla,' replied Titus. 'And Crispus championed your cause.'

Azhar studied the bandages on Crispus's arms. 'So explain why you did not slaughter them all?'

That was enough for Titus. He strode towards Azhar, the look on his face terrifying. 'You coward, have you no honour?' he shouted. 'First you assault my wife when there is no one to defend her, then you send your people into battle while you cower, and now you expect us to break our word and kill innocent people when we vowed that they would be respected under the ancient rules of engagement.'

He swung a fist at Azhar while the others looked on in shock. Azhar barely managed to duck the blow and reached for his sword, but Titus was well balanced, even in his rage. He hit him powerfully with his other fist and must have broken ribs. Azhar staggered back but recovered himself and leapt forward with a scream, fists raining futile blows. Titus punched from the shoulder, dislodging Azhar's helmet, but his right fist was bloodied on the bronze. He followed up with a knee to Azhar's groin, and the commander of Sicilia's troops doubled up in pain. His other knee came up forcefully into Azhar's chin and the peacock general went down.

Titus put his foot on Azhar's throat, oblivious to the shouts behind him.

It was Zerenia. She was running towards the four men. 'Stop! Wait!' she cried. 'You don't understand!'

'Give me a sword,' said Titus, his training and experience keeping him calm even in the euphoria of a fight. 'I will rid us all of this worm right now.'

Zerenia came up to them, panting with the exertion. 'You would kill an innocent man?'

'What?' said Titus.

'He may be evil, but he is not the man who offended me. His is not the father of Smudge.'

'Then who is that man?'

Zerenia's eyes flashed as she looked at Sextus. 'There is the man who defiled me,' she said, 'and I demand the right to pass judgement on him.'

Sextus was taken aback at the outburst.

'Find me a sword.' Titus's words carried death.

'No,' said Zerenia, calmer now. 'There have been many nights when I have wept myself to sleep, willing your death, Sextus Pompeius. And you should die, right here on my land, our land. You came to me when I was unprotected, and now who will protect you in your moment of weakness? Not Azhar, who lies in the sand with a foot on his throat.'

Sextus backed away, knowing that his men were too far away to prevent his death. 'You would not... You were willing. You wanted it more than I did...'

227

All four men could feel the fury that emanated from Zerenia in that moment. But when she spoke, she managed to stay calm, as if she knew that no one would ever believe such a lie.

'One word from me and my husband will kill you,' she said. 'I have longed for it. But I will not command it. Go now, and never set foot on our land again. Never come to our home. If you do, you will die, because this man —' she indicated Titus — 'is more a man than you will ever be, a man of honour, and if I asked he would kill you now. So go, and never let your shadow darken Pax Villius again.'

Sextus looked from Zerenia to Titus and Crispus and saw only grim vengeance there. Titus fought the urge to overrule his wife and, in his anguish, kill the man who had raped her years ago.

Slowly, he released his foot from Azhar's neck. 'You heard my wife. Go. *Now!*'

Azhar got to his feet, brushed sand from his embossed cuirass, picked up his helmet, and looked at Sextus, who simply nodded his agreement.

Four hundred Sicilian troops were marched away from Pax Villius. Although Rome had failed in its invasion of Sicilia, a seemingly inconsequential event on an obscure shore had changed the course of a war: the island's leaders had been shamed.

On the beach, Titus and Zerenia embraced.

'Is it over now?' whispered Zerenia, her mouth close to his ear.

'I doubt it,' he replied.

PART THREE: RECKONING

CHAPTER THIRTY-FOUR

Portus Julius, mainland Italy, Spring 36BC

Four men stood in the shade of a temporary awning. It was hot, but a gentle onshore breeze tugged at braided fringing and cooled the hilltop observation post. Three of the men, bareheaded, wore off-duty tunics, although they carried short *gladius* swords sheathed at the hip. The fourth, also bareheaded but not armed, wore a full-length Greek robe. Before them was a table bearing maps, anchored against the breeze with small rocks, a jug of water, four goblets and a bowl of fruit. Behind them, waiting in the sun's noon glare, was a team of freedman secretaries and servants and beyond these a squad of twenty fully armed guardsmen in two ranks, none daring to wipe sweat from their brow or swat away flies for fear of rebuke. Their officer was a stickler for discipline and not a man with a reputation for kindness.

To the left of the vantage point stretched the shimmering Bay of Puteoli, populated by sluggish merchantmen under sail and numerous fishing skiffs out of the bustling port that gave its name to these waters. In the distance, far to the south, a small fleet of four war galleys was rounding the Misenum promontory. But the four men were not there to enjoy the views across an open sea.

Directly in front of them was the first of two astonishing engineering feats. Rome's newest naval port was a seawater lake separated from the bay by a broad breakwater, a mile long, stretching from the harbour of Baiae opposite to the barracks and warehouses below where they stood. A section of this immense structure had been cut away to allow access into the lake. Its shores were lined with the hulls of a hundred new ships, huge quinqueremes built for war and low-slung *liburnians* designed for speed. Carpenters and engineers swarmed over them to step masts and fit weapons, all hidden from Rome's enemies. A massive chain looped across the harbour entrance, held just above the water by a powerful winch, seaweed dripping from massive rusting links. Even if the naval harbour was discovered, no enemy ships could enter and any vessels seeking access would do so with a forest of spears and arrows pointing at them from either side of the entrance.

But this was just one engineering miracle. The Greek, Strabo, a writer of around thirty who had attached himself to the Roman court, had been explaining that the breakwater, wide enough for two carts abreast, had been built by Herakles — the other men suppressed their mirth at this — but it had now been breached by Rome's newest hero, Agrippa, who was standing next to him. 'It is known as Via Herculanea,' he was gushing, 'but now perhaps we should rename it —' Agrippa silenced him with a subtle nudge. Because standing on the other side of Strabo was the triumvir Gaius Julius Caesar Divi Filius, son of a god, but known simply as Octavian in this company.

And Octavian was not listening. Hands on the table, he was leaning forward to look approvingly to his right, where in the past year thousands of mattocks and shovels had bitten deep into the ground, the spoil banked by cart, donkey and slave, to dig a canal of five-hundred paces to another lake, Avernus, concealed from prying eyes where crews trained on yet more newly built ships and learned Agrippa's new art of sea warfare. A large quinquereme was currently in this channel, being towed from the bank by a team of oxen, to be readied for sea trials.

A huge sea wall, a narrow entrance, a vast inner harbour and a concealed training lake. Rome would not suffer another defeat to the pirate ruler of Sicilia. Not if Octavian and Agrippa had anything to do with it.

Octavian looked at the fourth man. 'Does Sextus know anything of this?'

'Sir,' replied Titus, 'he does not.'

The four warships turned together, and their bows pointed towards the distant entrance to Rome's new west coast naval headquarters. Each shipped oars as their sails filled with the southerly and seven hundred rowers hoped the new course would give them an hour or two's respite. On the command platform of one of the triremes stood Menas, weathered features partly concealed by a thick beard, lank dark hair touching the shoulder straps of a leather cuirass. He spoke briefly to the *trierarch* standing next to him.

'Send word to the fleet. We hold this course for Portus Julius. Ready the signal flags and as we approach assume single file behind me.'

The pennants flying from his ships' masts were no longer the blue of Sicilia, but the red of Rome. Menas looked up at the symbol of his new loyalty and thought bitterly how little respect he had been shown by his new masters, cold-hearted Octavian and his jumped-up general, Agrippa. His shoulder throbbed with a dull ache where he had taken an arrow in Rome's cause almost two years previously.

'Remind the captains to keep all weapons hidden,' added Menas with a lopsided grin aided by the wine from the ship's rations. 'And have our precious cargo ready for a parade.'

'Now, let's see how we will deploy.'

Octavian clicked his fingers in the direction of a secretary, who promptly removed the top map of the Portus Julius harbour complex to reveal a second map, this time of Sicilia.

Agrippa picked up a thin rod, which he used as a pointer. Its tip rested on Messana, the port overlooking the straits between Sicilia and Italia.

'This is the closest and easiest place to land our troops, but it will be fiercely defended,' he said. 'Twice we have suffered much loss of ships and men in the seas between where we are now and the port of Messana.'

Titus stepped closer, conscious that a mere centurion should tread carefully in such company yet aware that his service had won their respect. 'Would it not be wiser to land troops elsewhere on Sicilia?' He pointed to the island's western coast. 'Panormus? Lilybaeum?'

Agrippa nodded. 'You would think so, but that would mean more time at sea for our troop ships. And those waters can be treacherous.'

Octavian placed a finger firmly on Messana. 'I have consulted an augur. The gods will not oppose us a third time.' Then he moved his finger to the smattering of small islands just to the north of Sicilia. 'The people of the Lipara islands are our friends. They do not love Sextus. From there we can take Mylae and Messana, supported by the Tarentum fleet, and our legions can sweep south and west.'

Titus thought it seemed well rehearsed, perhaps for his benefit.

Agrippa turned to Titus and smiled. 'If, the gods forbid, you are found out or captured, this is all you know.'

'So you are holding something back?' Titus asked.

Agrippa nodded. 'You are familiar with Lepidus?'

'Of course. The third triumvir. He rules in Africa.'

'And Africa is not so very far from Sicilia's southern shores.'

Titus knew this plan would destroy Sextus. This was not something he had always wanted, even when spying for Agrippa as one of his vipers, but Sextus was no longer his friend. He was a rapist, and Zerenia the victim. Yet he loved Sicilia and knew that what he was seeing could destroy an island where life was simple and free, and with it his home Pax Villius and the people he loved. All because the Sicilian pirates had blockaded Rome's vital grain supplies for so long and thumbed their noses at Octavian and his precious new order just across the narrow straits.

'So you see,' Agrippa was saying, 'we want Sextus to know that we will attack Messana, so he is unprepared for the arrival of Lepidus with twelve legions from the south.'

'I can do this,' said Titus. 'I can let it be known that Sextus need only worry about his northern coast.'

But Agrippa was shaking his head. 'We have other plans for you, for which you will be well rewarded. We have another agent who knows, or thinks he knows, what we are planning. His pockets are filled with gold for information that we already knew thanks to your messages, and we have let slip some of our intentions.'

'Then why do you need me?'

'I will come to that. But first you need to know who this other agent is, so that you don't kill him.'

'Why would I do that?'

'Because it is our understanding that you have had dealings with him and, by the way, he is not to be trusted. I think you know him as Azhar the Cruel?'

Titus was stunned. How could this be? The Sicilian general who had been implicated in the plot to overthrow both Rome's and Sicilia's leaders in a coup, who had been badly disfigured as he escaped a burning vessel, who had surprisingly been forgiven and accepted by Sextus. And the man responsible for torturing Titus, even to the point of removing a finger. A man Titus would very much like to kill — slowly.

Titus shook his head in dismay. 'You can be sure Azhar is not to be trusted. He would betray his own mother. He is selfish, heartless and, yes, cruel.'

'Very few of us are honourable in war,' observed Octavian, who had placed his forefinger on the centre of the map. 'We need to set up staging posts so that messages can be sent swiftly, north and south. Somewhere around here, midway between Agrippa and myself in the north, and Lepidus in the south.'

Titus studied the map. He was thoughtful for a moment, then looked up. 'There is a place midway between Messana and the western coast.' There was no town marked where his finger pointed. 'It is mountainous and well hidden. Jerax. The caves of the vultures.'

Strabo, who had remained quiet throughout this conversation, suddenly became interested. 'I have heard of this place. It is the door to the underworld, and it's guarded by the titan Crius —'

Agrippa laughed, cutting Strabo off, but Octavian seemed pleased.

'If this is the door to Tartarus and it is guarded by a fearsome titan, and we don't want any suspicious Sicilians snooping around, it could be the perfect place. What do you say, Marcus?'

Agrippa smiled his approval and Titus said, 'I have the ideal titan guardian in mind.' Crispus would revel in the role.

But Octavian was no longer paying attention, instead fixing his gaze on the approach of four warships, each reefing sails as oars were extended to control manoeuvres and come into single file.

'Menas, if I'm not mistaken,' said Agrippa. 'Showing off, as ever.'

Agrippa's engineers had rebuilt the new entrance to Portus Julius with wide stone quays to allow visitors to moor outside the harbour while presenting credentials for authorised entry. This was a top-secret naval base to which no vessel, no matter the friendly pennants or the reputations of their captains, could gain access without the authority of high-ranking duty officers — usually a prefect or an officious *navarch* hoping to climb the ranks in the navy Agrippa was building for Rome.

As it happened, on the day Menas came with four ships, the duty officer was neither, because his superiors had been summoned to the Avernus training lake where manoeuvres were taking place using the new harpax weapon devised by Agrippa's engineers. The man on harbour entrance duty that day was Maximus Lucianus, a centurion of questionable reputation who had served under Menas in Sardinia and came with the traitor when he switched sides from Sextus to Octavian.

Now, when Lucianus ran to the harbour entrance as the flagship came alongside, a dozen armed men behind him, Menas already had braziers alight and smoking, ready to cook a midday meal to serve with lashings of wine after the morning's labours.

Menas's flagship moored first, the other three standing off, each also lighting cooking braziers and breaking out skins of wine as if anticipating off-duty celebrations. Lucianus hailed his former superior.

'*Ave*, Menas,' he called. 'What brings you to Portus Julius?'

'Lucianus? Hail, old friend. Come aboard and we will talk together of old times and great triumphs.'

Lucianus, who was not properly dressed as the port's duty officer should be, hesitated.

'First I must make a record of your numbers and the purpose of your visit.' He hesitated, then added, 'Sir.'

'Then we will come ashore to provide everything you need to reassure your superiors that we come only to lend our might and our skill to Rome's great cause.' Menas grinned as a worried look crossed Lucianus's face. His sailors tossed ropes that would draw his flagship to the quay steps. 'And to show our goodwill, here is a gift for your men.' Menas snapped his fingers and several women, painted and dressed in the unmistakable manner of their trade, filed onto the deck. Lucianus's eyes lit up and his men at arms shuffled forward, necks craned. Menas didn't wait. He took the nearest siren by the hand and helped her to the landing step, then ushered the others to follow. 'Collect the money first,' he called. 'No charge to you, Lucianus, and my men will take care of releasing the chain.'

Poor Lucianus knew he risked his career and his life, but his men made his mind up for him. If he did not choose swiftly, he would have the poorest pick. He chose the woman that giggled the least and smiled with her eyes. Six burly crewmen leapt ashore as the shore guards and their new friends departed in the direction of the harbour barracks, one of them pulling the lynchpin to allow the entrance chain to splash into the murky water and settle in the mud below.

All four ships moved effortlessly into the outer harbour of Portus Julius.

CHAPTER THIRTY-FIVE

Titus Villius Macer watched the scene in the harbour below and knew something was wrong. Warships entering among so many moored vessels with fire braziers alight was forbidden, and downright dangerous. And one of them was hanging back close to the entrance. On its deck archers lined up, facing the dockside where the entrance chain winch was positioned. He heard Agrippa mutter, 'Neptune's scaly testicles, that can't be right.'

But Titus was already on the move, his centurion's instincts kicking in as he barked orders to Octavian's guard with such authority that the twenty men instantly obeyed. 'On me, at the double.' Their officer barely hesitated, recognising the command of a more experienced soldier and urging his men to follow this tough, middle-aged war hero who bore scars that marked him as a man not easily defeated.

Agrippa moved to join the small force, but Octavian pulled him back. 'Leave it to your viper,' he said. 'He knows what he's doing.' He knew better than to risk his best general.

As he ran through scrub that clawed at his ankles and calves, sensing the guards close behind in their full armour, Titus scanned the scene. Three ships were looping in single file to sweep past a row of moored ships; on each more braziers were being lit and archers stood ready with oil-soaked arrows. A fourth ship stood off just inside the harbour entrance, perhaps to ensure the defensive chain was not raised to trap the attackers within the harbour. Six armed men guarded the winch. The harbour officer and his detachment were nowhere to be seen. No one within the harbour lake or working on shore or on the ships seemed to have become alert to the danger.

Titus increased his pace, unencumbered by armour. The guards dropped back, panting now and sweating profusely. Wearing full battle dress and helmets, they carried heavy shields and each bore an iron-tipped spear. They were not equipped for a sprint over rough terrain.

Titus wished Crispus was with him. Together, they had never tasted defeat. Alone, things might be different. He pushed the thought aside.

He came up to the harbour guard's barracks and stopped running near the door when he heard laughter and bawdy singing. He peered in, took in a scene of indiscipline, drew his *gladius* and swept it against a stack of spears, sending them clattering across the floor.

'Who commands here?'

He was met with blank stares, just as Octavian's guards arrived, panting, behind him. One of the errant soldiers pointed to another door at the back.

'Tell your officer we are under attack,' said Titus, his voice menacing. He pointed his *gladius* at the shocked men and their painted women. 'You have much to do if you are not to be crucified to man.'

He turned, looked towards the six men who stood by the winch, then towards the Portus Julius harbour lake. Menas's ships were approaching the helpless hulls of Agrippa's new vessels. Extending from the bows of the rogue ships were long poles, each bearing a flaming brazier. He knew what was coming, wood planking caulked with pitch, decks and rigging scorched dry under relentless Italian sun, all at the mercy of the cruel flames.

Titus did not wait to see the braziers drop, the fire arrows fly and the inevitable inferno that must surely follow. He faced the six men at the winch who now turned towards him, sailors armed with curved falcata swords favoured by pirates, each standing tall and strong. He glanced at the one ship that had remained close to the entrance and took in the line of archers on the deck, bows drawn tight, aimed at him. He knew he would not survive the first volley. A swift hand-signal brought up Octavian's guard, each soldier locking shields with the man next to him, spears brought to bear outwards with a unified grunt, a disciplined performance that would have been impressive in a land battle but was pointless in these circumstances except to show that Rome trained its forces well.

There was only one thing Titus could do if he was to make a difference, and that was to get close to the men at the winch and hope the archers would not risk wounding and maiming their own men. He watched the ship's commander, hoping to use the time between his command to fire and the resulting arrow storm. And he recognised Menas, the traitor, whom he had met in the company of Octavian and Agrippa, and whom he had last seen wounded by an arrow in a sea battle not far from here.

As if slowed by Janus himself, Menas was at this very moment readying the first volley. His sword was arcing upwards and would sweep down with the command to loose. The men beside Titus tensed and crouched. The sword swept down. And Titus ran.

The arrows flew and with a familiar rushing sound fell on Octavian's guard, several clattering on the spot where a moment ago Titus had stood. Two of the harbour guard who were sheepishly leaving the barracks, strapping on cuirass and sword belt, were felled by stray arrows that fell out of the sky. Octavian's guard took the brunt of the volley on their shields, although two fell back, clutching feathered shafts at their necks and shoulders.

But Titus was running clear, straight at the six men. One of them stood closer, while the others fanned behind. This meant two were perilously close to the edge of the harbour wall. He focused on the man in front and commanded his muscles to ignore his fatigue and his lungs to take in air. He didn't have time to hope ageing limbs could still perform the tricks of a youthful centurion and pushed hard off his right foot, his left crunching horizontally into the neck of his target, who had barely had time to raise his sword. This slowed his momentum and at the same time he swept his *gladius* to the right, catching the next man beneath his ear and sending him sprawling to his left in a spray of red mist. He careered into the next man, who lost his balance and fell into the waters below.

But three remained.

Titus heard another volley fly and hoped Octavian's guard would not be pinned down. He needed them. He did not want to die on a harbour wall, miles from home.

He played for time. Facing the three men, just close enough to discourage Menas from shooting at him, he paused for breath. The three men had doubt in their eyes and Titus smiled at them.

'No need to die today,' he said. 'Unless you really want to.' He put as much menace into his voice as he could muster.

It was in this moment that Titus realised that several ships in the harbour were ablaze and there were shouts of alarm from all sides. And there were no more arrows flying. Octavian's guardsmen were jogging up behind him and the three ships that had attacked the fleet were making for the harbour exit.

Menas's ship was easing just ahead of them, the double traitor on the command platform, laughing.

'Jump or die,' Titus said to the three Sardinians.

They jumped.

'Man this winch,' Titus commanded the guard as they arrived. 'Four of you, the strongest, raise the chain fast as you can. The rest of you, arrest those lazy bastards who let Menas into Portus Julius.'

It took Octavian's squad precious minutes to choose the four strongest, some of them arguing, and then more time to work out how the long-levered ratchet winch worked, and who should have the pleasure of arresting the condemned harbour guards, most of whom stood shame-faced while the ships they were supposed to protect burned.

The winch groaned as two ships slid by and headed to the open seas. Menas positioned his ship above the place where the chain would rise, close enough to have a conversation with Titus while the men in the water were heaved aboard.

'Impressive,' smiled Menas. 'Not bad for an old man.'

Titus remained grim-faced and his knee throbbed painfully. 'So you fight again for Sextus?'

'Sextus is the Son of Neptune. I see that now. I fight for those whom the gods favour, and Sextus will always have the advantage over Rome.'

'That's not what you said when we met before, when you pledged your ships and your legions to Octavian.'

'Times change. Sextus has beaten Octavian's pathetic navy twice,' said Menas. 'Why should this time be any different?'

'We shall see. And Sextus is no son of Neptune, unless he wishes to join his fishy god in the depths!'

'And you, Titus Villius, you pretended to be his friend while you entreated with his enemy. I wonder what he will have to say about this?'

Titus felt the bottom fall out of his world. He had given no thought to the peril that he now faced. The moment Menas landed on Sicilia's shore, he would be revealed as a spy for Rome and vengeance would be visited on him and his people.

The chain grated on the keel of Menas's ship. It would rise no further, no matter how hard the men strained at the winch. The third ship sailed effortlessly past, then Menas ordered some of his oarsmen to shove his ship off the chain.

Menas waved his farewell as his ship followed the others into the wide bay of Puteoli. On the hill above the harbour, Octavian, Agrippa and Strabo watched as a pirate had once again got the better of Rome.

Lucianus was crucified right there on the dockside, but not before his back was whipped to a bloody pulp by Agrippa's execution squad. Whimpering and passing in and out of consciousness, he was crudely nailed to a beam and hauled against the wall of the barracks until his feet were off the ground, and a fire was lit beneath him. If he had been able to open his eyes, he would have seen the men of his guard clubbed and beheaded one by one. Agrippa had considered decimation, execution of every tenth man drawn by lots, but as there were just twelve of them, that would have spared all but one. Not enough to appease the anger of Rome.

The women were spared the spectacle. They would be a useful addition in the brothels of the small town that had sprung up around Portus Julius. None dared look back as they were led away to their new employment.

Titus was not interested in the fate of Lucianus or his guard. He stood on the harbour breakwater watching the departing ships, took three deep breaths and forced himself to think. He must return to Pax Villius, his home on Sicilia, by the fastest means possible and organise the evacuation of his family, servants and workers. They had to be hidden from Sextus's wrath before Menas revealed him as a spy. In the distance, out on the serene waters of the Bay of Puteoli, the four ships were putting distance between themselves and Portus Julius lest Agrippa send ships to avenge Rome. They were sailing south-west as all ships had to when leaving the bay, but soon they would either turn north around the island of Ischia and head for Sardinia or sweep due south around Capri, towards Sicilia.

They turned south.

CHAPTER THIRTY-SIX

'You face three choices,' said Agrippa.

He had led Titus to a dockside tavern where he ordered everyone out except the landlord and his staff, demanding food and wine to be placed before them. Agrippa had brought two others: one was Strabo, the wild-haired Greek writer and the other was Philotas, a fellow viper. Titus recognised him as the quiet servant who had tended his injuries after the battle at Philippi and had helped explain the spy codes and the wider purpose of new Rome. That was six years ago, but Titus never forgot a kindness.

'What do you suggest?' he asked.

Strabo fidgeted and Philotas remained still and thoughtful as Agrippa answered.

'You can wait until we have readied a fleet to chase down Menas and sink his ships, but it will take us half a day to provision and prepare,' said Agrippa. 'Maybe more.'

Titus said nothing.

'Or you can ride our best horses to Rhegium, changing mounts at our staging posts, then book passage to cross the straits to Messana.'

'That is most kind,' said Titus. 'But are horses faster than ships?'

Agrippa shrugged. 'Ships depend on the winds, the crew and the gods. If you want my opinion, your best chance is in one of our scout ships — your third choice. You can shadow Menas to see where he goes and then travel onwards to your home.'

'But Menas has been gone, what, two hours already?'

'The ship I have in mind is fast. No creature comforts, sleek and low in the water, and if there is even the smallest breeze she can use that because we have stolen your invention.'

Titus was too worried about his predicament to smile an acknowledgement of yet another example of Agrippa's resourcefulness. 'The underwater wing?' he said. 'That was Eshmun, my father-in-law, may the gods protect him in Elysium.' As a Sicilian, Titus held to trustworthy Greek religion.

'The same. It is a gift on smaller ships. Especially with larger sails.'

'I am glad,' said Titus. 'Everything Eshmun gave us was intended for mankind. But your scout ship, can you spare such a vessel?'

'Of course. So that's settled. I will have her ready within the hour, and you three will go after Menas.'

Titus looked at the others. Strabo, still wearing a cumbersome Greek robe, appeared too clumsy to be a sailor and Philotas perhaps too much a gentleman for such an adventure, yet both seemed eager.

'I know what you are thinking,' said Agrippa. 'These men are not sailors. But when I appointed you a viper, you did not baulk at the challenge placed before you. And both men will be useful to you, though none of you are dressed or equipped for such a mission.'

Titus agreed, knowing the value of leather trousers, a warm bodice and a cloak to wrap close.

'And neither are you armed or provisioned,' added Agrippa, 'so go now to the quartermaster, who has already been briefed and is expecting you.'

The quartermaster was an elderly but very efficient man. He had three neat piles of seafaring clothing ready for collection, as well as money-belts filled with gold and coin. He narrowed his eyes as if reluctant to outfit and provision three strangers, two of whom appeared to be Greek foreigners and the third, Titus, too gnarled and scarred to be of noble stock.

But Agrippa had spared no expense. This mission was important to him — and to Rome.

The small ship promised by Agrippa was moored outside the stricken Portus Julius harbour. She was indeed sleek, with two masts holding furled lateen-rigged sails. She had no fighting platform, just a plain deck with rowing benches to accommodate sixteen rowers. There were no below-decks cabins and no luxuries. Midships was the housing and pulley system for the retractable keel. This was familiar only to Titus, who smiled approvingly.

It was late afternoon, and the day was beginning to cool.

This will be at least two days of gritty open seas hardship, Titus thought, relishing the challenge.

Agrippa was waiting for them on the dockside. He admired the three men in their sailor's clothing, armed only with long knives and each carrying a shoulder-sack with dried provisions and waterskins.

'She is named *Diana*,' Agrippa told them, waving a hand towards the boat, 'a name most apt, as you hunt the enemy by moonlight!'

He hailed a lithe young sailor with bright eyes and a three-day beard, who seemed to carry authority. '*Ave*, Celer. You are ready to sail?'

Celer gave Agrippa a mischievous wink, which in other circumstances would have brought swift punishment. Agrippa chuckled. 'These men are in your care. You have your orders. Look after them well and do whatever they ask of you.

Especially this one.' He slapped Titus on the shoulder. 'He is important to Rome, and it is vital that you deliver him to Sicilia with all speed. Then report back to me. Bring me happy news.'

Celer winked again. It seemed to be a habit. 'You can trust me, sir.' Then, looking at his three charges, he added, 'Climb aboard. Adventure awaits.'

The scout ship *Diana* cut a smooth passage across the Bay of Puteoli and then heeled with the westerly as she chased due south past Capri. The rowers were no longer needed, each withdrawing their oar with knowing looks and gentle words of encouragement to colleagues seated fore and aft.

Celer was in the bow, laughing at *Diana*'s power and the spray lashing over him. Titus, Strabo and Philotas huddled on the deck, seeking protection from the stinging water, none of them fearful of Neptune but all of them grateful that the captain Celer knew what he was doing.

'What do we do when we catch them?' asked Strabo.

'It's more important that we find landfall on Sicilia before Menas,' said Titus.

'And if we don't?' Strabo was already looking slightly green, the sickness coming upon him.

'We will,' Philotas assured him. 'Have you ever experienced a ship with such speed?'

'Gods no,' said Strabo, and threw up.

Philotas ignored Strabo's plight. 'He is with us because he writes about geography and volcanos. I am with you because I know how Octavian has planned this invasion. Which would you prefer to discuss?'

Unwell though he was, Strabo managed, 'Vulcan plays with us in his lairs within Vesuvius, Strongyle and Etna. I go to meet him. He is far more powerful than Rome or Sicilia.' His chin rested on his chest and his eyes closed.

'Liar,' Titus smirked. He knew that Etna was unpredictable, continually rumbling with smoky threats and sometimes fire and ash, but right now his concern was his family. Vulcan could strike his anvil whenever he liked, but it would not deter Titus Villius Macer. Yet he knew that Strabo would not be on this mission unless Agrippa had given him a purpose beyond marvelling at volcanos.

Leaving the writer to sleep, he looked at Philotas. 'Tell me what you know.'

'We know two things,' replied Philotas, holding up one finger. 'One, that Sextus has only a powerful navy to defend Sicilia. His army is nothing. He may call them legions, but they are made up of slaves who have fled Italia and Greek freedmen like myself. No training, no order, and poorly equipped. Not like a true Roman legion, and Rome has many of those, and Africa even more. Land just a few legions on Sicilia and Sextus is finished.'

'This I can confirm,' said Titus. 'The Sicilians are no match for true Roman soldiers.'

Philotas lifted a second finger. 'But what Sextus does have is an awful lot of money. There is no limit to the number of ships he can build or men he can buy. He has hoarded millions of sesterces by stealing grain shipments and controlling the price of the supplies that Rome must buy to feed its people.'

Titus was no economist, but he could see where Philotas was going with this. He had always assumed Sextus just hated new Rome; it had never occurred to him to question just how much money Sextus was making from his piratical endeavours and the vast harvests that Sicilia itself could supply at inflated prices.

'Do you know what the current price is for a modius of grain?'

Titus shrugged. He did not know the answer, nor how many modii Rome needed each year, although he knew the value of an amphora quadrantal of good wine at current prices.

'Let's say the accepted price would be twenty sesterces for a modius,' Philotas continued. 'Sextus charges twice that at least, and he does not pay one sesterce for the grain he offers. Rome cannot get supplies from anywhere else while Sextus controls the seas. And Sextus has stolen millions of modii over the past six or seven years. That means he has taken an inflated price for enormous supply of grain. Octavian and Agrippa believe he has stashed nearly two thousand million sesterces somewhere on Sicilia. That's more than six hundred thousand talents!'

Not a figure Titus could understand. His limit was a centurion's pay and the trade he needed to feed the hungry mouths of his Pax Villius family.

'It would take a mule train a mile long and a fleet of ships to carry that amount of money, and Octavian wants it all. Not to mention Marcus Antonius, and Lepidus. Everyone wants to find the money.'

Titus understood. 'So Strabo is going to Sicilia, where he will pretend to be a writer studying volcanos and geography when in actual fact he is looking for a pirate's treasure hoard?'

'Correct.' Philotas looked Titus in the eye. 'But that is no concern or yours. You are returning for a completely different reason.'

'To save my family,' said Titus.

'Yes. You know that Menas has knowledge of you and can cause you great harm,' said Philotas. 'But you must look further than that. It will be down to you to meet Lepidus and guide him ashore on Sicilia.'

'What? Let me see to my family. Nothing is more important!'

'Of course. You must do this. But you have time. Lepidus will bring his ships to Sicilia in the month of Junius and you must be there to meet him. We have long been in discussion with him, and we know how many ships and how many legions will cross from Africa.'

'Meet him where? And why would he pay any attention to an old centurion like me?'

'Did you not know? You have been promoted to tribune and you have command of all of the landing sites around the south and west coast of Sicilia.'

'Tribune? Me? What use is that when Jupiter knows how many legions will swarm ashore not two months hence?'

'You will give Lepidus this.' Philotas pulled a small scroll from a leather pouch that he had carried in his provisions sack. Titus unfurled it. He read: 'To Lepidus, Triumvir, the bearer is my appointment as tribune and your guide in Sicilia. He is a Sicilian and true Roman warrior. Spare nothing in your care and respect for this man.' It bore Octavian's seal.

'I cannot...'

'Yes, you can.' Philotas looked Titus in the eye. 'You are a senior officer in the army. You will know what to do. And now you have enough gold and coin to buy everything you need — horses, men, provisions, anything your people might need. And I can tell you that Lepidus will land at Lilybaeum because it's closest to Africa.'

Titus said nothing. He trusted to inspiration and courage in everything he encountered, however unexpected.

Philotas leaned closer. 'You will also need to know the new viper codes. We think Sextus and that worm Azhar are aware of our methods and our code is too simple.'

The messages that passed between Agrippa and his viper spies always began with the word *vipera*, but with the letters advanced one or more in the alphabet. This indicated the code used for the message. It had been invented by Julius Caesar back in the days before the civil wars, when a Gallic tribesman would have great difficulty deciphering the messages, even if he knew Latin. It would not be too taxing for a Roman citizen of Sextus's pedigree should one of the messages fall into the enemy's hands.

Philotas explained the new code as the sun sank to the western horizon.

Titus had hoped they would catch Menas's four ships before nightfall, but he was disappointed. Knowing that Menas's vessels would be keeping close to land to seek shelter in a cove overnight, Celer ordered half-sail as darkness fell. They would cautiously hold their southerly course, trusting that a full moon would light their way, the dark mass of Italia to their port side just visible enough for them to steer away from the coast's rocky dangers. A rising swell where currents collided made Strabo's condition worse, but the crew slept in the bilges, hardened sailors all, while Titus went forward to watch through the night with Celer.

'We will see them at first light,' said a confident Celer. 'You should get some sleep.'

But with his family at such risk, Titus could not sleep, even with *Diana*'s soothing motion under shortened sail. The time was put to good use. Celer had often navigated around the Lipara islands, which would be somewhere off their starboard bow by dawn. But he knew little of Sicilia's coast and although he knew where Messana was, he had never been there.

'The currents in the straits between Sicilia and Italia can be treacherous,' said Titus, 'but I know the way and with fair winds we might reach my home before nightfall tomorrow.'

'You are a lucky man,' said Celer, wistfully. 'You have a family and a farm. Me, I just have this. A life at sea. *Diana* is my home and her crew my family. Tell me about yours.'

And Titus did. He spoke about Zerenia and the children, about the generous harvests and the folk who worked the land, his work for Agrippa and the sea battles they had won with the ancient Veneti ships *Boreas* and *Eurus*, which Eshmun had converted into small, fast warships equipped with scorpio weapons. He described the bloodshed on Pax Villius's beach and his wish that war against Sextus would soon be over so they could live a normal life.

They both knew that would not be any day soon.

CHAPTER THIRTY-SEVEN

Celer changed course as dawn threw a misty glow across a sea troubled only by a small breeze from the west. He narrowed his eyes and Titus followed his gaze towards Strongyle, a volcano that aeons ago had formed the northernmost of the Lipara islands. A column of smoke rose vertically from sea-level below the mountain, then spread outward towards them where the wind caught it. Behind the smoke column, the mountain was calm.

'That smoke is not Vulcan's doing,' Celer muttered. 'He vents his fires higher up.'

'Menas?' Titus asked hopefully. Perhaps the pirate had sheltered in Strongyle's lee and taken the opportunity to raid a local settlement. His greed would slow him down.

'Let's have a look.'

Serene in the morning's calm, *Diana* rounded a rocky point into a wide bay. Four ships were anchored in the shallows, stern on to the shore, and beyond them a settlement burned. Celer coaxed the small scout-ship closer and the crew, now all awake, stared in horror at the bodies strewn on the beach. Three more were slumped on torture stakes, no doubt the village leaders who had been forced to reveal where anything of value was hidden before being left to die in agony. Only a few huts remained. A woman crawled out from one of them, keeping low to avoid detection or more likely unable to stand and run. A brutish raider emerged, grabbed her by the hair and pulled her back inside.

A swarthy man, bearded with long, dark hair, staggered from another hut, scratching his crotch. He loosed his *braccae* ties and pissed onto the shingle, and while relieving himself looked up and stared at *Diana* two hundred paces off.

'Get us out of here,' whispered Titus, knowing that a raised voice would carry across the water. 'That's Menas, and there's nothing we can do to help these poor people.'

'No reason for him to suspect we are anything more than a coast-hopper,' Celer replied, hand-signalling a new course. Still at half sail, *Diana* began a lazy arc to point away from the settlement as if to say, *nothing to see here*. The man on the shore shrugged and went back to his stolen quarters. Strabo pulled a scroll from his satchel and began to sketch the mountain, making a soft grunting noise in his excitement, oblivious to the suffering they would leave behind.

No one spoke until they had rounded the next point. Then the crew came alive, sensing the urgency and the lead they had gained at the misfortune of an innocent Strongyle fishing settlement. Under full sail with a fair breeze, they would reach Sicilia's northern shores that day.

But none of the four winds would oblige.

They rowed. There were sixteen oars, shorter and lighter than those of a war galley, and sixteen men whose lusty songs dwindled to painful grunts before a westerly found its breath late in the afternoon. The rowers slumped, grateful to see the twin sails fill. *Diana* surged as if longing to reach Sicilia before the island descended into war once again.

Strabo used the extra space vacated by the oarsmen to finish his drawing. 'Volcanoes warn us when the gods are stirring,' he insisted on telling Titus, who had not slept since leaving Portus Julius and would rather rest. Celer was already asleep in the stern, wrapped in his cloak, trusting the watching crew, so Strabo turned to an equally weary Philotas. The words droned as Titus succumbed to sleep: Vulcan thrashing his anvil and sending fire into the heavens, but only when the gods were about to change everything.

May the Fates keep my family safe from Vulcan and the gods of war. And with that prayer, Titus slept.

Rough hands shook him awake, followed by hastily whispered words.

'You're a merchant, shipwrecked and rescued by us.' It was Celer's voice.

'What...?' As a veteran soldier, Titus came instantly awake and looked around, taking in the faces of a larger ship's crew peering down into *Diana*'s bilges where others stirred. He noted the several crew members straining on ropes that held their scout ship alongside what was clearly a *liburnian* warship. He focused on the blue pennant flapping loosely in the breeze, catching the last of the weak evening sun. It was a Sicilian patrol vessel.

He cast sleep and all thoughts of Rome from his mind, looked around and sensed they were standing off the entrance to Messana port.

So he was a Sicilian merchant and he had been rescued and brought home. The first part was true, the second a spur-of-the-moment cover dreamed up by Celer. Thank the gods. Now was not the time to be found out.

'How do we know you're not Roman spies?' The gruff voice belonged to a red-faced man wearing a blue bandana around his head. He wore no shirt over his bronzed, muscular torso, and he had authority in his eyes. He was clearly the Sicilian *liburnian*'s captain. His vessel was fast, lightly armed and crewed by tough marines.

Titus cursed in Greek. Then, in the local Sicilian dialect, he said, 'Is this any way for a Roman to sneak ashore, wallowing in the bottom of a poxy little ship with these animals for company?'

Celer and his crew looked bemused, and Titus was grateful they couldn't understand, but the Sicilian captain did. He threw his head back and laughed.

'What was your cargo?'

'Have you ever been to The Blue Flag and sampled Niko's Pax Villius vintage?'

'Never. Niko only serves me lizard piss.'

'What is your name?'

'Theron the Hunter.'

'Then put me ashore and I will tell Niko that from now on he is to serve Theron the Hunter only the finest Pax Villius wine. And charge it to my account.'

'I have a mind to do that,' the captain replied, still using Sicilian vernacular, 'but first, what Roman vessels have you seen on your travels?'

'Not one,' Titus lied. 'You sank them all two years ago.'

'Then you had better come ashore.' The captain turned to command his crew, then came back to his ship's rail. 'Did you say "Pax Villius"?' Titus nodded. 'Then that strange ship called *Boreas* is yours too?' Titus nodded again, slowly this time. 'Skippered by a woman?'

'Yes. Why?'

'They are unloading right now, in the port. You might want to divert some of it to me.'

Titus said farewell and expressed his gratitude to Celer and his crew, then the three men clambered aboard the Sicilian warship. Theron the Hunter put Titus, Strabo and Philotas ashore on a quay that was heaving with dockers hauling goods, mostly pirated, to the ramshackle warehouses that crowded the port surrounds. On the way in, they saw *Boreas* moored at a wooden pontoon and Titus whistled to Marina, who was overseeing the unloading of amphorae of wine and oil for Messana's inns and army barracks. She waved back enthusiastically, and teenage Leo at her side thumped his chest and saluted with outstretched arm.

'Meet me at The Blue Flag,' Titus called.

The three men ignored Theron's command to report to the harbour's military office. Titus led Philotas and Strabo straight to The Blue Flag, but a hundred paces off he held back and ushered them into a side street.

'The Flag is being watched,' he said. 'Look there, those men on the corner are not sailors, nor those opposite. They are Sextus's thugs.'

The two pairs of men had given themselves away by not concealing their armour and weapons with the cloaks that were meant to hide their true purpose. They were watching the inn's entrance. Titus knew immediately the island's military were on to Niko and probably the vipers too.

'Act happy,' he said. 'We're glad to be back home and just want to celebrate with a few jugs of ale.' He hummed the first bars of 'The Old Man of Syracuse'. 'Know that one?' Strabo and Philotas shook their heads. 'Just make it up, then. Put your arms around me and make like we're out for a good time.'

Titus sang and the three weary men pretended they were sailors out for a run ashore, arm in arm. They arrived at the inn's door and barged their way in, ignoring the suspicious watchers.

'Niko,' shouted Titus as he entered, 'bring ale for three thirsty travellers!'

The watchers shrugged and turned their attention to an attractive woman escorted by a tall teenager who had, it seemed, also developed a sudden thirst. They were inside the inn before either of the nearest watchers could react.

'Marina!' Titus smiled at the woman and Leo. 'Is all well back home?'

Marina smiled in the affirmative and Leo began an outburst of news, but Titus held up a hand. 'We have precious little time,' he said.

He explained that at any moment Menas and his ships would sail into Messana, and all would be lost because Sextus would know that he, Titus, was spying for Rome, and everyone at Pax Villius would face immediate annihilation.

Niko found them. 'You don't have time for a drink,' the landlord said. 'They are coming for me and from what I've just overheard, they are coming for you also.'

'Thought as much,' said Titus. 'Those thugs outside…'

'They've cracked the code,' Niko said with despair. 'They murdered my courier and went to work on the message he was carrying. Wasn't a difficult code, after all.'

Titus studied his feet. Strabo shuffled, confused. Philotas looked pensive.

'Wait a moment,' Marina said. 'You mean, every message you send now can be read by Sextus?'

Niko nodded.

'Then what *do* you want them to know, as opposed to what you *don't* want them to know?'

Philotas smiled. 'This young lady is way ahead of us all with her scheming. We want to divert Sextus from bringing vengeance upon your home, Titus, and we want him to think Rome is about to invade from across the straits.'

'Where is the main Sicilian fleet right now?' Titus asked Niko.

'Most of the ships are at Syracuse, in the south,' he replied. 'Sextus believes there is a big African grain shipment that will skirt the south of the island to avoid being trapped in the straits, and he wants to intercept the whole lot.'

'Then in theory, it would make sense for me to go there to observe and report back to Rome.' They all agreed with Titus's thinking. 'So if they think I am going there, they might not waste time looking for me at Pax Villius. It could give us time to evacuate.'

While Niko went to find writing materials, Titus and Philotas began to concoct a simple message that would say Titus was on his way to Syracuse because that was where the Sicilians were concentrated, and that Messana on the northern point of the island was the obvious place for the Roman fleet to land troops. He implied that this simply confirmed other messages and was being sent as back-up.

'Then all we have to do is make sure it falls into the hands of those thugs outside,' said Marina.

Niko returned with a stylus, a skin and a leather container. He wrote YLRGTC, the word *vipera* two letters advanced using the alphabet's twenty-three letters. This would provide the code for the rest of the message. Not too difficult, but neither was it the more obvious code of one letter removed. It took precious time to code the message that Titus and Niko concocted:

T. Villius Macer goes to Syracuse to confirm earlier message. Sicilian fleet gathered there. Messana undefended.

'Short and sweet,' said Philotas. 'Should do the trick. Now, how do we deliver it into the wrong hands, so to speak?'

'Leave that to me,' said Niko. 'I will drop it when I run for my life. But you must move fast and get your people to safety. There are horses in the stables, and you have your ship in the port. There are maps in my study showing the best landing sites on the island, north and south. Now go, and may the gods protect you.'

CHAPTER THIRTY-EIGHT

Pax Villius, near Messana, Sicilia

'Who knows the way to Jerax?' asked Titus, barely pausing for breath after leaping from an exhausted steed. He was alone. He had ridden at full gallop, leaving the others far behind. He had no time to greet Zerenia, nor hug his children. He did not salute Crispus or wave at the field workers who gathered to hear news.

'Husband, surely you are aware I know the place?'

Titus gave Zerenia a half-smile. 'Of course, of course, that's good. You will lead with Crispus.'

'I think you need to tell us more,' said Zerenia. 'You have been away too long. You are tired and probably hungry, so come — we have food inside.'

'There's no time for that. You are all in danger and we must leave immediately.'

Crispus stepped forward. 'Now that's most unlike you, Titus. Are we running away for the first time in our lives?'

'Only to protect our people,' Titus replied. 'Menas has turned back to Sextus and at this very moment will be informing him that right under his nose his old friend is actually a spy for Rome. That means we have only a few hours to get everyone to safety, because you can be sure he will want swift revenge.'

'I see your point. So what's the plan?'

Titus pulled a scroll from the horse's saddlebag and placed it on a table in the porch. Marina, Philotas and Leo rode in through the gates, their weary mules hanging their heads low.

'Where's Strabo?' Titus asked.

Philotas looked south where Etna stood proud, crowned with grey clouds that rumbled a complaint. 'Gone to talk to Vulcan. He said he wanted to look for a pirate's treasure and just wandered off. But he knows where we're going and will turn up in his own good time.'

Those that could get near crowded around the map and, with military precision, Titus laid out his plan. He explained he was needed in the south of the island. He did not say why, not yet. He would take their second Veneti ship, *Eurus*, with a small crew to sail past Syracuse down to Lilybaeum. Everyone else must be ready to leave within the hour. He pointed to a mark on the map where a crude X had been scratched. 'This is Jerax,' he said, looking around the small group. 'Zerenia knows the way and Crispus will lead, with the help of Barek and Felix.' His crew of twenty would leave Crispus in charge of around a hundred men, women and children.

'Now, gather your belongings — take only what you need for the journey,' barked Titus, clapping his hands together to instil some urgency in the bewildered community. 'There is no time to lose. Weapons, armour and cooking pots in one cart, provisions in the other. Round up the mules and donkeys, bring the dogs and goats, and find cages for the chickens.'

An old man raised a trembling hand and asked, 'When will we return here?' Pax Villius had been his home for many years; he had watched his children grow up and learn how to coax the finest grapes from the land.

Titus wanted to say it would all be over soon, but he knew how Roman wars dragged on. Against his better judgement, he made a promise he wasn't sure he could keep.

'This is our home and the gods have always smiled upon us. We will all return for the harvest.'

Crispus led the people of Pax Villius to within sight of a crumbling temple on the summit of Jerax mountain that must have predated the founding of Rome itself. He knew little of Sicilia's weaving tracks and rocky paths, but he organised the men, women and children, protected them from bandits and hid them from military patrols that may or may not have been sent by a vengeful Sextus Pompey.

It was Zerenia who provided the direction from her knowledge of the island. Practical as ever, she had organised the hundred or so people of the community and provisioned carts and mules, all the time following Titus's instructions to buy swift horses wherever they found them on the journey and pay well the headmen of the settlements they passed for food and the use of their wells.

Before they left Pax Villius, Titus had placed his hands on Crispus's shoulders and instructed the former gladiator to consult Philotas at every stage because he knew the whole plan. He also made him promise to protect the community with his life.

And so, within hours, Pax Villius was deserted and left to the foxes, rabbits and eagles. The journey took them eight days, never faster than the slowest cart, the one with the weapons concealed by blankets and baggage. Children and the infirm rode atop the carts, competing with caged chickens in their chatter. Any horse or mule that was lamed on the perilous tracks was dispatched, the meat salted for future hardships. Felix and Barek scouted ahead and ran relay to report to Crispus, whose military craft and deep suspicion of mountain tribes served them well throughout the journey. If Sextus and Azhar had concentrated their forces on the northern coast, fearing that was where the main threat of invasion lay, they were unlikely to send patrols into the interior where the Pax

Villius column snaked through hill country. Every settlement they encountered was treated with respect and good humour, sometimes leading to festivities around an olive-wood fire where village elders recounted exaggerated tales of ancient heroes and Barek, who had a remarkably tuneful voice, taught them bawdy drinking songs that brought much merriment.

On the eighth day they approached Jerax. They gazed at the high temple and knew it was too sacred and too exposed to be their home, but Zerenia ushered them onwards because she knew that at its base was a hidden settlement that served the oracle, rumoured to be an old crone with enough magic to transform herself into a beautiful maiden or an angry bear at will. This settlement was also protected by the guardian titan, Crius. That Crius had not been seen in human form for a thousand years was of no consequence; his power pervaded the entrance to the underworld where rites of passage were negotiated for the dead.

The reception was not warm. The travellers came at dusk to a disordered tangle of homesteads beneath two wide cave entrances, dark eyes in the side of the mountain lit by tallow candles. Together, viewed from afar, they had the appearance of a giant titan's war helmet looking south, a rocky escarpment forming a prominent nose. Above this was the helmet's plume, the remains of the old temple.

Around the base of the mountain were numerous stone hovels, housing for peasants and mountain men, all devoted to the oracle and her guardian. They could feel her power, a misty stillness that lay heavily upon the valley, silencing them all as they approached. The chickens were hushed in their cages, the dogs slinking beneath the carts, mules and donkeys reluctant to continue until coaxed forward with soft words. The travellers had all heard stories about the titan who guarded this place, and some, especially the children, expected an angry giant armed with a studded club to come storming out of one of the caves.

But there was no titan, although the village headman gave a good impression. He was tall, bulky and bearded, suspicious of these hundred who came to his territory. Behind him ranged the men of the village, tapping clubs and makeshift spears in their hands. The headman planted his feet apart to make it clear the travellers would not be allowed to pass.

Crispus began to advance towards him, but a soft word from Zerenia stopped him. 'No, Crispus, let me handle this.' She strode towards the big man, which meant hitching her skirts to cross a low wall that marked a boundary.

The man raised an eyebrow. He had been expecting to fight.

'We come in peace,' called Zerenia. Still the man said nothing, so Zerenia walked right up to him. 'We have been forced to flee our home, and war is coming. We have travelled far, we are weary and hungry, and we do not seek trouble.'

The man grunted. At least he understood and must have realised from her speech that she was a true Sicilian.

'And we bear gifts.'

The man shrugged.

'We can tell you what will happen when Rome comes to our shores.'

At last he spoke. 'What do you want of us?'

'To be able to live among you for a little while. We have much to share with you. And we wish to approach the oracle.'

The man turned to the men behind him. Some of them nodded.

'Then you are welcome. But you must build your own shelters, and he must keep apart from us.' He pointed to Crispus, who wore his Greek-style armour and helmet.

'He is a friend,' said Zerenia, 'a good man to have on your side when the enemy comes.'

'Then he must keep away from our people. You —' he pointed to the Pax Villius family arrayed behind Zerenia — 'you are welcome. Bring your gifts.'

CHAPTER THIRTY-NINE

A village near Lilybaeum, southern tip of Sicilia, early summer 36BC

Titus found lodgings for his crew, which included Leo. They had sailed in worsening weather past Syracuse, where no Sicilian warships challenged them. They sought respite each night in deserted bays, dining on bluefish and tunny. They used lures made from cloth or their women's discarded jewellery. Sicilia's lively fish were easily duped.

Their new home was carefully chosen, within sight of both the walls of Lilybaeum and the prime landing places where the cream of Africa's legions would come ashore if all went to plan. *Eurus* was safely berthed in Lilybaeum's harbour, and the port officials were convinced that Titus was a local trader seeking pottery, copper and trinkets imported from Africa. But the crew had not been permitted entry to the city, which was held by one Rufus Plenius with a single legion. A garrulous dockhand had let slip that Plenius was preparing to move his soldiers out, a snippet of news that hinted the disinformation put about by the vipers was paying off. It would make the arrival of Lepidus's legions that much easier; they would have no difficulty overcoming a single legion, and this might mean less bloodshed.

Titus knew the precise date when Lepidus would set sail from Utica and the harbours of Africa, but he had no way of knowing when the flotilla would arrive, especially with the cruel weather that often thrashed the seas across Sicilia's southern shores.

It was Titus's job to co-ordinate with the great triumvir. Lepidus, a man who was rumoured to be bitter at his treatment by Octavian and Antonius, had a vast army at his command, including hordes of feared Numidians. He had harnessed these fiercely proud people and ordered them to join him in his endeavour to grasp more power in Rome. They would be rewarded with much plunder and Titus knew Sicilia's meagre land forces would not be able to stand against the invader, especially when attacked on two fronts.

The crew of *Eurus* took it in turns to watch from hilltops and headlands while those off duty enjoyed the summer warmth and local hospitality. Titus negotiated with a wealthy farmer to buy supplies and hire several of his fleet-footed horses, not just for his watchers to move around but also to provide Leo with a mount to carry a message to Jerax as soon as the ships were sighted. He longed for news of his people and forced himself to trust in the abilities of Zerenia and Crispus, praying to Mercury for their safekeeping.

But he knew that Sicilia, his island of balmy weather and good wine, was about to be torn apart.

Leo saw the sails first.

'There are hundreds of them!' he cried, bursting into Titus's sparse room.

'Then we are about to meet Marcus Aemilius Lepidus, and you are about to ride to Jerax with the news,' said Titus as he grabbed his sword belt. 'How far off are they?'

Leo looked confused. He still wasn't good at counting or estimating distance.

Titus wasted no time. 'Show me.'

Both were wearing simple peasant trousers and summer tunics, easy for running but not appropriate dress for a newly appointed tribune to greet a Roman triumvir. There would be time later to don the basics of a military officer, although Titus would have to rely on the written authority Philotas had given him and persuasive speech to convince Lepidus of his position.

Leo raced ahead through the village towards the nearest hill for a good view, Titus lagging behind as his ageing joints refused to cooperate. As he ran, he heard the first peals of alarm bells sounding in Lilybaeum. The city would soon become rife with speculation and confusion. He reached the top of the hill, where Leo was gazing out to sea.

The ships filled the horizon. All were under sail in the brisk westerly. There were five hundred huge troop transporters, maybe more, aided by triple banks of oars in their lumbering progress, with impertinent war galleys patrolling the flanks. This was a fleet built by enslaving half of the people from Mauretania to Cyrenaica and taxing the other half to feed such a mammoth invasion project.

Lepidus meant business. There were enough troops here not only to wrest Sicilia from Sextus's grasp but also to control the entire island afterwards. Perhaps they could even face off against Octavian himself, should the triumvirs' reputation for disharmony present the opportunity.

'Look there.' Leo, whose eyes were sharper than Titus's, pointed to where three of the smaller warships had detached themselves from the main force.

Titus shaded his eyes. An advance party, probably Lepidus's elite marines, were making for the wide bay near to where they stood, the obvious landing for such a large army and the reason why Titus had chosen this place to watch for the invader. He estimated there was about an hour before the first three ships would nose onto shingle to disgorge the marines and form a bridgehead — on a beach that was completely undefended.

'Find the others,' he told Leo. 'Tell them to dress in their finest and come to the beach armed. Bring two horses, ready to ride, but remain unmounted. I will meet you on the beach.'

Titus always kept his hair respectfully short, not easy when his wife was many miles away, but Leo was handy with a sharp knife. He ran a hand over his face stubble and decided that the visitors would look worse. He stripped and splashed cold water over his head and shoulders, dried himself, pulled on knee-length *braccae* and donned an expensive linen undershirt.

He delved into his trunk and laid out his neck-scarf, leather cuirass, decorative shoulder guards, studded kilt and woollen cloak with the viper *fibula* clasp. When he had dressed, he clipped on his belt and attached his *gladius* and *pugio*. He tried to check his appearance in a bronze mirror but decided his reflection was distasteful; he was incapable of looking like a military tribune, so the authority he carried would have to suffice if questioned. He hoped his years of command as a centurion, etched on his features and confirmed by his posture, would be convincing enough. Although his centurion's helmet nestled in the trunk, he decided not to wear it as he came in peace, and this would be an encumbrance. But he did strap on greaves, because he considered his lower legs ugly. He laced his boots tight.

Leo and the crew of *Eurus* were already on the beach, watching the arriving ships which were now only a short distance from the shore, their sails furled, oars dipping and rising in perfect unison. Leo held the lead ropes of two horses — one would bear him away at Titus's command, and the other would act as a reserve for the long journey. Titus ordered the crew to stand in a line at the top of the shingle and beckoned Leo to bring the horses to the sea's edge.

Following the three ships was a larger quinquereme — probably Lepidus's flagship, Titus guessed — making slower progress under oars, as if hanging back until it was known who if anyone opposed them. Beyond this, the vast fleet grew larger, ready to land at the given signal to disgorge its thousands.

The lead ships approached at speed, lightly armed marines poised in their bows which bucked and plunged in the swell, scattering white spray. They surged onto the shingle together, their keels ploughing deep furrows, metal-tipped beaks leading the way. The first men leapt ashore just a few feet from where Titus and Leo stood, unflinching. The horses shied at the sight, but Leo calmed them.

The marines ignored them. They streamed from the ships and fanned out in a wide semi-circle where they stood, short spears pointing inland, watching for an enemy that wasn't there. They also ignored *Eurus*'s crew, who shuffled and fidgeted, trying not to look threatening. Titus noted their dark skin and lithe movements, their black-plumed leather helmets and unusual oval shields — these must be Lepidus's elite Numidians.

An officer watched his men from the central ship's command platform, his armour and burnished helmet setting him apart as the fleet prefect or a general. He was a head taller than the ship's captain and attendant soldiers, each silently awaiting orders. He scanned the shore, amused eyes alighting on Titus for the briefest moment, then spoke to the man next him, who snapped a command to the signalman amidships. Two brightly coloured flags were hoisted, a prearranged signal that meant nothing to Titus.

Almost immediately, the quinquereme increased speed.

The officer left his command platform and made his way past seated crew to the bows. He leapt down to the shingle right in front of Titus, who saluted. The officer did not return the gesture, just scowled beneath the helmet's cheek flaps.

'And you are…?'

'Titus Villius Macer, shore tribune appointed by Octavianus Divi Filius and posted by Marcus Vipsanius Agrippa to meet you here.'

The officer snorted and looked casually around, then watched the larger ship's approach.

Titus was offended. 'And you are…?' he asked.

The officer turned and looked into Titus's eyes. They were the same height.

'Nerius Panthera, commander of my Numidians. Don't get in their way.'

'They would do well not to get in my way,' retorted Titus, but Panthera had already turned away to whistle to his warriors. A series of hand signals told them to move inland, then a barked order to the remaining crew and troops in the three ships brought them pouring onto the shore. They formed up in six ranks, facing the ocean.

Titus made a mental note to teach this cocky commander some manners. He was a few years younger than Titus. His olive skin and strange language — though he had a Latin name — set him apart as some kind of adventurer made good on the edge of the Roman world.

Then Lepidus came to Sicilia.

The quinquereme was indeed the fleet's flagship. It was much larger than the three ships that had already landed, with a pompous command deck garishly decorated in red and gold, a vast canopy providing shade for the man who had come to conquer where Octavian had repeatedly failed. Marcus Aemilius Lepidus was seated on a curule chair, his well-groomed grey hair more suited to a toga than the fine gold-inlaid armour he wore. This man had sailed across miles of sea amid storms and looked as though he was arriving for a ceremonial parade. Around him stood true Roman legionaries, as befitting a triumvir, and the deck above the rowers' platforms was lined with archers. Titus could tell all of these men were disciplined elite marines, because not one of them lost balance as the great ship turned parallel to the shore, side-on to the swell, to lay off just ten paces from dry land.

Oars were shipped and a dozen bare-chested men leapt into the sea, somehow maintaining position despite the water reaching up to their chests. A lavish palanquin with an embroidered cover was passed over the ship's side. *This could be interesting*, thought Titus. *A wealthy Roman who doesn't want to get wet.* The men in the water tried to hold the litter steady.

Lepidus moved slowly and regally to the ship's side railings, where a section was removed. Servants risked their lives by reaching out to hold the great man's hands as he stepped gingerly onto the litter and took his place on the seat. He managed to look like a conquering monarch as he was brought to the shore. A squad of guards waded ashore beside him.

Titus studied his face and saw cruelty there. Patrician, consul, triumvir and *pontifex maximus* — here was a man past his prime but clinging to power as if by divine right. And now, frustrated at his treatment by Octavian and Marcus Antonius, he was bringing the might of massed legions and the wealth of Africa Nova to conquer a rebellious island.

Titus turned to Leo. 'Hold the horses here, listen carefully to what is said between us, and be ready to ride to Jerax.' He walked right up to the still seated Lepidus, who turned and glared scornfully.

Panthera probably saved his life by standing with him.

'What's this?' Lepidus asked Panthera.

'Sir, he is a tribune sent by Octavian to welcome you. His name is Villius.'

'Very well, Villius, report.'

'Over there —' Titus pointed towards Lilybaeum — 'is the nearest city, which is held by Rufus Plenius and one legion.'

Lepidus threw his head back and laughed. 'I came here with twelve legions to fight, and what do I find? One paltry legion! What about the rest of the island?'

'I wouldn't be surprised if Plenius isn't evacuating as we speak. He will have seen your ships approaching. And Sextus is gathering his forces and ships around Messana on the other side of —'

'I know where Messana is, you idiot.'

Now Titus knew exactly what sort of man he was dealing with. He indicated Leo and the horses.

'We have arranged to send messages to Agrippa and Octavian about your intentions, sir.'

'A child? You entrust my words to a child?'

Titus sensed Leo bridle. He was taller than this jumped-up nobleman and no doubt a better rider and a better swordsman. But Leo calmed when Titus laid a hand on his shoulder.

'You can leave that to us, sir. Your intentions?'

Lepidus heaved himself to his feet. He was running to fat with too much good living in Africa. He looked around and saw no resistance. 'My men will build our first camp on firm ground right here. This is now my island. We will crush all resistance in Lilybaeum and sack the city. Then we will do the same in every village and town around here. Then we will advance across my island and the day will soon come when we will crush Sextus Pompeius. After that, we will show Octavian who is the true master and how a rebellious land should be brought to book.'

Titus shuddered. These words did not bode well for Sicilia. He turned to Leo. 'Ride to Jerax and tell them what you have heard. Leave nothing out.'

CHAPTER FORTY

Lepidus didn't wait for all of his legions to come ashore. Hoping to catch Plenius before he fled, he sent the first two disembarked legions to the city with orders to show no mercy. But Plenius had deserted Lilybaeum, and the few remaining soldiers were butchered as the invaders went door to door slaughtering the men, raping their women and taking anything of value that they could carry. Two large pens were built just outside the city. One held children and young people who were now slaves and would serve at the whim of the African legions, and if they did not, they would be summarily executed. The other held animals rounded up from the surrounding farms — mules, oxen, cows, sheep, goats and chickens, each either a pack-animal or food for a hungry army. Dogs were instantly silenced. Cats hid in dark corners. The screaming gradually turned to weeping and despair before a deathly silence hung in the thick smoke that heightened the smell of blood and voided bowels.

Titus did not witness the horror, although he knew what was happening. He stayed close to Lepidus as an adviser should, answering questions from the triumvir and his officers in a command tent that had been erected at the centre of a vast military camp. Twelve legates crowded around Lepidus and Titus to study a large map; twelve legates, Titus realised, and therefore twelve legions. His suggestion that Lepidus march his legions into the rising sun to join Octavian's forces on the other side of Sicilia was met with a stony silence. Instead, Lepidus pointed to the ancient settlements on the southern coast. 'Destroy them,' he said, and called for more wine.

Then he summoned Panthera.

Titus could smell ambition as the Numidian commander stood between him and Lepidus, tense as a readied *ballista* yet cocksure and disdainful of those around him. A man not to be trifled with. He ignored Titus, turning his back on him as he smiled at Lepidus, his eyes cold.

Lepidus placed his finger on Lilybaeum. 'Within the week, my legions will hold all of this —' his finger swept south to coastal towns and fishing villages — 'and this.' His upturned hand indicated the coast to the north as far as Panormus.

Panthera said nothing.

'All of these places interest me,' Lepidus said. 'Do you know why, Panthera?'

'Because there are slaves to be taken and perhaps much plunder.'

Lepidus nodded slowly. 'But I want more than slaves and a few trinkets, don't I, Panthera?'

Titus could not see the Numidian commander's face, but he sensed the smirk.

'Indeed, sir. And if you allow me, I would like to introduce you to someone who might be able to help us find what you are looking for.'

'I hoped you would say that,' said Lepidus. 'What have you got for me?'

Panthera turned and beckoned to a Numidian soldier who stood near the command tent's entrance. 'Bring him.'

Twelve legates, the triumvir Lepidus, their attendants, and Titus all turned to see who this person might be. The soldier ducked out of the tent, and moments later returned with three men. Two were his fellow Numidians, fully armed, looking mean. Between them was a tall man dressed in casual riding gear, leather *braccae* and a woollen jacket, unarmed but clearly a well-muscled fighter. He was a Sicilian who showed no signs of having been mistreated.

But the striking thing about this new arrival was his face. Most of it was livid with burn scars from neck to scalp, his mouth a twisted grimace, his once golden hair now barely a few tufts. It was a face Titus knew well. T
oo well.

Azhar the Cruel, commander of Sicilia's forces, stood before them — a man who would stop at nothing to gain power and wealth; a sell-sword who had a strange ability to convince anyone he would support them, be it Sextus, Octavian or Lepidus.

Azhar approached and stared at Titus with unmistakable triumph. Here was a man who had finally found in Panthera and Lepidus likeminded ambition that would harness Hades himself in a quest for glory.

Titus stood expressionless and returned a cold stare that must have cooled the scars on Azhar's face.

Lepidus recoiled, but Panthera's smooth tones reassured him. 'This is Sextus Pompeius's right-hand man,' he said, holding up a hand to halt Azhar's advance. 'I believe he has information that you will appreciate. Noble Azhar, meet the triumvir Marcus Aemilius Lepidus.'

Lepidus gathered himself, knowing that this turn of events could speed his conquest of Sicilia. 'And what do you bring me, ah, Azhar the Ugly?'

Azhar did not rise to the insult. 'Riches,' he said. 'Untold riches.' He gave Titus a sideways glance with a hint of unease. That told Titus that Azhar the Cruel had not expected to meet his adversary in the invader's command tent at Lilybaeum.

'Go on,' said Lepidus.

'If you will allow me to explain a few things while looking at your map?'

Lepidus and Panthera gave him room to approach. Titus put his hand on the *gladius* at his side, a movement that Panthera noticed. A slight shake of the head indicated there was no need to worry — Azhar was not here to assassinate Lepidus. But as he moved towards the table with its map spread before them, Azhar found a moment to pass close to Titus and whisper, 'It's not over between us.'

Titus remained stony-faced.

'There are several places on this island that will interest you, noble triumvir,' said Azhar. 'Allow me.'

He pointed to Syracuse, then Messana, then Panormus. 'These are the obvious places,' he said, 'and I will show you precisely where to find what you seek.'

'Which is what?' asked Lepidus, though the gleam in his eye said he knew full well what was coming.

'Coin enough to pay your legions ten times over.'

'And you? What do you expect to gain from this?'

'I am not greedy,' Azhar replied, and Titus resisted the urge to laugh. 'A tenth should do it.'

Lepidus gave him a look that could be construed as agreement, but Titus suspected it meant Azhar would die before he received one sesterce.

'Show me.'

Azhar leaned over the map and pointed.

Titus craned around Panthera to see where Azhar pointed. The finger on the map showed a place he knew to be perilously close to Jerax, where his family and people were hiding out.

'Where is this?' asked Lepidus, the look on his face barely concealing the greed that drove him.

'There are caves here where no person in their right mind would dare to look because they are protected by unseen forces. Pain and anguish await anyone who enters; only two people know the rites of passage.'

'The perfect place to hide a whole heap of treasure?'

'Precisely.'

Titus's heart sank. He had a feeling he knew what was coming.

'And where is this place?'

Azhar allowed a pregnant pause. All twelve legates pressed in. Panthera allowed himself a quiet chuckle. Lepidus stared at Azhar.

'Jerax.'

For a second time, Titus felt the bottom fall out of his world.

Lepidus sent legions north and south along the coast to sack and plunder every town and settlement, then sat back in his palatial command tent to await news of the fall of Drepanum, Mazara and Panormus. The prettiest boys were liberated from the slave pens, washed, groomed and dressed in colourful silk, and paraded before him. He drank copious amounts of wine and had the cooks whipped when the dishes placed before him were not to his liking; the legions had laid bare the surrounding countryside and denuded forests so that local food was scarce. Many of the supply ships from Utica had been destroyed in storms or taken by pirates. Lepidus seethed, his anger growing like the fury of Etna.

Titus quickly learned to distance himself from the enraged and spiteful triumvir, choosing instead to spend more time with the crew of *Eurus*, watching for the return of Leo with news from Jerax and the expected invasion from the north. Not even summer days could lift the pall of gloom that hung over Lilybaeum and the Roman camp like a vast, suffocating cloak. No birds sang, soldiers grumbled and hungry camp dogs skulked with their tails between their legs. Titus knew the smell of mutiny.

His fear overwhelmed him when he learned that Lepidus had sent Panthera and Azhar with a small party of Numidians to scout the route to Jerax and discover if there was indeed a vast fortune waiting to be collected in the caves of the vultures. He sought audience with Lepidus and pleaded with the triumvir to allow him to travel to Jerax to protect his family and people. He explained how they sought refuge there and that Azhar was not to be trusted. Surely he could be allowed to lead his people to safety.

Lepidus merely scowled. 'I don't give a damn about any Sicilians,' he said. 'And you, Titus Villius Macer, have given me nothing. I do not need a guide and I do not need your advice. Get out of my sight.'

Titus needed no second invitation.

He left Lepidus for what he hoped would be the last time, and once out of the command tent, ran to his lodgings to arm himself and prepare to ride to Jerax.

When he got there, he found Leo bleeding on the floor.

CHAPTER FORTY-ONE

Jerax, Central Sicilia

Zerenia stoked the fire above which a blackened pot hung from a tripod of spears lashed together. Marina and Crispus squatted at her side.

'Leo must have returned to Titus by now,' said the navigator. 'I hope he is safe.'

Crispus put a reassuring arm around Marina. 'Of course he is safe. He has a way about him, melting into shadows and keeping out of trouble. He'll make an excellent spy.'

Zerenia said nothing. She worried for Leo, and she wondered how long her husband would remain with this monster Lepidus. She also worried for her people, who had their own camp apart from the Jerax settlement. They were kept separate by the suspicious headman and refused admission to the oracle in the caves.

The evening chill penetrated their woollen cloaks. Around them the camp murmured as little ones were put to rest beneath carts and makeshift tents, and adults gathered around crackling fires. Beyond, the two caves glowed with candlelight, neither menacing nor welcoming.

Strabo the Greek had arrived at their camp in time to add valuable intelligence for Leo to take back to Titus at Lilybaeum, and for Philotas to take to Agrippa. What he knew was vague, but Agrippa was landing his legions at Mylae after surging through Sextus's desperate shipping defences and now he was gaining a foothold in the north of Sicilia, close enough to Messana to take the city and its vital strategic port. That was the good news.

The bad news was that he believed a small force of Sicilians was heading their way. Rumour had it, said Strabo, that a vast store of Sicilia's own coin, some of it struck by Sextus and more by the defeated Murcus of Syracuse, was hidden in this very region. Chances were, he said, that Sextus needed money to pay his crews and his armies. If that hoard was here at Jerax, the people of Pax Villius were in a very bad place indeed. Instead of finding safety, they might be right at the centre of the very thing that every dictator, commander and general needed above all else — money.

That was the news Philotas carried east to Agrippa, but both Zerenia and Crispus knew they were on their own. They would just have to do their best to survive.

'We should consult the oracle.' Zerenia spoke to the flames. 'Perhaps she will show us what to do now.'

Marina stirred the pot. 'Oracles are never clear; they speak in riddles.' She had always preferred to seek inspiration from gazing at the stars. 'Let me approach the headman,' she said. She was as much a child of Sicilia as Zerenia, and probably one with more awareness of magic, the titans and the gods who protected this mysterious community.

'We'll go together,' replied Zerenia. She felt the need to lead, but not alone. Deep down, she was fearful of these people who did not take kindly to intruders. 'Perhaps we should take a token?'

'Like what? Pax Villius wine or a pair of fowl plucked and ready for the spit?'

'Perhaps a child, to speak for us…?'

'They'll likely as not sacrifice it to Crius!'

'Money?'

'We could try. Works for most people.'

At last Crispus spoke. 'These people don't care for treasure, and the oracle is an old crone, blind and infirm. What use would she have for money, especially if it is true that her caves conceal an emperor's ransom?'

'I take your point, Crispus, but however we do it, we must seek the oracle,' said Zerenia.

With nothing more to offer than the wealth they carried with them, Zerenia donated jewellery she had acquired in Messana's markets and Marina her best necklace. They placed their gifts in a string bag and, with barely a word between them, set off to see the headman.

It was not an easy meeting. After much questioning and gesturing, he reluctantly gave his name as Drago then told them to make themselves scarce. But a girl, perhaps Drago's daughter, begged them to stay. 'I am your friend,' she told them. Drago snorted and resumed his evening meal, which consisted mainly of a fire-blackened leg of pork.

'What is your name?' Marina asked the girl.

Her reply was incomprehensible, but they settled on 'Li', which was the first part of her long explanation.

'Li, we want to see the oracle,' said Zerenia. 'Can you take us to her?'

Li nodded. 'Now?' she asked. Her wide eyes, framed by radiant dark curls, seemed to combine innocence and confidence.

'Yes, now.'

Li did not seem to feel the heaviness in the earth, the oppressive weight of the mist that swirled around their feet. She skipped, turning every so often to laugh, 'Come on! This way!' Every step that Zerenia and Marina took seemed to be weighed down more, as if unseen hands reached for their ankles to drag them back.

But the child's unencumbered dance to the caves, or more specifically the left-hand cave, gave them hope. Its entrance was wide and dark, the glare of candlelight obscuring the interior. Li did not hesitate and ran straight in. Both Zerenia and Marina collapsed to their knees at the entrance, their bones heavy. When they looked up, there was no sign of Li.

As their eyes adjusted to the gloom they saw the spirit gods that lined a pathway to the interior, like familiar household gods but far more ancient. A vulture stood among the statues, glaring at them.

'Can you hear music, or is it just me?' Zerenia asked, her voice dulled in the presence of Hades.

'If it is music, I don't like it,' Marina replied, breathless.

It might have been a single note or even a chord, but it did not vary. It emanated from rock formations laid down when the gods were young.

The candles danced in unison, indicating movement within. The child appeared before them, now grave and stilled, and beckoned to them.

They entered.

The oracle was not a blind crone. The only part that Crispus had got right in his description was that the oracle was a woman. Zerenia was convinced she had seen this woman in the settlement, carrying a basket of bread on her head.

Now her dress was different. Her furs reached the floor, settling around the large rock on which she sat. Her aquiline nose gave her the appearance of a vulture, her eyes distant as though she slept with them open. Her hair was concealed by a fur-lined hood, and her hands were hidden by a sleeping animal that might have been a cat or a small dog. The girl Li took up a position beside her and watched the visitors with no hint of a smile. *An oracle in waiting*, thought Zerenia as she edged forward, signalling to Marina to hang back.

Not a flicker of response crossed the oracle's face, nor Li's.

Zerenia bowed low, then knelt, almost but not quite prostrated. Her neck ached as she kept eyes on the oracle. Still no response. The silence became overpowering and Zerenia wondered if she should speak first.

But it was Li's small voice that broke the constraint. 'Who attends the oracle?'

'I am Zerenia, the wife of Titus Villius Macer and leader of his people called Pax Villius who seek refuge here,' Zerenia answered solemnly.

'You are welcome because you come in peace,' said Li, 'and what do you seek from the oracle?'

'I wish to know if my husband is safe, and if his people are safe in your village.'

'They are as safe as they have ever been,' said Li, solemnly.

'And my husband?'

'You will see him sooner than you expect, and you can judge for yourself.'

Zerenia became impatient and began to ask why Li did not let the oracle speak. The woman remained impassive, unmoving. But Li held up a hand and continued.

'Bloodshed is coming and there is nothing you can do to avoid this, but your enemy will be your protector.'

Zerenia sat up straight, confusion and surprise crossing her face. She needed time to think this through. Should they stay here? Where else could they go? Why would soldiers come here when the war was at sea and on the coast?

Her father, Eshmun, had once told her that when life became confusing, it was best to think of something completely unrelated. In the same way, when someone was not making sense, it was best to change the subject and see what happened.

'Where is the titan Crius?'

Li did not change her icy expression. 'He is here and will kill the true enemy of Sicilia.' She turned and walked towards the rear of the cave. The woman did not move. She didn't even blink.

CHAPTER FORTY-TWO

Lilybaeum

The arrow had struck Leo in the small of his back, just above the hip. Snapping the shaft must have caused great pain, but Leo had managed it one-handed and somehow continued his journey back to Lilybaeum, despite the loss of blood.

Now he lay bleeding on Titus's floor.

With two strides the centurion, now tribune, knelt beside the boy, who immediately began a semi-delirious report, babbling about danger, treasure and Numidians.

'Shh.' Titus quietened him and turned him onto his side. He ripped Leo's shirt to expose the broken shaft and tutted when he could not see the arrowhead. He told Leo to stay still while he soaked a clean cloth in the freshwater bucket and wiped away crusted blood to reveal an inflamed entry wound. He had years of experience of war and knew this would fester unless he removed the arrow.

Leo began talking again. This time Titus encouraged him. He had seen veterans talk of their mothers, wives, children and campaigns while a knife dug deep into flesh, preferring meaningless chatter to screaming in agony. He himself preferred to bite on a wooden spoon, but he knew Leo looked up to him and would prove himself a man.

'Ships, hundreds of them … landing at … forget the name…' Leo was saying as Titus calmly gathered more cloths and the only flask of wine in the room, a mulsum mixed with honey, which he thought resembled that used by the Fifth Alaudae's surgeons. 'Many ships destroyed … attacking

Messana…' Titus lit a candle, tested his knife with his thumb, then held the blade in the flame. He put a piece of cloth in Leo's hand in case he preferred to bite rather than talk and knelt beside him. 'All safe at Jerax… Enemy may come…' Leo continued to talk to a table leg and barely hesitated when the knife began its work.

The arrowhead was deep enough to require considerable cutting of flesh, but Titus was as sure as he could be that no vital organ had been pierced. 'Men travelling north … Numidians … Azhar…' Titus pulled the arrowhead free with a ghastly sucking sound just as Leo mentioned the name of Azhar and the boy passed out. He had seen surgeons cauterise a wound such as this with a knife hot enough to cause flesh to sizzle and steam, but he had no blazing fire. He held the knife in the candle flame long enough for it be hot, but the effect when he pressed it to the wound was not as impressive as that achieved by the Fifth's surgeons. He soaked a cloth with mulsum and pressed it to the wound, pinching the flesh together, then reached for the larger cloth and bound the limp body securely.

Then he sighed, sat back and drank the rest of the wine.

Leo's return delayed Titus in his urge to ride east to Jerax. He needed to know what the boy had discovered. That cost him two days, because Leo was first delirious and then confused, but he had the strength of youth and showed signs of recovering well. Titus could find no medic or nurse to assist him, as Lepidus had murdered or taken into slavery all those who might have potential, and he refused to ask the invading legions for help. He had been exiled from this part of the invasion.

While Leo recovered, his gibberish making increasing sense, Titus ordered his crew to prepare *Eurus* for passage back to Pax Villius, which must surely be safe now that Sextus was focused on more pressing matters. 'Drive out any unwanted visitors and secure it for our return,' he told them. 'If you are challenged by Lepidus's officers in the harbour, act dumb — you are simply traders seeking a more peaceful port. And take Leo with you.'

Leo was sufficiently aware to object. 'You do not know the way to Jerax,' he said. 'I know all the shortcuts and the best taverns to rest and change horses.'

'But you are wounded, and cannot ride for at least ten more days,' said Titus, dismissively turning to his men to give further instructions.

'Pax Villius is my family too,' Leo said to Titus's back. 'If you do not take me, I will hide myself until I can steal a horse and follow you.'

'You will do no such thing,' Titus said without turning.

'Watch me.'

Titus knew he had lost the argument. He himself had fought many a battle while dripping blood into his boots and knew well the drive that kept a man going when in truth he should be dead in a ditch.

'We'll see,' he said with a half-smile.

Titus found enough food and wine in a deserted inn that had been overlooked by Lepidus's men and spent another day questioning Leo while he regained his strength. He heard all about the settlement at Jerax and the distrust shown by the headman. Above all, he was relieved to learn that his people were well fed and happy in their seclusion. But what worried him was the news that Jerax may be where Sextus had hidden some of his hoard — just as Azhar had said.

Then Leo told him about a chance encounter with the Numidian forces heading in that direction. 'There were no more than fifty of them, led by that unpleasant Panthera fellow and another man who I have seen before.'

'Tall, arrogant and a face like a smashed crab?'

'Yes. The man you call Azhar the Cruel.'

'So the chances are that our worst enemies could be closing in on Jerax from two sides,' Titus said with dread.

'And that's why I am coming with you. My part in this isn't over. They saw me and hunted me down. I almost got away but those Numidians are relentless, and my horse was tiring. They thought I was dead, but I swore to myself that I would have my revenge. Somehow my mare knew the way home — I owe her as much as I owe you. You must take me with you.'

Titus had seen this so many times — how the desire for honour and revenge could hold a man upright until his mission had been accomplished.

'You are a fool, Leo. But you are a son to me, and I will allow this — against my better judgement.'

It was impossible to hide horses from an invading force determined to have every living creature for miles around for food, or for its cavalry. Titus was not surprised to find the last horses had gone from their rented stable. So he decided to steal some from the legion.

Wearing his dress armour, he went to find a decurion in the paddocks that housed Lepidus's reserve cavalry, ready to bark orders in the hope that no officers knew that he had been dismissed from his duties. In the event, he did not need to bluff. He could hear the decurion and his fellow officers celebrating their good fortune with bawdy songs in their command hall. A dozen horses were tethered nearby. The vast tented barracks was being turned into a more solid construction with much chopping and hammering, enough of a distraction to elicit several salutes as the tribune passed by.

He took three horses, the ones that showed most energy, and was not challenged by anyone.

The unobservant officers raised their voices in the rousing climax to 'The Fair Maiden of Carthage' as Titus led a stallion and two mares away.

Back at his lodgings, Titus roused Leo, who seemed determined to impress with his mobility and swiftly recovered strength as they packed weapons, armour and supplies, saddled two of the horses and roped the armour and their belongings to the third.

They departed at dawn, just four days after Leo had stumbled onto Titus's floor.

'For Pax Villius,' muttered Titus as he leapt onto the stallion.

CHAPTER FORTY-THREE

The farms and forests inland from Lilybaeum had been ruined by the invaders. No birds sang and there were no wild forest sounds because there was no forest — just splintered tree stumps and churned ground where the boots and axes of Africa Nova had ruined nature's beauty and destroyed the livelihood of every farmer for miles.

Titus and Leo rode through the devastation in silence, their mounts hanging their heads low. Where they could, they chose a path away from groups of engineers and their slaves, but there were times when Titus relied on his rich tribune's cloak and gleaming *fibula* badge of office to avoid questions from lowly soldiers. He was an officer and Leo his servant. If challenged, their story was that they had been sent by Lepidus himself into the interior to support the Numidian task force that had gone before.

The day began to threaten intense heat, so they made for the nearest forest that had not yet been assaulted, seeking the shade of beech, chestnut and oak and the companionship of fleeing foxes and boars. A roebuck peered from the edge of the woods then fled in alarm. They followed a track through the forest that bore evidence of riders having passed not many days before. It was easy to follow the Numidians' trail, so they picked up the pace, Leo leading, the pair riding in silence for hours before Titus called a halt beside a stream that flowed out of the mountains where the ancient Sicani lived.

They dismounted to fill waterskins and let the horses drink and forage for sweet herbs.

'You have been here before?' Titus asked his young companion.

Leo nodded. 'Drank from this very stream.' He looked pale and his hand was shaking as he held the waterskin in the stream.

'Let me look at your wound.'

When the bandage had been unwound, Titus frowned. The wound was healing under a dark scab, but the flesh around it was inflamed. He told Leo to undress and lie face up in the brook. The flow of cool water would do its work and take heat from the wound.

'You said you knew every village and tavern between here and Jerax?'

Leo nodded. He was beginning to shiver.

'So where are they?' asked Titus.

Leo raised a hand and pointed east along the track. 'Not far that way. Maybe an hour's ride.'

Titus looked up to where the dappled sunlight pierced the canopy of trees. Midday. A rest would be good, then they'd push on with the last of the day.

'When your toes turn blue, we'll go there,' he said.

The tavern was at the centre of a small village that smelled of death. No one had been left alive. A solitary chicken meandered on the dirt track, lost and bewildered. Bloated bodies of men, women and children told their own story of hate and mindless cruelty. Vultures scattered as Titus and Leo rode into the clearing, silent in their dismay, dismounting to check for any signs of life. There was none. The innkeeper lay doubled over a fallen tree, a black-feathered shaft in his neck.

They knew this was the work of Panthera's Numidians.

Wrapping scarves around their noses and mouths to block out the stench, they entered the tavern where more bodies lay. These were simple people who lived off the land and probably traded among themselves with foraged food. They had no money and nothing of value. Their end was pure savagery.

Leo threw up beside the mutilated body of a young girl.

'I knew her,' he said through his tears, kneeling beside the body. 'Her name was Kerith. She was my friend.'

'There's nothing for us here,' said Titus.

His eyes were cold steel. They were a day's ride, maybe more, from Jerax. He feared for his people if Panthera could reach them first, and there was no reason why not. Would Crispus be ready for them? He knew that Marina, Barek and Felix would not take a step back and were as skilled as any Numidian swordsman, and the men of Pax Villius were well drilled with shield and spear, but would the people of Jerax also be capable of defending themselves?

'Come, Leo.' Titus took Leo's arm and lifted him gently to his feet. 'We must make haste.'

They rode until they could barely see the track ahead. They made no fire in their makeshift camp, so they dined on the dried meat and crusts of bread they had brought for emergencies, listening to the sounds of a hunting owl and the distant howling of wolves.

Leo slept on the hard ground, wrapped in his cloak. The horses, divested of their loads, stood forlorn, tethered to a tree. Titus sat and gazed at the stars. He wished he knew more about them, so he could divine what the gods had in store for his people. He knew they were speaking when he saw three stars fall to earth in rapid succession, then a wild display of smaller splashes of light. It could mean Pax Villius would fall, or that the Numidians would be defeated — or it could mean nothing at all. He turned his gaze to where he knew Etna rose proud above Sicilia, looking for the glow of Vulcan's fury, but there was nothing. He dozed upright, his hand clasping his sword, until the first birdsong told him dawn approached.

He nudged Leo awake. They readied the horses, and Leo led them towards Jerax even before first light touched the slopes of Etna.

The sun was high when their weary horses climbed a hillock, and at the top Leo pointed to a distant hill crowned with the ruins of an ancient temple.

'Jerax.'

Titus nodded grimly and they asked for one last effort from their mounts, riding side by side across rough terrain until Leo suddenly halted.

'What is it?' asked Titus.

'Listen — hear that?' Leo whispered.

Titus strained and, yes, he could hear it. The unmistakable sound of battle. Shouting, the clash of steel, the cries of pain and anguish.

They were too late.

Titus kicked his mount to a canter and the mare reluctantly found reserves of energy, Leo following. There was no time to don the armour carried by the spare horse.

If they could have heard anything over the noise made by three horses cantering over hard ground, they would have sensed the din of warfare diminishing. But they only knew that whatever fight had been taking place was over when they saw a handful of horses and then soldiers running towards them. Titus tried to make sense of their attire and appearance, but they were covered in grime, sweat and blood. He called out to one man but was ignored. He was grateful that he didn't know him.

He slowed and watched.

The retreating animals and men had kicked up a dust storm, which made it hard to make sense of the chaos, but none of the retreating men seemed interested in two riders approaching the battlefield. They just stumbled past.

Titus and Leo pressed on. Then they saw the bodies.

CHAPTER FORTY-FOUR

Dust and pollen swirled like gritty fog in the gentle breeze. Shadowy shapes moved among the prone bodies, seeking their own or perhaps dispatching enemy survivors.

Titus and Leo approached, their horses starting and snorting in the dust. The confusion, smell and horror following the battle was a familiar experience for Titus, but for Leo the shock was something new. Mouth agape and terror in his eyes, he stared at the scene as his mare whinnied and tossed her head.

They dismounted and calmed the three horses as best they could. The dust thinned, beginning to settle. They led their mounts on, picking a route between the bodies, staring reluctantly down on each in trepidation that it might be a friend or, worse, family. They came closer to those who searched the field and Titus called softly to the nearest — a woman, scarf wrapped tight across her nose and mouth. It was Zerenia.

She was frantically turning over bodies, looking at faces then moving to the next. She looked up. Titus could see her face was streaked with dust and tears.

'Titus?'

'Zerenia.'

He let go of the reins and ran to her, taking her in his arms. He held her tight as she heaved and sobbed against him.

'Titus ... oh, Titus, I... We...'

Titus tried to calm her, but he was desperate to know what had happened here. Leo also dropped his mount's reins, drew his short sword, and went ahead.

'Tell me,' said Titus, and Zerenia looked into his eyes.

'We were attacked,' she said. 'But we were ready.'

'Attacked by who?'

Zerenia shrugged. 'I don't know, but I think Crispus knew, and Drago.'

'Drago?'

'The headman in the village. He fights like a demon.'

'I can guess who did this, but why would they want to hurt these people and our family?'

'They wanted the treasure that is hidden here.'

'So it is true? There's a fortune hidden here? If I had known, I would never —'

'I know, this is the worst place we could have chosen. It was never safe. But the gods knew.'

'What do you mean?'

'The oracle said our enemy would protect us.'

'Eh? Our enemy, at least one of them, has been here and this doesn't look much like protection to me!'

'No, you are right.' Zerenia looked around at the scene of death and destruction. 'We have lost friends this day. But we would all be dead if it wasn't for our true enemy.'

Titus stepped back and held Zerenia at arm's length. 'Which enemy?'

'Sextus.'

'Sextus Pompeius is here?' He reached for his sword but found Zerenia's hand upon his where it clutched the handle.

'Be calm, husband. You had better come and see for yourself.'

Zerenia led Titus by the hand, picking a route among bodies and dead horses. He knew from her tears that Pax Villius had lost some of its people and he dared not look at the mutilated corpses and cold faces on the ground.

'The children?' he asked.

'Safe.'

'Crispus? Marina?'

'Wait, husband. It could have been worse.'

A crowd of fearful people parted to allow them to pass. Titus assumed they were Jerax villagers because he recognised none of them. Some women keened, while others bowed to Zerenia. A child met them, a knowing smile on her pale face, then stepped aside as they passed and came face to face with a large, bearded man whose hands rested on the handle of a double-bladed axe.

'This is Drago,' said Zerenia, bowing. 'We owe him much this day.'

Titus looked at the weapon. It was stained with blood and had clearly reaped many souls in the battle.

'You are Titus Villius Macer?' Drago's voice was a growl, coming from deep in the ground on which he stood.

'I am he, and my woman tells me I have much to thank you for.'

Drago's stare was intense. 'At first, we did not welcome your intrusion,' he said. 'But now, we are glad you came. And the oracle spoke truth, as she always does.'

'I have heard. Our enemy would protect us. And where can I find my enemy?'

Drago turned and pointed towards two caves in the hillside. In front of these were several wagons and dozens of mules. A small army of slaves was loading them with sacks and wooden crates, Sicilia's treasure, stolen or pilfered from Rome by a nation of pirates. As Titus followed his gaze, a brightly armoured officer emerged from one of the caves, gesticulating urgently to show where the load was to be placed. He wore no helmet.

Titus knew it was Sextus and his hand again reached for his sword. He had vowed to kill the man who had raped his wife.

A sixth sense must have told Sextus he was being watched. He hesitated and turned towards the knot of villagers that surrounded Titus and Zerenia. Titus thought a smile twitched at the corners of Sextus's mouth. The air between them crackled. He took a step forward, but Drago's hand stayed him.

'We are the guardians of these caves,' said Drago, 'and we have fought enough for one day.'

'Then I think you had better tell me exactly what has happened here and why I should forgive my worst enemy. And where is Crispus?'

'We three will go to my house,' said the headman, 'where all will be explained as far as we understand it, and we will decide what is best for your people and mine.'

Titus was glad to escape the anguished scenes around them. Drago's home was simple — a single room with a central fireplace, with beds, seats and low tables arranged around the hearth. It seemed that in the summer, food was prepared outside, where several amphorae of Pax Villius wine were stored in the shade of an ancient olive tree. Titus recognised the generous gift that must have oiled the relationship between his people and the inhabitants of Jerax.

And where there was wine, there was Strabo. The Greek writer did not appear to have been involved in the fighting, but Titus knew his skills lay in words rather than the sword. Strabo appeared to have invited himself into this inner circle, and neither Zerenia nor Drago objected as he took a seat, arranging his chiton elegantly around him. Only then did he greet Titus with a warm smile.

The wine, watered appropriately, was served in simple clay cups by the same young girl Titus had seen moments before. He was intrigued by the respect shown to her by Zerenia, who answered his raised eyebrow by mouthing 'oracle'. He almost laughed but caught his wife's shake of the head just in time to avoid embarrassment.

Zerenia sought the headman's permission to begin. He approved, and she took a deep breath.

'They say there is always a calm before the storm comes, and we awoke this morning to a still, bright day. We broke our fast and the children played while the women went about their work. I think because it was so still it was easier to see and hear the approach of men from the south.'

'Panthera. And Azhar with him,' muttered Titus.

Zerenia shrugged. 'We did not know who they were. They were coming up the slope between the trees and were some way off, but we could see they were soldiers by the way they moved. Crispus sent Felix to get a closer look and if possible find out if they were hostile, but I think Drago already knew because he was summoning his fighters. Crispus, too, and Barek were arming themselves.

'Then Felix came back. He had counted thirty mounted warriors and confirmed they appeared well trained, moving as a unit not a rabble. Although they appeared not to know the terrain, it was clear they were heading for Jerax.'

Titus interrupted. 'Did he say anything about their leader?'

'There were two. Both were tall and assured. Felix could see little of the one in charge as he wore a helmet, but the other did not. It was Azhar. Even at a safe distance he recognised that scarred face.'

'The warriors and their leader Panthera came here with Lepidus from Africa,' said Titus. He turned to Drago. 'They are Numidians, renowned warriors, and you have done well to defeat them.'

Drago shook his head. 'We have Crispus to thank for that, and after him, Sextus.'

Zerenia resumed her account. 'Drago is right. Crispus organised a defensive line at a place where the attackers would have to approach uphill. He ordered carts, barrows, anything to make a wall and summoned everyone including the women and older children. All of the men held spears upright, and those that did not have one were given tent poles and stripped branches. He placed our fighters in front of the barrier and had the women stand on the carts behind. With cloaks and shawls covering their hair and makeshift spears held high, and the sun behind us, we must have looked like a large host vastly outnumbering their thirty.'

'Clever,' said Titus. 'So tell me, where does Sextus come into this?'

Zerenia and Drago both looked at Strabo, who ran a hand through his unruly mop of hair and cleared his throat.

'Well,' he said, 'there are times when words are mightier than the sword.'

CHAPTER FORTY-FIVE

Strabo, unpredictable as ever, had wandered off long before the Numidians had approached. Before dawn, he had set out to climb to the ancient temple atop the mountain, there to seek the wisdom of the island's Greek gods and get an eagle's view of the land around for his next book on the geography of Sicilia.

'You can see Etna from up there,' he enthused, 'and the sea on three sides. Quite beautiful...' His eyes glazed over at the memory and the others fidgeted, willing him to get to the point. Zerenia, who sat nearest, gave him a gentle nudge. 'Ah, yes,' said Strabo. 'Where was I?'

'Communing with the gods on top of a mountain,' said Titus impatiently.

'And besides a volcano and the sea, what else did you see?' asked Zerenia.

Strabo described the approach of two separate groups of men. In the east, snaking through a rocky pass was a wagon train with a mounted escort and what he estimated was around eighty foot-soldiers, blue pennants indicating an important Sicilian with his retinue. He knew full well this must be Sextus coming to draw on his treasure trove.

He decided this would be an opportune moment to meet the ruler of the land, never mind politics and the war. He would go and plead for patronage, which would of course mean that Sextus Pompey would have a starring role as an upright and generous bringer of wealth and greatness to Sicilia. Naturally, he did not put it quite like this in his account of events —

rather he said that he was attempting to discover Sextus's intentions.

Strabo was gathering his scrolls and writing tools when his attention was drawn to the intermittent flash of sunlight in the south and west, which if he was not mistaken was likely the reflection from a polished cuirass or shield. He spent long enough watching this second group to ascertain a small column of riders was also approaching Jerax.

This presented a conundrum, but he decided he should seek out Sextus.

'How did you know it was Sextus?' asked Titus.

Strabo tapped the side of his nose. 'Because when I was in Messana, I stuck my over-large nose into his business. I struck lucky when trying the local brew with a couple of his officials and the alarm in my head sounded when the cave of the vulture was mentioned. You can reimburse me later for an enormous quantity of questionable ale.'

Titus ignored the Greek's suggestion. 'Go on.'

Intercepting Sextus wasn't easy as there was no clear path, just a rocky hillside where gorse and brambles took a liking to his shins, and he badly twisted an ankle. But a dishevelled Strabo got his meeting with Sextus by waving his arms as he limped towards the column's vanguard, which by now was barely a mile from the settlement.

'As you can imagine,' said Strabo, 'Sextus was in a hurry to inspect his ill-gotten gains, but he was intrigued to know why a famous Greek writer was wandering alone in this inhospitable wilderness. We had a lovely conversation about the good folk of Jerax and the travellers who had sought refuge there. I swear he was about to take me to his bosom and promise me untold riches for presenting him in a good light, when we were interrupted by the distant yet unmistakable sound of warfare.

You can imagine this alarmed a man who was within touching distance of his treasures. So I told him about the riders I had seen from the high temple. To say he was angry that I had not mentioned this earlier would be an understatement. He ordered his men to advance at a run and left me standing there beside the track, injured, thirsty and not a little offended. It took me an hour to limp back here, and by then my part in saving Jerax was completely forgotten.'

There was a moment's silence while the others in the room puzzled over this account, wondering if Strabo had actually done anything to help in the circumstances or had merely served his own interests.

'I think I know what happens next,' said Titus, 'but I would rather hear it from someone who was actually there.'

Zerenia looked at the impassive Drago before taking up the story.

Panthera could have come in peace, but that was not his way. Zerenia told how she stood with the other women behind the front row of pitifully few warriors in an attempt to give the impression of a meaningful defensive force. All of the children had been hurriedly herded into a secluded part of the settlement, including Gaia, Marcia and little Smudge, where they were guarded by Marina, who would give her life in their defence should the enemy break through. Crispus and Drago stood together a few paces ahead of the defensive line, Crispus in his Greek gladiatorial armour, Drago wielding his great axe, beard and bearskin cloak, giving him a fearsome look that no Numidian was likely to have ever witnessed. Behind them stood all of the Pax Villius men, hastily armed, who were being encouraged by lithe Felix and the giant carpenter, Barek. Further back were the aged and women pretending to be soldiers.

This was sufficient force to cause Panthera and his cavalry to hold their ground. Their approach would be uphill across two hundred paces of rocky ground, far enough away to be fooled into thinking the settlement was better defended than it actually was. This gave Crispus time to weigh up the odds. He counted thirty men, confirming Felix's estimate, lightly armed and all mounted. He had not seen warriors like these before. Although their leader wore Roman armour and a plumed helmet, the riders wore leather breeches and tunics, with black headgear. Each bore a short thrusting spear or curved longsword, with light oval shields strapped to their left arms.

Against them ranged a numerically superior force, but this was mostly a rabble of old men and women bearing farm tools and clubs. Though the women of Jerax were fearsome when roused to anger, they would be no match for mounted Numidians.

Zerenia watched the tense stand-off from where she stood on one of the Pax Villius carts, encouraging the women around her to be brave and make the enemy think they were so outnumbered they should retreat. No one here really wanted to fight. There would be no winners, whatever happened.

Zerenia felt a tug on her skirts and looked down. Her heart missed a beat when she looked into her daughter's eyes.

'Mama, look there.'

'Marcia! What are you doing here? Go back, *now*.'

But Marcia had reached that age when she was convinced of her own capability. She pointed back to the mouth of the caves.

Zerenia gasped.

There was a whole army there, Sicilians, drawn up in ordered ranks.

She looked to where the Numidians waited and sensed their tension winding ever tighter, ready to unleash terror and death. She turned back to the unexpected force that had arrived in Jerax. Friend or foe? Should she tell Crispus? She made up her mind instantly, leapt down from the cart, grabbed Marcia's hand and ran towards the caves.

There she came face to face with her tormentor. Sextus Pompey.

All this Zerenia had relived with her eyes closed for a better recollection. Now she opened her eyes and saw that Titus, Strabo and Drago were quietly captivated by her account.

'That cannot have been easy for you,' Titus growled, 'meeting Sextus after what he did.'

'My only thought was that we might be saved,' Zerenia said. 'In that moment, it did not matter to me — I only hoped that our people might survive this day.' Though the fight had been just that morning, it now seemed as though days had passed. She suddenly realised how weary she felt. 'I was telling him about this raiding party, and he could see the rear of our lines. But even as I spoke there was shouting and clamour, and he immediately ordered his men to advance. It did not seem to matter to him that I could be supportive of Rome's invasion, just that the community was under attack and likely as not it was his true enemy attacking a peaceful settlement.'

Now at last Drago played his part in the telling.

'Their horse charged head-on.' His voice was deep and resonant. 'That was foolish.'

Most of the animals shied as they approached what must have seemed an impenetrable barrier fronted by two enormous warriors swinging fearsome weapons above their heads. From somewhere, the whole front line of defenders yelled obscenities and raucous challenges and the charge seemed to falter. Drago described how he and Crispus charged together, the great axe felling the first two horses while Crispus used his experience to sidestep a rearing animal to pull its rider to the ground, his *gladius* taking the man in the throat. Drago swiftly adopted the same tactic, looking for the leader in the high-plumed Roman helmet — the man he now knew to be Panthera, commander of Africa's Numidians.

'I saw him, not leading from the front as a general should,' said Drago. 'Crispus was nearest and ran to meet him. There was another with him, a man with a face I cannot forget.'

'Azhar,' breathed Titus.

'But we never reached them,' said Drago. 'Our line was buckling. Where we had shouted the challenge, there were now screams of fear. The attackers had mostly dismounted and spear and sword bit deep.'

Neither Drago nor Crispus knew at this stage that a powerful force led by Sextus was at that very moment advancing towards the fray. They had no option but to defend their people, which they did with all fury, but they saw several fall to the skill and ruthlessness of the Numidians. The Sicilian soldiers poured around both sides of the defensive line and gave the remaining Numidians no quarter. After a moment's confused hesitation, Crispus and Drago lent axe and sword to furious slaughter. It was over in minutes, with only a few managing to escape. The Numidians had expected a handful of helpless mountain folk and had instead been put to flight, outnumbered and humiliated.

'How many have we lost?' asked Titus. 'And what of Crispus?'

Zerenia studied her feet. 'Eight dead, both ours and the men of Jerax. Drago's women are skilled in healing the wounded, and that includes Barek and Felix, who both fought like lions. Crispus, and Drago here —' she looked at the giant headman with gratitude — 'were true heroes, but if it hadn't been for Sextus I fear we would have all been slaughtered by those demons.'

Crispus had been torn between entreating with Sextus and pursuing the enemy to make sure they did not have reinforcements.

'I think I know what you are going to tell me,' said Titus. 'But first, Panthera and Azhar escaped?' Zerenia and Drago both nodded. 'And Crispus went after them?' Zerenia nodded again. 'Alone?'

'With Marina. She will keep him out of trouble.'

Titus leaned back and sighed. 'Now I want to embrace my children. And then I will speak with Sextus.'

CHAPTER FORTY-SIX

Sextus Pompeius Magnus Pius, last remaining son of Pompey the Great and self-appointed pirate ruler of Sicilia, was overseeing the loading of chests containing around half of the island's wealth. Six wagons groaned under the weight. Uncomplaining mules would carry more treasure.

He watched his old friend Titus Villius Macer approach from the direction of the settlement, followed by a small knot of women and three children. One of the women was Zerenia, hand in hand with a small boy of about eight years. Two girls, twins he had seen before at Pax Villius, walked beside the woman who always made his heart skip a beat, and the child he knew to be his son.

Titus stopped a few yards short of the man he had sworn to kill. Behind him the women and children stood still, uncertain whether they would witness vengeance or a truce. Sextus waved his soldiers away; he did not want them to witness his shame.

The two men stared at each other in what silence was allowed to them by the distant screech of cicadas. High above the Jerax caves and temple, an eagle cried. Titus realised he didn't know how to begin, so he stared hard. The late afternoon sun burned hot on bared heads.

Eventually Sextus spoke. 'You came late to the fight. Where were you?'

'With Lepidus, until two days ago.'

'I hear you have been helping Octavian all along. And now Lepidus also. What news of his legions?'

'They are merciless, and they destroy everything in their path. These Numidians were simply scouts, looking for your hoard of coin so that Lepidus can add to his riches. He has already proclaimed himself king of Sicilia. He is a madman and ten times worse than Octavian will ever be.'

Sextus laughed hollowly. 'And you helped him to lay waste to *our* island.'

Titus felt a pang of guilt and fingered his viper brooch. Sextus was right; he had helped Rome and now Sicilia would be destroyed by the legions of Lepidus. But there was one small hope.

'Take your money and go straight to find Octavian,' said Titus. 'Make your peace with him. He needs money because you have strangled Rome with your theft and piracy. He will welcome you with open arms, and then you can deal with Lepidus together.'

Another hollow laugh, more of a snort. 'Rome killed my father. Octavian would smile sweetly at me while his knife finds my heart. I am not stupid.'

'Then what will you do?'

'I can destroy any enemy at sea,' replied Sextus, but Titus saw doubt flicker across his face.

'But on land? Rome comes for you from your left and your right. It's over, Sextus. Can't you see that?'

Sextus said nothing, and suddenly understanding struck Titus. Sextus was not going to fight, at least not on land. He would load his fortune onto his ships and flee to some far-off land to begin again, with untold riches and not a little seafaring skill as a pirate king.

Sextus turned his gaze to the women and children behind Titus and changed the subject. He was about to take a huge risk with his next words. Before him was a veteran centurion, older by some years, and Sextus had noticed the slight limp of a man past his prime, but he knew he and Titus would be evenly matched. Sextus preferred to fight only when the odds were firmly in his favour, but he spoke anyway.

'Is that my child?' He pointed directly at Smudge.

Titus had gladly taken the boy to his heart, as a father should. But now the lad's true father was looking at his son. Titus could not help himself. He reached for his sword.

'Titus, *no!*'

At the sound of Zerenia's shout, Titus froze. She was right. She always was. Killing Sextus in front of his own men, and in front of Zerenia and his children, would serve no purpose. He looked at Sextus. *If he so much as smiles at me, I will kill him right here and now.*

But Sextus didn't smile. In fact, Titus thought he saw a slight dimming in his eyes. Regret? Remorse?

'Yes,' said Titus, taking his hand from the pommel of his sword. 'But he is my son now.'

Sextus gazed at the boy. 'What's his name?'

There was a long silence while Titus thought about his answer. What kind of name was Smudge? It did not fit a boy who would quickly grow into a man and one day own the Pax Villius vineyards and estates in Bruttium, and perhaps go to war for Rome where a soldier should not bear the name of an inkblot on a vellum scroll.

'Titus. His name is Titus.'

He heard Zerenia gasp with pleasure at this pronouncement, while Sextus merely nodded his approval.

'A noble name,' he said. 'But there remains one item of business between us.'

'And what might that be?'

With a wave of his arm, Sextus indicated the caves from which his men had carried chests of treasure, probably violating the rule of a child oracle who, as it happened, cared nothing for earthly riches.

'In there,' said the pirate, 'there is more coin. We cannot carry it all away. When we are gone, what remains is for you and the people of Jerax to share. There should be enough for you to build better ships than those ancient vessels of yours, and enough for these good people to build a shrine more fitting for the Oracle of Jerax and the titan Crius who guards her. Perhaps a bronze statue? Use that oaf Crispus as a model!'

And with that, Sextus turned to summon his men to get ready for the road. His soldiers put their shoulders to six treasure-laden carts as drovers cracked whips above docile but determined mule teams, and Titus watched Sicilia's pirate ruler walk away.

Zerenia and his three children, Gaia, Marcia and little Titus, came to stand with him.

'Sextus!' Titus called to the retreating dictator. 'If I see you again, I *will* kill you.'

'No you won't,' Sextus said over his shoulder. 'You haven't got it in you.' He carried on walking.

'Is it over now?' asked Zerenia softly, her hand finding Titus's. 'Can we go home?'

'The answer to your second question is yes, when Crispus and Marina return to us.' Titus looked into her eyes and saw weariness there.

'The answer to my first question?'

He did not answer. Instead they embraced.

CHAPTER FORTY-SEVEN

Marina was much better at stealthy tracking than Crispus. Her man might be a brute in battle, but he was too large and muscular for sneaking around in woodland unseen. But somehow they managed it. They kept up with the small party of retreating Numidians who were too intent on reuniting with the main force to notice that they were being followed.

They were lightly armed, Marina with her bow, Crispus carrying a long knife. They wore no armour, just leather shirts, trousers and tough boots appropriate for the terrain. They had no intention of fighting and if discovered would use words as weapons, or just flee. This was simply a reconnaissance exercise. They foraged for food and ate mushrooms and berries. They drank from cool mountain streams and slept in turns on beds of bracken. They made no fires, but then it wasn't cold. And they had each other for warmth, whether needed or not.

The Numidians were not so cautious. Their leader was a bully, and his angry voice could be heard for miles as he berated his men. All Crispus and Marina had to do was follow the voices and watch for disturbed birds taking flight.

On the second night they crept close to observe the Numidian camp. There was a blazing fire, men illuminated as they spit-roasted a young boar, and there, slightly apart from the others, the distinctive figure of Azhar the Cruel — sullen and brooding, a man with no limit to his treachery. Crispus felt the point of his knife and imagined taking Azhar out right there.

'Don't even think it,' whispered Marina.

The next day, they understood what was going on. Crispus knew all the sounds and smells of a Roman cohort, and this one was not far distant. The sun was high when they heard them — not the rhythmic tread of a legion, because this part of Sicilia threw up too many obstacles for an orderly advance, but rather the sound of scouting cavalry picking their way among the trees and boulders. Leo had reported twelve legions under Lepidus, an enormous force that would be divided in two, one half to secure the southern coast, the other the northern coastline as far as Messana. Perhaps six legions in each direction.

But the central part, with its mountains, forests and gorges? This terrain called for a different type of advance. And to Lepidus, it was important territory not just because Azhar had told him about Sextus's hidden fortune, but also because he needed to mop up Sicilian resistance across the whole island.

So, a nimble force. Men and riders who did not need roads to march on. Probably elite troops selected from the best of each of the twelve legions. Probably led by Lepidus himself.

It all made sense to Crispus.

And Jerax would be right in their path.

They watched long enough to see the Numidian leader report to the cohort commander. That could not have been easy for him. In effect, he was reporting his own miserable failure. And it got worse for him when, after being ordered to wait in the shade of a terebinth, a high-ranking Roman in full parade gear, accompanied by a mean-looking mounted guard, arrived to hear the story for himself.

Crispus was a gambling man, and he would have put every last sesterce on this nobleman's identity. The Numidians stood to a man and shuffled their feet nervously before flinging salutes laden with respect, fake or otherwise.

It had to be Lepidus himself.

If the Numidian had any sense, he would be explaining to the triumvir that he had come face to face with the full might of a Sicilian army under Sextus Pompey and had barely escaped with his life after personally slaughtering dozens of the enemy.

The only one who didn't show true Roman military respect was Azhar, who, with customary arrogance, remained seated while all the salutes and explanations were going on. Eventually he stood and sauntered over to the Great Man on his immaculate mount. He pointed east and was no doubt adding to the story that Sextus and a small fortune lay in that direction.

Marina and Crispus lay side by side, shrouded by bushes, watching and learning.

'Time to get back to Jerax?' whispered Marina.

'We need to know numbers,' said Crispus. 'But then whether it's five hundred or five thousand, they're going to wipe out Jerax, especially as that Numidian bastard has a score to settle.'

'So we need to get back as quickly as we can.'

They shuffled backwards with an awkward reverse belly crawl, melted into woodland, then set out at a trot to warn the Pax Villius family and the Jerax community of what was heading their way.

Three days after starting their mission, they returned to find the Pax Villius column preparing to move out, possessions being loaded onto carts and wagons, wounded being made comfortable ready for the journey, and a neat row of graves where two communities had paid their last respects to friends bound together in honour. Crispus saluted Titus, just as he had so many times when serving with him in the Fifth, but Titus was not in a mood for formalities. Instead, he embraced his former *optio* and expressed his gratitude to the man who would stop at nothing to defend Pax Villius and this innocent community.

'Where's Sextus?' asked Crispus. 'Is he rotting in the ground or running from your angry sword?'

'Neither,' said Titus. 'I was persuaded to see sense and have left his fate in the hands of Octavian and Agrippa — unless he crosses my path again. But he did leave us a parting gift.'

'Interesting. Pray tell.'

'Guilt money. He couldn't carry all of his treasure. What's left now belongs to us and the people of Jerax, but I think we'll leave it all here.'

Marina interrupted. 'I can think of ways that money could be used, helping the poor to get back on their feet as soon as these power-hungry monsters go back home.'

'Where is this treasure?' Crispus asked Titus. 'Hope it's well hidden. There's a whole army not far behind us, and they won't be sharing it with the poor.'

'Who leads? How many? How long until they get here?' The probabilities and various options were colliding in Titus's head.

'We think it is Lepidus himself and the Numidian will return with him as a guide. That rat Azhar too.'

'Panthera, Lepidus and Azhar,' breathed Titus. 'None of them known for their kindness.'

'They can only travel as fast as their supply wagons, all told at least five hundred men. They will be here tomorrow, unless —'

'Unless they send an advance party.' Titus was thinking fast. 'It's what we would do in the circumstances. They don't know if Sextus is still here, so they will send enough men on horseback to throw down a challenge. Sextus is the big prize.'

'And he is long gone. So we find ourselves in the middle of a fight again, and it's one we can't win.'

'Not if there's no one here for them to kill,' said Marina.

'So we move out, but that still leaves Drago and his people. And the oracle.'

'They can leave too. Plenty of places around here to hide. It's their country, after all.'

'That leaves Sextus's stash, or what's left of it,' said Titus. 'Azhar knows it was hidden here at Jerax. They'll tear the place apart looking for it. And if we take it, they'll come after us.'

Marina looked around, surveying the community that had lived in peace until Sextus had tainted it with gold and a mountain of filched coin. She looked towards the caves of the vulture, where an oracle was protected by a titan, then she looked at Crispus and saw a titan in human form. She turned her gaze to the high temple.

'I have an idea,' she said quietly.

CHAPTER FORTY-EIGHT

'Where would you hide your treasure?' Marina asked Drago, looking up into the big man's dark eyes.

Titus and Crispus stood with her. They trusted her wisdom, and always had since she had guided their ships by the night's stars. Leo was there too, his wound now healed and fit again to run messages wherever required.

'I would dig a hole and bury it,' replied Drago.

'Right. And how many chests are there to bury?'

'We have counted thirty left behind by Sextus.'

'Containing?'

'Coin, mostly. Denarii, sesterces, some gold coins.'

'Heavy, then?'

'Very.'

Marina studied the ground around, then looked back to where a Roman cohort would soon appear.

'We don't have much time,' she said. 'Have your young men dig a hole big enough for half of the chests.'

Drago immediately understood at least half of the plan.

'Close by, but not too obvious?'

'Correct,' smiled Marina. 'Have more of your people empty a good part of those chests before they are buried. Put the money in sacks, anything that can be carried, then hide them along with the remaining chests.'

'Where?'

'There.' Marina pointed upwards towards the high temple ruins. It was a steep climb up a little used track where only sure-footed donkeys and the strongest men could carry such a load. A plainly ridiculous place to hide such a heavy hoard. 'If the ancients could carry stone to build it, your people can carry a few sacks and chests. But we must be quick about it; we don't know how long we have.'

They sent Leo to relay the message and whip up support, and soon a team of men were digging in a clearing at the edge of the settlement. Satisfied that Drago had everything under control and clearly understood the plan, including the need to move the entire settlement to safety in the surrounding woods, Marina turned to Titus and Crispus.

'All those of Pax Villius should leave now,' she said. 'We must put distance between our people and this place.'

Titus agreed. 'If the column goes south towards our home, that is a direction Lepidus will not want to take while Sextus goes east. Especially if he thinks the remaining treasure is buried here.'

'Precisely.'

'But I am not going.'

Marina rolled her eyes.

'Then neither am I,' said Crispus. 'He can only be *primus pilus* if his *optio* is with him.'

'All right, all right,' said Marina. 'I understand. If there's danger, you men want to puff your chests and flex your muscles.'

Both men smiled. She was right, of course, but Titus had a more intelligent motive.

'Remember I am tribune appointed to guide Lepidus, whether he asks for help or not,' he said. 'I don't care for him one bit, nor those two bastards with him, but it is my duty to point out to him the swiftest route to Messana in the east, where his conquest will be complete. That it just happens to be the same direction that Sextus has taken with an enormous fortune is by the by. You and Zerenia can lead our people to safety, and I will make sure you are not pursued by Lepidus and his bloodthirsty followers.'

Marina was indignant. She folded her arms and her eyes flashed a warning. 'I'm staying right here with you both, if only to make sure you don't do anything foolish.'

Titus was about to protest, but Crispus held him back with a hand on his arm. 'Marina knows what she's doing,' he said. 'She should stay. Zerenia has Leo and the men of Pax Villius to help her on the road home, and Felix and Barek are sufficiently recovered to lend a hand. And there's Strabo to keep them all entertained. The three of us can stay here to see this through.'

Titus knew he was right. He stared at the point where a track from the west emerged from woodland and wondered how long it would be before he faced Lepidus again.

And Panthera.

But above all Azhar, the man nobody should trust.

His hand throbbed at the memory of Azhar's gleeful cruelty when his torturer had removed a finger after accusing him of spying on Sextus. And now Azhar himself had betrayed Sextus and was helping Lepidus.

He took my finger. I will take his head.

Drago's people were used to tilling the land and had all the tools they needed to dig a wide hole for a dozen half-filled chests. Taking the rest of the hoard to the temple ruins was not so easy. The path was rocky, a challenge even for the village's donkeys, but by dividing much of it into smaller, more manageable quantities, this was also achieved within two hours of Marina's suggestion.

The Pax Villius column had moved off after tearful farewells and promises of a return in more peaceful times. Titus, Crispus and Marina were each now clothed in distinctive dress armour with plumed helmets tucked under their arms, swords and daggers at their hips. They watched their friends and families depart, Zerenia and Strabo in the lead, Leo riding his mare to police the flanks and the rear. As if on cue, a breeze picked up to disperse the dust cloud as they made their way slowly into Sicilia's hill country and out of sight of Rome's aggressors.

Crispus suddenly became aware of a small girl standing next to him. Her matted hair framed her grubby face and her tunic was soiled; even the children had been digging.

'Hello, little girl,' said Crispus, and at the sound of his voice Marina turned, then crouched beside her.

'Hello, Li,' she said. She looked at Crispus and Titus. 'This is Li, the Jerax oracle.'

Neither man was surprised; they had heard the stories.

'You were right, Li,' said Marina. 'Our enemy was our protector.'

Li said nothing, just smiled at them. Then she looked up at Crispus. 'Hello, Crius,' she said.

'My name's Crispus, but it's quite similar, I suppose.'

Li then looked into Marina's eyes. 'You are the sea goddess. Your name is Eurybia. You saved Crius and now you are married.'

Marina laughed and Crispus scratched his head. Titus merely snorted. Then Marina remembered that this little girl had been right before, so she showed her due respect.

'Li, what should we do when the bad people come?'

Her people were leaving to hide from the troops who would soon appear, but she didn't seem concerned.

'Crius will know what to do.'

'Do you mean Crispus?'

'No, Eurybia, I mean Crius.' And with that, she turned and walked towards her cave.

'She's not the only child who can't say my name,' said Crispus.

'She thinks you are the titan who guards her cave of the vulture,' said Marina. 'If you think about it, you do act like an arrogant god sometimes. And as it happens, you *are* guarding her cave.'

'If he's Crius, that makes me Zeus,' said Titus. 'But who in the name of the gods is Eurybia?'

'Oh, a real goddess,' said Marina with a chuckle. 'Power over the seas, knows her way around the oceans.'

Crispus looked at her. 'How did Li know you are a navigator? Although power over the sea is a bit far-fetched.'

'Better watch out, Crispus, or is it Crius? Legend has it we will have three children with terrible powers.'

Titus interrupted their banter. 'Listen.'

They listened. The sound was like waves on the shore falling back on pebbles. There were no trumpets, shouts or even the clank of armour, although birds scattered in alarm. The three could feel it, a growing certainty that a force was moving towards them through the trees. Titus knew no fear — he had learned to push that away years ago — but strangely his bones ached, and his stiff joints reminded him that he was past his prime.

Now they could see movement in the woods. Splashes of colour, the sway of horses, branches pushed aside, the crack of hoofs on dead wood.

All three instinctively loosened the blades at their hips.

Lepidus, Panthera and Azhar had come.

CHAPTER FORTY-NINE

The first riders to break cover from the woodland were not Numidians. They had been discredited. These were true Roman cavalry, a lightly armed scouting detachment of twenty horse. They wore no garish plumage, just woollen riding breeches, leather cuirasses and light helmets without cheek pieces. Sensible, in the heat of the day. Their swords were strapped to their thighs, and their bows and short spears were to hand for swift action.

The moment they saw Titus, Crispus and Marina standing together, they fanned out into a semi-circle and reined in, facing the trio. Although armed and helmeted, three soldiers on foot posed no threat. The riders waited, horses patient and obedient, watching expressionless.

Next to appear was Lepidus. Only a man of extreme arrogance and ambition would wear so much gold and purple. His helmet and heroic cuirass were inlaid with gold, his greaves fashioned in polished silver, his tasselled saddle blanket woven with red and gold thread. He wore a purple cloak, a statement, like Caesar before him. Even the black stallion sparkled with bronze, gold and silver adornments. His weapons — a sword and *pugio* — looked too delicate to be a threat, but this was a man who let others fight his battles for him.

Behind him and to his right was Panthera, more simply dressed and armed, returning to the scene of his shame just a few days ago. On his left was Azhar, armed to the teeth with his favoured falcata and at least two long knives thrust through his belt. He wore a patterned leather cuirass and a helmet decorated with a black ponytail plume. The cheek-plates could not disguise his gruesomely scarred face, and he scowled when he saw Titus.

The three riders did not allow their horses to break stride as they rode towards the Pax Villius trio.

Titus, Crispus and Marina stood their ground.

Lepidus halted a spear's throw in front of them. Titus thumped his chest and saluted, as a tribune should. He looked the part, his helmet held respectfully under his left arm, his firm jaw thrust forward.

Lepidus stared at him while Azhar scowled and Panthera stood, unmoved.

Titus knew that Crispus would be weighing up the three men as his opposition, watching for signs of doubt and weakness, but he also knew that his *optio* was pragmatic and any show of aggression would mean certain and merciless death. Marina would be looking on with a woman's common sense: *nothing to see here, move on, your enemy went that way.*

Lepidus was first to become bored with the silence. 'Speak,' he ordered.

'Titus Villius Macer, tribune, reporting for duty, sir.'

'And who are these with you?'

'Crispus, my *optio* from the Fifth Alaudae, and his woman, Marina.'

Lepidus scowled. Like so many before him, he was a misogynist, but he had too much on his mind to be bothered that a woman was standing before him dressed in armour.

'Report, tribune.'

'Your enemy, Sextus Pompeius Magnus Pius, was here not three days ago. He has retired with one century towards Messana.'

'And why was he here?'

328

Of course, Lepidus knew the answer, so Titus was careful with the facts.

'He came to collect money that he had hidden here.'

'Did you try to stop him?'

Titus knew from experience that it was prudent to be succinct with men like this.

'I wasn't here, sir.'

Lepidus looked around as if expecting Sextus to be loitering nearby, but all he could see was a deserted settlement. No soldiers, no people, not even a dog sniffing for scraps of food. He narrowed his eyes.

'I have reports that there was an armed unit here guarding the Sicilian deposit. What do you know of them?'

'My people were here. They are not soldiers and I have sent them home.'

'Why were they here?'

Titus had that stomach-churning feeling that he had forgotten something very important and was unprepared for what was coming next. He had failed to order his thoughts to match the suspicions of the men he now faced, men who were about to accuse him of being in collusion with Sextus. And one of those men had a devious mind and hated him enough to have him tortured. As Titus shifted his gaze to look at Azhar the Cruel, he could feel the venom emanating from him.

'This man is not your ally,' said Azhar. 'He is here purely to line his own pockets. He has betrayed us to Sextus Pompey.'

Betrayed *us*? If he knew anything about Lepidus, Titus was sure that Azhar had just made a big mistake. He should have said *you*, not *us*. Lepidus confirmed the mistake with a regal turn of his head and a hostile stare at the Sicilian traitor.

Titus said nothing.

'We will search this place and then decide who lives and who dies,' said Lepidus.

He nudged his horse forward, Panthera and Azhar falling into line, followed by the twenty riders as more elite troops came up behind them. Their commanders called the entire cohort to a halt and ordered them to dismount to await further orders.

Azhar spat as he passed Titus, the spittle landing on his boot. Titus decided today would be Azhar's last and he knew without looking that Crispus concurred.

Lepidus made himself the priority. He sent men to find a table and chair and his personal servants emerged from the ranks of soldiers with an ornate umbrella, refreshments, a flagon of wine and his favourite goblet. *The longer they take over this*, thought Titus, *the safer for my people*. He didn't care about Sextus, and he wanted Lepidus to follow his enemy. *Let them fight it out among themselves*.

Once settled, Lepidus sent Panthera and several men to search the caves. This alarmed Marina, who feared they would harm Li, so she followed them. It took them an age to gather materials for torches and even longer to light them. Marina watched as they entered, ready to go to Li's defence. She waited patiently, hearing no commotion, not even the men talking to each other. Other men searched the Jerax homes, recklessly overturning furniture and disturbing pots and pans, smashing pottery and storage jars. Then Panthera's men began to emerge from Li's cave, blood drained from their faces and each shivering, although it was not cold.

'What is in there?' Panthera asked Marina as he emerged into the light.

She decided to be vague. 'What did you see?'

'Nothing, but we heard whispering voices.'

'And what did those voices say?'

Panthera shrugged. Marina was pleased to see uncertainty and fear there; she had expected him and his men to behave with coarse ribaldry. She built the tension.

'You have been in the presence of the oracle. She only reveals herself to the pure of heart. You are lucky you were not struck down by the titan that protects her.'

Had she gone too far? It seemed not, because Panthera ordered his men into the second cave — they obeyed with evident reluctance — but he himself did not follow.

'Have you seen this oracle?' he asked her with surprising respect.

'Yes. I have spoken with her. She foresaw your defeat when you came here before.' Marina could see confusion and fear of the unseen on Panthera's face.

'Can I speak with her?' he asked.

'Why would you wish to do that?'

'There are things I would like to know.'

Marina decided to probe a little deeper. 'What sort of things?'

Panthera looked across to where Lepidus feasted alone beneath his garish shade, and again Marina read his mind. He hated the triumvir. But he was not prepared to give voice to his disloyalty. Marina filled the silence and watched his face for further signs.

'She foresees the fall of your commander, Lepidus.' A lie, but what harm could it do?

Marina was right to watch closely. She saw several emotions cross Panthera's face and took pleasure in knowing that Lepidus did not command the respect of his men. She wondered how far this insurgence went, hoping it was as infectious as a plague of boils.

She was waiting for his reply when a commotion distracted both her and Panthera. The soldiers had found the disturbed ground where Drago had buried the decoy chests. She saw Lepidus rise from his table, Azhar sprinting to see what had been discovered. Titus and Crispus walked towards the gathering crowd. She ran to them as Panthera summoned his men from the second cave.

A hundred army-issue spades made light work of the pit where the soil was already loose. Azhar led the detail — it had been his word that treasure lay at Jerax, and he could hardly contain his delight that he was about to be proved right.

While the soldiers scrabbled in the deepening hole, Marina whispered to Titus that Panthera had found nothing, not even an oracle, in the caves and the three of them watched the Numidian leader making his report to Lepidus.

The first chest was brought up to solid ground. Necks craned as it was opened before Lepidus, who bent and scooped a double handful of coins.

'Bring me more!' he bellowed.

Eventually a dozen chests were laid before the triumvir — a small fraction of that now safely hidden in the vaults of the high temple ruins. Titus knew what was coming next and kept his eyes on Azhar. So did Crispus and Marina. The scarred Sicilian was pacing towards Lepidus, a mixture of delight and anger on his face.

He spoke to Lepidus but Titus could not hear, such was the din made by excited soldiers who were toasting their efforts by passing skins of water around, playing that hopeful game soldiers could not resist in their assumption that plunder and riches were coming their way. Lepidus listened and glanced towards Titus. He called for silence, which took some moments as the squad commanders called their men to order. When all was quiet, Lepidus addressed Titus directly, Azhar beaming at his side.

'This man has accused you stealing what is rightfully mine and betraying Rome by lying to me. What do you say?'

Titus was ready. He did not hesitate. 'Then I challenge him to combat. Just me and him. Let the gods decide who speaks truth.'

He felt Crispus and Marina stiffen and heard the murmur that went around the soldiers within earshot.

It was then that Crispus kneed him in the groin.

CHAPTER FIFTY

'I will defend the honour of Titus Villius Macer.'

Crispus had planned this move all along. Marina knelt with Titus, who was groaning 'bastard, bastard, bastard' over and over. She told him he was too old to fight Azhar and his creaking bones would not see another day unless he allowed his *optio* to represent him. Titus writhed in pain. Crispus's Greek-style shin guard had a pointed top that had stabbed his groin right next to his manhood, and blood now ran down his left leg. It was worse than anything he had encountered in battle with the Fifth.

He tried to stand up but couldn't. He collapsed and looked up to see Crispus standing straight and strong. He knew he could not fight Azhar. He raised a hand in acknowledgement and through the pain managed, 'I will kill you for this, Crispus!'

He heard Lepidus announce, 'Over there. Form a circle. Panthera to take wagers. Mine is on the gladiator.'

He used this term because Crispus had already donned his Greek helmet, an all-in-one bronze piece that made him look like an avenging demon, topped with an undyed horsehair plume running front to back. His leather cuirass was reinforced with iron bands, not the elaborate gold or silver of a Roman officer, but the stronger for it. A skirted kilt did not disguise powerful thigh muscles, and his studded boots were a weapon in themselves.

He drew his *gladius* and a vicious-looking long knife. He carried no shield.

He walked towards the circle, Azhar beside him.

The Sicilian carried his piratical falcata in his right hand, a vicious curved weapon that could decapitate a man with ease when the timing was right. In his belt were two long knives, useful back-up weapons. As he walked, Azhar called for a shield and was rewarded when one of Panthera's men offered a light Numidian shield. This was no place for heavy Roman *scuta* used in shield-walls for shunting the enemy backwards. This was an occasion for speed and dexterity.

Both men looked straight ahead as they approached a small gap in the circle of men, the place where they should enter. The noise around them swelled as they walked into the circle, a full ten spear-lengths across. Lepidus pushed his way to the front, opposite the point where they had entered, and Crispus thought that was probably the first time in his illustrious career the triumvir had allowed himself to touch a sweaty, filthy soldier of the lower ranks.

'Gentlemen!' shouted Lepidus, and the circle of men fell silent. Lepidus looked around. Crispus and Azhar stood side by side, watching him. 'Gentlemen, this is a fight to the death. Do not give either man any assistance.' For a moment, Crispus wondered if Azhar had any allies among these soldiers. He thought not, but he could not be sure. He would have to watch his back. 'The winner will go free without fear or favour; the loser will be left for the birds and foul rodents of this place.'

A long, deep growl of approval from the onlookers greeted this announcement.

'Begin.'

Crispus backed off at a crouch, as did Azhar. They faced each other, Azhar with his oval shield on his left arm, his falcata circling menacingly in his right. Titus watched the sword's movement, seeing how it was wielded, establishing whether Azhar was a skilled swordsman or a slashing brute.

Then he looked at the shield. It was strong enough to deflect a sweeping blow, but would it survive a direct thrust from a sharp *gladius*?

Crispus and Azhar began to circle each other. The crowd became impatient.

Azhar made the first move. He came in hard and straight, leading with the shield, falcata held wide to sweep low and decisively at Crispus's legs. Crispus read it. He took the shield on his shoulder and then spun around and away as the blade hissed through the air.

But Azhar had followed through in the same direction and deftly reversed the action of his sword. Still low. Not so much force this time, but it took Crispus on his right greave. The blunt side of the weapon crunched into the shin protector and numbed his leg from ankle to thigh, causing the big former gladiator to stumble.

The onlookers gasped. Azhar had showed speed of thought and arm. Was it the nimble against the muscular? Tradition had it that speed always beat strength.

Crispus ignored the lack of response in his right leg and aimed a thrust with the knife in his left hand that would have taken Azhar's eye if the Sicilian had not dodged, again showing speed and fighting craft. If Crispus's right leg had not been so unresponsive, he might have finished it there with his *gladius*, but now he found himself blocked by the shield while his weight took him forward into a clumsy embrace with his opponent, shield crushed between them.

Sweat made them slip apart. Both men backed off to start again. The crowd noise swelled and someone shouted, 'Give us blood!'

During his years in the arenas of Rome and the provinces, Crispus had learned never to respond to the crowd, at least not until it was all over. Time and again he had seen an opponent interact with onlookers and strut around, and even as he heard the words he was on the move — just in case Azhar was that stupid.

He was.

The tip of his *gladius* found Azhar's shoulder just as he pranced for the crowd. It wasn't deep, but it was a start. The soldiers roared their approval as Azhar yelped, a bright stream of blood running down his shield arm.

Crispus backed off, hoping the wound would slowly weaken Azhar, allowing more time to goad and probe.

But it made the Sicilian angry, and Crispus realised too late that backing off allowed him more room to swing his falcata. It came in low and hard to Crispus's left, where his only defence was the long knife that now spun wildly away after deflecting the blow, leaving him with only a *gladius*. His enemy's eyes shone with joy as he lined up a backhand, knowing that Crispus had no weapon in his left hand to take advantage of the opening.

But Crispus still had a weapon in his left hand: a fist. Bone and gristle, hard as iron. His *gladius* parried the blow, steel sliding off steel, and his left fist slammed into Azhar's ribs — right on the edge of his cuirass, which gave way like paper. If he hadn't been off-balance, Crispus knew it would have broken two or three ribs, but it was delivered with sufficient force to bring a winding grunt and hopefully a slower performance.

But the falcata had done its damage. When it glanced off the short sword, it then bit deep into Crispus's own cuirass, crunched against a rib, and bit into his chest a hand's width below his shoulder. Crispus felt it bite. He knew the wound would bleed and that sharp pain would follow in just a few

337

seconds. His *gladius* arm would gradually lose its function, and soon he would have no choice but to fight left-handed.

It was now or never.

He doubled over, clutching his wound. He could feel the blood seeping between his fingers, the pain now kicking in. The crowd roared.

Azhar had his sword raised high for the despatch, his shield flung out to his left.

Crispus mustered everything he had left and thrust upwards with his right arm.

The *gladius* entered somewhere around Azhar's sternum and continued its upward passage, slicing through chest and throat until it almost touched his brain. But it didn't need to go that far. Azhar's eyes were wide with shock, his mouth gushing blood. It spilled down his chin, over his chest and onto Crispus's forearm.

The crowd gasped again, then fell silent. The clatter of Azhar's sword as it fell to the stony ground was deafening. Crispus held him upright, his sword still buried in Azhar's chest, and studied his opponent's face.

'Kiss goodbye to your riches,' he hissed and twisted the blade.

Azhar seemed confused, his eyes fading.

'Kiss goodbye to your island.'

Pink bubbles formed at the corners of Azhar's mouth. Was he trying to speak? Crispus twisted the *gladius* again.

'That's for my friend Titus,' said Crispus.

He let the body drop.

There was a long silence. The soldiers were stunned by the suddenness of the bloody conclusion.

'Never liked him. You've done me a favour,' Lepidus growled at last. 'Load up the money so we can move out. We will go to find Sextus Pompey.'

Within the hour, Marina had Crispus bandaged and feeling like a hero. Titus, on his feet again, although looking a little green, forgave his friend.

'Let's go and catch up with the family,' he said. 'I've a feeling that this will be all over by Saturnalia, and we can all go back to living a normal life.'

EPILOGUE

Pax Villius, two months later

The pipes played Bacchus's joyful tune and drums built a rhythm for Zerenia and her wine dancers. Skirts hitched high, long legs stained with rainbow colours, she laughed as she trod the grapes with Marcia and Gaia, holding hands and oblivious to the skins in their tangled, dripping hair. In three huge vats, women and children stamped in frenzied celebration of the best harvest in many years.

The Pax Villius family clapped and danced. Barek's rich voice sang of the gods' benevolence, while younger children screamed with excitement.

Titus couldn't dance, not that he ever did. It wasn't down to the knee in the groin delivered by Crispus — that pain had disappeared within hours — nor was it due to old wounds inflicted by Rome's enemies. The throbbing ache in his knee and now in his hip told him he was getting old, too old to fight and certainly too old to dance. Let the young show Dionysus their gratitude.

He sat on a rock apart from the revellers, in his favourite spot overlooking their bay. On his knee was his son, Little Titus, a thoughtful lad who had a quiet, assured nature — unlike his true father.

Crispus sat with them. Since delivering that sudden blow to the tenderest parts of his *primus pilus*, he had studiously avoided all jocularity about blunting Titus's spear and had kept close to him, assuaging his guilt by acting almost as a manservant. He kept Titus's cup full, opened doors for him, polished his weapons and didn't let him carry anything heavier than a spoon. It annoyed Titus, but in a quiet moment alone Zerenia had told him not to complain and let Crispus work it out for himself. Besides, she had said, poking him in the ribs, he *was* getting old, and he'd have to learn to let everyone look after him.

But he still wore his viper brooch with pride, even though his spying days were over.

He told Crispus he should join the celebrations. 'Go to Marina,' he said. 'An occasion like this always leads to a happy event.'

But Crispus didn't hear him. He was watching the ships as they passed through the Messana straits where two months earlier some six hundred war galleys had waged war in a final showdown. Sextus had all but lost the land battle yet had somehow persuaded Octavian their differences should be settled at sea. After all, Sextus was 'Son of Neptune' and the sea was his favoured domain. But what Sextus didn't know was that Octavian's friend and general, Agrippa, had built an entirely new navy, trained thousands of oarsmen and marines, and developed a fearsome weapon called the harpax which could grapple enemy ships and draw them to close-quarter destruction like a spider pulling a fly to its deadly fangs.

The Pax Villius family had watched from this very spot as the two navies engaged, Octavian's larger ships with red towers fore and aft, Sextus's smaller vessels flying Sicilian blue pennants. And Sextus had been soundly trounced. Wreckage had been washed ashore on the Pax Villius beach in the following days _ masts, shattered planking and bodies. Reports and rumours had drifted inland, bit by astonishing bit, that Octavian was now master of Sicilia.

Lepidus's men had deserted him and gone over to Octavian, who had promised them more. With Marcus Antonius languishing in the east, and Lepidus banished to live a solitary life, Octavian was now the First Man in Rome.

But the rumours didn't stop there. It was said that Sextus had escaped with just seventeen ships, all that was left of the three hundred he had ranged against Octavian.

Little Titus tugged at Crispus's sleeve. 'Can we go to the beach and catch some crabs?'

'Eh? Yes, of course, but later.' He didn't take his eyes off the sea. Instead he pointed. 'What do you make of that, young Titus?'

Father and son looked to where he pointed.

Four ships were passing the northernmost point of their bay, coming from the direction of Messana port. They were triremes, under oars with sails furled, each flying an array of colourful pennants. There were no archer towers, harpax weapons or bristling spears. The shrill of pipes giving the rowers an easy pace could easily be heard across the calm sea. They were ships on a peaceful mission, for a change.

'Now who might that be?' mused Titus.

Little Titus was jumping with excitement. Like all boys, he loved ships as much as he loved toy soldiers. Titus ruffled his hair and told him the ships were probably sailing around to Tauromenium.

'Oh no they're not,' said Crispus.

All four ships had begun a lazy turn to starboard and were heading towards them.

Pax Villius was off its guard, celebrating a bounteous harvest. Even if the ships were coming in peace, they bore someone of importance or even a delegation. It was not an occasion to assemble a guard of inebriated farmers.

They watched the ships until they were certain. The triremes were in line, heading for the shore.

Titus crouched beside Little Titus. 'Go find Leo and tell him we have visitors on the shore. And send Strabo to us.'

The boy ran off. Leo would know what to do: he'd pass the problem to Zerenia and Marina while the men straightened themselves out, and act as a runner to pass messages between the shore and the main house.

A whistle sounded and the four ships turned together to face out to sea, rowers dropping oars into a slow forward motion as anchors were let go with perfect timing to leave the vessels stationary, side by side.

'At least they're not beaching,' said Titus. 'Not so many mouths to feed.'

'Unless they swim ashore,' laughed Crispus.

A skiff was being lowered from the lead ship. Ten crewmen climbed over the trireme's side, five of them holding the small boat steady as two men made their way across the deck. Their white braided tunics contrasted sharply with the duller clothing of the crew.

Titus had no doubt who these visitors were.

Octavian looked older; Agrippa didn't. Both men were in their late twenties or thereabouts, but Marcus Vipsanius Agrippa thrived on planning campaigns and winning battles. The man Titus knew as Octavian but who was now Imperator Caesar Divi Filius still had a pale, cold look, but his forehead now bore lines of worry. He was thin and bony, clearly not a warrior like the more thickset Agrippa, but both men found it easy enough to leap across the skiff's bow onto shingle without getting their feet wet.

Titus and Crispus gave perfect military salutes to disguise their casual dress and the lack of appropriate house servants to meet their visitors' needs. Octavian did not return the salute, instead extending a hand to clasp wrists with first Titus then Crispus.

'*Ave*, Titus. *Ave*, Crispus.'

Agrippa did the same, his eyes alighting on the viper brooch.

'Sir, if we had known —' Titus began, but Octavian held up a hand.

'This is what you might call a flying visit,' he said. 'We are on our way to Syracuse to appoint a new governor, but our visit here is long overdue.'

Strabo arrived, panting with the exertion a young man should not feel unless he was as overweight as the Greek writer. Agrippa turned to the sailors who had remained on the skiff, its bow held by cloying shingle. He clicked his fingers. Two of the men lifted a small chest by its rope handles, manoeuvred it across the bow and placed it before the four men.

'Here are the orders for my best viper,' he said.

'Sir, I cannot. I have a family now and a business to run. My knees hurt and I walk with a limp.'

Agrippa smiled. 'You are still Titus Villius Macer. Without you, we would have achieved nothing.'

Titus knew this was not true. 'What of Niko?' He needed to know if The Blue Flag's landlord had survived Sextus's ruffians. 'He is your best viper, not me.'

'Ah, Niko. A great man. He was treated badly, but we found him in Messana's dungeons. He is now in Rome; he has a villa and a new inn to manage. You must visit him soon.'

Titus had no intention of ever going to Rome again. 'I am pleased for him. And Philotas?'

Agrippa looked towards the ships, put his fingers to his lips and whistled. Then he shouted, 'Philotas!' A man came to the stern rails of the lead ship and waved. 'Vipers all present and correct,' he said, and Titus breathed a sigh of relief.

He turned and saw that his people were flooding onto the beach, all of them dishevelled and most of them staggering after their revelry. 'It seems you are about to be invited to our celebration of a good harvest.'

'Not us,' put in Octavian with a broad smile that belied his cold image. 'But I have one more request.'

Titus bowed from the neck and waited expectantly. His people had stopped halfway from the visitors. They sensed this was a private conversation.

Octavian pointed out to sea, past the four ships and beyond where Italia's toe was all that was between them and the world under Rome's control. 'Sextus went that way. He had seventeen ships and some of them may have contained treasure.'

Then he pointed to the two old Veneti ships beached in the corner of the bay, near the Pax Villius repair sheds. 'You have these two ships, and I am told they are swift as the winds after which they are named. Take them and pursue Sextus, then report back to me.'

Titus thought he saw Agrippa smirk where he stood just behind Octavian.

'I cannot. As I have told you, I have business here.'

Octavian laughed. 'I thought not. It was just my little jest.'

'Very funny,' muttered Crispus under his breath, just loud enough for Titus to hear.

The two giants of Rome's military might turned and climbed over the skiff's bows, taking their place midships. Agrippa turned back and beckoned to Strabo.

'Come aboard, Strabo,' he called, 'and tell us what these miscreants have been doing while my back was turned.'

Strabo didn't hesitate. He had much to report of Sicilia's defiant stand and, more specifically, the bravery of an innocent community. It would make a good story for the Greek writer to tell. He climbed aboard and said his farewell with a heartfelt wave of his hand.

Titus and Crispus helped push the boat away from the shore.

They took the chest back to Pax Villius and left it unopened in the weapons room. Seven days later, Crispus reminded Titus about it, and was ignored. Fifteen days later, Zerenia reminded him. About twenty days later, he went to the weapons room, looked at it, tapped it with his foot, and left it there. If he had opened it, he would have found a map and the deeds to another farm in Bruttium and a further one on the nearby island of Melita. And three gold ingots.

But Titus Villius Macer did not open the chest. Not yet.

A NOTE TO THE READER

The story of the Sicilian Revolt fascinates me. It is so full of rich characters — from an international pirate, Sextus Pompey, to the would-be emperor of Rome, Octavian, later Caesar Augustus.

Sextus throttled Rome by controlling the seas all around southern Italy, reaping a vast fortune by seizing grain supplies to control prices. This caused years of famine for Italy and almost brought a premature halt to Octavian's aspirations.

But his right-hand man, Agrippa, had other ideas. He knew that to win, you must fight fire with fire. Or just build a better navy, which he did. And he supported it with a spy network that would make 007 proud.

Titus Villius Macer was a reluctant spy (and entirely fictional). We know from history that Julius Caesar invented a spy code that today would be laughable — for A write B and so on — but in its day it was quite revolutionary. Agrippa was a smart general, architect and statesman, and no doubt spymaster to boot. Yes, he was ruthless, but he was also convinced that Octavian's goals were the right ones. Marcus Antonius could have used someone like that.

Octavian's story now moves on to the tragedy that is Antony and Cleopatra and the climactic events of the Battle of Actium and its aftermath. The battle itself is central to my novel, *Sea of Flames*, featuring the crew of a plucky Greek ship plunged into the struggle for world domination. There are many more stories yet to be told — history is rich with heroes and anti-heroes, honour and betrayal, oppressors and liberators.

I hope you have enjoyed this series. If you want more, in addition to my novels *Libertas*, *Line in the Sand* and *Sea of Flames*, I recommend some of my favourite writers: Douglas Jackson, Conn Iggulden, Simon Scarrow, Robert Harris and from the past, Mary Renault, Mary Teresa Ronalds and James A. Michener. Special thanks to Amy Durant at Sapere Books for her faith in my work at a difficult time in my writing career, and to my amazing editor, Natalie Linh Bolderston.

Reviews by knowledgeable readers are an essential part of a modern author's success, so if you enjoyed this novel, please spare a moment to post a review on **Amazon** and **Goodreads**. You can also connect with me on **Twitter** or on **my website** and **sign up to my newsletter on Substack**.

Alistair Forrest

alistairforrest.com

Sapere Books is an exciting new publisher of brilliant fiction and popular history.

To find out more about our latest releases and our monthly bargain books visit our website: **saperebooks.com**

Printed in Great Britain
by Amazon

45224715R00195